MAVERICK
LEGEND OF THE WEST

MAVERICK
LEGEND OF THE WEST

by ED ROBERTSON

FOREWORD BY ROY HUGGINS

POMEGRANATE PRESS, LTD.

LOS ANGELES   LONDON

This is a POMEGRANATE PRESS, LTD. book.

MAVERICK
LEGEND OF THE WEST

Copyright 1994 by Ed Robertson

MAVERICK™ © 1957, 1994 Warner Bros. Pictures, Inc.

Library of Congress Catalog Card Number: 94-065746

Tradepaper Edition ISBN: 0-938817-35-3

First printing: May 1994

10 9 8 7 6 5 4 3 2

For POMEGRANATE PRESS, LTD.:

Editor: Kathryn Leigh Scott
Cover design/Book design: Benjamin R. Martin
Cover photographs: Gene Trindl
Typography consultant: Leroy Chen

Printed and bound in The United States of America

by
McNaughton & Gunn, Inc.
Saline, Michigan

POMEGRANATE PRESS, LTD.
Post Office Box 17217   Beverly Hills CA 90209-3217

To my father. He would have liked this.

ACKNOWLEDGMENTS

They say a writer works alone. And that's true — but only to a certain extent. Nobody who writes non-fiction works alone, and this writer is no exception. I hope that I have not overlooked anyone.

For their time, patience and professionalism in granting interviews and answering dozens and dozens of questions, I thank Roy Huggins and Adele Mara, Bill Orr, Budd Boetticher, Marion Hargrove, Coles Trapnell, Howard Browne, Leslie Martinson, Richard Bare, Bob Colbert, Iris Chekenian, Luis Delgado, and Roger Moore.

For providing access to a treasure of information on both the *Maverick* series and Warner Bros. television in general, I am indebted to the entire staff at the Warner Bros. Archives, School of Cinema-Television, University of Southern California. I am particularly thankful to Stuart Ng, Bill Whittington, Ned Comstock, and Leith Adams.

A big Thank You to the staff at San Francisco Public Library for all their help, particularly my sister Jo-Ann Collins and her husband Selby Collins.

I also wish to thank: Steve Imura; Tricia Stanley; Frank Fiorenzano; Jim and Melody Rondeau; Kenny Stone; Peter and Cheryl Youngman; Dan Falatico; Dave Landis; Linda Brevelle, Stuart Shostak; David Martindale; David Chin; David Miller; Mikel Burton; Garry Yaggi; Sal Mauriello; Dana Boyd of KSHB-TV, Kansas City; Richard from WOIO-TV, Cincinnati; and Ann Eliot of Nielsen Media Research.

And: Gene Trindl; Bob Rubin; Chris Anderson; Rusty Pollard; Dave Brown; Ann Mathis; Kay McAfee; Milton Moore; Mary DeBoom and Jon Strauss; Frank Free; Bob Charger; and Barbara and Thom Anderson.

Special thanks to:

Mick Martin, co-author of *Video Movie Guide*, for the generous use of his interview with Jack Kelly, which he conducted just two weeks before Kelly's death in 1992;

Jerry Pam, for making possible my conversation with Roger Moore;

Louise Renne, Burk Delventhal, Mariam Morley, Scott Emblidge, Linda Ross, Mary Jane Sylvia, Ron Baxter, Irene Carter, Georgia Tynan, Cathy Pearson, Marjorie O'Toole, and Katherine Djanikian — for reasons too numerous to mention;

At Pomegranate Press: Kathryn Leigh Scott and Ben Martin.

Geoff Miller, for all your warmth and hospitality;

Michael Wright; my mother Josephine Robertson; my family; my friends;

And Cathy McCarthy, with much love. Thanks for putting up with me.

FOREWORD

No series in the history of television passed through as many mutations, cast changes and major tonal shifts as *Maverick* and still managed to capture and hold firmly onto cult status. *Maverick* has had more lives than an alleycat, and it's still out there, the ultimate loner, alive and thriving. I was with the series for only its first two seasons, so I hope I can say this without undue immodesty.

The man who should be allowed generous bragging rights is Ed Robertson, who has studied and described this entertainment phenonenon from its beginning in 1956 to its most recent return, the Warner Bros. movie, in 1994. Robertson not only makes that history suspenseful and absorbing, he has discovered and analyzed the unifying elements that have been present in the series from the beginning to...well, I can't "end" because I am persuaded, after reading *MAVERICK: Legend of the West*, that *Maverick* is nowhere near the end of its illustrious history.

Warner Bros. as of the date of the Foreword, is in discussion on a sequel to their movie version of *Maverick*. Can yet another television series be far behind?

Roy Huggins
March 10, 1994

JAMES GARNER AND JACK KELLY

TABLE OF CONTENTS

INTRODUCTION

In the late 1950s, prime time television was saturated with Western series featuring traditional cowboy heroes. Very few of those shows stood out, and for that reason very few are still remembered.

Maverick is one of those exceptions. When it debuted on the ABC television network in September 1957, *Maverick* looked very much like a straightforward Western — it told typical Western stories, and it had what appeared to be a typically handsome hero in the person of Bret Maverick (James Garner). But Bret Maverick (and, later, his brother Bart, played by Jack Kelly) didn't relate to problems in the ways we've come to expect from our Western heroes. The traditional Western hero is a stalwart cowboy who wouldn't hesitate dropping everything and risking his life to help a damsel in distress. If that same damsel went to Maverick, however, he'd more than likely point her in the direction of the sheriff's office. Or sometimes Maverick would help the damsel, but before getting involved, he'd ask her, "What's in it for me?"

Maverick was also one of television's first openly mercenary heroes. If there was a reward, Maverick wouldn't hesitate becoming involved, although he did prefer making money the easy way — at the card table, and at the expense of less-experienced poker players. He was also an ardent believer in self-preservation (his own, of course), and as such, he did his absolute best to avoid troublesome situations: if a gunman came into town looking for him, Maverick wouldn't think twice about ducking out the back door. He was not so much cowardly as simply reluctant to get involved (as his dear old Pappy once told him, "Love your fellow man, but stay out of his troubles if you can"), but if faced with no other choice, Maverick would tackle the situation head on. Unlike most cowboy heroes, he wasn't the fastest gun in the West — and he knew it — so he always tried, whenever possible, to use his wits to solve his problems.

Maverick took many of the conventions that had characterized TV Westerns and turned them inside out. Its hero was not an altruistic lawman or a noble vigilante, but rather a card-playing grafter — the basest of professions, at least in the eyes of the fictional Old West. Yet as con artists go, Maverick was not an absolute scoundrel — he may take advantage of your good nature, but he always intends, in the back of his mind, to make up for it. "I love money," he once said, "but I hate jails." In fact, the only people Maverick cheats are cheaters themselves. Ironically, he plays poker on the level — he doesn't need any trickery to take your money because he already knows he's a better player than you are. (He wouldn't play cards with you unless he knew he could win, because he doesn't like to gamble.) Still, unlike most TV heroes, Maverick didn't always come out on top. By the end of any given show, he may find himself broke, swindled, thrown out of town, or even (as is the case with one episode) hog-tied in the middle of nowhere.

Maverick not only took the conventions of the Western and threw them for a loop, the show also upset the conventional wisdom in television. At a time when the networks were teeming with Westerns, ABC scheduled *Maverick* on Sunday evenings against three prime time powerhouses (*The Jack Benny Program*, *The Ed Sullivan Show*, *The Steve Allen Show*) — and got away with it. For two years (1957-59), *Maverick* was the hottest show on television: millions of people dropped what they were doing every Sunday at 7:30 p.m. to watch the fresh, hip show that became *the* Western among Westerns. *Maverick* was the first bonafide commercial success produced by Warner Bros. Television (it won an Emmy Award for the studio in 1959), but the show's impact went beyond that: it launched Roy Huggins, its writer/creator, on his way to becoming one of the top producers in television; it solidified ABC at a time when the network was struggling; and it catapulted James Garner into superstardom.

Maverick's appeal has endured over the years: reruns of the 124 episodes have played continuously on independent stations in this country and abroad since the series ended its network run in 1962. *Maverick* also had a tremendous influence on the work of many people who first watched the show, and who then later became television producers themselves, such as Frank Price, Jo Swerling Jr., Glen A. Larsen, and Stephen J. Cannell; in fact, the "next generation" at Warner Bros. attempted to revive *Maverick* on three occasions in the late 1970s and early '80s. Columbia House Home Video has distributed 30 episodes of the original series on videotape, and in 1994 Warner Bros. adapted *Maverick* as a major motion picture starring Mel Gibson, Jodie Foster and James Garner.

Maverick has remained in the public consciousness despite the fact the series itself was a hit only two of its five seasons on ABC. The show failed just as quickly, and as spectacularly, during its final three seasons; by the time it was finally cancelled in 1962, *Maverick* had lost over fifty percent of its original audience. *Maverick* has also survived despite its lack of a singular identity: there isn't one *Maverick*, per se, but many different *Maverick*s that spawned themselves over the course of the show's network run. You could divide *Maverick* into four separate series, for example, with each show starring one of the different actors who played Maverick: Garner, Kelly, Roger Moore, and Robert Colbert. Or you could break it down into two kinds of series, based on a more fundamental approach. Whereas the humor of *Maverick*'s first two years had a wry, understated but wicked bite, the show became increasingly broader during the final three seasons — to the point where *Maverick* had changed from a Western with humor to a Western resembling a slapstick comedy.

Maverick dominated television for only two years, a relatively modest stretch compared to the two other major prime time Westerns that have remained in the public eye (*Gunsmoke* ruled for 20 years on CBS, while *Bonanza* ran for 14 seasons on NBC). Yet *Maverick* exploded into prime time with a bang so overwhelming, the fact that the show ended with a whimper only four years later has been overlooked. *Maverick* has burned itself indelibly in the hearts and minds of its followers in a way that few television series can. *Maverick* wasn't just a popular TV show about "the legend of the West," as its theme song proclaimed. *Maverick* became a legend unto itself.

Maverick's history before it burst onto the airwaves is also the stuff of legends. *Maverick* was entirely the creation of its producer, Roy Huggins, but Huggins nearly had to abandon his project simply because Warner Bros. refused to pay him the royalty to which he was entitled as the show's creator. The studio would not produce a TV series unless the program was based on material owned by Warners, and if Huggins hadn't found a suitable property, there would not have been a *Maverick*. Also, series star James Garner became a folk hero of sorts by virtue of how he left *Maverick*. When the studio tried to bully him in 1960, Garner stood up to the challenge; when the matter made its way to court, Garner won, and found himself freed of his contract.

But, like most legends, *Maverick*'s history contains many elements that have taken on mythic proportions. As we trace its life on television, we'll examine the myths and the realities; we'll find out what made *Maverick* work during its first two years and what changed the show in its final three seasons. We'll take a look at the three *Maverick* revivals — *The New Maverick*, *Young Maverick*, and *Bret Maverick* — as well as the *Maverick* movie. We'll also meet many of the key people who brought *Maverick* to life: Roy Huggins, Coles Trapnell, Bill Orr, Marion Hargrove, Doug Heyes, Howard Browne, Leslie Martinson, Budd Boetticher, Richard Bare, Luis Delgado, Iris Chekenian, Robert Colbert, and Roger Moore.

The history of *Maverick* is a fascinating story, filled with as many plot twists as any given episode of the series. We hope you'll enjoy it.

PART I: BIRTH OF A LEGEND

1. THE GENTLE GRAFTER

The classic Western hero is a fiction that Americans have embraced time and again in novels, film and television over the past century. The cowboy has it made: he has no family, no goals, no obligations, and no apparent anxieties. Compared to modern times — which require flashing a driver's license, Social Security number, or some other means of personal identification every time we turn around — the classic Western cowboy can ride into a strange town and ask for a job, or walk into a bar and ask for a drink, with absolutely no questions asked. He never seems to worry whether there's a roof over his head — more often than not, he's likely to dismount, lie on the ground, and sleep under the stars. And he never seems to go hungry — even if he hasn't money to pay for food, he's usually enterprising enough to find a way to earn his keep. In modern parlance, the classic Western hero is an irresponsible drifter who never comes across as irresponsible.

The appeal of the Western hero — that sense of total freedom — was one reason for the boom in Westerns that hit prime time television in the 1950s. But few of the early TV Westerns differed much from each other. The likes of The Lone Ranger, The Cisco Kid, Hopalong Cassidy, Roy Rogers and Gene Autry were mostly plot-driven, with the emphasis on "good guys versus bad guys" and "Cowboys and Indians," and they were almost always written for kids. By the mid-1950s, however, television's approach to the "oater" began to change with the onset of the so-called "adult Western" — shows that incorporated interesting, multi-dimensional characters into the traditional Western environment. Gunsmoke led the movement of "adult Westerns," and soon prime time saw such complex protagonists as Wyatt Earp (The Life and Legend of Wyatt Earp), Vint Bonner (The Restless Gun), Paladin (Have Gun, Will Travel), and Cheyenne Bodie (Cheyenne).

Cheyenne took the "adult Western" movement one step further: as the first hour-long Western, it showed that TV could present stories that were as sophisticated as those told in full-length motion pictures. But Cheyenne did not begin that way. Although ABC advertised Cheyenne as an "adult Western," the network instructed Warner Bros. to design the series, which aired at 7:30 p.m., specifically to attract a young audience. Knowing how much Westerns appealed to children, the network figured that a strong showing among younger viewers would translate into a strong audience share for the show. But the strategy backfired. After a few episodes, Cheyenne did not pull the numbers the network had anticipated; in addition, the stories were too simplistic, more juvenile in their approach than adult. Cheyenne's sponsors were enraged — they wanted the series to attract adult viewers, who, after all, were the ones who were going to buy their products. Warner Bros. immediately retooled Cheyenne; the key change was the innovative approach introduced by the series' new producer, Roy Huggins.

Huggins, born July 18, 1914 in Pierce County, Washington, began his career as a novelist in the 1940s. His first success came about after he sought the advice of respected mystery writer Howard Browne (The Taste of Ashes, Thin Air, Scotch on the Rocks), around 1945. Browne recalled his first encounter with Huggins. "I was editing pulp magazines in Chicago at the time," he said. "I had written several novels in the Chandler vein, when I received a letter from Roy asking me to take a look at his first novel, which

ROY HUGGINS WITH AWARDS IN BACKGROUND

was also written in the same style. He sent me his manuscript, and it was a hell of a story, but about three-quarters of the way through, it began to fall apart. But the talent was there — believe me, the man could write.

"I wrote him a long letter, spelling out what I would have done if I had written the book. A little time passed, and back came the manuscript with a note from Roy: 'I did exactly as you told me, so you're obligated to buy this.' I read the book again, and he'd done exactly that. It was one hell of a book [*The Double Take*], and I bought it, and William Morrow published it in hardcover. Then Roy sold the movie rights to Columbia Pictures [for what eventually became the film, *I Love Trouble*]. Roy insisted on writing the screenplay himself, even though he'd never written one before; but he did such a great job the studio signed him to a contract. He was off and running."

Huggins remained at Columbia Pictures for several years, where he flourished as a screenwriter of such films as *I Love Trouble*, *The Fuller Brush Man*, *The Lady Gambles*, *Hangman's Knot* (which he also directed), and *Pushover* (the picture that introduced Kim Novak, the last of the studio-created stars). In the meantime, the television industry was beginning to take off. Huggins recognized the tremendous opportunities the new medium offered, particularly to writers, and he started looking for a way in. That chance came about in 1955, shortly after he'd left Columbia, when Huggins received a phone call from his friend, director Richard Bare.

"I was producing a show called *Joe Palooka*, and I needed someone who could help me produce the scripts," remembered Bare. "I was producing and directing that show, and I didn't have time to work with the writers, so I asked Roy to come aboard. He helped me out for about twelve weeks. That was his first experience in television."

It was around this time that Warner Bros. Pictures decided to move into television. The studio had just worked out an arrangement to produce programs exclusively for the ABC television network, beginning in the fall of 1955. "Jack Warner had been resisting going into television for five years," explained Bare. "Early in my career, I shot a lot of B-pictures and short subjects for Warners; J.L. wouldn't allow me, or any of his other directors, to have a TV set any place visible on the set. That's how adamant Warner was against television: 'I'm not going to give those bums free advertising — they're already eating away at my box office.' But after he'd seen 20th Century-Fox and Columbia enter television about a year earlier, Warner changed his mind. He knew I could shoot fast, so he hired me as the first Warner Bros. television director.

"But Warners also needed producers, and so I told Bill Orr, who was in charge of Warners' television department, about my friend Roy Huggins. Bill asked, 'Has he ever produced anything?' And I said, 'No. But, I'll tell you: this guy can produce, because I worked with him on the *Joe Palooka* show, and I know that he's the greatest story mind I've ever run into.' I knew that Roy was available, and that he'd wanted to get into television. I called him at Columbia, where he was cleaning out his desk, having come to the end of his contract. 'Come over to Warners this afternoon and meet Bill Orr. He's looking for a TV producer.' Roy came over after lunch and I introduced him to Bill, who took my word for it and signed him on the spot. The first show he produced was *King's Row* [which, along with *Cheyenne* and *Casablanca*, aired under the umbrella *Warner Bros. Presents*].

"*Cheyenne* was the first [of those *Warner Bros. Presents* shows] that got off the ground, and I directed the entire first year of *Cheyenne*. But Bill and I were very unhappy with the producer that had done the first two or three *Cheyenne*s. The stories were mundane, and the sponsor sent us a wire that told us how bad they were. ABC was ready to cancel us. That's when Roy came over — and I was just delighted to work with him again.

"After Roy took over *Cheyenne*, we got another telegram from the sponsor — this time, it read, 'Now you're on the right track.' So that solidified Roy as a producer."

Under Huggins' guidance, *Cheyenne* became the only hit series on *Warner Bros. Presents* — the other two shows disappeared by the middle of the 1955-56 season. Huggins produced *Cheyenne* for the remainder of its first year. Although he was happy to experience the show's tremendous commercial success, Huggins felt somewhat restricted by *Cheyenne*'s Western format. So when an opportunity arose to take over another series for the 1956-57 season, Huggins left *Cheyenne* to produce *Conflict*, an anthology series depicting how people reacted to sudden changes in their lives. Shortly after he began working on *Conflict*, Huggins first came up with the idea for what would become his breakthrough series.

"The three or four shows that had been done before I took over *Cheyenne* reminded me of what was wrong with the usual, run-of-the-mill Western: there was a fascinating sameness about them," Huggins explained. "In every show there was either a gunfight, a saloon fight, or both; and in most instances the outcome of the story was predictable within five or six minutes. The cliches were always there, and to me, the Western had become a rather boring thing. It seemed to me that if there was any fun to be had from doing a Western, it would require a good-natured but irreverent assault on the entire Western formula.

"So I began to think about doing a Western that would take on these cliches in a subtle way. It would be a Western infused with humor — meaning, on the surface, it would look like a straightforward Western, and tell Western stories, but underneath, it would poke fun at the conventions of the traditional Western. I wanted to do a Western series that would turn every cliche inside out — even to the way the hero dressed. For example, in most Westerns, the dude gambler is the 'bad guy,' and he dresses in black. So I would make the dude gambler dressed in black the 'good guy,' but a good guy whose attitudes are the reverse of the typical Western hero."

The hero of the traditional Western is an altruist, someone who wouldn't hesitate to risk his life if someone ran up to him and asked for help. The hero Huggins had in mind would be more of a pragmatist. "My character would say, 'You need help? You see that building over there? That's the sheriff's office. Go over there and ask him for help,'" explained Huggins. "Or he'd say, 'Sure, I'll help you — but what's in it for me? Is there any money in it?' The typical Western hero was dedicated to serving the good of his fellow man, but my character would be dedicated to serving his *own* good.

"That was the idea I had in mind — it would be a Western, but with a different spin. I thought the audience might like it, because it would be a fresh approach to the Western."

The hero of Huggins' conceptual Western would be patterned after a popular literary character known as "the gentle grafter." "There were dozens of books about grafters written in the early part of the 20th century and in the latter part of the 19th century," the producer explained. "It was a character that people in the Gilded Age liked. In fact, there's a great deal in *Maverick* that I didn't invent. The reluctant hero, for example, was something I borrowed from popular film. You can find him in almost every movie Bogart made — in fact, all of the *film noir* heroes tended to be reluctant heroes."

However, the concept of the reluctant hero would be new to television at the time, and certainly new to the standard TV Western. Huggins was confident that viewers would like his idea; however, he couldn't develop it right away because he was busy producing *Conflict*. Huggins kept the idea in the back of his mind and waited for an opportunity when he might be able to pursue it. Such an opportunity came up in late 1956, while Huggins was preparing an episode of *Conflict* called "The Man from 1997." "Something accidental happened on that show that altered the lives of a number of people, including my own," he recalled.

"The show contained one of those thankless supporting roles usually played by a contract actor. The role was that of a smalltime hustler — the kind of guy who's always betting on horse races — and it had a number of lines that could be funny in the hands of a good actor. Bill Orr [the executive in charge of television at Warners, and as such, *Conflict*'s executive producer] asked me to use an inexperienced actor he had signed to a contract about a year earlier — a big, good-looking young man from Oklahoma named James Garner. I had used him in another thankless role on *Cheyenne* and, frankly, had not been impressed.

"On the second day of production on 'The Man from 1997,' I went to the regular run of the dailies to see how Garner was doing. I made it a rule not to look at dailies at the regularly scheduled time, when they were seen by the crew, the executives, and the network liaison. I watched them alone or with the film editor because it's enough of a problem to judge scenes soundly, shot as they are from three or four angles and out of sequence, without adding other distractions, like comments on wardrobe, makeup and hair style. Or, worse yet, laughter at something that is forced or cute or false.

"One of Garner's scenes came on. Jim read a line, and the whole room burst into laughter. And they were right. The editor turned to me and said, 'Christ, I had no idea that line was funny!' I wanted to think that I had stumbled onto hidden treasure. I knew for certain the reading hadn't come from the director — that kind of purity can come only from the actor.

"I had talked with Jim Garner at length more than once. He looked and sounded like an amiable cowboy, and I had never heard him say anything remotely funny. But as the scene went on, other lines that had been written with only a forlorn hope that they might evoke a chuckle were being made funnier than they had any right to be by Garner's skewed and underplayed delivery.

"I really had stumbled onto something wonderful, the rarest thing there is in Hollywood: an actor with an unerring instinct for a funny line. Some lines are funny almost no matter how they are read (punch lines, joke lines), but humor that genuinely works is the kind that comes out of character, and is funny only if the actor knows how that character would read the line and why.

"After I saw the dailies on 'The Man from 1997,' I knew I had the actor who could play the character I had in mind. I could build that Western around James Garner."

Fate brought James Garner not only to Roy Huggins' attention; it had brought him to Warner Bros. and to acting in general. James Scott Bumgarner was born in Norman, Oklahoma on April 7, 1928. His mother died when he was five. At age 16, he quit high school to join the Merchant Marines, where he served for one year. Jim then moved to Los Angeles, where his father had relocated, and attended Hollywood High School for about a year. One of his first jobs was modeling swim trunks for Jantzen Sportswear. After a year on the West Coast, Jim Bumgarner returned to Oklahoma, where he starred in football at Norman High School, and later joined the State National Guard. In 1950, he was drafted for the Korean War; as an infantryman, he served 14 months in Korea for the Fifth Regimental Combat Team of the 24th Division and was awarded two Purple Hearts for wounds suffered in action. After his discharge in 1952, Jim enrolled at Norman University (he completed his high school education while in the Army), but he dropped out after one semester and returned to Los Angeles to work with his father, a carpet layer.

Then fate stepped in. One day, while driving up La Brea Avenue in Los Angeles, Jim Bumgarner noticed a sign that read PAUL GREGORY AND ASSOCIATES. When he lived in L.A. before the War, Jim had met Paul Gregory, who worked at a soda fountain across the street from the gas station where Jim worked after school. Back then, Gregory, who had wanted to become a talent agent, suggested that Jim take up acting; now Gregory was a successful agent and producer, so Bumgarner, who was now exploring career possibilities, decided to pay his old friend a visit. "Here's the part where fate steps in," Garner told *Playboy* in 1981. "If I get an urge to do something but it's not convenient for me to do it, I won't do it. Well, there was a parking space in Paul's building — and if that space hadn't been there, I never would have driven around the block to look for one."

Soon after meeting with Gregory, Jim won a role as one of the judges in the national stage production of *The Caine Mutiny Court-Martial*. Jim never spoke a word of dialogue during the year he was in the play, but he learned a lot about acting from watching the stars of the show — Henry Fonda, Lloyd Nolan, and John Hodiak. (He cued Fonda and Nolan as they learned their parts, and later became Hodiak's understudy.) In 1954, after 512 performances, Bumgarner was offered the role of Lt. Steve Maryk in the *Caine Mutiny Court-Martial* in a new national tour directed by film great Charles Laughton. After a few performances, Laughton met with the young actor and gave him an indispensible word of advice.

"I was sure Laughton was about to can me, because, although I knew my lines, I wasn"t very good," Garner told *Playboy*. "He told me, 'Jim, your problem is that you're afraid to be bad. Therefore you do nothing. You go down the middle of the road and you have no highs and you have no lows."And he was right. I was still afraid of being laughed at, of trying not to be bad instead of focusing on being good....Laughton told me that if I wans"t any good, he'd let me know , and to leave it to him And ever since then, I'll stick my neck out and leave it to the director to chop it off if he has to."

After touring with this second *Caine Mutiny Court-Martial* production for seven months, Garner returned to Los Angeles in 1955, where he filmed a commercial for Winston cigarettes that has become somewhat famous. According to Garner, the ad took off because one of his lines contained a grammatical error—"Winston tastes good like a cigarette should," instead of *as* a cigarette should. The slogan did become very popular, while the struggling young actor survived off the income he made from that commercial for nearly one year.

In the meantime, the fledgling television department at Warner Bros. had decided to keep an eye out for new acting prospects. "Jack Warner had told Bill Orr that as long as the studio was going to make all these films for TV, he was going to need a lot of new faces," said Richard Bare. "Warner didn't want to pay established stars — he wanted to develop new talent, mostly because it would be cheaper to do it that way. So Bill gathered all the TV producers and directors and asked us to look for new faces.

"As it so happened, I had seen a 'new face' the night before, at a restaurant bar in Los Angeles called the Rondelay. I couldn't remember the fellow's name, but a friend of mine named Bob Lowry had introduced me to him. I called Bob and asked for the guy's name. Bob said, 'Oh, yeah. That was Jim Bumgarner.' Bob didn't know how to get hold of him; he'd just been meeting Jim at the bar. But I also knew the bartender at the Rondelay, so I called him and left a message for Bumgarner to call me at Warner Bros.

"Now, coincidentally, we were about to shoot the first episode of *Cheyenne*, which was also going to be the first television show filmed at Warners. We had completely cast the show, with one exception — we had not found an actor to play a young Union Army lieutenant. It was a one-scene, one-day part.

"Hoping to fill this part, I kept calling the bartender — 'Has Bumgarner come in?' 'No,' replied the bartender. 'Well, please tell him to call me.' This went on for three days. Finally, Jim called me. 'Mr. Bare, I understand you're looking for me,' he said. 'Yeah, Jim,' I said, 'it's two-thirty in the afternoon, can you come right out to the studio?' And he said, 'I'll be there in twenty minutes.' Which he was.

"I gave him the scene to read, and he auditioned. He wasn't very good, but there was some quality that I saw in him, and so we read the scene a couple of times, hoping he might loosen up a little bit. So, finally, after an hour or so, we had a chance to read in front of Bill — Bill had to okay everything in those days, and since this was the very first TV film with Jack Warner's name on it, everything had to be just right."

Several hours passed by the time Garner finished auditioning in the office of William T. Orr. The scene with the Army lieutenant was scheduled to begin shooting the following morning, so it was vital that Orr approve the casting of Bumgarner — there simply was no time to look for anyone else. Orr and Bare stepped outside into the anteroom. Orr immediately liked Bumgarner, but he was concerned about about the actor's lack of experience. "Bill asked if we could get somebody better," Bare continued. "I said, 'Bill, we are going on location tomorrow morning at six a.m., and I need to know if I can have this guy play this role. It's an important role.' Bill said, rather begrudgingly, 'Well, all right, if you think you can get a performance out of him . . .' I said, 'I'll guarantee I'll get you a performance.'

"We went out the next day, and we shot the film. And Jim was fine. The day after that, Jack Warner was looking at the dailies with Bill Orr. When Jim came on, Warner asked, 'Who's that guy?' — he even called out to the projectionist and said, 'I want to look at that tall kid again.' And as he watched Jim, Warner turned to Bill and asked, 'What's his name?' 'Jim Bumgarner,' said Bill. And Jack Warner said, 'Take the 'bum' out and give him a seven-year contract.'"

Since Bare was directly responsible for bringing both Roy Huggins and James Garner to Warner Bros., you might say that he is, in a sense, *Maverick*'s "true" creator.

"I certainly didn't create *Maverick* from a conceptual form — that was Roy's doing altogether," Bare said. "But I did a have a hand in bringing together the two ingredients that made *Maverick* the success it was — Roy and Jim."

Shortly after signing Garner, Warners wasted little time in putting him to work. In addition to guest roles on *Cheyenne* and *Conflict*, the studio put the young actor in two of its 1956 feature films, *Shootout at Medicine Bend* (directed by Richard Bare) and *Toward the Unknown*.

2.   A TALE OF TWO PILOTS

Meanwhile, shortly after the completion of "The Man from 1997," an opportunity arose for Roy Huggins to pitch his idea for his prospective series about the gentle grafter. In October 1956, ABC president Leonard Goldenson assigned Robert Lewine, one of the network's programming executives, to arrange a meeting with Warner Bros. to discuss possible new series ideas for the 1957-58 season. Among those who met with Lewine were Warners TV head William T. Orr, executive story editor Jack Emanuel, and Roy Huggins. At this meeting, Huggins presented Lewine with two ideas that the network executive immediately liked. The first proposal was for a series based on the adventures of Stuart Bailey, the private detective whom Huggins had created for a series of novellas written for *The Saturday Evening Post*; the second was for his series about the gentle grafter.

After receiving the go-ahead from Lewine and Orr, Huggins went to work on the pilot script for his Western series, which he eventually named *Maverick*. "A 'maverick' was originally, as one of the *Maverick* scripts once put it, 'a calf who has lost his mother, and whose father has run off with another cow,'" Huggins explained. "Later, the word came to refer to anyone who doesn't run with the herd — a stray. And I have a feeling that *Maverick* itself may have contributed to the ultimate meaning of the word as a kind of good-natured, unaggressive nonconformist." The name "Bret Maverick" was derived from two sources: Samuel A. Maverick (1803-1872), a Texas cattleman renowned for his independence; and Huggins' oldest son, Bret.

Huggins laid out the basics of the Maverick character in his pilot episode, "Point Blank." "First, Maverick is flat broke, and he cons a cowboy out of five bucks with a game you can't win — if you're the cowboy, you can't win. It's called the 'belt game,'" he explained. "I spent a large part of my childhood in a private school, an oldtime military school called the Hill Military Academy, founded in the 19th century, located on the outskirts of Portland, Oregon. My father died when I was very young, and my mother wanted my brother and me to have male role models, so she sent us to Hill Military Academy. Well, Hill Military Academy had a habit of hiring ex-military officers and noncoms. If you spent enough time at Hill, it was like being in the Army for four years. And among the many things I learned were a lot of Army con games. I learned the belt game, among others. The belt game was a very simple game, which Maverick uses in 'Point Blank.' [Maverick takes off his belt, rolls it up, and challenges the cowboy to push a pencil inside one of the loops so that the pencil comes out inside the belt when he unrolls it. Whether the pencil is in or out of the loop depends on how Maverick unrolls the belt.]]

"Maverick cons a dumb cowboy out of five bucks. With his five bucks, he gets into a poker game — and when he sits down at a poker table with ordinary cowboys, that's a form of cheating, too, because they don't know what they're doing. They're there to have fun and gamble, and Maverick's there to take their money. Maverick came out okay in the game, and after the game, he gives the cowboy whom he'd cheated ten bucks — his original five dollars, plus 100% interest. However, the sheriff arrests Maverick for running a con game!

"Also in this original *Maverick* pilot, he has a love affair with a beautiful girl, but she's an accomplice in a murder, and there's a reward for proving that she's guilty. And Maverick proves it. He turns her over — and then quibbles about the size of the reward! The sheriff, who also loves this girl, says 'I want you out of this town in ten minutes.' And Maverick says, 'Sheriff, I've gotten out of towns this size in *five* minutes.'

"That was pure *Maverick*, and it never changed. I did shows that were more complex in their con, but that was the one of the better *Maverick*s."

But Huggins encountered a stumbling block that would prevent him from proceeding with "Point Blank" as *Maverick*'s pilot episode. Several years earlier, the Writers Guild of America had won a history-making concession in the basic contract with the major film studios — the "created by" royalty, which rewarded a royalty to any writer who created a TV series based on his own characters and his own original story. In 1957, the royalty on a one-hour series was $500 for each weekly episode for the life of the series. However, the writer would not be entitled to a "created by" royalty if the Guild determined that the series was based on material (a novel, a film, etc.) that was already owned by the studio or which had previously been published or released. Since Jack Warner had already determined that he wanted to produce his television shows as inexpensively as possible, he demanded that the pilot episode of every Warner Bros. series had to be based on a property owned by the studio. Each of the first three series produced by the studio was based on Warner Bros. films — *Cheyenne*, *Casablanca*, and *King's Row*.

Huggins was informed that, because the story and characters in "Point Blank" were entirely his creation, he could not use them as the basis for the pilot of *Maverick*. "J.L. Warner had laid down the law: 'If we have to give up a series, we'll give it up; but I will never pay a royalty to any writer,'" Huggins explained. "It was Bill Orr's unfortunate job [as the head of the television department] to enforce that edict. Orr informed me in writing that my original story could not be used for the pilot, and that I would have to find a wholly-owned Warners property on which to base *Maverick*, or else there would be no series.

"I didn't want *Maverick* to die because I really *wanted* to do the series. I must have known that the series would take off: it was fresh and it needed to be done. The airwaves were full of tired old traditional Westerns and I knew that this would just grab the audience; they would love it and it would be a smash. I said to myself, I've got the actor in Jim Garner — he's under contract to Warners, and I can't take him with me. I'll have to find a way to get this thing done under their rules."

A short time later, Huggins found what he needed in a non-fiction book that Warners had purchased some time before — C.B. Glasscock's *The War of the Copper Kings*, the story of how a clever lawyer used an obscure but still operational law to beat the Amalgamated Copper Company out of a fortune. Although Huggins' story (which he eventually called "The War of the Silver Kings"), as well as the Maverick character, were completely different from the Glasscock book, he did incorporate the guileful legal device into his adaptation; therefore, Warner Bros. could assert that *Maverick* had originated from a studio-owned property. Thus, "The War of the Silver Kings" became the pilot of *Maverick* because the studio would not have to pay him a "created by" royalty. ("Point Blank," the original pilot, became the second episode of the series.) This explains why Huggins' name never appeared on the series' credits as the creator of *Maverick*. To solidify its claim of ownership, Warners commissioned the drafting of several proposals in 1957 (*Concho, Cameo Kirby*) whose concepts were strikingly similar to the one which Huggins presented to Robert Lewine in October 1956. The studio even went so far as to purchase a treatment that Huggins had written for Columbia Pictures (see the discussion of the episode "The War of the Silver Kings"). However, in fairness to the Warner Bros. of today, it should be pointed out that the *Maverick* movie produced by Warner Bros. in 1994 prominently displays this credit: "Based on the Series Created by Roy Huggins." Huggins did not ask for this credit, and Warners was not under any legal compulsion to give it.

In early 1957, Huggins assigned James O'Hanlon to write the teleplay for "The War of the Silver Kings," which was scheduled to air as a segment of *Conflict* in April 1957. In the meantime, the star of the series was in Japan making a feature. Director Joshua Logan (*Mr. Roberts*) had cast James Garner to play Marlon Brando's sidekick in *Sayonara* (1957), a role which proved to be the young star's big screen breakthrough — later in the year, Warners cast him as the lead in *Darby's Rangers* (1958).

3. SHOOTING THE PILOT

By the time Garner had returned from location shooting on *Sayonara*, Warners had hired Budd Boetticher to direct the pilot episode of *Maverick*. Boetticher, a former pugilist and professional bullfighter, had already established himself as a major film director with such films as *Bullfighter and the Lady*, *Wings of the Hawk*, *East of Sumatra*, *The Man from the Alamo*, and *The Magnificent Matador*. By 1957, Boetticher had completed the first two [of what would eventually amount to seven] Westerns between 1956 and 1960 that would secure for himself an enthusiastic following of connoisseurs of the genre both in this country and abroad.

When he agreed to direct the pilot, Boetticher wasn't aware that James Garner, or that any actor, had been cast as Maverick. In fact, Boetticher had never heard of Garner, with good reason — prior to *Sayonara*, Garner had not been well known outside of Warner Bros. By coincidence, however, Boetticher happened to "discover" his star while watching some early footage of *Sayonara*. "I was at Warner Bros. one day, and I was walking down the street on my way to lunch when I ran into Jack Warner, with whom I'd always had a great relationship," Boetticher recalled. "Warner said to me, 'Budd, come with me, I want to take you into the projection room and show you one of the worst things I've ever seen in my life.' And I said, 'Colonel [one of Warner's nicknames], I really am late for lunch. I have to—' He said, 'Please come in with me.'

"So we went into a projection room, and I sat down with all of his executives — Steve Trilling, Walter McKuen, Bill Orr. The lights went out, and on came a scene from *Sayonara*. Naturally, I recognized Brando right away, and with him was a most attractive, slightly overweight, very athletic-looking young actor in a green Navy uniform. And Brando looked [into the camera] to where Josh Logan was sitting, and he said 'Okay, Josh, are we rolling?' Logan's voice said, 'We've been rolling for quite a while. I said Action, Marlon. Action.' Then Brando asks him, 'Where do I look?' Logan says, 'Marlon, you look over there to the bridge — there's a fellow waving to you where you should.' Then Brando says, 'Jesus Christ, I can't play a scene if I have to look at some fellow waving to me with a handkerchief. Will you get him off of there?' So they get the poor fellow off the bridge, and then Marlon said, 'Are we still rolling?' Logan said, 'We've been rolling for some time, Marlon. Action!'

"Brando then asked, 'What do I say?' So, you hear the script girl's voice in the background: '"Here she comes now,"' Mr. Brando. "Here she comes now." That's what you say.' Brando then turns to the nice-looking fellow in the green uniform, and asked 'Do you have your line?' and the young fellow said, 'I'm all ready, Marlon. Go right ahead.' Brando asks again, 'Are we rolling?' 'Yes, we're rolling,' said Josh Logan, 'Action!' Then Brando said, 'But I don't know who she is, do I?' Logan: 'You know who she is, Marlon. She's the woman that you fall in love with — you already know this if you've read the script.' 'So I'm happy to see her?' 'Yes, you're happy to see her, Marlon.'

"This went on for the entire nine minutes — at 25 cents a foot, and at 1 1/2 feet-per-second Technicolor film. They never got the shot. Watching Brando was driving

Jack Warner crazy, but it hadn't bothered me, because I had been paying attention to the young actor in the green uniform. I stood up and I said to Warner, 'Maybe he could play Maverick.' Warner blew his top — he said, 'That son-of-a-bitch is never going to work for this studio again.' And I said, 'Why?' Warner said, 'We need Marlon Brando like we need —' And I said, 'I'm not talking about Marlon Brando. Who's the other fellow, the one in the green uniform?' And someone said, 'That's James Garner.'

"Whenever you have something as enormously successful as *Maverick*, everyone involved has his or her story on how it came to be. And that's my version of how Jim became Maverick. I don't think I discovered Jim — I would be very proud if I had. I understand, from what I've read, that they [Orr and Huggins] already had him in mind to play Maverick. But that's the first time that I ever saw Jim Garner."

Garner returned from Japan sometime in February 1957. He and Boetticher hit it off immediately; they worked out together and played golf every day in the weeks before shooting began on the pilot. "Jim thought he was a little overweight when he came back, so we went to the gym every day, and from that point on we became dear, dear friends," said Boetticher. "We worked our tails off — I think Jim lost about thirty pounds for the pilot. But, in addition to becoming friends with Jim, I also discovered what a master athlete he was. There's a sequence in the pilot where Maverick's supposed to dive behind a table and shoot a gun out of some cowboy's hand. When you watch Jim perform that stunt on film, you'll see how smooth and graceful he carries it out. Everything Jim did athletically, he did tremendously well."

Production began on "The War of the Silver Kings" on March 4, 1957. Although Boetticher did have prior experience with the frenetic pace of television (in 1951, he shot a one-hour adaptation of *The Three Musketeers* in just three days), he advised Warners TV department head William Orr that he would need more than the standard length of time allotted for filming a one-hour television picture (six days). "Bill had assured me that *Maverick* was an important project," said Boetticher. "The script was excellent; Roy had created a great character, and I had a great personality in James Garner. Bill said, 'Do whatever you want. Just help us sell this pilot.'"

Production on the pilot lasted ten calendar days. Boetticher initially shot *Maverick* as he did his other Westerns — that is, as a big screen feature, emphasizing vast panoramic views over tight shots of the actors. This prompted Orr to send the director a friendly reminder of the need to film *Maverick* within the confines of television. "I received a very formal letter from Mr. Bill Orr, but it was written with his sense of humor," Boetticher recalled. "'Dear Mr. Boetticher [he wrote], I've admired your work for the past two days, but we are not making *Gone with the Wind*. It's more important that we see who the people are as close as we could get, because this is not your usual wide screen feature, and I would appreciate your cooperation.'

"I didn't say anything about the letter. The next day, I shot all the closeups I figured I needed for the entire picture. I sent Bill a whole day's worth of closeups, nothing else, and it became a joke around the studio.

"A few days later, as we were nearing the end of the pilot, I received another message from Bill Orr, that we were 'behind schedule', and that if I hadn't wrapped up the production by four o'clock that afternoon, he was going to come down to the set and pull the plug himself. We decided to play a joke on Bill.

"At four o'clock, Bill came down to pull the plug, which he did. The lights were out for about a minute. But when he turned them back on, there was nobody there — we had all gone across the street to the local bar! A few minutes later, Bill came over, and he said, 'Come on back, Budd, I was only kidding!'

Boetticher completed the pilot, but "The War of the Silver Kings" did not air on *Conflict*, as scheduled. Instead, the film went into the hands of James Aubrey, the executive who ran the entire programming department at ABC-TV. The network decided to show the pilot to a prospective sponsor, billionaire metals industrialist Henry Kaiser, who at the time owned the third largest aluminum company in the world. Kaiser had made his fortune paving highways in Cuba in the 1920s, and he also built Bonneville Dam, Grand Coulee Dam, and Hoover Dam. Kaiser's company played an instrumental

role in the outcome of World War II by providing hundreds of Liberty Ships to the Allies.

Kaiser informed ABC network president Leonard Goldenson that he wanted to broaden his base of appeal (Kaiser Industries was not well known outside the West Coast) by sponsoring a weekly Sunday night program. Kaiser had suggested a series of feature films, newly released for television, that would air from 8:00 p.m. to 10:00 p.m. When the network was unable to accommodate Kaiser's first request, Goldenson promised Kaiser that he would look for something that would pique the industrialist's interest.

Kaiser was something of a maverick himself: he had prided himself on pulling off accomplishments that no one believed were possible. The network had proposed scheduling *Maverick* on Sunday evenings from 7:30 p.m. to 8:30 p.m. — directly against two Top Ten shows on CBS (*The Jack Benny Program*, *The Ed Sullivan Show*) and a third proven audience favorite in NBC's *The Steve Allen Show*. Kaiser's friends advised him not to back *Maverick*; one of them, famed TV personality Art Linkletter (*House Party*, *People are Funny*), warned him that "there are already a zillion Westerns on the air, and you'll be up against three champions in Sullivan, Allen and Benny; your *Maverick* will die like a dog."

But Kaiser bought *Maverick* simply because he liked what he'd seen — and specifically, because he loved James Garner in the role. ABC, Warner Bros. and Kaiser Industries became partners in the series, with each sharing one-third of the show's profits and merchandising revenue. ABC scheduled *Maverick*'s debut for Sunday night, September 22, 1957.

4. THE MAVERICK APPROACH

In the meantime, while ABC was courting Kaiser Industries, Roy Huggins continued producing *Conflict*; among the segments he completed was "Anything for Money," the first of two pilots for what became *77 Sunset Strip*, the second series he'd proposed to ABC programming executive Robert Lewine in October 1956. When *Conflict* was cancelled at the end of the 1956-57 season, Huggins immediately threw himself into the making of *Maverick*. The series' creator/producer was very clear on what *Maverick* was — and what it wasn't. "I never intended *Maverick* to be a satire on Westerns, because I didn't think that satire could work on a weekly basis," he explained. "I never intended it to be an 'anti-Western,' either, although I *did* use that term for publicity purposes. But describing *Maverick* as an anti-Western is misleading because *Maverick* was a Western: it had to be confined to a certain period and geographical area, which limited the kinds of stories we could tell. Although Maverick was a dude gambler and a con artist, those characteristics also restricted the scope of the series."

What Huggins had designed, therefore, was a series that would have all the trappings of a straightforward Western, but with one element that had been rarely evident in the genre: a sense of humor. But the series was never intended as a comedy Western. "I wanted the writers and directors to understand that when Maverick slipped out the rear window, he wasn't trying to be funny," said Huggins. "The humor of the show was generated from Maverick's character, never from the situation. Even in those stories later on [in my two years on the show] where the premise of the story was relatively light — such as 'Shady Deal at Sunny Acres,' 'The Rivals,' or 'The Saga of Waco

Williams' — I strived to place Maverick in situations that were plausible, never farfetched. *Maverick* was not a 'comedy Western.' *Maverick* was a Western with humor."

In other words, Huggins played it straight more often than not, particularly in the first season. The majority of the episodes during his two-season tenure with the show depicted straightforward Western stories that did not always allow for infusions of humor. Although *Maverick*'s approach to humor began to resemble more that of a "situation comedy" after Huggins departed the series, the same holds true for the majority of the third-through-fifth-year episodes. "Which leaves me with an opening to say that *Maverick*'s reputation isn't what it's cracked up to be — as much as I hate to say that," Huggins added. "*Maverick*'s reputation was based on its attitude, and on maybe ten or twelve unusual scripts. The rest of the shows were pretty much straight-forward Western dramas."

Huggins devised a list of ten "guidelines" to writing and directing a *Maverick* episode that became well-publicized during the height of the series' popularity in early 1959. "If I had known that those 'ten points' were going to be as widely read and analyzed as they have been, or will be, I'd have left a couple out," he admitted. "In some cases, whenever I referred to 'Maverick's essential indolence,' I was having fun at the character's expense; and I'm sure that I contributed a lot to some of the misconceptions of the show when I said that 'in a *Maverick* story, the situation is always hopeless, but never serious.'"

Having been advised by Huggins himself to take some of this with a grain of salt, here is "The Ten-Point Guide to Happiness While Writing or Directing a *Maverick*:"

1. Maverick is the original disorganization man.

2. Maverick's primary motivation is that ancient and most noble of motives: the profit motive.

3. Heavies in *Maverick* are always absolutely right, and they are always beloved to someone.

4. The cliché flourishes in the creative arts because the familiar gives a sense of comfort and security. Writers and directors of *Maverick* are requested to *live danger-ously*.

5. Maverick's activities are seldom grandiose. To force him into magnificent specu-lations is to lose sight of his essential indolence.

6. The *Maverick* series is a regeneration story in which the regeneration has been indefinitely postponed.

7. Maverick's travels are never aimless; he always has an object in view: his pocket and yours. However, there are times when he is merely fleeing from heroic enterprise.

8. In the traditional Western story the situation is always serious, but never hopeless. In a *Maverick* story the situation is always hopeless, but never serious.

9. "Cowardly" would be too strong a word to apply to Maverick. "Cautious" is possibly more accurate, and certainly more kind. When the two brothers went off to the Civil War their old Pappy said to them: "If either of you comes back with a medal I'll beat you to death." They never shamed him.

10. The widely held belief that Maverick is a gambler is a fallacy. In his hands poker is not a game of chance. He plays it earnestly, patiently, and with an abiding faith in the laws of probability.

Some of these points, however, are right on the mark. Maverick was never as much of a coward as he's purported to be; he'd certainly make a lousy poker player if he was. A true coward never attempts *anything*, let alone a bluff. Also, "fleeing from heroic enterprise" doesn't necessarily make him a coward. One of Maverick's primary rules (second only to "Line thy pockets") is "Preserve thyself," which would entail avoiding troublesome situations — if there was any way to get out of the matter, he would do so. However, as episodes such as "Day of Reckoning," "A Rage for Vengeance," and "The Ghost Soldiers" depict, when faced with no other alternative, he would shed his reluctant facade and tackle the situation head on. And while "gamblin' is his game," Maverick was not a gambler, per se. Maverick laid out his philosophy in the episode "Duel at Sundown:" "Only one man in a hun'red plays poker with regards to the odds. Luck's important only when you sit down with men who play as tight as you do. When I find that out, I quit — it's gambling."

Some of the guidelines to *Maverick* which were not included in the "ten points" were nevertheless present in the character, if not always presented explicitly in the series. "Sometime early in the first season, after he had directed one or two shows, Budd Boetticher suggested that Maverick should have a horse of his own," said Huggins. "Budd thought that Maverick should ride the same horse every week. I think I knew why he'd said that, because Budd knew the genre (he made all those great Westerns with Randolph Scott), and on top of that, *he* was a horseman. I said to him, 'Budd, I've got to tell you something important but secret about Maverick: he doesn't like horses. Maverick would *sell* his horse in a minute if he needed a stake in a poker game.' Now, I don't believe we ever saw that in any of my shows, but that was part of what I had in mind for the series." (Apparently, Maverick changed his mind about horses after Huggins left, because in *Bret Maverick* he had a regular horse, Lowball.)

Huggins and Boetticher apparently did not see eye-to-eye on one other character aspect. "Maverick was a hero who didn't like being a hero," said Huggins. "At best, he was a reluctant hero, always ready to go out the rear window of a saloon. I had a sequence written into 'According to Hoyle' with Maverick and Big Mike McComb (Leo Gordon); Big Mike was supposed to say 'Let's go back in there and get this guy,' and Maverick's supposed to say, 'Hey, wait a minute now, Mike, let's think this over,' or something like that. But when I watched that sequence in the dailies, the lines had been switched: McComb now had the reluctant lines that were written for Maverick.

"I found out that Budd had switched the lines. When I asked him why, he said that he didn't believe that heroes should talk that way. I explained to him that what he had done wasn't what I had in mind for the character. Now, don't get me wrong: Budd Boetticher is an excellent director, but we didn't agree on that concept of *Maverick*."

Boetticher was already an established director prior to *Maverick*, and he felt well within his rights to change the dialogue to suit what *he* wanted. Huggins disagreed with Boetticher. While Boetticher may not have agreed with the final decision, he did respect the producer's right to maintain control over his creation. Boetticher had always realized one of the key differences between shooting television and shooting for the big screen. "Television is a producer's medium — it has to be — and the producer has the final say," he explained. "Feature-filmmaking is a director's medium — at least, it *should* be." Given that difference, as well as the fact that both Boetticher and Huggins are strong personalities, it's no surprise that they had a difference in opinion. Boetticher did not direct any more *Maverick*s after "According to Hoyle" — he went on to film *Buchanan Rides Alone* (1958), the fourth in his series of seven classic Westerns starring Randolph Scott.

It should be noted, however, that Boetticher and Huggins were not always at odds when it came to *Maverick*; both agreed as to how to approach the humor of the show. "Laurel and Hardy were paid to be funny, and they did pratfalls and did funny things. But that was not *Maverick*," Boetticher said. "There's nothing in the world worse than when you have an actor who looks into the camera and says, 'Boy, this next line's gonna kill you. It's really funny.' You don't see any of that in the *Maverick*s I directed. You don't expect Jim to be funny, but when he is, he's really funny, because he played it straight. The humor was already in the script."

Boetticher was not pleased to see the broader, slapstick humor that characterized *Maverick* in the years after Roy Huggins' departure. "I think I saw two *Maverick*s [from the last three seasons], and my reaction is still as it was then. I said, 'Jesus Christ, look what they've done to *Maverick*!' and I never saw them again," the director said. "So I'm intentionally no authority on what happened to *Maverick*. But it shouldn't have happened to *Maverick*, and it did."

5. MAVERICK'S WRITERS AND DIRECTORS

Having devised a definite scheme for the show, Huggins went about developing stories for the 26 episodes scheduled for *Maverick*'s first season. In the meantime, he also began to assemble a team of writers and directors who also understood his approach to the show. Douglas Heyes (11), Marion Hargrove (9), Howard Browne (8), Russell Hughes (4), Gene Levitt (4), Montgomery Pittman (3), and Gerald Drayson Adams (3) combined with Huggins to write 42 of the 53 *Maverick* episodes produced in the first two seasons. After Boetticher directed the first three segments of the series, the majority of Huggins' episodes were helmed by three directors: Heyes, who directed 11 shows (including ten of his own scripts); Leslie Martinson (13); and Richard Bare (9). Martinson also directed five episodes in the third-and-fourth seasons; Bare directed two third-season shows.

Howard Browne, Douglas Heyes and Marion Hargrove were the core members of Huggins' writing team. Browne, of course, played a key role in Huggins' early writing career; Huggins reciprocated by bringing Browne into television in 1955. "Roy telephoned me around the time he first came to Warner Bros.," remembered Browne. "This was several years after he sent me his first manuscript; we had since met each other, and became friends. I was still in Chicago editing pulp magazines and quite happy.

"One day Roy called me and said, 'Howard, I want you to quit your job and come out here and write television for me.' I said, 'Roy, I wouldn't know a screenplay if it bit me in the ass!' He said, 'Well, we'll give you a couple of samples; all you have to do is come up with the story, and then you write the screenplay. Come on out. But quit your job — I know you can do it.'

"I told Roy that I wasn't going to quit my job, but I did take a leave of absence, and I came out to L.A. Everything was set up for me. I looked at the two scripts Roy had sent me, then I thought for a while, then I came to the studio to meet with Roy. I told him I had an idea for *Cheyenne*, and I described how I was going to open it. I wasn't very far in my presentation, when I noticed Roy was beginning to laugh.

"I asked him what was so funny. Roy said, 'That's pretty fancy, Howard. Let's see, the opening is in Omaha, and you have a train of the period pulling into the station. Behind an ornamental fence, you see people getting in at the front of the train. We have a bunch of settlers, their wives, their children, their luggage and everything. I've got to tell you, Howard, that you've just blown the entire budget of the picture in the opening sequence!'

"I thought, 'What did I know about budgets?'

"Roy continued, 'I'll get a call from the Prop Department, and they'll say, 'We have your ornamental iron fence, Mr. Huggins. It'll cost $15,000, but we have it.' So I then said to Roy, 'All right, let's do this: suppose we make the couples newly married and they don't have any children yet. And since they're poor people, they're travelling very light; instead of having a train, can you mock up the front of a train with some engine sounds, and they won't be boarding it, they'll be disembarking.' When I finished, Roy said, 'Now you're talking like a television writer.'

"I enjoyed working for Roy Huggins more than any other producer I worked for," Browne continued. "Roy was perceptive: he knew what made a good story, and so did I. We worked well together. This man was a hell of a talent — and still is. He was born to be creative in this business, and his record shows it. Just look at all the shows he started: *Maverick*, *77 Sunset Strip*, *The Fugitive*, and so many others.

"Roy Huggins is the smartest, most talented man I've met in Hollywood in the 40 years I've been out here — but don't tell him I said that!"

Marion Hargrove is the best known of the *Maverick* writers for two reasons. He wrote both "The Jail at Junction Flats" and "Gun-Shy," two of the most famous episodes of the entire series. But long before *Maverick*, Hargrove had made a name for himself as a bestselling humorist. Hargrove was a writer for *The Charlotte News* when he was drafted into the Army in 1941; once inducted, he began a column that related his experience in basic training. In 1942, these articles were turned into a book, *See Here, Private Hargrove*, which in turn became the basis of two smash motion pictures (*See Here, Private Hargrove* and *What Next, Corporal Hargrove?*).

After receiving his discharge from the Army in 1945, Hargrove went back into freelance writing, and in 1948 published another novel, *Something's Got to Give*. In 1955, Hargrove was invited out to Warner Bros. to begin work on another motion picture. "J.L. Warner read a story in *Life Magazine* about a young Army draftee in training camp who had trouble keeping his two girlfriends apart," he recalled. "Warner thought it would make a great picture, which he wanted to call *The Girl He Left Behind*, and he wanted me to write the picture." Hargrove went up to Fort Ord, California to do some research; when he returned to the studio two weeks later, he felt that his story would work better as a novel than a film. After Hargrove informed the studio of his thoughts, Warners worked out a deal with Viking Press [Hargrove's publisher] that enabled Hargrove to complete the book at the studio. Guy Trosper wrote the screenplay almost simultaneously. "Carl Stucke [an assistant story editor at Warners] would come around once or twice a week to pick up my manuscript pages," said Hargrove. "Then Carl would pass them on to Trosper for use in the screenplay. We finished [both the novel and the screenplay] in about eight weeks." The feature version of *The Girl He Left Behind* starred Tab Hunter, Natalie Wood, David Janssen, and a young James Garner.

Shortly after finishing that novel, Hargrove moved into television. "Finley McDermid, the story editor at Warners, called me and said 'Marion, you should come across the street to the television side. We're just getting started over there,'" he recalled. "I said, 'Finley, there are two things that God did not intend me ever to write. One is Westerns, and the other is television.'"

Hargrove, of course, soon entered both. "Dave Dortort, whom I had known at Warners, gave me a call; he was producing a show called *The Restless Gun*, which was based on an old radio show, and he had a lot of radio scripts," he continued. "Dortort said, 'I've got a hell of a story here, and I can't think of anybody who can write it but you.' So I told him about television and Westerns, but he said 'Will you at least come out to talk about it?' And I did — and it clicked. It was a very good story ['Silver Threads'], and I believe Chuck Connors played the guest lead."

Word had spread about Hargrove's work on *The Restless Gun*, and soon other producers began approaching him — including Roy Huggins. "I knew who Marion was, and I figured anyone who could write a book as funny as *See Here, Private Hargrove* was someone I could use on *Maverick*," Huggins explained. Over the next several years, Hargrove contributed many scripts for Warner Bros.: the pilot for *Colt .45*; *Girl on the Run*, the second pilot for *77 Sunset Strip*; *Cash McCall*, a feature starring Garner; and nine episodes of *Maverick*.

Roy Huggins and Marion Hargrove have known and respected each other for nearly 40 years. Hargrove had a bead on the approach to Westerns that Huggins had in mind for *Maverick*, so they were a good match. But their working relationship wasn't always smooth. "Marion's writing was pretty straight in the beginning," Huggins recalled. "Later on, he loosened up, and his scripts would be filled with wondrous inventions, and funny bits of dialogue. In fact, a lot of the humor in Marion's scripts never got on film, because it was in the 'business' — the stage directions. He would write things like

'Maverick rides into town, and like his sponsor, he is quilted,' because one of the products Kaiser sold was quilted aluminum foil.

"I'd always encouraged writers to 'live dangerously' when it came to writing *Maverick*, but never to go so far that it wasn't plausible. Marion was probably my most 'dangerous' writer in that regard. However, we often disagreed over what was funny, and our problems were unfailingly in accordance with the following sequence of events:

"I would give Marion a story, and he'd write the teleplay, but he would turn it into a comedy. I would say, 'Thank you, Marion, but I'm now going to bring it to where its feet are touching the ground, just maybe lightly, but touching the ground, not floating three feet in the air.' He'd ask me why, and I'd tell him, 'Because it's not funny. Only the truth is funny, and I don't believe any of the things these people are doing.' 'What do you know about humor, for Christ's sake, Roy?' he'd say. 'Marion, all I know is that when I told you this story, I thought it was funny and I believed it. Now I don't believe it and it ain't funny, so I'm going to do some work on it.'

"I would rework his script [as I did with all the other writers, except Howard Browne and Douglas Heyes]. Marion would read it and tell me he'd prefer not to put up with any more aggravation of this kind.

"The show would go on the air, and Marion — a man with many, many friends — would get calls not just from Hollywood, but from the South and from New York. His friends would tell him he was back in form, and that *Maverick* was the best thing on TV. The following Monday, he'd walk into my office and say, 'Roy, if that esoteric imagination of yours has come up with another yarn, let's go to work.' And, of course, the reason his friends liked it was that it was still 80% Marion Hargrove."

Hargrove also recalled the sequence of events, which went on for about two years. "Roy and I complemented each other, in that I was always strong on style and he was always strong on story," he said. "And it's true that we didn't always agree with each other when it came to preparing the scripts. But I think basically both of us figured that while the other guy could be a real pain in the neck at times, he also had something tremendous to contribute, so he was worth the extra effort. I think that was a mutual thought."

It was. "I kept working with Marion because he wrote funny stuff," said Huggins. "He wrote great dialogue and created singular characters; all I had to do was apply a correction to the implausibilities that he had introduced into a very plausible story. Marion was of enormous importance to me and to the success of *Maverick* because I didn't have anyone else like him — in fact, I usually gave my best ideas to Marion. So I would always welcome him back, the Monday after one of his shows appeared, with joy and relief."

Iris Chekenian has a third-party perspective on the Huggins-Hargrove tandem: as Hargrove's secretary, she often sat in on those meetings in which the writer and the producer argued over the script. "Roy and Marion have always respected each other, but they were also diametrically opposite kinds of people," she observed. "Roy had a strong, 'Type A' personality back then, whereas Marion was always more laid back, understated. Their styles were so opposite that I think it was their styles that clashed. And they fought each other — a lot. But it was always over the work product. It was never anything personal."

Leslie Martinson and Douglas Heyes alternated as *Maverick*'s regular directors during the first two seasons: they were the two directors who best seemed to understand Huggins' approach to the series. "Doug usually directed his own scripts, so I never had to worry about his shows," Huggins said. "Les Martinson was an excellent director. Les was a mystery to me — I never understood what it was about Les that made him get it right. But he clearly understood what we were trying to do, and that's why he directed so many of our shows."

Martinson's explanation: he respected what he called the "purity" of Huggins' creation. "There were certain things that *Maverick* did, that were laid out in the scripts; what I tried to do, as the director, was keep out anything that would take away from the purity of the concept," he said. "For example, I remember when we filmed that scene in

'Gun-Shy' [the famous parody of *Gunsmoke*] where Jim has the shootout with Ben Gage. We had a lot of fun that day. Ben did such a perfect take-off on James Arness; he had everyone on the set in stitches, he was that funny.

"But, in order to keep it pure — because the script itself was pure satire — I remember saying something like, 'The one thing I don't want is 'Hey, this is really funny, folks.' Let's have some fun, but let's not enjoy ourselves so much that we lose sight of the purity of the straight farce.' Because, if you're not careful, then you're a little 'over the top,' and it comes out on film.

"I tried to keep those moments of 'impurity' out of the *Maverick*s that I directed. The humor of the show was already there."

6. JAMES GARNER

The secret to *Maverick*'s success — particularly that of its first two seasons — is simple. It had scripts that catered to a definite kind of humor, and it had a performer in James Garner who had the charm to make it work. "There's no question that Jim was the perfect vehicle for the Maverick character," said Huggins. "It was no accident — I just *discovered* it by accident. I don't think there's ever been anyone like Jim Garner playing that role. That is a traditional role — the sly con man with a twinkle in his eye, who is willing to change his opinion *in a second*. It is the country bumpkin who is really *very* smart, who surprises you by being smarter than the city slickers — but who also is modest, and wry, and underplayed. And also, of course, a man who tries *never* to appear to be stalwart and brave.

"For example, this is one of the greatest readings that Jim Garner ever did: He is being beaten up, and the heavy, who has four or five cohorts, has got Garner down. He's grabbing him and saying, 'Now, you're gonna do that, right?' And Maverick says, 'Right.' And the guy says 'Wrong! You're not gonna do that!' And Maverick says, 'You're right, I'm not gonna do that.'"

Marion Hargrove has written for Garner on many occasions since *Maverick*: he wrote the screenplays for many of Jim's films (*Cash McCall*, *Boys Night Out*, *The Wheeler Dealers*), as well as two episodes of Garner's *Bret Maverick* series. "Meta Rosenberg [Garner's former agent, and later an executive at Cherokee Productions, Jim's film company] figured out why Jim and I have always fit as actor and writer," he said. "We're both essentially rural comics. A lot of it has to do with background. We're both from the South [Hargrove is from North Carolina], and I think the southern background is a richer environment to grow up in than any other in the country. You can get to know more people — you watch them, you know what they're like. That can be a great benefit to a writer or an actor, I think.

"And, of course, Garner went through many odd jobs before he settled onto acting, so he would've met a lot of different people. He told me that he learned a lot from listening to people while he worked at the filling station [where he worked while attending Hollywood High in the early 1950s]. He'd take in the different conversations people had as they passed through."

Garner has never been afraid to assert himself, and his relationship with Warner Bros. during his *Maverick* years was occasionally stormy. The battle ground usually concerned the studio's frugal spending policies. Garner was realistic enough to know that many of his early film roles had as much to do with his salary as his performance. In 1957, his contract paid him the minimum salary of $250/week, and the studio

JAMES GARNER AND DIRECTOR LESLIE MARTINSON

capitalized on it as much as possible by starring him in features rather than paying established, and therefore higher-priced, movie actors. Prior to *Maverick*, Warners doubled Garner's weekly salary, but the actor later discovered that of his $500/week pay, $285 was straight salary; the remaining $215 was an advance against residuals from *Maverick*. When *Maverick* took off in the ratings, the studio raked in the money, while Garner, despite having a major impact on the success of the series, was not allowed to share in any of the show's profits. When *Maverick* made him a household name, Garner now had the kind of clout he did not have before, and he didn't hesitate to use it.

"I was once offered $7,500 to appear on *The Pat Boone Chevy-Showroom* in 1959, and the studio wanted me to be on it," he told *Playboy* in 1981. "But contract players at Warners didn't receive personal-appearance money — it was paid to the studio. Warners wanted the entire $7,500, and that represented a lot of money to me. All the rest of ABC's TV cowboys were going to be on the show — Jack Kelly, Clint Walker, Ty Hardin, Peter Brown, but I refused to go on if I wasn't paid. I settled for $2,500 and a Corvette with everything on it. The others wound up getting $500 each, and Warners tried to teach me a lesson a little later on." (Warners suspended Garner's salary in early 1960 after claiming that a strike by the Writers Guild forced the studio to shut down production of its TV shows. Garner challenged the suspension, and the matter eventually went to court. See the discussion of *Maverick*'s "Fourth Season, 1960-1961.")

Garner never brought his problems with the studio on to the *Maverick* set; in fact, if anything, they made him more sensitive to the plight of the other members of the crew, particularly those on the lower end of the totem pole. "I remember one show where I had a small part, along with about five or six extras," said Luis Delgado, Garner's stand-in on *Maverick*. "It was a bar scene, and we were all playing cowboys, and we each had one line to do in the scene. It was late at night, and this was the last shot that they were going to do for the evening. The director wanted to finish it quickly, because if we went another five minutes, we'd all go into overtime — which, in my case, and the case of the five or six extras, would mean an extra 50-60 bucks apiece, which was a lot of money back then.

"I said to Jim, 'We only have five minutes to go, and then we go on overtime.' Jim turned around and walked up to the assistant director and said, 'Hey, man, I gotta go to the bathroom!' So he took off and went to the bathroom. He came back a few minutes later, but before he walked in, he kind of motioned to me with his eyes, as if to say, 'Are you guys on overtime?' I said or I nodded, 'Yeah, we're on overtime,' and so Jim came in. He helped six guys, who were making small money, make an extra $50 apiece. That's Jim. He does that all the time."

Because Garner's fiery relations with the Warners executives were so well-publicized, he has occasionally been misconstrued as a temperamental performer. But that's not the case. "Jim can be bad-tempered, but that's not the same as being temperamental," said Roy Huggins. "He's a very conscientious performer. He may not always agree with you, but he'll respect you, and he'll let you do your job. Every now and then, on *Maverick*, he'd come to my office, or he'd ask me to comedown to the set, and we'd talk over whatever the problem was. Then he'd leave, or I'd leave, and I wouldn't hear from him for another three months."

Director Leslie Martinson and Garner liked each other personally, but they didn't always work well together. Their styles clashed: Garner brought a loose and easygoing approach to work, while Martinson was a little more intense. Garner often vented his frustrations with Martinson to producer Huggins. "Jim would say, 'You've got to get rid of this guy; he's driving me crazy!'" Huggins recalled. "And I would say, 'Jim, I've tried other directors. They get it wrong. Les gets it right.'"

Garner, to his credit, never badmouthed Martinson in front of anyone else. In fact, Martinson did not become aware of Garner's complaints to Huggins until he read about them in Raymond Strait's *James Garner: A Biography*. "I was raised at MGM, and I worked for 15 years there as a script clerk, with such master directors as Vincente Minelli; and while it may not have been the 'divine right of kings,' so far as the weight of the director was concerned, it was pretty close," said Martinson. "But that's the background in film that I grew up in. I work closely with my actors, and I've become good friends with a lot of them, but when it comes to work, there is a line that the director must draw.

"Everyone has moments in their life when we've said something that we've come to regret. There is one such moment in my life that concerns Jim Garner — it was a misunderstanding, but I did not use tact as a director. I went a little overboard.

"We were filming a scene [for the episode 'The Ghost Soldiers'] on the back lot; it was 116 degrees that day, and we're up on a parapet, so it's even hotter, and there's no wind — it was blocked off. We were shooting a long scene, about four or five pages, with Jim Garner and Jim Westerfield. I was trying to get the perfect angle on a two-shot, and Garner was fighting the dialogue.

"After about eight or nine takes, Jim said, 'Leslie, are you going to break this up?' I said, 'Oh, Jim, we've almost got it; hang in there with it, will you?' He said, 'Okay,' and he did. Around take 15 or so, I finally get the shot I wanted.

"I was about to call 'Wrap' when I suddenly realized that I needed to film a couple of closeups of Jim. So I took a deep breath, and I said, 'Gentlemen, put a four-inch on here and give me a closeup of Jimmy.' Although I had already told Garner that I had wanted the scene done using only the two-shot, I tried to explain why I now needed a closeup. Jim was, understandably, tired and a little upset, and he said, 'You so-forth-and-so-forth.'

"This is the moment that I've always regretted: I came down pretty hard on him. It was 116 degrees, and I wasn't about to argue with him. I told Jim in rude, harsh terms that I wanted the closeup, and we finally shot it.

"That was the last time I ever worked with Jim Garner. I had been scheduled to direct him in *Cash McCall*, but I was taken off that assignment. I was never told why, but I have a feeling that incident on 'Ghost Soldiers' had something to do with it. That's why I wish I had that moment back, because I've always enjoyed working with him."

However, Garner and Martinson have remained amicable over the years. "Jim would stop by and visit me while I was directing other shows on the Warners lot," Martinson said. "And over the years, when I see him socially, he's always warm. I remember once, several years ago, I was filming something down in Paradise Cove, and Jim's company was also there, shooting *The Rockford Files*. Jim came down to my set and we had lunch. And whenever I see him, I always say, 'You're still getting along without me, huh, Jim?' And he says the same thing to me: 'Better than ever, Leslie!'"

James Garner's most enduring aspect as a performer, the one quality that has always appealed to his audience, is how likeable he comes across in all his characterizations. When Garner was a young actor, John Hodiak, for whom Garner had understudied (and whose role of Lt. Steve Maryk he would take over after Hodiak's untimely death in 1955), once gave him an invaluable word of advice: "Ninety-nine out of a hundred people instinctively like you. Forget the one percent who don't; you won't change them. That means that ninety-nine out of one hundred people watching you will also like you."

It's often said that Garner is not an actor — that he merely plays himself. Garner himself once said, "I don't act — I react to what someone says. People want to see someone who they enjoy, and I've tried to give them that by being natural and part of the scene, whether it was in films, television, or on the stage. If an audience gets the idea that you're acting, you're finished. You've got to look real, and I think that comes from being real."

Garner is such a gifted actor that he hasn't always received the credit for how hard he works. It isn't easy to make yourself look natural and easy. Luis Delgado, who has known the actor since long before Jim entered the motion picture business, thinks that the industry has only recently realized how talented a performer Garner is. "Jim is a much more talented actor than he was when he first started," he said. "I say this from my heart: I think that Jim is an Academy Award-level performer today, and I think he's been at that level for the last 20 years. But I think a lot of producers typed him as a 'tongue-in-cheek' actor, because that's what he mainly did on *Maverick*. That's why Jim enjoyed that picture that he did with Julie Andrews, *The Americanization of Emily*

[Garner's all-time favorite role] — there was a little comedy in that film, but Jim's role was mostly a serious role. The same holds true with his character in *Murphy's Romance*.

"I think a lot of people are starting to realize what Jim can do, instead of going back to that old label of him as a 'tongue-in-cheek actor.' I think they are now realizing that they have missed something with him. They are giving him roles that really mean something — you'll see that most of the shows he's done for *Hallmark Hall of Fame*, such as *Promise* and *Breathing Lessons*, are dramatic shows. Practically every one we've done has won some sort of Emmy Award for Jim, so he must be a pretty good actor."

John Hodiak was right about James Garner: people instinctively like him. "Jim is the most-loved actor in the business," added Delgado. "Ask the members of the crew, ask anybody who's ever acted with him. Everybody wants to work with Jim."

Even his adversaries can't help liking him. Roy Huggins recalls bumping into Jack Warner shortly after Garner had beaten the studio in court in late 1960. "I was discussing something with Warner, and at some point I brought up Jim Garner's name," said Huggins. "Warner fumed, and he carried on at great length about 'Jim Garner, that no-good son of a —.' But suddenly Warner stopped and said, 'Hey, why am I talking about him like this? I *like* him.'"

7. ENTER BART MAVERICK

Warner Bros. was one of the pioneers of early dramatic television. Although *Warner Bros. Presents* was not the first one-hour dramatic program (anthology programs such as *Studio One* and *The U.S. Steel Hour* were already on the air in 1955), it was the first weekly hour-long filmed dramatic series. While the anthology shows were performed live on the night of broadcast, the Warner Bros. shows were filmed in advance and had to be delivered to ABC prior to their scheduled airdate. The studio "invented the wheel," so to speak, in terms of production of a weekly one-hour series. Roy Huggins explained the set-up: "We shot the shows in six days — we'd start filming on Monday, for example, work through Friday, break for the weekend, then finish on the following Monday. On Tuesday, we'd start filming the next show, and so forth. That meant that there were eight calendar days for every show. That was the minimum. So it was already taking a day too long: the shows took a minimum of eight days to shoot, but they were being aired every seven days."

But, on any given day, there were other factors that often contributed to further delay in the production. Sometimes a particular set or a stage wasn't available; or it may have rained on a day scheduled for exterior shooting; or an actor was sick. As a result, the eight-calendar-day turnaround time becomes nine or ten days. "Today, the networks could remedy some of the problems brought on by delay with a pre-emption — meaning, they'd air another program to run in your regular time slot for one week, then you'd return the following week," Huggins explained. "Pre-emption is a very common practice in television now, but back then, the networks were very rigid: they believed that if you broke the viewing habit [of tuning in each week to watch a given show], the viewers wouldn't come back. So, since pre-emption was not an option available to us, we really had to work hard in order to meet the network's deadlines for airdates.

"Before *Maverick*, I had not experienced any problems with making airdates, and neither did any other producer at Warners, because the shows we produced did not air

JAMES GARNER AND JACK KELLY

every week — they rotated with the other shows on *Warner Bros. Presents*. In the first year [1955-56], *Cheyenne* alternated with *King's Row* and *Casablanca*; then the next year [1956-57], *Cheyenne* alternated with *Conflict*. So I wasn't faced with having to get a show ready to go on the air every week; I had to get one ready every other week — so if the average TV season lasted 40 weeks, I would only have to produce a maximum of 20 shows a year. I had more room for error in my production schedule.

"But *Maverick* brought about a new situation: it was the first show Warners produced that aired every week, and which featured only one star. The network had ordered 26 episodes, so I now *had* to get a new show ready to air every seven days. We started filming in August 1957; by the first of September [after we'd completed about three shows], we were behind schedule. I realized I couldn't deliver 26 shows without pre-emptions. But since we couldn't pre-empt, I decided I'd have to bring in a brother, whom I eventually named Bart. Bart's character would have the same attitude as Bret Maverick; as much as possible, he would be an identical twin. Once we had a second lead, we'd get together a second production unit and shoot two *Maverick* episodes simultaneously. I brought this to Bill Orr's attention, and we began interviewing actors to play Bart."

While Huggins interviewed and tested numerous actors for the part, Warner Bros. television head William T. Orr apprised ABC and Kaiser Industries of the production problem. Orr knew that Huggins had intended "Bart Maverick" as a permanent fixture — whoever played the lead would alternate with Garner as the lead each week. But ABC and Kaiser Industries had other ideas. "We had a meeting in Hawaii [where Kaiser owned a string of hotels], and everybody had this suggestion: we would have the other Maverick, but he would be a 'with' — a supporting character," Orr recalled. "I told them, 'No, he has to be a co-star.' If the audience thinks he's just a secondary actor, those segments would go down the tube, because the audience will figure 'he's not the star.' I insisted that he had to have star billing along with Jim Garner." Orr assured the network and the sponsor that Garner would appear in as many episodes as possible. ABC and Kaiser approved the casting addition, but there was one slight hitch — although Kaiser's representatives cleared the change, apparently no one informed Henry Kaiser himself of what was happening with his own TV program. Kaiser didn't find out about the addition of "Bart Maverick" until the night the character first appeared on Maverick — and he was not at all happy about the change in plans. See the discussion of the episode "Hostage!"

In the meantime, Richard Jaeckel, Stuart Whitman, Rod Taylor, Tom Gilson, Don Durant, Barne Williams, and Brad Jackson were among the many actors considered to play Bart Maverick. "Eventually I decided on Jack Kelly, who starred on *King's Row*, and whom I liked very much," said Huggins.

Jack Kelly was born on September 16, 1927 in Astoria, New York. You could say that acting was in his genes — his mother Ann had been a stage performer; his older sister Nancy won a Tony Award for her role as the mother in the Broadway production of *The Bad Seed*; and his younger sister Carol became a television actress. As a child, Jack performed on stage and worked as a model (he posed for a soap company when he was only two weeks old!); by the time he was 11, he had already acted in four Broadway plays, and had done some radio work. But Kelly didn't want an acting career at first; he had originally chosen to become a lawyer. But when his studies were interrupted (the Army drafted him at age 18; Jack served as a weather observer in Alaska for one year), he concentrated on acting. In 1947, Kelly moved to New York for two years, where he found a lot of work in radio and television. He then moved back to Hollywood, and landed a two-year contract at Universal Pictures. Kelly then moved on, and worked for other studios in such films as *The Country Girl*, *To Hell and Back*, *Cult of the Cobra*, *Hong Kong Affair*, and the science fiction classic *Forbidden Planet*.

James Garner never complained about the sudden loss of his sole starring role, nor did he ever question the necessity of hiring Jack Kelly; rather, he welcomed his co-star, quite literally, like a brother. "Jim could have made me look bad," Kelly told *TV Guide* in 1958. "But he made me feel right at home." Kelly enjoyed a lengthy and happy run on *Maverick* ("I whistled all the way to work on that one"); in fact, by the end of the series, he had appeared in more episodes (75) than had Garner (55). Yet, because he did not join the series until the eighth episode ("Hostage!"), Bart Maverick was always seen as a secondary character. This would be a difficult set of circumstances for any actor to endure, yet Kelly approached the situation realistically and professionally.

"At the time we hired him, I think Jack had come to realize that he wasn't going to have the kind of career that he might've thought he was going to have when he was under contract as a young actor at Universal," said Roy Huggins. "And I think he regarded the job on *Maverick* as a nice steady income for a number of years — maybe seven. And he was happy with that.

"I think Jack also knew that, no matter how much he tried, he was never going to equal Jim Garner — that he was always going to be 'Maverick's brother.' Maybe he didn't realize it, but outwardly, he gave the feeling that he did. And he may have been very realistic about it. Jim was there first, and Jim was going to cross the line first, because he'd already had a head start. But, however he may have rationalized it, Jack *always* gave his all."

Kelly was an extremely hard-working performer who was always open to any suggestions to make himself better. Not that he needed any improvement — with nearly twenty years of experience under his belt, he was already an accomplished actor by the time he started *Maverick*. The "knock" on Kelly's performance — if it can be called one — is that he wasn't James Garner. "I've always thought Jack was very, very good," said Huggins, "although I will admit that I was never quite as happy with him as Maverick as I was with Jim Garner. That's because I always judged Jack on the basis of how Jim would play the role — which, I realize, wasn't very fair.

"After Jack had done about two or three shows, Bill Orr came to me and said, 'What can we do to get a better performance out of Kelly?' And I said, 'Why don't we run one of his shows that you feel has the most examples of his failing to do as much with the part as he could, and we'll talk to him about it.'

"I wasn't any more specific than that, because I didn't think there was anything you could talk to Jack about. He was only 'bad' relative to Jim Garner — that, without Garner there, we would have been very happy with him!

"But we brought in Jack, and told him that we weren't very happy — Bill Orr said it very nicely. Orr was always a gentleman.

"We went into a projection room and ran the show — I'm sitting behind Jack, Bill Orr's sitting next to Jack, and Hugh Benson [Orr's executive assistant] is sitting on the other side. The show goes on, scenes are played, and I'm waiting for someone to say something — to push the button, say 'Hold it here,' to talk to Jack Kelly. But they *don't*.

"A reel is changed and no one has said anything. And then, finally, there's a scene in which Kelly is carrying a tray, I think, in his hands. But he bumps into somebody and drops the tray! I said, 'See, Jack — you're clumsy. That's your problem.'

"Everybody laughed. Bill Orr stopped the film and said to Jack, 'Well, Jack, go on, keep doing it. It looks all right to me.' No one offered any criticism. There was really none you could offer."

The sudden addition of another character several weeks into the series brought on another delicate problem. "That was a real blow to the audience: suddenly, out of nowhere, a brother appears, and I had to be very careful how I handled it," Huggins recalled. "I eased Kelly in, very slowly, by using Garner as a kind of 'safety net.' We'd have Bret Maverick introduce the shows with Bart, particularly the solo shows with Bart."

The viewers embraced Kelly immediately. After his first four broadcasts, he received over 3000 letters from fans who assured him that they enjoyed Bart Maverick as much as they did brother Bret. In fact, despite the fact that he was always overshadowed by Garner, Kelly actually outdrew his co-star on a consistent basis throughout *Maverick*'s first two seasons (when the show was as its peak of popularity). "The shows with Jack always rated slightly higher than the shows with Jim," Huggins said. "The average rating for Jack's shows was something like 8/10 of a percentage point higher than the average for Jim's shows. That's too small a figure to have any significance whatsoever — but it's strange only because it was consistent."

8. THE WISDOM OF BEAUREGARD "PAPPY" MAVERICK

Roy Huggins and Marion Hargrove each had a hand in the creation of one of *Maverick*'s most memorable characters. "I was dictating my first *Maverick* script to my secretary, Iris Chekenian," recalled Hargrove. "Iris didn't do shorthand — she took longhand on long legal pads, and a page of her longhand was a page of script. While I was dictating, I was also usually watching her expression, or watching her fingers. At one point, I thought of a very clever line of dialogue for Maverick — and suddenly Iris' fingers slowed down. I asked her, 'What the hell is wrong?' But I knew what the hell was wrong. I said to Iris, 'That's too good a line for a dumb cowboy, right?' and she said, 'Right.' So I said, 'Let's start it off with something like, "As my old Pappy used to say . . .'"

"I told Roy about Pappy, and he immediately realized the possibilities — which I hadn't — of what we could do with the character. And that is how Pappy was born."

Huggins saw Pappy as a means of providing a buffer for some of Bret and Bart's more outrageous attitudes. "The things that were attributed to Pappy were much more emphatic than *Maverick* usually was," said Huggins. "I decided that there were some attitudes that I wanted, that I knew Maverick had — and I say 'Maverick,' meaning both Bret and Bart — that I might want to express through a third person. That was the original reason for Pappy, to say outrageous things that were a part of the *Maverick* philosophy. For example, something like 'If either of you comes back with a medal, I'll beat you to death' invited them to act cautiously, or possibly even cowardly."

"According to Hoyle" was the first episode to feature one of Pappy's aphorisms ("Faint heart never filled a flush"). "Roy was very good at those lines, which he called Pappyisms," said Hargrove. "Howard Browne was very good at them, and I enjoyed writing them, too. One of my favorite Pappyisms was a line I used in 'The Thirty-Ninth Star' — 'Work is fine for killin' time, but it's a shaky way to make a living.'"

The best Pappyisms are featured in *Maverick*'s first two seasons. However, Coles Trapnell (who succeeded Huggins as *Maverick*'s producer in 1959) and his writers came up with a few gems, such as "Hard work never hurt anybody — who didn't do it" (from "Last Wire from Stop Gap") and "If you're ever served a rare steak that is intended for somebody else, don't bother with ethical details — eat as much as you can before the mistake is discovered" (from "Pappy"). All three *Maverick* revivals (*The New Maverick*, *Young Maverick*, and *Bret Maverick*) also incorporate Pappyisms.

PART II:
THE EPISODES

FIRST SEASON: 1957-1958

PRODUCTION CREDITS

Starring James Garner as Bret Maverick
and Jack Kelly as Bart Maverick

Executive Producer: William T. Orr
Produced by: Roy Huggins
Created by: Roy Huggins

Directors of Photography: Ralph Woolsey, Harold Stine, Edwin DuPar, Carl Berger, Wesley Anderson, Carl E. Guthrie, Frank Phillips
Camera Operators: Lucien Ballard, Robert Tobey, Marvin Gunter, Ben Wetzler, Jerry Finnerman, William T. Cline, William Rinaldi, Fred Terzo, Phil Eastman, Dick Doran, Harry Davis, Elmer Faubion, Lou Schwartz, Eddie Albert, Luis Molina, Roy Clark, George Nogle, Robert Higgs, A.E. Green
Art Directors: Howard Campbell, Perry Ferguson, Arthur Loel

Supervising Film Editor: James Moore
Film Editors: Frank O'Neill, Walter S. Stern, Tom Biggart, Elbert K. Hollingsworth, Folmar Blangsted, Carl Pingitore, Robert T. Sparr, Robert Watts, Harold Minter, Rex Lipton

Music Supervision: Paul Sawtell, Bert Shefter
"Maverick" Theme by David Buttolph

Production Manager: Oren W. Haglund
Sound Mixers: M.A. Merrick, Theodore B. Hoffman, Samuel F. Goode, Franklin Hanson Jr., Charles Althouse, Dolph Thomas, Stanley Jones, David Forrest, Eugene F. Westfall
Script Supervisors: Wanda Ramsey, May Wael, Ruth Brownson, Doris Miller, Mary Yerke, Marie Halvey, Irva Ross
Chief Electricians: Lee Wilson, Robert Farmer, P.D. Burt, Glen Bird, Joe O'Donnell, Ernie Long, Paul Burnett, Francis Flanagan
Assistants to Chief Electrician: James Patton, Everett Miller, William Sayres, Francis Black, Chris Whitsel
Key Grips: Weldon Gilbert, Ken Taylor, Ken McIrvin, Bickford Carroll, Louis Maschmeyer, William Classen, George Mumaw, Dick Thoelsen

Set Decorators: Ben Bane, William Wallace, Faye Babcock, Frank Miller, Ross Dowd, Pat Delaney, M.F. Berkeley, Ralph S. Hurst

Property Masters: Robert Turner, Limey Plews, Archie Neel, John Moore, Fred Kuhn, Ed Edwards

Assistant Directors: Lee White, C. Carter Gibson, Rusty Meek, Robert Farfan, Mecca Graham, Bill Lasky, Claude Archer, Earle Harper, Bill O'Donnell, Don Page, Victor Vallejo, Alan Pomeroy

Wardrobe: Ted Schultz, Claude Barrie, Russell B. Coles, Jane Leonard, Geoffrey Allen, Henry Fields

Hair Stylists: Jean Reilley, Margaret Donovan, Tillie Starriett, Helen Lierley, Marian Vaughan, Irene Beshon, Helen Berkeley.

Makeup Supervisor: Gordon Bau

Makeup Artists: Norman Pringle, Bill Phillips, Newt Jones, Lou LaCava, Henry Vilardo, Nick Behr, Dan Striepeke, Al Greenway, Ray Romero

Announcer: Ed Reimers

"[*Maverick*'s] well-staged action, leavened by nice touches of humor, serve to make a better than fair TV entry," wrote *Daily Variety* on September 24, 1957. "James Garner impresses as a fresh and rugged young personality with a strong future in pictures. Expert support is forthcoming from John Litel, Edmund Lowe, and Leo Gordon. Budd Boetticher's direction is definitely a series plus. However, with the video landscape a-crawlin' with adult westerns, producer Roy Huggins will have to come up with better scripts to survive in the rating race."

Its remarks about the script notwithstanding, *Variety* had a point. The consensus in television was that *Maverick* didn't have a chance to survive against such well-established Sunday night greats as Ed Sullivan, Steve Allen and Jack Benny. "When they told me they were going to throw me in against Steve and Ed, I asked, 'Why are you wasting film?'" James Garner told *The Saturday Evening Post* in 1958. "It's ridiculuous. Sullivan has been up there for nine years and Allen is great, too. Everybody I talked to felt the same way; they said they all commiserated with me."

But, as the star of the show continued, there were signs that things were going to be all right. "My friends all told me, 'They're going to knock you off, Jim, but I'll watch you anyhow. I'm up to here with the Sunday night variety shows. After all, how many jugglers, dancers and comedians can you stand without getting an ache behind your eyeballs? Maybe yours will be different.' So I had a sneaky hunch that we had a chance."

Indeed. Maverick averaged a respectable 28 share after its first six weeks on the air against the "impregnable" trio — meaning that of all the households with televisions in use at 7:30 p.m. on Sundays, almost 30% were watching *Maverick*. Either Garner had a lot of friends watching his show, or Roy Huggins had hit on something. "*Maverick* definitely struck a nerve," said Huggins. "I think people were bored with the hero who had no flaws of any kind, who was 'hero' through and through. People were tired of the hero who was an absolutist — they wanted a hero who had some moral ambiguity.

"See, Maverick wasn't merely a spoof on the Western formula — it was also intended to make a point. Inside every conforming American there is a rugged individualist trying to get out, and *Maverick* aims to help him do it. The show premiered at a time when the growing suspicion was that we'd become a nation of security-seeking, contented conformists — in contrast to our pioneer ancestors, who looked to themselves for rules, and who prized venture over security."

Huggins designed the Maverick character as the essence of the self-reliant, freedom-loving individualist of our past. He is motivated by profit, curiosity, anger, sex and self-preservation— motives that are always derived from himself, and never from others, or "The Community." Whereas the traditional fictional hero doesn't hesitate to involve himself in the plight of others, Maverick thinks before he gets involved — and his first thought is, usually, "Is there a reward?" This is a real reaction, something we've felt more often than we'll admit. It certainly is the kind of reaction we are trained not to voice precisely because it is socially unacceptable.

"The audience glommed onto those moments when Maverick behaved like a reluctant hero, or even an anti-hero," said Huggins. "When he quibbled about the size of the reward in 'Point Blank,' he wasn't behaving like a hero, because the classical 'hero' would never consider taking the reward. Yet the audience accepted Maverick — they recognized in him their desire to make a profit. They also saw in Maverick someone who lived life fully, joyfully, and without any of the doubts and anxieties of modern conformity."

Another aspect of *Maverick* that appealed to audiences: Bret and Bart preferred using their heads to get out of trouble over using their guns. Part of that was out of necessity. By their own admission, the Mavericks were at best average with a gun, so if they found themselves facing a crack shot, they usually had to think up an advantage. "Maverick, very often, resorted to trickery whenever he faced somebody who was holding a gun on him," said Huggins. "He was often in situations where he'd have to decide whether to use his gun and see how he does, or try to think his way out of it. For example, there's a scene in 'Point Blank' where two guys confront him — they want Maverick to do something he doesn't want to do. So Maverick pretends to go along, and says, 'Okay, I'll help you. Look, here's how we'll do it.' He smooths out the ground as if he's drawing a map, but once he gets a pile of dirt together, he grabs it and throws it in the eye of one guy, pulls his gun on the other guy, and gets out of it!

"Another instance that was particularly pleasing to me was the episode ['Relic of Fort Tejon'] where a gunman is hired to kill Maverick. The gunman strolls into town, and Maverick says 'Well, you seem mighty sure of yourself and that puts me in a spot. You see [Maverick takes off his hat], I'm not the fastest gun in the world.' The gunman says 'start for your gun,' and Maverick says 'That won't be necessary. I've already got a little derringer in this hat pointed right at your heart.' The gunman thinks Maverick is bluffing but Maverick dares him to call it. So the gunman says 'Drop the hat and show me the derringer,' but Maverick says 'I'll show you the derringer after I pull the trigger.' The guy drops his gun, and he's humiliated when he finds out that Maverick didn't have a gun in his hat! By the time he could react, it was too late — Maverick had the drop on him.

"That was the kind of thing that young adults remember about *Maverick*. They weren't asked to admire a great hero who pulls his gun and wins, but rather a guy who uses his mind and gets out of trouble by being smarter than the other guys."

Although the tone of *Maverick* shifted more toward comedy after Huggins left the series at the end of the second season, this fundamental aspect of Maverick's character — the desire to resolve conflict, whenever possible, without resorting to violence — never changed throughout the remainder of the series.

Huggins realizes he wasn't always consistent on how well Maverick could handle a gun. For every instance where Maverick would say, "Look, half the people in this town are better with a gun than I am," there would be instances where he would prove otherwise. Early in "Point Blank," for example, Maverick disarms a rowdy saloon patron by diving behind a fallen table and shooting the gun out of the other man's hands. "Who knows — maybe he got lucky," joked Huggins. "Back then, whenever I gave interviews to promote the show, I'd say that whenever Maverick got into a shooting scrape, he has to win by cunning or by sheer necessity — after all, we couldn't let him die, not with 26 shows to produce a year."

But there was also the practical side of the matter. "Good storytelling requires that you have a hero, and you're not going to have a successful series with a hero who is a Hamlet, who can't make up his mind," explained Huggins. "In every series I've ever done, the story always came first. Always. There are certain rules that you can never break, and one such rule is that you must always tell a story that will grip the audience, get them interested or surprised, and provide them with a satisfactory ending. Then they'll come back and watch you the next week.

"In other words, the Maverick character was always there in every episode I produced; but Maverick wasn't always able to express that character, given the confines of a particular story. Whenever possible, I would have Maverick act reluctant to take on somebody, or deny having any skill as a gunfighter, or anything like that — so long as it wasn't at the expense of the story. But if I put him in a situation that clearly demanded a heroic response, or else the story wouldn't make sense, then he'd act accordingly."

Huggins is addressing a facet of the Maverick character that has become one of the many myths that have grown out of the series. Maverick — whether Bret, Bart, Beau or Brent — is unfailingly remembered, in both television reference books and the hearts and minds of fans who grew up watching the series on ABC, as an "anti-hero." But look at the character over the course of the series' 124 episodes, and you'll find dozens of instances where Maverick must risk his life to resolve the dilemma, in the tradition of the very best of heroes.

"I realize that, while I was hyping the show, I often referred to him as an 'anti-hero,'" said Huggins. "Again, that was for publicity purposes. A true anti-hero is *not* a hero. Maverick was a hero. He didn't always behave like a conventional hero, but I believe he was always internally consistent. If someone he loved or deeply admired had been killed, or had been treated abominably, Maverick would become angry and take on heroic enterprise [as he did in 'A Rage for Vengeance,' when he avenged the death of the woman he loved]. He had an inescapeable sense of honor.

"I think the audience loved it whenever Maverick shed his 'reluctant' facade and acted like a damned hero!"

Again, the record speaks for itself. By the time Jack Kelly joined the series as Bart, *Maverick* had developed a strong following, and if there was any apprehension as to whether Kelly could maintain the audience, it was quickly put to rest. "As a matter of fact, a show that I did was the first one to beat out *The Ed Sullivan Show* and *Jack Benny*," Kelly told Mick Martin in 1992. "I remember getting a very large charge out of the fact that one of the shows I did, being considered Maverick's brother instead of Maverick, was the [first] one that won the rating race."

The audience for *Maverick* continued to grow over the course of the 1957-58 season, regardless of which actor played the character (Garner or Kelly), or how the stories portrayed the character (gentle grafter or conventional hero). The series averaged a solid 38.5 share of the Sunday night viewing audience over its final 16 episodes that year. What made the difference, Garner told *The Saturday Evening Post*, "was that grownups as well as the kids, liked our show. Also we jumped off a half hour before Sullivan and Allen; that way we had a half-nelson on their audience before they came to grips with the situation."

The Television Academy of Arts and Sciences honored *Maverick* in 1958 with Emmy nominations for Best Dramatic Series and Best New Series. Although the series did not win in either category, Roy Huggins did score a tremendous personal victory. "When the nominations came out that year, I was notified by the Academy that if *Maverick* won in either category, the award would go to William T. Orr as executive producer and Roy Huggins as producer," Huggins recalled. "Bill was the executive producer because he was Executive in Charge of Television at Warners, so his name was on every Warners show [as Executive Producer] regardless of whether he did nothing, or a great deal. I suspect that Bill Orr had a great deal to do with some of the other shows at Warners, but he had absolutely nothing to do with *Maverick* for the entire two years that I produced the show. He didn't read the scripts, he didn't cast the shows, and he didn't edit them.

"I wrote the Academy and explained exactly what I just stated, and I asked if this was sufficient evidence for a decision to be made on who should accept the award for *Maverick*. And it was, apparently. I don't know if they asked Bill to comment on that letter, although I would guess they did. In any event, they took Orr's name off that list — although, of course, we didn't win that year. But we did win the following year." (Huggins alone accepted the Emmy in 1959, when *Maverick* won.)

Film editor Robert Sparr was also honored with Emmy nominations for the episodes "The Quick and the Dead" and "Rope of Cards."

Perhaps the most remembered element of the original *Maverick*, second only to James Garner's performance, is the theme song written by Paul Francis Webster and composed by David Buttolph. Both the *New Maverick* reunion TV-movie and the *Young Maverick* series reprised the original theme, while *Bret Maverick* interspersed bits of the old song into its musical score. The TV theme was also foremost in the minds of the makers of 1994 *Maverick* feature film. Writer William Goldman, in an early draft of his screenplay, suggested the playing of the original song over the film's opening credits, while director Richard Donner had the song's lyrics printed on the back of the special T-shirts he distributed to every member of the film's crew.

Surprisingly, however, Webster's lyrics did not officially become a part of the series until the second season. The first season episodes used only an instrumental version of the song to accompany the closing credits. However, in some rerun packages, the first-year shows have been re-edited to include a music-and-lyrics version of the closing theme. For example, if you were to catch a rerun of "Point Blank" or "According to Hoyle" on a local TV station that carried *Maverick*, you'd notice that the closing credits of these episodes featured a resounding vocalized rendition of the *Maverick* theme song that did not actually appear on the show until the fifth season (see below). However, if you were to watch these shows as part of the *Maverick: The Collectors Edition* series available through Columbia House Home Video, you'd notice that both episodes actually closed with an instrumental version of the theme song. (Columbia House duplicates the original prints — the actual film that aired on the night the episode was first broadcast. The original prints of the first-year *Mavericks* feature an instrumental at the end of each show.)

There are three versions of the vocals that were recorded for the series. The first, a rather simple version, appears just once (in "The Day They Hanged Bret Maverick") and uses its banjo-and-percussion accompaniment to create a rhythm that effects the sound of a horse galloping. The second recording of the vocals — the one that most viewers remember (its tempo is more robust and upbeat) — is featured at the end of second-, third-, and fourth-season episodes. The third rendition of the *Maverick* theme song is even more resounding than the second — it uses sound effects to punctuate such lyrics as "Riverboat, ring your bell" (at which point, we hear a bell ringing) and "Fare thee well, Annabelle" (we hear a riverboat horn sounding). The third and last vocalized version first appeared in the fifth-season episodes, although, as mentioned earlier, it has been dubbed onto some first-season (and, occasionally, second-season) shows for syndication.

Also of interest: Every episode of the first season opens the same way — the "teaser" (a short scene from the episode), followed by a cut to *Maverick*'s logo (a silhouette of Maverick playing cards with three men), while Ed Reimers' booming voice announced "*Maverick*, Starring James Garner and Jack Kelly; Produced for Television by Warner Bros." This sequence did not alter (except to indicate changes in the cast) during *Maverick*'s entire five-season run. However, the closing sequence for each of the first 13 episodes of the first year differed slightly, insofar as each of these shows had a logo card of its own. "The War of the Silver Kings" had as its logo a picture of a mine shaft; "Point Blank," a figure emptying a bank vault; "According to Hoyle," a copy of *Hoyle's Book of Games*; and so forth, on through the 13th episode, "Naked Gallows" (whose artwork depicted an empty hangman's noose). Beginning with the 14th show, "Comstock Conspiracy," *Maverick*'s logo served as the backdrop for the closing credits, and the series followed this pattern for the remainder of its run.

Key episodes of the first season: "War of the Silver Kings," "Point Blank" (the original pilot, and in Roy Huggins' estimation, one of the few "pure" *Mavericks*), "According to Hoyle" (introducing Diane Brewster as Samantha Crawford), "Hostage!" (Jack Kelly's debut as Bart), "Stampede" (the first show with Efrem Zimbalist Jr. as Dandy Jim Buckley), "The Wrecker" (based on the 1891 novel by Robert Louis Stevenson and Lloyd Osbourne), "Rope of Cards" (the episode that introduces "Maverick Solitaire"), and "Black Fire," a takeoff of Agatha Christie's *And Then There Were None*.

Familiar faces this season: Adele Mara, Mike Connors, Karen Steele, Edd Byrnes, Joanna Barnes, Dan Tobin, Kathleen Crowley, Gerald Mohr, Sherry Jackson, Werner Klemperer, Ruta Lee, John Russell, William Reynolds, Gene Nelson, Whitney Blake, John Vivyan, Hans Conried, and Claude Akins.

1. THE WAR OF THE SILVER KINGS

(a.k.a. "Easy Come, Easy Go" and "The Last Chance")

ORIGINAL AIRDATE: SEPTEMBER 22, 1957

Teleplay by: James O'Hanlon
Based on the book War of the Copper Kings by C.B. Glasscock
Directed by: Budd Boetticher

Guest Cast: Edmund Lowe (Phineas King), John Litel (Josh Thayer), Leo Gordon (Big Mike McComb), John Hubbard (Bixby), Carla Merey (Edie Stoller), Robert Griffin (Fennelly), Donald Kirke (Crane), Fred Sherman (John Stoller), Bob Steele (Jackson), Lane Chandler (Lawson), Tyler McVey (Kriedler)

Synopsis. Soon after arriving in the mining community of Echo Springs, Maverick wins a high-stakes poker game with the unscrupulous town magnate, Phineas King. King doesn't take kindly to losing — he has Maverick beaten up, and later tries to have him killed. Maverick, who knows that King is as much a cheater as he is a millionaire, is determined to beat King at his own game.

"The War of the Silver Kings" plays very much like a straightforward Western story — Maverick rides into Echo Springs, rights the wrongs (in this case, he negotiates a new working agreement between King and the miners, and gets Judge Josh Thayer back on his feet), then leaves the town "a little better than he found it." But this first episode establishes the key elements of Maverick's character. Twice, Bret beats King by sheer bluff — he stayed in the poker game, and later won the game, by betting with an envelope filled with clipped newspaper; then he snows King into settling with the miners even though Maverick knew that the court had reversed the decision upholding the apex law. Upon accepting defeat, King thinks back and then realizes exactly how Bret did it — "It was guts, nothing but guts," he said, with clear respect for Maverick's abilities.

Although he does get a tremendous amount of personal satisfaction in attaining retribution, Maverick, for one of the few times in the series, does not benefit financially from his victory. "That was another concession I had to make with both ABC and Warners in order to get *Maverick* on the air," recalled Roy Huggins. "In my original story for 'War of the Silver Kings,' Maverick kept a part of the settlement with the mining company. Neither the studio nor the network wanted him to keep the money (even though he'd won it legally); both insisted that Maverick turn the money over to the miners. I insisted that Maverick, of course, would *never* do that, but I later learned that ABC's objection came from Standards and Practices (the network censors). I wanted *Maverick* to sell, so I conceded that point. That's why I played it a little more 'straight' in that first show — but that was the *only* show of mine that was deliberatley inconsistent with the tone and concept of *Maverick*."

"The War of the Silver Kings" became the pilot episode of *Maverick* as a result of Jack Warner's mandate against paying royalties to writers for the creation of series based on their own original material. Huggins had designed the "Point Blank" episode as *Maverick*'s pilot, but once he was informed about the "no royalties to writers" policy, he had to write another pilot that was based on a property owned by Warner Bros. "I started looking in the Warner Bros. catalog for something I could use — an old movie, a book, anything that they owned — and eventually I found the Glasscock book, *The War of the Copper Kings*," said Huggins.

The War of the Copper Kings was a non-fiction book that described how an attorney named Augustus Heinze defeated a copper company in court on the basis of an obscure but still operational law known as the apex theory. But Huggins recalls stumbling onto that bit of history prior to *Maverick*. "Years before, when I was at Columbia Pictures, I had been asked to do a remake of *Gilda* [a 1946 picture starring Rita Hayworth] that would have a Western background," he recalled. "I did a lot of research on mining in Montana for this treatment [for the film, which was called *Antonia*], and at some point I came across this old law known as the 'apex' law, which said that if a miner found an outcropping mineral vein, he had the right to follow that vein downward into the ground, even if it led him underneath the holdings of other miners. On that basis, a lot of people were 'mining' under other people's mines. It was a law that eventually became outmoded, but for some reason, it was never taken off the books. When I read about the apex law, I thought it would make a wonderful device for a story, and I used it in *Antonia*." Huggins completed the treatment for *Antonia*, but the film was never made.

On the basis of the apex theory, Maverick convinces the townspeople to raid the ore in Phineas King's mine. When King takes the matter to court, Maverick simply waits for the opportunity to play his hand — because the apex law was never repealed, the miners are within their rights to loot King's claims. "Maverick played it masterfully, and it wasn't even a con game," said Huggins. "He had found a gimmick in the law books — an interesting and historically accurate gimmick — and used it to his advantage."

Warners was satisfied that "War of the Silver Kings" would be based on a property they'd owned, although Huggins' story is completely different from Glasscock's book. The only element Huggins pulled from *The War of the Copper Kings* was the apex theory, which wasn't even Glasscock's creation — it was an old law, and therefore already in the public domain. The story itself — and the Maverick character — was Huggins' creation entirely. Warners' lawyers apparently saw this as a possible loophole in the event Huggins chose to dispute the matter (which he did) before the Writers Guild. If "War of the Silver Kings" was not based on a Warners-owned property, then Huggins could still claim ownership of *Maverick*, and therefore be entitled to "created by" royalties. In order to play it safe, the studio purchased Huggins' treatment for *Antonia* from Columbia Pictures. Warners could then state unequivocally that "The War of the Silver Kings" was based on a property the studio had owned. The Writers Guild reviewed the matter, and suggested that Huggins not proceed because the Warners case looked fairly strong.

Ironically, Huggins did not realize that the studio had purchased *Antonia* until many, many years later. "Well, that shows you just how far they went to protect themselves," he said. "I'm sure someone in the Legal Department advised Warners that they'd better cover all the bases — because there's really no other reason for their buying my treatment for *Antonia*. *Maverick* had nothing to do with *Antonia*; *Antonia* was a remake of *Gilda*. But I'll tell you the really funny thing about this: I probably told Warners about *Antonia* myself."

The roan horse that Maverick rides in this picture belonged to director Budd Boetticher, an expert horseman (and onetime professional matador). Boetticher didn't care for any of the horses that Warners had available (the studio rented horses from a nearby stable), so he arranged to have a horse named Gitano brought in from his own private stable. "I've always had wonderful horses, and I thought, 'Why would I use any of the stock horses at Warner Bros. when I already have a horse that's perfect for the part?'" Boetticher reasoned. "Gitano was a big horse. You just can't ride a horse like that unless you're a superb horseman. And Jim Garner was a great athlete, as well as a great horseman — everything he did athletically, he did well. As soon as I realized that about him, I knew Jim could handle my horse. When you see him ride into town on a horse like that, and see him handle that animal so beautifully, you say to yourself, 'This guy's a hell of a horseman.' That's the whole idea."

2. POINT BLANK

(a.k.a. "The Third Cross" and "Burning Sky")

ORIGINAL AIRDATE: SEPTEMBER 29, 1957

Teleplay by: Roy Huggins
Based on a Screenplay by: Howard Browne
Directed by: Budd Boetticher

Guest Cast: Karen Steele (Molly Gleason), Mike Connors (Ralph Jordan), Richard Garland (Wes Corwin), Mitchell Kowal (Fletcher), Zon Murray (Callahan), Benny Baker (Mike Brill), Robert Foulk (Moose), Peter Brown (Chris Semple)

Synopsis. Maverick settles temporarily in the small railroad town of Bent Forks, where he soon falls in love with Molly Gleason, a woman with a somewhat disreputable past. Unbeknownst to Maverick, Molly and her lover, a bank teller named Ralph Jordan, plan to use him as a pawn in their scheme to embezzle $100,000.

"Point Blank" was originally conceived as the pilot for *Maverick*, and as far as Roy Huggins is concerned, it's still the "real" pilot. "If you compare the first two shows it's easy to see which was intended as the pilot," he said. "In 'Point Blank' I created a classical Western hero [the sheriff] — a brave, honest, loving man, honorable and courageous — in order to contrast him with Maverick. We also showed Maverick cheating someone but making up for it; and we indicated that he could come close to falling in love and still keep his self-interest clearly in focus. I deliberately made Maverick look bad in the eyes of the sheriff, and even to some of the audience, when he quibbles about the reward — actually *bargains* over this woman he's turned in. The sheriff is disgusted with Maverick and throws him out of town.

"I didn't do many *Mavericks* that were as pure as 'Point Blank.' But it didn't become the pilot because Bill Orr was notified by the legal department that he couldn't use it. The studio would be on the hook to me for a royalty: $500.00 per episode for as long as the series ran. So Orr said to me, 'Sorry, J.L. Warner says no. You'll have to find something that we own to base that series on,' — which I eventually did [*The War of the Copper Kings*]."

Huggins also explained the background behind the rather unusual writing credit for "Point Blank" — teleplay by Huggins, based on a screenplay by Howard Browne. "I had written a story called 'The Saga of Onyx O'Neill,'" said Huggins. "The story of 'Onyx O'Neill' had all the elements of what became the 'Point Blank' story, but it did not have the Maverick character — the gentle grafter. I asked Howard Browne to write a script based on 'Onyx O'Neill,' which he did. Howard's script was a screenplay — a straight Western for theaters, not for television.

"After the meeting with Robert Lewine [in which Huggins first presented the concept of *Maverick*], I decided that I wanted to use Howard's script, which was by then called 'The Burning Sky,' as the basis for the pilot of *Maverick*," Huggins continued. "It was a good script — all we needed to do was adapt it to fit the Maverick character. However, Howard was not available to revise the script — he was ill, and was still recuperating. So I wrote the teleplay myself, and it went on the air as 'Point Blank,' although the show itself became the second episode."

Huggins' teleplay for "Point Blank," therefore, was based on the "Burning Sky" screenplay by Howard Browne, which in turn was based on Huggins' original story, "The Saga of Onyx O'Neill." "That is the official credit for 'Point Blank,' but as you can see, that's a rather clumsy-looking credit," said Huggins. "So I removed my name from where it would have appeared the second time ['based on a story by']."

During the Writers' Guild strike of 1960, Warner Bros. managed to continue producing their shows by taking scripts that had been written for one series and tailoring them for use on another. In one such instance, "Point Blank" was redone as a segment of *77 Sunset Strip* called "Perfect Setup."

Director Budd Boetticher had been friends with Executive Producer William T. Orr since long before the days of *Maverick*. "I first met Bill around 1950, when I was filming *Bullfighter and the Lady*," said Boetticher. "Bill's wife, Joy Page, was my leading lady in that film, and she was an excellent actress. I'd had gotten to know Bill then, and I've always liked him ever since."

3. ACCORDING TO HOYLE

(a.k.a. "The Gambler and the Lady")

ORIGINAL AIRDATE: OCTOBER 6, 1957

Teleplay by: Russell B. Hughes
Based on the Story "A Lady Comes to Texas" by Horace McCoy
Directed by: Budd Boetticher

Guest Cast: Diane Brewster (Samantha Crawford), Tol Avery (George Cross), Jay Novello (Henry Tree), Ted de Corsia (Joe Riggs), Esther Dale (Ma Braus), Leo Gordon (Big Mike McComb), Walter Reed (Bledsoe), Tyler McVey (Hayes), Sailor Vincent (Man), Don Turner (Hamhead), Robert Carson (Kittredge)

Synopsis. Bret loses over $17,000 playing poker with Samantha Crawford, a con artist employed by George Cross — who once lost $50,000 to Maverick and is determined to get it back. Samantha claims that Cross is her father and that he needs to recover the money in order to get out of jail. Bret also needs money (two riverboat owners staked him to $5,000, which he promptly lost to Samantha), so he forms a partnership with Samantha. Maverick purchases gambling equipment (with money loaned by Samantha) as part of a scheme to put a crooked game room owner named Joe Riggs out of business. But Samantha and Cross decide to doublecross Maverick by selling the equipment to Riggs.

The rule of Hoyle referenced in this episode is authentic — it first appeared in *Hoyle's Book of Games* in 1876:

"In five card stud poker, straights are not played, unless it is determined at the commencement of the game that they are admitted."

Once Roy Huggins discovered this obscure condition for the game of poker, he knew that he could work it into a story for *Maverick*. But Huggins recalls learning something even more important from his experience with this episode. "I learned that if you're going to write about poker, you have to write about it realistically and accurately," he said. "In 'According to Hoyle,' Samantha Crawford's plan was to play very carefully until Maverick got a straight, at which point she'd nail him with the rule from Hoyle. Several hours into the game, Maverick gets a hand that's building toward a straight — a six, a seven, an eight and a ten. His hole card is a nine.

"I received several letters from viewers who pointed out to me a detail about poker that I had overlooked in this story: Maverick never would have stayed with his hand unless he had an ace in the hole. Unless Samantha's cards were absolutely lousy (and they weren't, because she had at least a pair of nines), he would have thrown his cards away in a real poker game. But that wasn't the way I played it, and as I said, I received several letters from viewers who had caught that error.

"And I thought, 'They're right, I was being careless.' I had just violated the one rule that I'd tried to follow all throughout my career in television. I'd always strived for my shows to cater to the intelligence of the upper 20% of the audience — in other words, if there was something in the script that I knew would offend, or be otherwise unacceptable to, the upper tier of the audience, I would remove it. And I have never compromised with that rule in all my 40 years in this business."

James Garner worked hard to make his cardhandling expertise look as authentic as possible. "Jim's a pro, and he worked like hell to learn how to handle those cards," said Budd Boetticher. "We photographed Jim so that everything he did well — and he could do a lot of things with cards exceptionally well — we would, naturally, use a full shot of Jim shuffling in the picture." *Maverick* also occasionally used footage of professional card dealers — specifically, close-ups of the dealers' hands — to compensate for what Garner, Jack Kelly or the other actors could not do themselves.

Pappyisms: "Faint heart never filled a flush;" and "Man is the only animal you can skin more than once."

4. GHOST RIDER

ORIGINAL AIRDATE: OCTOBER 13, 1957

Written by: Marion Hargrove
Directed by: Leslie H. Martinson

Guest Cast: Stacy Keach (Sheriff), Joanna Barnes (Mary Shane), Dan Sheridan (Sideburns), Willard Sage (Burt Nicholson), Edd Byrnes (The Kid), Rhodes Reason (Hank Foster), Charles Tannen (Stableman), Richard Collier (Barfly), Charlotte Knight (Mrs. Clemmer), John Cliff (Deputy), Tim Graham (Hotel Clerk), Jim Hope (Player)

Synopsis. Maverick has a bad day in the town of White Rock. First, he's robbed of $3,000 by a young punk known as "The Kid." Then he discovers that the Kid not only lost all of his money playing poker, but was shot and killed for cheating. Then Bret loses his coat (containing the $1,000 bill he keeps for emergencies) after helping out a redhaired woman who, according to the townsfolk, died ten days earlier. When Maverick returns to town, he's nearly shot to death by the undertaker. When the undertaker, a very popular man in town, is later gunned down by a man named Foster (who matches Bret's general physical appearance), Maverick becomes the likely suspect.

Although Marion Hargrove was not under contract to Warners (like most freelance television writers, he worked on an episode-by-episode basis), the studio did provide him with an office where he could work. However, Hargrove's office was not completely furnished — specifically, it lacked a couch, and it took a series of inventive memos to Warners television head William T. Orr (mostly penned by Hargrove) to remedy the matter. "I sent a memo to Bill, from myself, and I reasoned that without a couch, my writing tended to be 'vertical' — I needed to lie down sometimes and work things out," Hargrove recalled. "That went nowhere, so I faked a memo from Roy Huggins that took the same tack: I had Huggins saying, 'Even though Marion's doing good work, it's all vertical writing — what I need is horizontal writing. Please give him a couch, etc.'

"After those two memos, Joanna Barnes volunteered a memo of her own, which was added to the stack. Then I sent one from the head of the studio's Prop Department that read, 'Bill, can you help us out? We are up to our asses in couches!' And then that memo was followed by a memo by J.L. Warner himself: 'Bill, for Christ's sake, what is all this nonsense about couches? Give Hargrove a couch.'"

After several requests, but still no couch, Hargrove finally resorted to drastic measures. "I sneaked into Bill's office one day and taped one last memo over his toilet bowl," he said. "When I came to work the next day, I found a couch in my office."

Shortly thereafter, Hargrove sold the "memos" to *Playboy*, which printed the entire collection as an article in 1958.

5. THE LONG HUNT

(a.k.a. "Dangerous Quest")

ORIGINAL AIRDATE: OCTOBER 20, 1957

Written by: DeVallon Scott
Directed by: Douglas Heyes

Guest Cast: Tommy Farrell (Lefty Dolan), Richard Webb (Ben Maxwell), Joan Vohs (Martha Maxwell), James Anderson (Whitey), Harry Harvey Sr. (Stagecoach Driver), Troy Melton (First Pursuer), Will J. White (First Holdup Man), Mark Tapscott (Player #1), Jack Gargan (Player #2), Rory Mallinson (Local Sheriff), Richard Crane (Jed Ferris)

Synopsis. Maverick befriends Lefty Dolan, a bank robber who rescued Bret from "a parcel of very disappointed poker players." Their friendship is cut short when Lefty is gunned down by two other holdup men, but before he dies, Lefty tells Bret an incredible story. Several years earlier, he and three others had pulled a bank robbery in Dry Springs, Arizona. A man named Jed Ferris, who bore a slight physical resemblance to Lefty, was arrested and convicted for the crime. Lefty, whose conscience has bothered him over the fact that an innocent man has paid for his crime, asks Bret to do whatever he can to clear Jed's name.

Some of the best lines of the early *Maverick* episodes were never filmed — they were included in the "business" of the scripts (the stage directions and character descriptions). In his *Life Magazine* feature article on the series, Marion Hargrove characterized *Maverick* as a writer's show: creator/producer Roy Huggins developed most of the stories for the first two seasons; Douglas Heyes and Montgomery Pittman usually directed their own scripts; and Hargrove often served as the show's "unpaid associate producer." The voice of the writer was so strong on *Maverick* that it permeated all aspects of the scripts.

"From the writer's standpoint, a movie or television script is the least satisfying form of literary expression," Hargrove wrote. "An actor often reads only his own dialogue, the technicians read only what is addressed to them, and many a writer has questioned whether the director reads anything at all. The freedom given to *Maverick*'s writers has led to a new school of script writing which is designed to remedy this. In a *Maverick* scenario, the writer's tone of voice is so contemptuous and his instructions so grumpy that everyone reads every word in a dazed and wary sort of fascination."

Hargrove headed up this "school," and his scripts usually contained any number of zingers. For example, in the list of characters that headed up the script, Hargrove would often describe Maverick as "an itinerant aluminum salesman" [Kaiser Aluminum was *Maverick*'s primary sponsor]; "the clean-living country boy who beat Shirley Temple in a fair fight;" "the celebrated jumping frog of Calaveras County;" "author, lecturer, columnist, and four-time candidate for President on the Socialist ticket;" or simply "awr hero."

Hargrove's stage directions ranged from "Maverick flashes that winnin' smile that scored a 49 in last week's ratings;" "Maverick looks at her as if he's lost his place in the script;" and, the most famous example, "Maverick looks at him with his beady little eyes."

But Hargrove was not the only *Maverick* writer who took such liberties with his scripts. In his teleplay for "The Jeweled Gun," Roy Huggins characterized Maverick as "a shy, introverted young man studying for the ministry." And DeVallon Scott's cast list for "The Long Hunt" describes the characters Rex and Whitey as "gamblers who we later find out are outlaws. . . . Both die young. Also known as Rosencrantz and Guildenstern."

The reference to Maverick's "beady little eyes," by the way, has been the subject of one of the most often repeated myths about the *Maverick* series. According to the legend, *Maverick* was a straightforward Western whose humor did not surface until *after* James Garner had seen Hargrove's reference to Maverick's "beady little eyes" and decided to play it for a laugh. Although that may be how a lot of people remember it, the fact is that *Maverick*'s sense of humor was present from the very beginning. Look back to the very first scene of the first episode, "The War of the Silver Kings," when Maverick fools the officious hotel clerk into thinking that he's deposited an envelope containing $4,000. The envelope, of course, was actually filled with clipped newspaper.

Pappyisms: "Hell has no fury like a man who loses with four of a kind;" and "Love your fellow man, and stay out of his troubles if you can."

6. STAGE WEST

ORIGINAL AIRDATE: OCTOBER 27, 1957

Teleplay by: George Slavin
Based on the Magazine Story "That Packsaddle Affair" by Louis L'Amour
Directed by: Leslie H. Martinson

Guest Cast: Erin O'Brien (Linda Harris), Ray Teal (Mart Fallon), Edd Byrnes (Wes Fallon), Peter Brown (Rip Fallon), Chubby Johnson (Simmons), Michael Dante (Sam Harris), Jim Bannon (Matson), Howard Nagley (Sheriff Tibbs), Fern Barry (Ella Taylor), Buddy Shaw (Dave Taylor), Ollie O'Toole (McLean)

Synopsis. Bret and the widow Linda Harris are held hostage by rancher Mart Fallon and his two sons. Fallon murdered Linda's husband, a miner who has found gold near Indian territory. Unfortunately for Fallon, only Bret knows where the mine is located. Maverick takes advantage of the situation — and of Fallon's greedy nature — by selling a map indicating the mine's location. What Bret doesn't tell Fallon is that the mine is worthless.

The teleplay for "Stage West" was later adapted to comic book form, and appeared in *Maverick* No. 945, published by Dell Publishing Company, Inc. in 1958. Dell published 18 issues of *Maverick* between 1958 and 1962.

This episode features several well-remembered **Maverickisms**, such as "Nothing's for certain, but some things I'll put money on, like a straight flush or a crooked mind;" and "Where money's concerned it could be dirty, dusty or soggy, just so long as it's money."

7. RELIC OF FORT TEJON

ORIGINAL AIRDATE: NOVEMBER 3, 1957

Teleplay by: Jerry Davis
From a Magazine Story by Kenneth Perkins
Directed by: Leslie H. Martinson

Guest Cast: Maxine Cooper (Donna Seely), Fredd Wayne (Honest Carl Jimson), Dan Tobin (Howard Harris), Sheb Wooley (Sheriff), Tyler MacDuff (Drake), Oliver Blake (Brimmer), Lou Krugman (Ferguson), Kem Dibbs (Connors), Earl Hodgins (Johnson), Alan Austin (Tommy Norton), Rush Williams (Deputy), Harry Strang (Delivery Man), Irving Mitchell (Doc Nelson)

Synopsis. Bret wins an old Army camel named Fatima as partial payment in a poker game. After several unsuccessful attempts to sell Fatima, Bret travels to Silver Springs, where he hopes to trip up Carl Jimson, a notorious cardshark who has snowed the entire town into believing his reputation for an "honest deal." Among those whom Jimson has fooled is Donna Seely, his fiancé — and a former girlfriend of Bret's. After Maverick exposes him as a fraud, Carl tries to kill him.

Apparently Maverick started to pay a little more attention to the rules of Hoyle after Samantha Crawford burned him with the "straights don't count unless we say so" gimmick in "According to Hoyle." In this episode, Maverick angers Jimson by asking for a cut of the cards in the middle of a poker game (Bret's trying to catch Jimson in the act of cheating). When Jimson objects, Maverick says, "According to *Hoyle's Book of Rules*, a player is entitled to call for a cut at any time during the game."

When Jimson still objects, Maverick says, "Well, I guess I misunderstood. You see, I thought this was a poker game. You make up rules for any game you like, but don't call it poker — it's misleading."

"Relic of Fort Tejon" was based on a story that first appeared in the December 20, 1947 issue of *Collier's*.

8. HOSTAGE!

(a.k.a. "Showdown at Midnight")

ORIGINAL AIRDATE: NOVEMBER 10, 1957

Written by: Gerald Drayson Adams and James Gunn
Directed by: Richard L. Bare

Guest Cast: Don Durant (Jody Collins), Laurie Carroll (Yvette Devereaux), Wright King (Rick), Jean De Val (Anton Riviage), John Harmon (Ziggy), Stephen BeKassy (Andre Devereaux), Mickey Simpson (Jubal), Trevor Bardette (Inspector Marvin), Roy Glenn (Straw Boss)

Synopsis. Introducing Jack Kelly as Bart Maverick. Bret and Bart seek their way onto the exclusive passenger list for the maiden voyage of *The River Princess* owned by

Andre Devereaux, a wealthy Creole aristocrat who is contemptuous of Americans. After Devereaux's daughter Yvette is kidnapped by Jody Collins, a muskrat trapper from the Bayous who has a strong hatred for the Creoles, the Maverick brothers try to rescue Yvette.

Henry Kaiser, the multibillionaire president of Kaiser Industries, became a partner in *Maverick* solely on the basis of watching James Garner in the pilot, "The War of the Silver Kings." Kaiser saw himself as a "maverick," and he became particularly enamored of Garner's performance. After extensive negotiations between his company, Warner Bros., the ABC network, and the advertising firm of Young & Rubicam (Kaiser's agency), Kaiser became *Maverick*'s primary sponsor, purchasing one-third of the show's ownership (ABC and Warners held the other two shares).

Kaiser was not pleased when he found out that another Maverick brother was going to be brought into the picture. ABC and Warners had met with representatives of Kaiser Industries to inform them that the creation of "Bart Maverick" was brought on by practical necessity (Roy Huggins decided that the only way that *Maverick* could meet its production schedule on time was to have two episodes in production simultaneously; Garner would film one episode, while Jack Kelly would star in the other). However, either Kaiser was never apprised of the situation, or he simply did not care. As far as Kaiser was concerned, he'd purchased *Maverick* on the basis of what he'd seen in the pilot — and what he'd seen in the pilot was James Garner.

On the Monday following the telecast of "Hostage!," Kaiser telephoned ABC president Leonard Goldenson and let him know that he wasn't happy with the addition of Bart Maverick. Goldenson flew out to Kaiser's headquarters in Oakland to discuss the matter. Goldenson recalls the meeting in his book, *Beating the Odds* (Charles Scribner's Sons, 1991):

"Leonard, I bought from you a bushel of red apples," he said. "I like red apples. But after I got through the top layer of red apples, I found nothing but green apples. I don't like green apples."

"Mr. Kaiser, if you're referring to the fact that we have Jack Kelly along with Garner, this was cleared with your advertising agency."

"Leonard, I made that deal with *you*. Not with my agency. I expected you to contact me if you're going to make any change involving Garner."

Goldenson had presumed that Young & Rubicam had cleared the change with Kaiser, but apparently that did not happen. However, the mishap in communications was not Goldenson's fault — he did not have any contact with Young & Rubicam. Warner Bros. and ABC's Sales Department had handled all negotiations with the agency.

The matter was soon settled, but the resolution wasn't cheap. "Eventually ABC had to pay Kaiser $600,000 to keep him happy," wrote Goldenson. "But it was worth it. *Maverick* became the foundation of our growing success on Sunday nights. And it launched not only Jim Garner, but it also helped Roy Huggins, who brought many fine programs to ABC over the years following."

Pappyism: "Never hold a kicker or draw to an inside straight."

9. STAMPEDE

(a.k.a. "No Holds Barred")
ORIGINAL AIRDATE: NOVEMBER 17, 1957

Written by: Gerald Drayson Adams
Directed by: Abner Biberman

Guest Cast: Efrem Zimbalist Jr. (Dandy Jim Buckley), Pamela Duncan (Coral Stacey), Joan Shawlee (Madame Pompey), Chris Alcaide (Tony Cadiz), Mike Lane (Noah Perkins), Pat Comiskey (Battling Kreuger), Rand Brooks (Jack Blair), Marshall Bradford (Marshal Hunt), Jim Hayward (Miner), Mark Tapscott (Deputy)

Synopsis. Bret teams with Dandy Jim Buckley to settle the score with Tony Cadiz, a cadaverous gambler who took the both of them for $12,000 (and left Bret for dead). Cadiz is travelling to the North Dakota mining town of Deadwood, where he plans to make a fortune by showcasing Battling Kreuger, the bare-fisted pugilist whom he manages. Cadiz offers to pay 2-to-1 odds to any man who can last ten rounds with "the Battler." After staking themselves to $4,000 (their reward for recovering two bags of gold stolen from the Wells Fargo Bank), Bret and Jim meet Noah Perkins, a giant of a man and, apparently, the perfect opponent for Battling Kreuger. Bret and Jim set up a high-stakes showdown between Noah and Kreuger — but when Noah bows out at the last minute, Maverick has to take his place.

This episode marks the first appearance of one of *Maverick*'s most famous characters, Dandy Jim Buckley. "I wanted to do a story with a character who was similar to Maverick," recalled Roy Huggins. "I wanted to contrast Maverick, the gentle grafter, with Dandy Jim, the *all-out* grafter. In many ways, both characters are alike; the biggest difference is that Buckley has absolutely no conscience, whereas Bret has an ethical 'system.' Maverick is what you would today call a 'situational ethicist' — if the situation adds up to a plus morally, and no one gets hurt, he's all for it. Buckley's code, on the other hand, is 'If it's good for me, I'll do it — the other guy's got to watch out for himself!'"

Buckley was originally intended as a one-shot character. "But I liked him so much, because I liked Efrem Zimbalist Jr.," said Huggins. "I got such a kick out of what Efrem brought to the role, that I brought back the character whenever I could."

10. THE JEWELED GUN

(a.k.a. "The Big Break")
ORIGINAL AIRDATE: NOVEMBER 24, 1957

Written by: Roy Huggins
Directed by: Leslie H. Martinson

Guest Cast: Kathleen Crowley (Daisy Harris), Miguel Landa (Henrique Felippe), Roy Barcroft (Cattleman), Stephen Colt (George Seevers), Norman Frederic (Mitchell), Terrence deMarney (Snopes), Edwin Bruce (Young Book Salesman), Tom McKee (La Mesa Sheriff), James Parnell (Sheriff), Alfred Hopson (Carter), Ezelle Poule (Mrs. Adams)

Synopsis. Daisy Harris, a wealthy woman with many secrets, hires Bart to pose as her husband ("John Haskell") and accompany her on a business trip to Laramie, Wyoming. Bart doesn't realize that Daisy is planning to kill him — long ago, the real Haskell was murdered by Henrique Felippe, her attorney (and lover). Daisy and Felippe are plotting to cover their tracks by staging an elaborate murder (and burial) of "Haskell."

"Except for when both brothers were in an episode, all scripts were written for Bret Maverick — written for Jim," Roy Huggins explained. "We'd have to make last-minute script changes wherever the first name, 'Bret' or 'Bart,' had to be used. We used their first names sparingly, always referring to the lead as 'Maverick,' so that few last minute changes had to be made. 'Maverick' would always head up the dialogue blocks. That helped us to be really true to the character and to the series — to believe, at the moment it was being written, that Jim would be playing the role."

Although the script for "The Jeweled Gun" was completed in August 1957, filming on the episode did not begin until sometime in October, shortly after Kelly joined the cast. Initially, the script was tailored for Garner, with Kelly appearing only in the vignettes that open and close the show. However, a last-minute switch resulted in Kelly starring in the episode (and Garner appearing in the vignettes), making "The Jeweled Gun" the first solo Bart adventure.

Hawaiian Eye took the script for "The Jeweled Gun" and refilmed it as the episode "Dead Ringer."

11. THE WRECKER

ORIGINAL AIRDATE: DECEMBER 1, 1957

Teleplay by: Russell Hughes
From the Novel by Robert Louis Stevenson and Lloyd Osbourne
Directed by: Franklin Adreon

Guest Cast: Patric Knowles (Paul Carthew), Karl Swenson (Captain Near), Bartlett Robinson (Longhurst), Mervyn Vye (Craven), Tom Browne Henry (Auctioneer), Maurice Manson (Bellairs), Allen Kramer (Jerome Braus)

Synopsis. After buying them their way into an exclusive ring of auction bidders, the Maverick brothers try to purchase *The Flying Scud*, a beached brig containing a cargo of Oriental rice and silk valued at $10,000. Bret's scheme to sell the goods for a quick profit runs aground when he gets into a bidding war with a man named Bellairs, who raises the price to $21,000 before dropping out. Bart soon discovers that Bellairs acted as a middle-man for James Dickson (whose real name is Paul Carthew). Carthew believes that the wrecked ship contains evidence that could link him to a crime which took place at sea many years ago.

"The Wrecker" shows that while Bart may not have been the "original" Maverick, he is still every bit as crafty as his brother. By the end of the story, Bart has found the log that implicates Carthew to a murder that took place on *The Flying Scud*, although he also knows that Carthew is innocent. The two men are adrift at sea, when Bart spots a rescue ship in the distance. Carthew has his back to the ship, so he doesn't realize what Bart has seen. Maverick uses this advantage to negotiate a reward ("Suppose we were rescued — what would you do?"). Carthew tells Bart that he has $50,000 in the bank, and that Bart would be entitled to half that amount. Once Maverick gets Carthew to put that in writing, he tells him about the approaching rescue ship. Carthew realizes that he's been had, but we get the impression that he doesn't mind.

"The Wrecker" marks Bart's first visit to San Francisco (Bret offers to take his brother out on the town). Bart also gets seasick in this episode.

12. THE QUICK AND THE DEAD

ORIGINAL AIRDATE: DECEMBER 8, 1957

Written and Directed by: Douglas Heyes

Guest Cast: Gerald Mohr (Doc Holliday), Marie Windsor (Cora), John Vivyan (Stacey Johnson), Mort Mills (Parker), Sam Buffington (Ponca), Roy Turner (Fred Turner), Hal Hopper (Jim Elkins), Herbert C. Lytton (Gus), Gordon Barnes (Marshal)

Synopsis. Bret becomes an accessory to robbery after a crook named Parker repays a debt to Maverick with stolen money. Parker reluctantly leads Maverick to the town of Bandero, where he meets Stacey Johnson, another of the robbers. Stacey, who possesses an incredible amount of bravado, has become something of a local legend because he once challenged Doc Holliday to a gunfight — and Holliday backed down. When Holliday arrives in Bandero to settle the score, Maverick must keep Stacey alive in order to clear himself of the robbery.

Lee Van Cleef was among writer/director Douglas Heyes' early considerations for Doc Holliday, according to a memo that Heyes sent to producer Roy Huggins shortly before filming began on "The Quick and the Dead." Van Cleef later guest starred in the fourth season episode "Red Dog."

The Television Academy recognized film editor Robert Sparr for his work on "The Quick and the Dead." Sparr was among the nominees for Best Editing of a Film for Television for the year 1957, although the award went to *Gunsmoke*'s Mike Pozen (for the episode "How to Kill a Woman").

13. NAKED GALLOWS

(a.k.a. "The Third Woman")

ORIGINAL AIRDATE: DECEMBER 15, 1957

Written by: Howard Browne
Directed by: Abner Biberman

Guest Cast: Forrest Lewis (Alec Fall), Mike Connors (Sheriff Fillmore), Sherry Jackson (Annie Haines), Morris Ankrum (Joshua Haines), Bing Russell (Tyler Brink), Fay Spain (Ruth Overton), Ed Kemmer (Clyde Overton), Jeanne Cooper (Virginia Cory), Don Dillaway (Ben), Richard Cutting (Cardoza)

Synopsis. Following a successful beaver-hunting trip, Bart arrives in Bent Spur, South Dakota, where he begins to investigate the death of Milo Ballard. Although he pretends to be a friend of Ballard's, Bart is really acting on behalf of Clyde Overton, the man accused of killing Ballard eleven months earlier. Clyde was convicted and sentenced to hang when he was mysteriously broken out of jail. Bart knows that Clyde is innocent.

Maverick was one of four Westerns produced by Warner Bros. during 1957-58 (*Cheyenne*, *Sugarfoot* and *Colt .45* were the others). All four series shared the same facilities: i.e., the sets that were used on *Maverick* were the same as those that were used on the other Western series filmed at the studio. "There were a few occasions where there would be three or four different Westerns, all out on the back lot, and all shooting at the same time," said Luis Delgado, who was James Garner's stand-in on *Maverick* at the time. "You would literally have the camera operators positioned practically back-to-back."

"I remember one time when that happened — we were back there filming a *Maverick* episode that happened to have both Jim and Jack, and there was also a *Cheyenne* and a *Sugarfoot* being filmed back there. Jack and Jim made a joke out of it. While we were getting ready for another camera setup on our show, Jack and Jim decided to 'drop in' on one of the other shows. *Cheyenne* was filming a shootout on horseback that day, so Jack and Jim got up on their horses, loaded their guns with blanks, and just rode right into the scene, shooting their guns with everyone else!"

Richard Bare recalls a similar instance occuring. "One time, we were out in the back lot filming *Maverick*, while another show was filming a chase scene, practically right behind us, at the same time," he said. "There were bandits in the chase scene, and they were supposed to get on their horses and tear down the road, and make their escape. We were in the middle of shooting *Maverick* when all of a sudden a couple of the bandits rode their way onto our set, right as we were filming. I've always wondered if the actors who played those bandits got two checks that day."

Mike Connors, who also appeared in the "Point Blank" episode of *Maverick*, starred as private eye Joe Mannix in the long-running CBS series *Mannix*.

"Naked Gallows" was refilmed on *Hawaiian Eye* as the episode "Shadow of the Blade."

14. COMSTOCK CONSPIRACY

ORIGINAL AIRDATE: DECEMBER 29, 1957

Written by: Gene Levitt
Directed by: Howard W. Koch

Guest Cast: Ruta Lee (Ellen Bordeen), Oliver McGowan (Jerome Horne), Ed Prentiss (John Bordeen), Werner Klemperer (Alex Jennings), Percy Helton (Mr. Vincent), Arthur Batanides (Brock), Terry Frost (Sheriff), Bill O'Brien (Doctor), Joy Rogers (Woman Passenger), Red Morgan (Stagecoach Driver)

Synopsis. Jerome Horne and John Bordeen run the largest railroad company in Virginia City. Bordeen owes Bret $10,000, but he'd rather shoot him than pay him. Maverick kills Bordeen in self defense — but after reporting the shooting to the sheriff, he discovers that the body (and all other evidence) has been removed. Maverick becomes further confounded the next day, when Horne pays him the money — and insists that Bordeen is alive and well.

"Comstock Conspiracy" features an exchange that encapsulizes what Roy Huggins had in mind when he created *Maverick*. In this sequence, Ellen Bordeen asks Maverick for help:

Ellen: If my father's posing as John Bordeen, he's doing it against his will, Mr. Maverick.

Bret: Possibly.

Ellen: Probably. But what can I do about it?

Bret: Go to the sheriff, I guess.

Ellen: Jerome Horne put the sheriff in office. Can you help me?

Bret: No, ma'am.

Ellen: Because you have your $10,000?

Bret: Yes, ma'am.

Ellen: You aren't very noble.

Bret: No, ma'am.

Maverick decides to help Ellen — but only after she convinces him that she knows how to handle a gun. "Comstock Conspiracy" also features this pearl from Pappy Maverick: "Stick your nose in other people's business, and you'll get it bent."

In a memo to Warners written after it had reviewed the script for this episode, ABC voiced a slight objection to Maverick's hiccupping at the end of the picnic scene with Ellen. The network admitted that if it were done lightly and in good taste, the hiccupping "would not be unseemly," but it still requested eliminating the hiccups from the scene. The hiccups stayed in.

Werner Klemperer starred as Colonel Klink on *Hogan's Heroes*. Director Howard W. Koch acted as Executive Producer of Frank Sinatra Enterprises during the early 1960s, and later became Vice President in Charge of Production at Paramount Pictures in 1965.

15. THE THIRD RIDER

ORIGINAL AIRDATE: JANUARY 5, 1958

Written by: George F. Slavin
Directed by: Franklin Adreon

Guest Cast: Frank Faylen (Red Harrison), Michael Dante (Turk Mason), Barbara Nichols (Blanche), Kasey Rogers (Dolly), Dick Foran (Sheriff Edwards), Morris Libbert (Jimmy Ellis), William Boyett (Collins), Robert Contreras (Jose), Charles Kane (Conductor), Felice Richmond (Woman Passenger), Dan White (Cowpoke)

Synopsis. Bart stumbles onto a pair of bandits who stole $80,000 from the Elm City Bank, then is later arrested by Sheriff Edwards, who mistakes him for one of the gang. Maverick escapes Edwards and heads after the robbers, hoping to recover the money and claim a five-percent reward. Bart locates Red, one of the robbers, but he's knocked unconscious before he can locate the money. Edwards arrests Maverick again and holds him for trial. But a murderous young couple, believing that Maverick knows the money's location, breaks him out of jail and hold him hostage.

Maverick becomes really scared in this episode. Twice he's abducted by people who think he knows the money's location (first by Turk and Blanche, then by Dolly and Red). Maverick honestly believes he's about to be shot to death by Red — until Turk and Blanche ride in at the last minute. Turk kills Red, but that only means that Maverick reverts to becoming Turk's prisoner. However, Maverick's keen sense of human nature saves his life: he manages to play Blanche against Turk by convincing Blanche that Turk would kill her in an instant.

Frank Faylen played the long-suffering Herbert T. Gillis, father of Dobie, on *The Many Loves of Dobie Gillis*. Kasey Rogers, who also guest-starred in "The Devil's

Necklace" and "Three Queens Full," was the second actress to play Louise Tate on *Bewitched* (she replaced Irene Vernon).

16. A RAGE FOR VENGEANCE

(a.k.a. "West of Laramie")

ORIGINAL AIRDATE: JANUARY 12, 1958

Teleplay by: Marion Hargrove
Story by: Roy Huggins
Directed by: Leslie . Martinson

Guest Cast: Catherine McLeod (Margaret Ross), John Russell (John Grimes), Gage Clarke (Bradshaw), Russ Conway (Sheriff), Lewis Martin (Andrew Wiggins), Jonathan Hole (Desk Clerk), Phil Arnold (Porter), William Bailey (Doctor), Carl Hodgins (Charley), Charlotte Knight (Mrs. Walker), Billie Benedict (Denver Porter), Rusty Westcoatt (Second Passenger), Luis Delgado (Gunman)

Synopsis. A mysterious woman named Margaret Ross hires Bret to accompany her as she transports $200,000 from Denver, Colorado to North Span, Montana. Maverick's curiosity becomes unbridled when he discovers that the money is counterfeit.

"A Rage for Vengeance" is one of those rare instances in the series in which Maverick allows himself to fall in love. "If you ever decide to get out of [the newspaper business], I can make an honest housewife out of you," he tells Margaret. Even though Margaret does not love him, Maverick is so taken with her that he stays to help her fight John Grimes, the ruthless cattleman who drove Margaret's husband to his death. When Grimes has Margaret killed, Bret avenges her death; when the town honors Margaret for all that she did, Maverick protects her memory by breaking into the bank and removing the $200,000 in counterfeit money that Margaret had deposited [in a strongbox inside the bank's safe].

"A Rage for Vengeance" also went through a rather interesting metamorphosis. "It often happens that the finished story [on *Maverick*] is a pole away from the original idea," wrote Marion Hargrove in 1959. "Howard Browne once toyed with a situation in which Maverick would play poker desperately for money that he knew was counterfeit. Getting nowhere with the idea, he gave it to Roy Huggins, who began working it like taffy. The end product was a four-handkerchief story which involved Maverick's taking honest work, falling in love, proposing to the girl and being turned down, shooting it out with a prospective governor of Montana, robbing a bank, being wounded and talking a sheriff out of jailing him. The show had everything but Browne's poker game."

Luis Delgado, James Garner's longtime professional stand-in and personal friend, has a silent bit in this episode (he's the gunman who shoots down Margaret's wagon at the beginning of Act IV). "That happened a lot, on *Maverick*, and on other things I've done with Jim," said Delgado. "When you're tied in with an actor, as I was with Jim, the actor will often ask the director or assistant director if they can work you into the picture — that way, the actor feels that he's taking care of his man, because if you're an extra or a stand-in, you could make a little more money if they took an individual shot of you [as is the case with Delgado in "A Rage for Vengeance"]."

Delgado has had regular roles on *The Rockford Files* (as "Officer Billings") and *Bret Maverick* (as "Shifty Delgrado"), but he has no ambitions of becoming a fulltime actor. "To me, acting is terribly hard," he said. "For some people like Jim, acting comes very easily. But when I see the camera staring at me, I get scared and panicky. If I have no dialogue, or maybe two or three words to do, I can get through that very easily. But if I have a lot of dialogue to do, I mess it up."

Delgado is also related to *Maverick*'s creator/producer, Roy Huggins. Luis' sister, Adele Mara, is Roy's wife.

17. ROPE OF CARDS

ORIGINAL AIRDATE: JANUARY 19, 1958

Teleplay by: R. Wright Campbell
Story by: Robert Ormund Case
Directed by: Richard L. Bare

Guest Cast: Will Wright (Jabe Hallock), Joan Marshall (Lucy Sutter), William Reynolds (Bill Gregg), Tol Avery (John Sloan), Hugh Sanders (Blaine), Frank Cady (Hamelin), Don Beddoe (Price), George O'Hanlon (Caldwell), Emile Meyer (Pike), Harry Cheshire (Judge), Harry Harvey Sr. (Store Owner), Donald Kirke (First Juror), Robert Lynne (Doctor), Ken Christy (Sheriff), Tom Monroe (Slim)

Synopsis. While playing cards in a small town, Bret is hoodwinked into performing civic duty — sitting on the jury for the murder trial of young Bill Gregg, who is wrongly accused of murdering an unscrupulous cattle rancher named John Sloan. But Bret turns out to be Bill's only hope. While the rest of the jurors are swayed by the largely circumstantial evidence against Gregg, Maverick has a reasonable doubt, and he alone votes for Bill's acquittal.

In "Rope of Cards," Maverick witnesses Sloan goad Bill Gregg into anger: Sloan turned down Bill's request for a $3,000 loan, then threw dirt on the name of Gregg's late father, whom Sloan accused of being a cheat. A furious Bill lunges after Sloan, but Maverick intercedes (an action for which Bill laters thanks Bret). However, no one witnessed what happened the next day, when Sloan does a 180-degree turnaround: he apologizes for dishonoring Bill's father, and offers to loan Gregg the money, after all. Sloan's about-face, however, was all part of his design to frame Bill for robbery. Sloan knew that, given the great number of witnesses who saw him turn down Gregg the day before, no one would believe Bill if he claimed that Sloan had suddenly decided to give him the money.

Maverick knows that Bill is innocent, and he proceeds to sway the rest of the jurors — except Pike — into voting for acquittal. But Bret also understands why Pike consistently votes "guilty" — Bill's story, though truthful, *is* hard to believe, given the events of the previous day. So he uses Pike's stubbornness against him. Maverick proposes to Pike that the odds of making five pat hands out of 25 consecutive cards (in a full, regular deck, shuffled without any tricks) are about a hundred-thousand to one — approximately the same odds of Bill Gregg's story being true. Pike shuffles the deck, then deals Maverick 25 cards face down. Bret proceeds to make five pat hands from the cards Pike dealt him. Pike is astonished, but Maverick tells him he shouldn't be: you can make five pat hands out of any 25 cards practically every time. (Pike changes his vote to "not guilty.")

Bret called his little demonstration "Maverick Solitaire." Although Pike thought that he'd been tricked, what Maverick did "is not a card trick at all," explained Roy Huggins. "Anybody can do it. In other words, you could take a deck, shuffle it, deal out 25 cards, and make five pat hands out of those 25 cards. *They're there.* Try it: nine times out of ten, it works. It's nothing I invented — it's just an interesting fact that a lot of people don't realize. They think it's impossible. They think the odds are a thousand to one."

Huggins adds a final note that'll give you an idea of just how many people were watching *Maverick* in 1958. "The Monday after we introduced 'Maverick Solitaire,' sales of playing cards had skyrocketed like you wouldn't believe," he said. "Everywhere you'd go, people who had seen the show were buying cards to see if they could do it. I was told by several people that by the end of the day, you couldn't get a deck of cards *anywhere* in this country. Every store that sold cards had sold out."

Richard Bare won the coveted Directors Guild Award as best TV Director of 1958 (for the *77 Sunset Strip* episode "All Our Yesterdays"). Robert Sparr received a second Emmy nomination, for Best Editing of a Film for Television for 1958-59, for his work on this episode (he had also been honored with a nomination in 1957, for "The Quick and the Dead").

18. DIAMOND IN THE ROUGH

(a.k.a. "The Great Diamond Swindle")

ORIGINAL AIRDATE: JANUARY 26, 1958

Teleplay by: Marion Hargrove
Story by: Roy Huggins
Directed by: Douglas Heyes

Guest Cast: Jacqueline Beer (Henriette), Lily Valenty (Madame), Fredd Wayne (Van Buren Kingsley), William Reynolds (Reynolds), Sig Ruman (Captain Steeger), Paul Power (Pyne), Robert Fairfax (Shelbourne), George Baxter (Vincent), Bob Stevenson (Sailor), Louis Mercier (Beaujean), Lela Bliss (Mrs. Shelbourne), Catherine Barrett (Mrs. Kingsley), Terrence deMarney (Murphy), Mason Curry (Second Teller), Jack Chefe (Butler), William Remick (First Millionaire), Stephen Ellsworth (Second Millionaire), Carlyle Mitchell (General Marvin), Patrick White (Selby), Otto Waldis (Scharf), William Bailey (Banker), I. Stanford Jolley (McClure)

Synopsis. Van Buren Kingsley, a ruthless New Orleans aristocrat now operating in San Francisco, stands to make a fortune by selling worthless stock in a diamond company. Kingsley claims he found his diamonds in Nevada, but he actually purchased them from a dealer in Pennsylvania. Kingsley's undoing begins when he rolls Bart for $17,000 and has him shanghaied to New Orleans. Bart returns to San Francisco, determined to put Kingsley out of business.

Bart spends four months aboard *The Silent William* without incident, so he appears to have gotten over his initial problems with the sea (in "The Wrecker," he'd gotten seasick). Over the course of the trip, Bart read the complete works of William Shakespeare (three times!), Prescott's *Conquest of Peru* (twice), *The Swiss Family Robinson*, and six books on navigation. He also claimed to have had the time to teach himself how to speak Dutch, French, and a smattering of Javanese. Of course, Bart might be pulling our leg as to some of this, but he *did* have a lot of time to kill.

Madame asks Bart if he's a man of wealth ("It depends on the cards I draw," he replies). Madame is pleased to learn that Bart is a gambler. "It's a good life, a worthwhile pursuit," she tells him. "There is no more exquisite art than the art of wasting one's time when one has the time to spare. But it is a dying art in these times."

CHARLES FRANK, JAMES GARNER AND JACK KELLY (THE NEW MAVERICK)

19. DAY OF RECKONING

(a.k.a. "A Terrible Day")

ORIGINAL AIRDATE: FEBRUARY 2, 1958

Written by: Carey Wilbur
Directed by: Leslie H. Martinson

Guest Cast: Jeanne Willes (Lily), Tod Griffin (Jack Wade), Mort Mills (Red Scanlon), Willard Sage (George Buckner), Russ Thorsen (Marshal Hardie), Virginia Gregg (Amy Hardie), Jon Lormer (Summers), Gus Wilson (Roy Hingle), Morgan Sha'an (Slim), Troy Melton (Harry), James McCallion (Charlie), Sammy Ogg (Boy)

Synopsis. When the marshal of Kiowa City, Kansas is gunned down in cold blood, a timid printer named George Buckner publishes a scathing report of the incident and plans to send it to the governor. The killers discover the report and demand that the town turn over Buckner by nightfall, or else they'll "tree" (i.e., wreck) the town.

In "Day of Reckoning," Maverick describes himself as a "fence straddler," because his line of business requires that he stay out of trouble, eat well, and mind his own business. But Bret also has a conscience that will gnaw at him whenever he "straddled" at a time when he should have interceded. Maverick tries to convince Marshal Walt Hardie to ride out of town and avoid the gunfight with Red Scanlon. When Hardie refused to back down, Bret let him face Scanlon — even though he knew the marshal would be facing a certain death.

Maverick doesn't like George Buckner ("A man who shouts brave and loud, then runs when he gets answered, makes me sick"), but he agrees to help him after Buckner strikes a nerve in Maverick's conscience. Buckner reminds Bret that just as he [Buckner] stood by and watched Jack Wade's men beat Charlie (the young newsboy) to death, Maverick also, in effect, stood by and did nothing while Wade and Scanlon gunned down Walt Hardie. Maverick becomes angry when he hears that, because he knows what Buckner said is true.

"Day of Reckoning" is based on Carey Wilbur's play "A Terrible Day," which was originally performed live on *Westinghouse Summer Theater* on July 19, 1955. The episode also features one of the most famous **Pappyisms** of all: "If either one of you comes back with a medal, I'll beat you to death."

20. THE SAVAGE HILLS

ORIGINAL AIRDATE: FEBRUARY 9, 1958

Teleplay by: Gerald Drayson Adams and Douglas Heyes
Story by: Gerald Drayson Adams
Directed by: Douglas Heyes

Guest Cast: Diane Brewster (Samantha Crawford), Peter Whitney (Gunnerson), Thurston Hall (Judge), Stanley Andrews (Sheriff Gait), John Dodsworth (Clayton Palmer)

Synopsis. In the Dakota Territory, Bart meets Samantha Crawford — whom he remembers from her encounter with brother Bret (in "According to Hoyle") — and discovers she is searching for a counterfeiter named Gunnerson. Hoping to collect some of the reward money, Bart leads Samantha to Gunnerson, whom they both discover is a Secret Service agent. When Samantha escapes with the counterfeit plates, Bart and Gunnerson trail her, but she eludes them by diving into the river. Bart follows Samantha to an island, where they protect each other from a savage tribe of Sioux Indians. However, upon reaching Nebraska Territory, Samantha disappears with the plates — while Gunnerson arrests Bart.

"The Savage Hills" marks the second appearance of Diane Brewster as Samantha Crawford, and provides some background on Samantha's character. Samantha's parents moved west with the wagon train out of Springfield; they settled in Dakota when she was five. She has learned how to survive on her own ever since her parents were killed by Arapahoe Indians when she was twelve years old. "That explains quite a few things," observes Bart.

Samantha Crawford is a fun character, and Brewster's performances certainly contributed greatly to the success *Maverick* enjoyed during its first two years. "I had used Diane Brewster before, and I knew that she was a good actress," said Roy Huggins. "She had played a similar character in an episode of *Cheyenne* I called 'The Dark Rider,' and I'm sure that I thought of her when I came up with the character Samantha Crawford."

"The Dark Rider" is the focus of an interesting chapter in the history of *Maverick*. In "The Dark Rider," Brewster's character — a con artist — leads a group of men on a cattle drive to Kansas. Cheyenne (Clint Walker) joins the group, and eventually saves their lives by unmasking a killer who had been disguised as a priest. Cheyenne also prevents the con artist from running off with all the money earned from the drive, but she gets the last word (she steals Cheyenne's money at the end of the picture). The name of Brewster's character in "The Dark Rider" is Samantha, a fact which has led to one of the biggest myths surrounding *Maverick*: i.e., that "The Dark Rider" was designed as a prototype for the *Maverick* series, and that the "Samantha" played by Brewster in that show was the same character she played on *Maverick*. Ironically, Roy Huggins himself created that myth when he told *TV Guide* in a 1959 interview that "*Maverick* really started with Samantha."

Huggins remembers making that remark, but he also cautions that comments such as "*Maverick* really started with Samantha" have to be understood in their proper context. "Sometimes when you're interviewed, you make statements that are exaggerations for the sake of the moment," he explained. "And sometimes these exaggerations are taken quite literally, and are repeated, and the exaggerations grow with each translation until they become mythic in proportion. Since I was the one who started this particular myth about Samantha Crawford, let me be the one to end it: *Maverick did not* start with Samantha, even if I said that in *TV Guide*, and 'The Dark Rider' *was not* a forerunner of *Maverick*. If *Maverick* started with any one character, or any one show, it was the James Garner character in 'The Man from 1997,' which was a segment of *Conflict*."

Richard Bare, who directed "The Dark Rider" for Huggins, concurs. "There was never a test show for *Maverick* on the *Cheyenne* series, and I ought to know, because I was the regular director on *Cheyenne* at the time Roy produced it," he said. "I know that Diane played a character named Samantha on that show, but there's no other connection between 'Dark Rider' and *Maverick*."

There are, however, two interesting footnotes to the "Dark Rider" myth. Besides Diane Brewster, Samantha Crawford on *Maverick* and the Samantha on *Cheyenne* have something else in common: Roy Huggins named both characters after his mother ("My mother's name was Samantha, and Crawford was her maiden name," he said). And there *is* a connection between "The Dark Rider" and *Maverick* — Huggins took the script and had it rewritten as a *Maverick* episode, "Yellow River."

21. TRAIL WEST TO FURY

(a.k.a. "The Tall Man")

ORIGINAL AIRDATE: FEBRUARY 16, 1958

Teleplay by: Gene Levitt
Based on a Story by: Joseph Chadwick
Directed by: Alan Crosland Jr.

Guest Cast: Efrem Zimbalist Jr. (Dandy Jim Buckley), Aline Towne (Laura Miller), Gene Nelson (Jim Hewlit), Charles Fredericks (Jesse Hayden), Don Kelly (Jett), Paul Fierro (Miguel), Paul Savage (Tall Man), Russ Bender (Doctor), James Hope (Lieutenant), Mike Hagen (First Johnny Reb)

Synopsis. In Colorado, Bret, Bart and Dandy Jim Buckley seek shelter in a cabin amidst a massive flood. While waiting out the storm, Bret and Bart recall their return to their hometown of Little Bend, Texas after the Civil War, where they worked as trail bosses leading a herd of cattle to Arizona, and encountered the unscrupulous rancher Jesse Hayden, who would do anything to derail the cattle drive — including framing the Maverick brothers for murder. The herd safely arrived in Arizona, but Hayden died before retracting his false testimony. For this reason, the boys explain to Buckley, they can never return to their native Texas. (Although a witness — a mysterious "tall man" — can clear the Mavericks, the man vanished, and the boys have never found him. However, given how much they enjoy roaming about, they aren't exactly in a hurry to find him.)

"Just before the war ended, Bart and I, like a lot of Johnny Rebs, joined the Union army of Indian fighters to keep from rotting in a Yankee prison," Bret tells Dandy Jim Buckley in this episode. Bart had also mentioned this story to Samantha Crawford in "The Savage Hills."

22. THE BURNING SKY

ORIGINAL AIRDATE: FEBRUARY 23, 1958

Teleplay by: Russell Hughes
Story by: Howard Browne
Directed by: Gordon Douglas

Guest Cast: Gerald Mohr (Johnny Ballero), Joanna Barnes (Mrs. Baxter), Douglas Kennedy (Connors), Whitney Blake (Letty French), Phillip Terry (Chick Braus), Syd Saylor (Depot Master)

Synopsis. Bart is among six passengers stranded in the Arizona desert after a group of Mexican bandits wreck their stagecoach. The bandits are after one of the passengers, a dance hall entertainer named Letty French, who they believe has stashed away $500,000 that once belonged to a prominent Mexican family. Without water, and without the likelihood of another stagecoach passing through, Bart and the others face a perilous situation: if the bandits don't finish them off, the merciless desert heat will.

Gerald Mohr, who starred as Doc Holliday in "The Quick and the Dead," and James Garner have one role in common: both played Raymond Chandler's classic private eye Philip Marlowe. Mohr was the voice of Marlowe on radio, while Garner starred on the big screen in 1969's *Marlowe*.

23. THE SEVENTH HAND

ORIGINAL AIRDATE: MARCH 2, 1958

Teleplay by: Russell Hughes
Story by: Howard Browne
Directed by: Richard L. Bare

Guest Cast: Diane Brewster (Samantha Crawford), Sam Buffington (Logan), James Philbrook (Simon), Myrna Dell (Anita), Gerald Perry (Pritchard), Byron Foulger (Hotel Clerk), Damian O'Flynn (Mr. Taber), Francis deSales (Mr. Gilling), Bob Steele (Wells), Sidney Mason (Mr. Lockridge), Charles Quinlan (Mr. Beaker), Jay Jeston (Mr. Folger)

Synopsis. In Kansas City, Bret bumps into Samantha Crawford, who offers to stake him $20,000 if he plays in a high-stakes poker game with wealthy businessmen. Unaware that Samantha was hired by a man named Logan to set up the game, Bret agrees — however, Samantha doesn't realize that Logan intends to use the game to stage a robbery. Bret regrets his decision after Logan's men interrupt the game and escape with $100,000. What's worse: the other card players accuse Maverick of orchestrating the heist and threaten to use their influence to blacklist him from any card game in the country. In order to clear his name, and recover the money, Bret and Samantha pursue the robbers.

In addition to bringing both Roy Huggins and James Garner to Warner Bros., Richard Bare had a hand in adding another member to the *Maverick* fold. "Diane Brewster was a key ingredient to *Maverick*'s success," he said. "Diane was my girlfriend once, and I brought her out to Warner Bros., and got her a couple of bit roles in some of the shorts that I was making (the old *Behind the Eightball* series). One time, she played a nurse, and one of the Warners talent scouts, who had seen her in the dailies, called me and asked if I thought Diane was good enough to do a Western. I told him, 'You're damn right — she's a terrific actress.'

"Soon after that, I was directing *Cheyenne*, and I cast her in a couple of early shows, but other producers and directors were also becoming acquainted with her work. Roy, of course, knew what Diane could do. When he began to work on *Maverick*, he created this conwoman who was going to be Garner's match, and he cast Diane, and then she went on and she did a bunch of *Mavericks*."

Diane Brewster also had recurring roles on two other popular ABC series: she was Miss Canfield, Beaver Cleaver's first teacher, on *Leave It to Beaver*; and she played Helen Kimble, the doomed wife of Dr. Richard Kimble, who appeared in flashbacks on *The Fugitive*. Diane Brewster died in 1991.

Pappyism: "Marriage is the only game of chance I know of where both people can lose."

24. PLUNDER OF PARADISE

ORIGINAL AIRDATE: MARCH 9, 1958

Written and Directed by: Douglas Heyes

Guest Cast: Ruta Lee (Sally), Joan Weldon (Grace Wheeler), Leo Gordon (Big Mike McComb), Jay Novello (Paco Torres), Rico Alanes (Fernando), Gene Iglesias (Ricardo), Nacho Galindo (Chucho Morales), Roberto Contreras (Alfredo), Manuel Lopez (Diego), Jorge Moreno (Ubaldo)

Song "Virtue is Its Own Reward"
Written by: Douglas Heyes and Jack O'Brien

Song "Ballada a la Luna"
Written by: Eugene Iglesias

Synopsis. In the Mexican town of Paraiso, Bart, Big Mike McComb, and Grace Wheeler search for the legendary *El Piaje del Paraiso* ("the Plunder of Paradise") — a fortune in gold, diamonds, doubloons, and rubies that has been buried for over one hundred years. Grace's husband, a geologist, discovered the treasure — along with a plan to smuggle it out of Mexico — but he was killed by bandits who are also searching for the hoard. As Bart, Mike and Grace close in on the treasure's location, they must also protect themselves from the same group of bandits, who have been following them.

When he first began producing at Warner Bros., Roy Huggins began a practice for writing stories that he would follow for the rest of his television career. Whenever he needed stories for his shows, he'd get in his car and take a three-or-four-thousand mile drive, and dictate stories while he drove. When he returned to the studio seven or eight days later, he had stories for eight or ten episodes — not just a few paragraphs here and there, but *complete* stories, including dialogue, stage directions, and fleshed-out characters.

"The stories I developed were longer than the script when they were transcribed," Huggins explained. "I would start with a situation and develop the story, following this theory about story development: start with something intriguing, and when you get to a point where you're not certain where the story is headed, ask yourself what might logically happen next that is truly interesting. That carries the story one more step. I never knew what that next step might be, but the method worked."

25. BLACK FIRE

ORIGINAL AIRDATE: MARCH 16, 1958

Teleplay by: Marion Hargrove
Story by: Howard Browne
Directed by: Leslie H. Martinson

Guest Cast: Hans Conried (Homer Eakins), Will Wright (General Eakins), Theona Bryant (Cousin Hope), John Vivyan (Cousin Milford), Jane Darwell (Mrs. Knowles), George O'Hanlon (Cousin Elmo), Edith Leslie (Cousin Elizabeth), Charles Bateman (Cousin Jim), Emory Parnell (Cousin Lonnie), Harry Harvey Jr. (Cousin Seeby), Don Sheridan (Luther), Jimmy Horan (Cousin Pliney), David McMahon (Sheriff)

Synopsis. Bret impersonates his friend Homer Eakins, who along with his other relatives, has been summoned to the Black Fire Ranch by his wealthy uncle. General Eakins wants to survey his relations for a two-week period in order to see who is most worthy of inheriting his $2 million fortune. However, one by one, each of the potential heirs is mysteriously murdered.

Bret has to impersonate Homer because he owes Homer "a substantial favor" (presumably, a lot of money). When Bret learns that the General wants to inspect his potential heirs for the next two weeks, he arranges for his friend "Maverick" (Homer) to stay with him. Homer, who never got along with his uncle, wanted to avoid meeting the old man; but Bret knows the scam won't work unless Homer is present to tip him off.

The General soons discovers the ruse, but he immediately takes a liking to Maverick: he feels he can trust Bret precisely because Maverick isn't a relative. The General wants Maverick to help him find the killer, although Bret initially declines — as Pappy used to say, "A man who can't find his own troubles doesn't deserve to share somebody else's." But Maverick soon changes his mind when the General offers him $2,000 to stay. "Did your Pappy have something funny to say about money?" cracks the General. "No, he spoke very highly of it," replies Bret.

Jane Darwell won the Academy Award for Best Actress for her performance as Ma Joad in the 1940 film adaptation of John Steinbeck's *The Grapes of Wrath*.

26. BURIAL GROUND
OF THE GODS

ORIGINAL AIRDATE: MARCH 30, 1958

Written and Directed by: Douglas Heyes

Guest Cast: Nancy Gates (Laura Stanton), Robert Lowery (Paul Asher), Claude Akins (Paisley Briggs), Charles Cooper (Philip Stanton), Saundra Edwards (Lottie), Raymond Hatton (Stableman)

Synopsis. Philip Stanton was convicted of murder and sentenced to hang, when a twist of fate saved his life — Sioux Indians raided the stagecoach transporting him to the place of execution. Although long presumed dead, Stanton actually escaped to the Waconda Mountains in Wyoming. When a scoundrel named Paisley Briggs finds a wedding band, he presents it to Laura Stanton as evidence that her husband is still alive (although Briggs has never seen Phil). Briggs knows that Laura plans to marry wealthy Paul Asher (Phil's former business partner) and demands $5,000 for his silence, but a skeptical Asher forces Briggs into leading Laura and him into the Wakondas. Briggs tries to abandon Laura and Asher before they discover his lie, but Bart, whom Briggs had robbed of $850, catches up with him. Bart joins the party for the rest of the expedition.

Claude Akins appeared in such films as *From Here to Eternity*, *The Caine Mutiny*, *The Defiant Ones*, *Comanche Station* (directed by Budd Boetticher), *Rio Bravo*, *Inherit the Wind*, and *How the West Was Won*. Akins, who co-starred with James Garner in *A Man Called Sledge* and Jack Kelly in *The Gambler Part 4: Luck of the Draw*, died in 1994.

Pappyism: "Flattery is like perfume — smell it, but don't swallow it."

27. SEED OF DECEPTION

ORIGINAL AIRDATE: APRIL 13, 1958

Written by: Montgomery Pittman
Directed by: Richard L. Bare

Guest Cast: Adele Mara (June Mundy), Gerald Mohr (Doc Holliday), Joi Lansing (Doll Hayes), Myron Healey (Jim Mundy), Frank Ferguson (Sheriff McPeters), Bing Russell (Ross Aikens), Frances Morris (Mrs. Pierce), Ron Hayes (Max Evers), Herb Lytton (Dr. Teller), Guy Wilkerson (Cecil Mason), Terry Rangno (Grady Lester), Clem Fuller (Stage Driver), Chuck Cason (Henchman)

Synopsis. The townspeople of Bonita welcome Bret and Bart with open arms — they believe that the Mavericks are Doc Holliday and Wyatt Earp, and that they've arrived in town to take care of Jim Mundy and his gang of troublemakers. (Bret and Bart try to clarify the misunderstanding, although Bret adds to the problem when he playfully refers to his brother as "Wyatt.") The sheriff thinks that Mundy is planning to rob the payroll of a nearby mining company from the bank, and he knows that the town will lose the company's business if Mundy is successful. The Mavericks try to stay out of the matter, but Bret becomes involved after Bart is shot by a henchman of Mundy's who believed Bart had stumbled onto their plan.

Adele Mara, who has been married to *Maverick* producer Roy Huggins for the past 40 years, stars in this episode as June Mundy (a.k.a. June Collins), a professional dancer whose role in the scheme is to cause a diversion by dancing in the bar at ten o'clock — precisely when Mundy and his boys are drilling a hole through the floor of their hotel room, which is located directly above the bank vault. The more June works the saloon patrons into a lather, the louder they will yell, and the less likely Mundy will be heard.

For the dance scene, Mara wore a diaphonous costume that prompted one irate viewer to write Roy Huggins with a complaint about putting a "half-naked woman" on network TV. Huggins responded to the viewer, "That was no half-naked woman, that was my wife."

Also in this episode, Bret admits that he's "not too good with a gun, but then I like to think that the next man is worse."

James Garner later played Wyatt Earp in the films *Hour of the Gun* (1967) and *Sunset* (1988).

MYRNA FAHEY AND JAMES GARNER

SECOND SEASON: 1958-1959

PRODUCTION CREDITS

Starring James Garner as Bret Maverick
and Jack Kelly as Bart Maverick

Executive Producer: William T. Orr
Produced by: Roy Huggins
Created by: Roy Huggins

Directors of Photography: Harold Stine, Ralph Woolsey, Perry Finnerman, Robert B. Warwick, Edwin duPar, Wesley Anderson
Camera Operators: William Riesboard, Eddie Albert, Fred Terzo, William Rinaldi, Robert Tobey, Stewart Higgs, Luis Molina, Herbert Fisher
Art Directors: Howard Campbell, Percy Ferguson, Leo K. Kuter

Supervising Film Editor: James Moore
Film Editors: Carl Pingitore, Robert Watts, Elbert K. Hollingsworth, Walter S. Stern, Robert T. Sparr, Harold Minter, Frank O'Neill, Fred M. Bohanon, Basil Wrangall, David Wages, Robert B. Warwick Jr., Marsh Hendry

Music Supervision: Paul Sawtell, Bert Shefter
Music Editor: Joe Inge
"Maverick" Theme Music by David Buttolph,
Lyrics by Paul Francis Webster

Production Manager: Oren W. Haglund
Sound Mixers: Stanley Jones, Samuel F. Goode, Robert B. Lee, B.F. Ryan, Francis E. Stahl, Earl Crain Sr., Francis J. Scheid, Theodore B. Hoffman, Leslie G. Hewitt, Oliver Garretson, Dolph Thomas
Script Supervisors: Rita Michaels, Doris Miller, Marie Halvey, Mary Ann Wale
Chief Electricians: Ernie Long, Vic Johnson, Joe O'Connell, Paul Burnett, Gibbie Germaine, Charles O'Bannion
Assistants to Chief Electrician: James Patton, Glen Bird, Harold Sherman, Ernie Long, Harry Whip,
Key Grips: Louis Maschmeyer, Harold Noyes, George Mumaw, Kenny Taylor, Weldon Gilbert, Dick Thoelsen, Howard Clair
Set Decorators: Frank M. Miller, Albert E. Spencer, Ben Bone, Faye Babcock, Jerry Welch, William Wallace, Mowbray F. Berkeley

Property Masters: Levi Williams, Fred Kuhn, Robert Turner, Harry Goldman, John Moore, Charles Mason, Robbie Cooper

Assistant Directors: Don Page, Claude Binyon Jr., C. Carter Gibson, Rusty Meek, Robert Farfan, Charles L. Hansen, Eddie Prinz, Claude E. Archer, Bill Kissel, Bill Lasky, Mecca Graham, Cliff Reed

Wardrobe: Claude Barrie, Russell Coles, Jane Leonard, Leonard Mann, Ralph Hibbs

Hair Stylists: Marian Vaughan, Jeannette Marvin, Tillie Starriett, Ann Saunders, Jean Reilley, Carl Silvera, Esperanza Corona, Arman Forgette, Lenore Weaver, Sally Berkeley, Merle Reeves

Makeup Supervisor: Gordon Bau

Makeup Artists: Henry Vilardo, Louis Phillippi, Lou LaCava, Fred Williams, Jack Obringer, Del Armstrong, Howard Smit

Announcer: Ed Reimers

I f its season opener is any indication of what's to come, ABC's *Maverick* will tighten the ratings noose around the collective necks of Ed Sullivan, Steve Allen and all the big name armies both can muster throughout the coming season," wrote *Daily Variety* in its review of "The Day They Hanged Bret Maverick," the first episode of the second season. "It is with a high degree of technical proficiency and dramatic punch that this series has launched its new season. A zinging self-confidence seems to emerge from the results of last season, when it forged well into the lead of the Sunday night ratings race. This is not a Western, per se: it is a highly mature dramatic presentation that combines the best elements of mystery and action with a professionally subtle sense of humor. [*Maverick*'s] appeal is not limited by age or sex barriers. If the quality is sustained, there seems to be no foreseeable reason why its audience acceptance will diminish."

Far from diminishing, *Maverick*'s audience increased by nearly 30% during its second and most successful season. People from all walks of life dropped what they were doing every Sunday night at 7:30 p.m. to watch the adventures of Bret and Bart Maverick. The series averaged a whopping 45% share of the total television audience in the U.S.

"*Maverick* was such a huge success that year that it became a kind of cult," said Roy Huggins. "I was told that you couldn't get a date on any college campus in this country on Sunday nights between 7:30 and 8:30 p.m. The girls were watching *Maverick*, but so were the guys!" In 1959, *Look Magazine* published a letter from a Pennsylvania woman who echoed the same sentiment. The woman chastised the magazine for overlooking *Maverick* in its Annual *Look* TV Awards. "After all," the woman wrote, "everything social in town closes Sunday night when 7:30 rolls around."   ABC and Warner Brothers parlayed *Maverick*'s success into a solid block of Sunday night Westerns, starting with *Maverick*, with *The Lawman* and *Colt .45* following.

As to the emerging self-confidence which *Variety* noted in its review of "The Day They Hanged Bret Maverick," that became evident as Huggins felt the freedom to experiment even further within the format of the traditional Western story. "*Maverick* was a Western, so the stories had to be confined to a certain part of the country, and within a particular period in time," Huggins explained. "They had to be 'Western stories.' Good guys and bad guys. But once *Maverick* became a huge success, I became a little looser about the kinds of stories I could tell. I could take risks. That's when I started doing things like 'The Rivals' [an adaptation of the 1775 Restoration comedy by Richard

Brinsley Sheridan], 'Black Fire' [the first season takeoff of *And Then There Were None* by Agatha Christie], and 'Gun-Shy' [the famous parody on *Gunsmoke*]."

The second season features five episodes that illustrate the kind of freedom to experiment made possible by *Maverick*'s phenomenally successful first season. Two of these episodes ("Shady Deal at Sunny Acres" and "The Rivals") stand out, among other reasons, because they contain little or no horses and gunplay — two of the most essential elements of a Western story. The other three ("The Jail at Junction Flats," "Gun-Shy," and "The Saga of Waco Williams") are a little more daring, in that each ventured into the realm of satire. Not all of these experiments worked, but that's not the point. What matters is that they were done. The following, then, is a closer look at these five important *Maverick*s, in the order in which they were broadcast:

The Jail at Junction Flats. One of Roy Huggins' professed goals with *Maverick* was to invert as many rules and clichés associated with the standard Western story as possible. One such rule is so basic that it often goes unsaid: the hero *always* wins in the end. But by this time, *Maverick* had already established that such would not be the case. Although Bret and/or Bart would right the wrong and cheat the cheater by the end of the story, the resolution didn't always come across smoothly. More often than not, particularly if the story involved money, the Mavericks ended up with their pockets picked, especially if they were involved with the likes of Samantha Crawford or (as is the case with "The Jail at Junction Flats") that all-out grafter Dandy Jim Buckley.

"Roy had that idea [that Maverick wouldn't always win in the end] from the moment he thought of *Maverick*," said Marion Hargrove, who wrote "The Jail at Junction Flats." "I was given to believe that's the approach the show was going to take. Although I played it 'straight' on my first assignment ['Ghost Rider'], I fitted in very well with Roy's idea after that."

But while that most elementary of conventions may have already been bent in previous *Maverick* episodes, it wasn't completely snapped until "The Jail at Junction Flats." What makes this episode stand out is the image we see before the final fade to black — the hero (Bret) ends up robbed and hog-tied in the middle of nowhere while the "heavy" (Dandy Jim) rides off into the sunset, singing a happy tune.

To anyone who thought of *Maverick* in conventional terms, the ending of "The Jail at Junction Flats" was a little jarring. "The audience, I'm sure, expected to see 'To Be Continued' flashed on the screen at that point," said Roy Huggins. "I remember receiving a ton of letters after that show aired. Many viewers protested — 'There are some things you can't do,' and 'We'll never watch your show again.' But there were a lot more people who loved the show, simply because it was different and unexpected. And, most importantly, I did not receive any complaints from the advertising agency, ABC, or Kaiser."

"The Jail at Junction Flats" scored a 46 audience share when it first aired on November 9, 1958, a figure that made it the most-watched episode of *Maverick* to that point. ("Gun-Shy" and "The Saga of Waco Williams" would both top that mark within a matter of weeks.) However, the true measure of "The Jail at Junction Flats" did not come forth until the following Sunday, when *Maverick*'s audience *dropped* nearly ten percent from the previous week. ("The Thirty-Ninth Star," which aired on November 16, 1958, registered a 42 share.) Considering *Maverick*'s total audience numbered well into the millions, that's a sizeable decrease in audience. The viewers clearly had spoken.

However, the protest did not last too long. Apparently convinced that the ending of "The Jail at Junction Flats" was not a harbinger of things to come, *Maverick*'s audience returned the following week. "Shady Deal at Sunny Acres," which aired November 23, 1958 (two weeks after "The Jail at Junction Flats"), recorded a 46 share, the same figure as "Jail." The prodigal viewers had come home.

A final word on "The Jail at Junction Flats." Thanks to Walter Doniger's innovative direction, it is one of the most visually interesting episodes of the entire series. ("Gun-Shy," featuring the wide-angle lens close-up of Ben Gage's backside, is the other.) Doniger's use of extreme close-ups [particularly in the sequence where Maverick and Buckley tie each other up] gives the picture a tremendous sense of depth that's not often explored enough in television. "Doniger believed in close-ups, and very tight shots, and things like that," said Marion Hargrove. "He was a good director, although I remember that Garner and Zimbalist kidded him about using a lot of close-ups. One day, Jim showed up for work wearing just about enough makeup for an Academy Aperture: extreme closeup of his face, from his eyebrows to his lower lip."

Shady Deal at Sunny Acres. Whenever possible, Roy Huggins would give James Garner a choice of which Maverick to play whenever both brothers appeared in the same story. (The episodes featuring just one Maverick were doled out to whichever actor was available, although all of Huggins' scripts were written with Garner in mind.) "In the case of 'Shady Deal at Sunny Acres'," explained Huggins, "I handed the script to Jim and said, 'We've got a pool going on which role you'll choose.' One role was the Maverick who sat on the porch carving out a wooden donkey for most of the story after his money had been stolen by the banker. Every now and then, one of the townspeople would ask him 'How are you gonna get your money back, Maverick?' and he'd say 'I'm workin' on it.' Meanwhile, the other Maverick in the story runs the entire con — he wines and dines the banker, he gets all the recurring characters (Dandy Jim, Samantha, et al.) to play their parts, and he operates the whole thing.

"Jim picked the role I thought he would pick — the Maverick who does nothing except carve the wooden donkey and say 'I'm working on it' for the entire picture."

Garner's role in "Shady Deal" may have been much smaller than Jack Kelly's, but his presence dominates the entire hour. Although much of the actual legwork in the story is done by brother Bart, it is clear that Bret's the one who is really orchestrating the scam. When Bret flatly tells the banker that he'll recover his money within two weeks, he's taking two factors into consideration. It would take about a week to assemble all the players and set the scheme in motion (Bart doesn't arrive in Sunny Acres until seven days have passed), and another week to carry it out (by the end of the second week, Bart has recovered the money).

Jack Kelly once said that the true essence of the *Maverick* series could be found in Garner's performance in "Shady Deal at Sunny Acres." "Jim blew us all away sitting there on the front veranda, simply whittling and reacting," he told Raymond Strait in *James Garner: A Biography* (St. Martin's Press, 1985). "You saw the whole thing through his eyes and his facial expressions. That is real acting. It was lovable and fun."

Director Leslie Martinson also had high praise for this episode. "Without question," he said, "the most beautifully constructed caper of all the *Maverick* shows was 'Shady Deal at Sunny Acres.' Out of all the *Mavericks* that I directed — and I watched so many others — that show stands out.

"There's a line in that show that I always remember — a typical Roy Huggins line. Bart (Jack) is having dinner with the banker (John Dehner) — who doesn't realize that he's sitting down with Bret Maverick's brother. They're discussing some possible investment or whatever, and then the banker says, 'After all, Bartley, if you can't trust your banker, whom can you trust?'

"I always remember John Dehner delivering that line. He played such an evil, swindling character in that show, which made it all the more delightful when he got his just desserts at the end. And the look on John's face when he realizes he's been had is priceless."

Writer Edmund Blair Bolles also found that particular line memorable. "*Maverick* was a Western that avoided violence," he wrote in an open letter to Bret Maverick that was published in *TV Book* (Workman Publishing Company, 1977). "The plot of the great 'Shady Deal at Sunny Acres' was typical [of the entire series]. There was a crooked banker whose pitch was 'If you can't trust your banker, whom can you trust?' You soon fell afoul of him and sought to settle the score, but characteristically you avoided the complications of violence. Instead you sat on a porch and let your friends prepare a great swindle.... By the end of the hour, the banker was tricked, you — Bret Maverick — were avenged, and no violence had been necessary."

Bolles considered the Maverick character as a sort of prophet. "In the years after you left [the air], people began to say things like, 'If you can't trust your President, who can you trust?' and they argued that violence was the only way to treat some situations.

But you had taught me better. . . . I realize now that you were the true prophet of the sixties, and constituted a lost ideal for the seventies."

Maverick's steadfast aversion to violence unless absolutely necessary is definitely one reason why the series has continued to appeal to TV audiences for nearly 40 years. "Shady Deal at Sunny Acres" neatly encapsulizes that entire perspective in one hour. It is no surprise that this episode is one of — if not *the* — most beloved segments of the entire series.

Roy Huggins agrees that in many respects "Shady Deal at Sunny Acres" is quintessential *Maverick*. "In many ways, it was, in that Maverick is cheated, but decides to get his money back without resorting to violence, and it had both brothers in the story," he said. "All of this was very deliberate. But, you could also make a case that it was *not* the quintessential *Maverick*. It was almost atypical, in that it featured every character in the series at that time — both brothers, plus all the recurring characters [Dandy Jim, Samantha, Gentleman Jack Darby, Big Mike McComb, and Cindy Lou Brown]. Nothing like that had ever been done before on *Maverick*, and nothing like that was ever tried again."

Huggins' personal assessment of "Shady Deal at Sunny Acres" is rather modest: "It was a very interesting *Maverick*."

Gun-Shy. Without question, the most famous episode of the entire series. "Gun-Shy" aired in January 1959 — at the height of *Maverick*'s popularity. It received an extraordinary amount of national publicity, including writeups in the nation's top three weekly news magazines — *Life*, *Time*, and *Newsweek*. Marion Hargrove himself wrote the three-page feature for *Life* ("This is a Television Cowboy?", Jan. 19, 1959), a whimsical look at the secret of *Maverick*'s success. The episode scored a whopping 49 share, a figure that would be topped just once — by "The Saga of Waco Williams," which would air just a few weeks later.

"Gun-Shy," of course, is a parody of the perennial No. 1 Western series *Gunsmoke*, which in 1959 was in the fourth year of its prosperous 20-season run on CBS (1955-1975). *Gunsmoke* depicted the adventures of U.S. Marshal Matt Dillon and his efforts to keep law and order in Dodge City, Kansas. It was television's first so-called "adult Western," in that it aimed to present more realistic characters and situations than the simplistic good-guys-versus-bad-guys settings seen in like of *The Lone Ranger*, *The Cisco Kid* and many of the early TV westerns. Although he was above reproach, Marshal Dillon was far from perfect — he didn't always get his man, and he didn't always know what to do. Yet Dillon in many ways served as the prototype for the stalwart altruistic Western heroes (such as Cheyenne Bodie) that dominated television throughout the '50s and '60s. *Gunsmoke*, as Marion Hargrove put it, "was the solemn daddy of all TV westerns."

But, like *Maverick* itself, "Gun-Shy" has a glow about it that transcends the truth. "Gun-Shy" is remembered in its idealized form, no doubt because of the enormous publicity the episode received prior to broadcast and the massive audience who tuned in to see it. But from the vantage point of the key people behind the episode, the reviews, at best, are mixed. "'Gun-Shy' itself was a mediocre success," said Hargrove. "But that episode is an important part of the history of *Maverick* — it represented a climactic point in both my professional relationship with Roy at the time, and in the future of the show itself." Hargrove completed one more script for *Maverick* after "Gun-Shy" (his adaptation of Sheridan's *The Rivals*), then departed the series. Hargrove was the first member of *Maverick*'s core group of writers to leave the show.

Roy Huggins and Marion Hargrove had clashed before, and they would clash again (Hargrove joined Huggins at 20th Century-Fox in 1960, when Fox hired Huggins to run their Television Department). It was always for the same reason: it was always a matter of style. Seen in that light, "Gun-Shy" becomes a kind of microcosm of Huggins and Hargrove's characteristically bumpy relationship.

The idea of parodying *Gunsmoke* first came to Hargrove while he was at a dinner party hosted by *Maverick*'s executive producer, Bill Orr. "It may have been on a Saturday night, which was the night when *Gunsmoke* aired back then," Hargrove recalled. "*Gunsmoke* had a classic beginning — every episode would open with Matt Dillon entering a long street, and then he'd fire his gun five times. I'd thought it would be fun if we worked that sequence into a *Maverick*, only we'd take it a step further. So I said to Bill at some point, 'I'd like to open a picture with a shot of Marshal Dillon's fat ass right in the camera, and then he'd fire his gun — POW-POW — only he'd miss each time, because we'd then zoom or cut to Garner, as Maverick, who would say, 'Shall I stand a little closer, Marshal?'

"Bill absolutely loved the idea. But when I told it to Roy . . . well, we went ahead and did the show, but Roy never quite warmed up to the idea. It was never one of his favorites."

Huggins explains his side of the story. "It wasn't a matter of liking or not liking the idea," he said. "We took the elements that poked fun at *Gunsmoke* — the marshal firing his gun, the Dennis Weaver character [the eccentric Chester Goode, who became the eccentric Clyde Diefendorfer on 'Gun-Shy'] — and worked them into the story, but they weren't the focal points of the story. The main thrust of 'Gun-Shy' was Maverick's search for gold that was hidden by a now-deceased Confederate Army soldier. The *Gunsmoke* elements were secondary.

"My problem with 'Gun-Shy' had to do with execution. Marion and I disagreed — as we often did — on what was funny and what wasn't. For example, whenever Mort Dooley would go out and do something stalwart and brave, the saloon matron [who's supposed to be the Amanda Blake character on *Gunsmoke*] would say, 'Mort, be careful.' In response, Mort would turn to her and tap her wrist — once, twice, then three more times — always in the same rhythm, and precisely five taps. The problem was, the taps on the wrist were meant to be funny, but I didn't think they were. There were a number of little nuances like that in the first act of the film. Marion had a lot to do with that show — he worked closely with Les Martinson on that one — and he thought the finished cut was fine. I felt just as strongly that it wasn't. And since I had a profound respect for Marion's talent and opinion, I had a problem."

A couple of days later, Huggins found a solution. "If 'Gun-Shy' had not been made for TV, Marion and I would not have quarrelled. We'd simply take the film to a theatre and let an audience give us the answer," he explained. "So I got an audience together and I showed them the Martinson-Hargrove version of 'Gun-Shy.' They hated it — in fact, Howard Browne was there, and I remember that he stood up and said, 'Roy, I suppose you showed this to us because you thought we would enjoy it, but I didn't, and I think you ought to bury it.' I re-edited the film, then assembled another audience and showed them the re-edited version. This time they liked it, and so we sent that print to the network, but I still had serious reservations about the show."

Because it attracted nearly 50 percent of the entire television-watching audience on the night it first aired, "Gun-Shy" tends to be remembered in an idealized manner. The irony is that the episode didn't quite live up to all the hype. Jack Gould of *The New York Times* thought the parody seriously backfired. "The take-off merely suggested that Marshal Dillon and his deputy Chester were stupid oafs," he wrote in his column of January 12, 1959. "It was heavy-handed satire without the saving grace of well-intentioned humor."

"Gun-Shy" did go a little too far in making Mort Dooley so feeble-brained he becomes annoying. The episode works when it ribs *Gunsmoke* not on *Gunsmoke*'s terms, but on *Maverick*'s. For example, in most *Maverick* episodes, Bret or Bart narrate the story. But "Gun-Shy" is told entirely from Marshal Dooley's point of view — with one exception. Halfway into the story, Bret Maverick cuts into the marshal's narrative following an apparently germane exchange between Dooley and Doc Stucke about cattle rustling. "I hate to butt into the Marshal's story like this," Maverick interjects, "but *somebody* has to tell you — the conversation you have just heard has nothing to do with the story. There will be no further reference to rustling."

That one line is the best line of the script, and does more damage to Dooley's character than any wrist-tapping or misfired gunshots. Although the narrative returns to Dooley for the remainder of the story, his point of view can no longer be trusted. That one line is the one element of "Gun-Shy" that is true *Maverick*: it ribs a convention (in this case, the unquestioned judgment of a stalwart marshal) within the confines of the convention (Maverick interrupts the narrative and tells us that the marshal is misleading us).

The New York Times was the lone dissenting voice. Every other review of "Gun-Shy" was positively glowing. Roy Huggins believes he knows the reason why. "Gun-Shy' benefited from the Hovland Effect," he theorized. "If people have been convinced that what they are about to see is the greatest thing ever done, they're going to think it was the greatest thing ever done." (Carl Hovland was a professor at Harvard who once gave two groups of students an identical newspaper editorial. He told one group that the editorial appeared in the Russian newspaper *Pravda*, but led the other group to believe that the article would appear in *The New York Times*. The first group attacked the editorial as being full of propaganda and lies, while the second one praised it for its truth and insight.)

"By the time 'Gun-Shy' aired, *Maverick* had the audience by the throat," Huggins continued. "We had also established such a great reputation with the reviewers — if it was a *Maverick*, it had to be good. That's why we got away with 'Gun-Shy.' It had benefited from such a tremendous amount of advance publicity that every one assumed it would be good."

The Rivals. "*Maverick* was probably the only Western on television that didn't require its writers to write 'Westerns,'" said Marion Hargrove. "Actually, Roy figured out that *Maverick* as a formula was an anthology show. It had one central character, and aside from that you could do anything."

Daily Variety picked up on the same point, and took it a step further. "The series with running characters in some ways permits more freedom than the anthology series, although the reverse is generally believed to be true," the trade paper observed in its review of "The Rivals." "In the important areas of characterization and tone of a particular segment, these elements are already determined for the audience, with the result that much more ambitious projects can be undertaken than by the straight anthology." *Maverick*, concluded *Variety*, was the perfect vehicle for an adaptation of Richard Brinsley Sheridan's 1775 Restoration classic *The Rivals*.

Variety also had high marks for the lead performers: "With Patricia Crowley turning in a fine performance as the addle-brained but beautiful heiress who wants to marry somebody poor but honest, and Roger Moore fine as the sharp but incurably romantic scion who wants to be loved for himself alone, James Garner had himself a field day as the man in the middle. . . . [Garner does] a variety of takes and reactions that adds a point of view to the proceedings."

Like "Shady Deal at Sunny Acres," "The Rivals" is not a "Western," per se. Neither episode has any gunplay ("The Rivals" does feature a pistol duel, but that's mostly a ploy by Van to lure Lydia to his side). Nor, except for a brief occasional sequence, does either show feature any horses. But "The Rivals" stands out for a more important reason. "That was the last episode I wrote for *Maverick*," Hargrove said. "We took the play — a satirical story which had to do with the romantic mind — and made it into a *Maverick*, and it worked. Jim and Roger were both gorgeous in that show.

"We were all quite pleased with it. Roy and I didn't squabble over it, like we did over 'Gun-Shy' — well, there was one point we had to work out. Originally, the Roger Moore character was going to kill himself. Roy and Les Martinson didn't want that — they kept asking me why. And I said, 'Because he's in love and he's crazy and he's romantic and he loves to *think* that he would do this.' They still wouldn't buy it. So we worked out another resolution — he *pretends* he's going to get killed. 'That,' Roy and Les said, 'we would buy.'"

"The Rivals" also stands out as the only episode to feature the three "principal" Mavericks — James Garner, Jack Kelly, and Roger Moore. Although Moore plays another character — millionaire and incurable romantic John Vandergelt III — the main thrust of the plot requires Van to switch identities with Bret, so in that respect, Moore "plays" Maverick — which he would eventually do, of course, in the fourth season.

The Saga of Waco Williams. Perhaps to show the producers of *Gunsmoke* that he could take it as well as dish it out, Roy Huggins came up with an idea of parodying another major TV Western. Only this time, the target was *Maverick* itself. "I wanted to put *Maverick* on, to a certain extent," Huggins explained. "I wanted to have a little fun with the Maverick character, and I came up with an idea for a story which eventually became 'The Saga of Waco Williams.'

"This is what I was thinking: Maverick would fall in with Waco Williams [played by Wayde Preston, who had been starring in the Warners series *Colt .45*]. Waco was an honorable, brave soul who always found himself smack in the middle of situations that Maverick would avoid at all costs. Waco would pick a fight, and Maverick would tell him, 'Waco, don't do that — they could *kill* you." And Waco would say, 'Well, what do you mean? What would you expect me to do?' And Maverick would say 'Duck — hide — run!'

"I don't believe the show was as good as it could have been, although at the time I thought it came off very well. But later on, when I looked at that show, I thought, 'Well, that really isn't what I had in mind. I didn't quite accomplish it.'"

Huggins has a point. The main plot of "The Saga of Waco Williams" — a cattle baron thinks that Maverick and Waco were sent by rustlers to wreck his empire — is incidental. The real draw of this episode is the dialogue. Maverick explains his philosophy of living to Waco in a series of exchanges, such as:

Bret: Waco, I've never seen a man do so many things wrong. Have you ever been in a gulf hurricane?

Waco: Nope.

Bret: Well, it's the big pine trees and the thick oak trees that get uprooted first. The palm trees are smart: they give with the wind.

Waco: That sounds like pretty good advice — for trees.

Bret: They live a long time.

Although Huggins believes that "Waco Williams" was not as good as it could have been, as a parody the episode works for the very reason that "Gun-Shy" did not work. In "Gun-Shy," the main story was good, but the satirical characterizations were a little heavy-handed. In "Waco Williams," the main story is not as strong, but the satirical commentary works without harming Maverick's character — because at the end of the story, it's Maverick who takes the ribbing.

"Everything Waco does works," said Huggins. "And at the end of the show, Waco is a hero: he's got the girl who is the daughter of a big rancher, and the townspeople are talking about running Waco for sheriff. And all this time, Maverick had been saying 'Don't do that, Waco.' Now Maverick gets on his horse and is about to ride out of town. No one even knows he's there, because they don't give a damn about Maverick. He's not the big hero — there's Waco, he's the hero! And Maverick hears this roar go up, then he looks into the camera and says, 'Now, he did everything a man shouldn't do — but he's still alive, it looks like he'll be elected sheriff, and I know he'll end up with the biggest ranch in the territory. And I'm broke. Nobody even knows I'm leaving — or cares. Could I be wrong?'"

That last line neatly summarizes what "The Saga of Waco Williams" is all about. "It was a gentle spoof of *Maverick*, but it didn't hurt his character," Huggins said. "I wanted to juxtapose Maverick with Waco — the typical Western hero — only Waco would win and Maverick would lose. And it was all summed up in the last line — 'Could I be wrong?' I'm sure the audience liked it."

They certainly did. "The Saga of Waco Williams" was the most-watched episode in the entire series.

Roy Huggins remembers that final sequence for another reason — he directed it himself. "It was *essential* that Jim look directly into the camera and say, 'Could I be wrong?' That's exactly how I had written it into the script," Huggins explained. "In that sequence we broke one of the 'fundamental' rules of filmmaking — never break the

so-called fourth wall. [Director] Les Martinson couldn't bring himself to do that — which I understood completely. I could understand why a director who has been trained never to break that rule would not want to direct something that would require him to do that. So Les shot Jim looking off past the camera, and delivering the line.

"Of course, when I watched that footage in the dailies, I said, 'No, it's critical that he look right into the camera.' So I went down to the set — which I never did unless it was absolutely necessary. I don't recall if they were still shooting 'Waco Williams' that day or if they had moved onto the next show, but that wouldn't have mattered, because Maverick's costume stayed the same. All I had to do was wait until they were on that 'Western street' again. I explained to Jim what I was going to do, and he got back on his horse, and we reshot that sequence."

Did Garner mind having to reshoot the entire sequence? "Jim didn't care," said Huggins. "He left those things to the people who were getting paid to do them. From a producer's point of view, that's the greatest thing about Jim. He doesn't try to change scripts, and he doesn't try to fight the authority of the guy who's responsible for the show. It's as if he were an actor from the old studio days. He didn't come from that era — but he has that attitude. He does his job, and he lets you — whether you're a writer, director, or producer — do yours."

Maverick not only cracked the Top 25 list of most-watched programs, it nearly bullied its way to the top. The series finished its second season as the sixth most-watched program on television — no mean feat, considering not only its competition (*Ed Sullivan* and *Jack Benny* were still going strong), but its time slot. *Maverick* aired from 7:30 to 8:30 p.m., when the total prime time audience was at its lowest. (The audience usually builds from 7:30 to 9:00 p.m., and reaches it peak in the 9:00 to 10:00 time slot.) Four of the five programs that finished ahead of *Maverick* in 1958-59 had the advantage of later time slots — *Gunsmoke* (No. 1) was a 10:00 p.m. show; *Have Gun, Will Travel* (No. 3) aired at 9:30 p.m.; *The Rifleman* and *The Danny Thomas Show* (Nos. 4 and 5, respectively) were both 9:00 p.m. shows. *Maverick* also aired on Sunday nights, traditionally not a high viewing night. CBS scheduled *Have Gun, Will Travel* and *Gunsmoke* back-to-back on Saturday nights, while *Wagon Train* (the No. 2 show that year), *Rifleman* and *Danny Thomas* were all weeknight shows. *Maverick*'s finish in 1958-59, given these factors, is all the more impressive.

But the true measure of *Maverick*'s popularity went beyond the numbers — it had an impact on the Television Academy itself. *Maverick*, the trade papers reported, was a shoo-in for winning the Emmy Award for Best Dramatic Series of 1958-59 — so much so that nobody wanted to run against it. A number of the major advertising agencies, whose clients sponsored such highly-rated dramatic shows as *Perry Mason*, lobbied the Academy to create a separate category for Westerns so that their clients' programs would not have to compete with *Maverick*. "They knew that they would lose if they went up against *Maverick*," said Roy Huggins. "The advertisers who had a stake in the top dramatic shows that year put a lot of pressure on the Academy to create a new category. They wanted to give their shows a chance to win an Emmy for Best Dramatic Show — an award they wouldn't have won if they ran against *Maverick*."

The Television Academy conceded, and as a result the nominations for 1958-59 included a new category, Best Western Series, whose nominees were *Gunsmoke, Have Gun, Will Travel, The Rifleman, Wagon Train*, and *Maverick*. The Emmy Awards ceremony took place on May 6, 1959. Ironically, Jack Benny, whose Sunday night series competed directly against *Maverick*, was chosen to announce the winner of the Best Western Series Award. Earlier in 1959, Benny had made a friendly wager with Roy Huggins concerning *Maverick*'s "Gun-Shy" episode and Benny's parody of *Gaslight*, the 1941 MGM classic starring Ingrid Bergman and Charles Boyer, which were scheduled to air on the same night (January 11, 1959). Benny's *Gaslight* satire had been filmed five years earlier, but it had been kept off the air because of a lawsuit filed by MGM. The legal battle went all the way to the Supreme Court, which ruled in favor of Benny. Given the tremendous national attention the case received, Benny bet Huggins that his *Gaslight* show would trounce "Gun-Shy" in the ratings that week. Instead, "Gun-Shy" clobbered Benny.

Huggins picks up the story. "Here we are, on the night of the Emmy ceremonies, and the man who had lost that bet was about to open the envelope that might reveal *Maverick* as the winner of an Emmy," he recalled. "Jack Benny was not one to let an opportunity like this pass unexploited. When Jack Benny read the list of nominees, he paused and grimaced when he read '*Maverick*.' The Hollywood audience, who was in on the joke, laughed heartily. Jack then asked for the envelope and gave the audience a pained look as he began to open it. He removed the card gingerly and refused to look at it, holding it away from him and giving the audience another mournful stare — which got a larger laugh. When he finally managed to look at the card, he cried 'Oh, no!' At that point I knew that *Maverick* had won. But Benny hadn't announced the winner yet, and so I sat frozen in my seat, waiting. He then gave the audience a long, Jack Benny look of cosmic resignation, glanced back at the card, and groaned, '*Maverick!*'

"I stood up, only faintly aware of the applause that *Maverick*'s victory was receiving. As I started toward the stage, I saw a young man squatting in the aisle. He was holding up a sign that read 'No speeches! We're running out of time! Please no speeches!' About twenty strides closer to the stage, I noticed a young woman who was also squatting and holding an identical sign. As I approached the steps leading up to the stage, I noticed another young man holding a sign that read simply 'NO SPEECHES.'

"I arrived on stage to an embracing burst of applause and stepped over to Jack Benny. I had already resolved to ignore the signs and take a few seconds to tell the audience that the Emmy belonged to Jim Garner and Jack Kelly, and Douglas Heyes and Marion Hargrove. But Jack Benny hadn't seen any of those desperate messages that were flashed at me — he was too busy having fun. When I reached for the statuette he pulled it away, and the audience roared. Jack went into a five-minute routine of just not being able to put this prize into the hands of the man whose show had defeated his. What Benny was doing was good comedy, and having no choice I laughed along with it.

"When Jack finally let me take the Emmy, the audience's laughter had reached such a peak that I knew I would have to stand there another minute or more before anything I might say could be heard. I finally managed to say 'Thank you very much,' and then the show went on. But that's something that has always bugged me — I mean, to this day, I ask myself, 'Why did I pay attention to those signs?' Why didn't I just say 'To hell with it,' and go ahead and make the damned speech?"

Huggins reflected further on winning the Emmy. "I received the award, but it was the show that was nominated," he said. "The television community had seen *Maverick* and realized that the quality was there every week, no matter who wrote it, who directed it, or who played it. I mean, Jim was Maverick, but the show was just as popular with Jack Kelly. I'm gratified to have received the Emmy, but it was the whole show that won."

Maverick's Emmy is worth noting. Because the Television Academy eliminated the Best Western Series category following the 1958-59 season, it was the first and only winner of that particular award. No Western series has ever won an Emmy since. *Maverick* was also nominated in the category of Best Editing of a Film for Television in 1958-59 (Robert Sparr for "Rope of Cards," Robert Watts for "The Saga of Waco Williams").

The Television Academy honored James Garner with a nomination for Best Actor in a Leading Role in a *Dramatic* Series for 1958-59. Although Garner did not receive the award, his day would come. Garner won Emmys in 1977, for Outstanding Lead Actor in *The Rockford Files*, and in 1987, as executive producer of *Promise*, a segment of *Hallmark Hall of Fame* which was recognized as that year's Outstanding Dramatic Special. Garner was inducted in the Television Academy's Hall of Fame in 1990.

The Association of Motion Picture Sound Editors named *Maverick* Best Sound Edited Television Series of 1958. "That award was really won by the Sound Department at Warner Bros.," said Huggins. "Warner Bros. was the studio that pioneered sound. They brought sound to Hollywood, with Vitagraph, and they developed, by far, the best sound department that you could find anywhere in Hollywood — better than MGM, better than anyplace. You could do things with sound at Warners that you couldn't do elsewhere, because their technicians were so good."

Familiar faces to look for this season include Clint Eastwood, Abby Dalton, Adam West, Connie Stevens, Robert Conrad, Julie Adams, Patricia Crowley, Neil Hamilton, and Roger Moore (two years away from joing the series as Cousin Beau Maverick).

28. THE DAY THEY HANGED BRET MAVERICK

ORIGINAL AIRDATE: SEPTEMBER 21, 1958

Written and Directed by: Douglas Heyes

Guest Cast: Whitney Blake (Molly Clifford), Ray Teal (Sheriff Chick Tucker), Jay Novello (Coroner Oliver Poole), Robert E. Griffin (Mayor), John Cliff (Cliff Sharpe), Burt Mustin (Henry), Hal Hopper (Stanley), Roy Erwin (Claude)

Synopsis. In the town of Hallelujah, outlaw Cliff Sharp breaks into Bret's hotel room and plants evidence linking Bret to a $40,000 robbery-and-murder scheme. After the town convicts him on circumstantial evidence, Bret faces the gallows. When greedy Sheriff Tucker offers to fake the hanging if Bret leads him to the stolen money, Maverick goes along with the ruse but ditches the sheriff at the first opportunity. When Bret discovers that Molly Clifford (Sharp's wife) arrives in Hallelujah, he trails her to New Mexico in the hopes of finding the money and clearing his name.

According to "The Day They Hanged Bret Maverick," Bret was born on April 7, 1847, and "died" on September 21, 1876. April 7 is James Garner's actual birthday (he was born in 1928), while September 21 is the date on which the episode aired in 1958.

Pappyism: "There's more than one way to please a lady."

29. LONESOME REUNION

ORIGINAL AIRDATE: SEPTEMBER 28, 1958

Teleplay by: Gene Levitt
Story by: Gene Levitt and Robert Mitchell
Directed by: Richard L. Bare

Guest Cast: John Russell (Edgar Maxwell), Joanna Barnes (Abigail Johnson), John Qualen (Leland Mills), Claire Carlton (Flora), Richard Reeves (Monty), Byron Foulger (Clerk), Robert Carson (Masher), Jon Lormer (Newspaperman), Tim Johnson (Billy), Ruth Warren (Local Gossip)

Synopsis. In Denver, a hat box puts Bret on the trail of Edgar Maxwell, an escaped convict (who also robbed Bret of his clothes), and Abigail Johnson, the wife of one of Maxwell's partners in a $100,000 bank robbery that took place eleven months earlier. Maxwell and Abigail head for the nearby town of Lonesome, where Maxwell buried the money (and, unbeknownst to Abigail, her husband) somewhere on the grounds of the old

Mills ranch. Bret's plans for capturing Maxwell and recovering the money are temporarily derailed when he is accused of murdering Monty, another of Maxwell's accomplices.

In the fall of 1958, James Garner was featured on NBC's *This is Your Life*, a weekly testimonial series that toasted celebrities and other prominent figures. Each week, host Ralph Edwards would surprise the unsuspecting guest of honor, either at work or at some location nearby the NBC studios, by informing him or her that "this is your life;" the guest was then transported to the program's studio, where he or she would be reunited with longlost relatives and friends who would help Edwards tell the audience the guest's life story.

Richard Bare played a hand in helping Edwards and his crew spring the surprise on James Garner. "Somebody with the Publicity Department at Warners came up to me and said, 'We're going to play a joke on Jim,'" said Bare. "'We've got it all arranged, and we'd like you to play a part: about two-thirty or three o'clock, pretend you've come down with some stomach cramps, so that we'll have to shut down the production.' I said, 'Okay, I'll go along with it,' because I figured at the very least I'd get a free afternoon off.

"So, about two o'clock, after lunch, I went into my act. My assistant director, who was also in on the gag, said, 'What's the matter, Richard?' And I said, 'Oh, I don't feel well!' The assistant director said, 'Do you think you'll be able to work?' And I said, 'No, I'm sorry — I've got to go home!' 'Okay, everybody, that's a wrap.'

"Now, the publicity people were all there, and they said to Jim, 'As long as you've got the rest of the day off, and you're in your makeup and costume and everything, we'd like you to do us a favor. NBC has been wanting us to help them test out their new color system. We've already got Jack Kelly standing by — would you come over with Jack and help us shoot some stills? It's only around the corner.' 'Well, okay,' said Jim. 'Hell, I'm under contract — I have to do it.' So they went over to NBC, and they got all the lights and everything set up, and they began to shoot . . . when all of a sudden, in walked Ralph Edwards. 'Jim Garner, This is Your Life!'

"Well, as it turned out, Jim hated surprises — he became absolutely infuriated, and he was particularly mad at Jack Kelly, because he figured that Kelly had something to do with it."

Garner's reaction, it should be noted, was not atypical. Although *This is Your Life* relied on the element of surprise, many of the program's guests of honor did not appreciate being "trapped" into an instant testimonial, particularly one that was going to be broadcast on national television. After his initial outburst, however, Garner calmed down and went along with the program. Richard Bare appeared on the show and related the circumstances of how he brought Garner to the studio.

John Russell starred as Marshal Dan Troop on the Warner Bros. Western series, *Lawman*.

30. ALIAS BART MAVERICK

(a.k.a. "The Best of Enemies")
ORIGINAL AIRDATE: OCTOBER 5, 1958

Written and Directed by: Douglas Heyes

Guest Cast: Richard Long (Gentleman Jack Darby), Arlene Howell (Cindy Lou Brown), I. Stanford Jolley (Sheriff), Richard Reeves (Rafe Plummer), Charles Briggs (Little Jeb Plummer), Jack Lomas (Sheriff), Hal Hopper (Horace), X Brands (Sioux Indian), Ted White (Sioux Indian #2), Michael

Carr (Sioux Indian #3), Harry Seymour (Piano Player), Phil Arnold (Man), Joe Walls (Poker Player)

Synopsis. Outside Crescent City, Bart encounters Gentleman Jack Darby, a fugitive wanted for embezzlement by the Missouri Surety Company. Although innocent of that charge (a dishonest bank clerk stole the money), Darby is no angel — in order to collect the $1,000 reward money, Darby convinces the Crescent City sheriff that Bart really is Gentleman Jack. While Bart sits in jail, Darby wins $2,600 playing poker, but leaves town after he kills one of the troublemaking Plummer brothers in self defense. Darby then frees Bart, only to rob him later. With an assist from entertainer Cindy Lou Brown, Darby's charming but not-too-bright girlfriend, Bart trails Gentleman Jack to Deadwood.

This episode marks Richard Long's first appearance as Gentleman Jack Darby, another "all-out" grafter meant to contrast Maverick's gentle grafter. "Gentleman Jack was created simply to replace Dandy Jim," said Roy Huggins. "They're exactly the same character. I probably had Efrem in mind for a story, but he wasn't available, because I think he had just started *77 Sunset Strip*. So we made a few changes, then cast Richard Long."

There are, however, a few marked differences between Darby and Buckley. Darby has some semblance of a conscience, because he helps Bart when the Plummer brothers go after Maverick toward the end of the story. "I'm only intruding because these gentlemen are after me," Darby explains. Dandy Jim Buckley, of course, would *never* get involved.

Also, whereas Bret's relationship with Buckley has been acrimonious at best, Bart and Darby develop a genuine rapport and friendship with each other that continues throughout the series. In fact, in Darby's next appearance ("The Spanish Dancer"), Darby and Bart become business partners for a short time. Darby does share one character trait with Buckley — neither ever seems to get himself dirty. When Darby told Bart that he had to crawl through the brush to escape the Plummer brothers, Bart wonders how he could have done so without dirtying his clothes.

Like their onscreen characters, Jack Kelly and Richard Long also developed a longtime friendship. "I had known Dick a long time before we did the *Maverick* shows," Kelly told Mick Martin in 1992. "We were at Universal together and did *Cult of the Cobra* there. I was at the studio in '51 and '52 as a contract player, and [I introduced him] to his first wife, Suzan Ball, who was also under contract there. I had some tickets to a baseball game, and I awarded them to Dick as a friendly gesture. He said, 'Aren't you going? I don't know who to take.' I said, 'There's a gal here you've got to meet,' and I introduced him to Suzan. They were married about two weeks later."

Sadly, Long's marriage to Ball was short-lived — Ball died in 1955 from cancer that had developed from a knee injury she had sustained while filming *East of Sumatra* in 1952. Long co-starred with Arlene Howell in the Warner Bros. detective series *Bourbon Street Beat* (ABC, 1959-60), and with Peter Breck in *The Big Valley*. He also co-starred with Juliet Mills in the ABC comedy *Nanny and the Professor* before his death in 1974.

31. THE BELCASTLE BRAND

ORIGINAL AIRDATE: OCTOBER 12, 1958

Written by: Marion Hargrove
Directed by: Leslie H. Martinson

Guest Cast: Reginald Owen (Norbert), Joan Elan (Ellen), Seymour Green (Albert), Gordon Richards (Butler), Rusty Westcourt (Outlaw Leader), Walter Barnes (First Outlaw), Robert Nash (Foreman)

Synopsis. In Wyoming, Bret collaspes outside Belcastle Manor, the home of an eccentric family of British aristocrats. After the Belcastles nurse him back to health, Bret earns his keep by leading the family on a bear hunt across the desert. But the expedition comes to a sudden halt when the Shaughnessy gang robs the group of their supplies — and leaves them to die in the desert.

Marion Hargrove came up with the suggestion of basing a *Maverick* story on *The Admirable Crichton*, the classic play by Sir James Barrie about a butler who is stranded on a deserted island with the wealthy family who employs him.

"The butler turns out to be the one with the leadership and intelligence to guide the family," explained Hargrove. "At that time, Roy and I met every Saturday afternoon to talk over story ideas — one week he'd come out to my place, the next week I'd go over to his. So, one Saturday, we'd gotten together, and I said, 'Roy, what are we gonna do this time? We've stolen everything but *Macbeth* and *The Admirable Crichton*.' Roy said, 'Well, I don't like the heavy in *Macbeth*, so we'll go with *The Admirable Crichton*.' And I said, 'All right, we'll go with *The Admirable Crichton* — we'll make the desert island the desert, and Maverick will play the butler.'"

After Hargrove and Huggins worked out the story for what became "The Belcastle Brand," the conversation eventually turned to casting. "Roy said to me, 'Who do you think should play Belcastle?'" continued Hargrove. "I had in mind Reginald Owen, who was one of the greatest character actors of our time — he'd played Scrooge, he'd played Louis XV, he was just a magical actor. But I didn't think we could get him, so I said, 'Roy, you can't get Reginald Owen, so it doesn't make any difference who plays Belcastle.' And Roy said, 'We could get Reginald Owen.'

"Somebody found Reggie out on the golf course and asked him if he was interested. 'Oh, by Jove, yes!' he shouted. And Reggie and Jim just clicked together. There was also a couple of real pros [Joan Elan and Seymour Green] playing the other Belcastles. Jim could play on the same level as Reggie and the other actors, and they all meshed."

Owen also made a small contribution to the dialogue. "There was one point where Maverick tells Belcastle something, and my line for Reggie was 'That's almost interesting,'" said Hargrove. "Reggie went up to me and said, 'Marion, if I may — the line should be 'That's interesting, almost.' And I thought, 'Yeah, that's right. In England, 'all most' is two words, and so 'that is all most interesting' would have a completely different meaning than what I'd intended. So we changed the line."

Pappyisms: "Always keep a thousand dollars pinned on your person. You're both so shiftless that if you didn't, you'd starve to death;" and "It would be a pitiful thing if you had to work for a living. Son, use your wits; the good Lord didn't give you brains."

32. HIGH CARD HANGS

(a.k.a. "The Death Card")

ORIGINAL AIRDATE: OCTOBER 19, 1958

Teleplay by: Tom Blackburn
Based on the Story "The Death Card" by Ralph Berard
Directed by: Richard L. Bare

Guest Cast: Efrem Zimbalist Jr. (Dandy Jim Buckley), Lilyan Chauvin (Sydney Sue Shipley), Frank Ferguson (Genessee Jones), Charles Fredericks (Joe Hayes), Martin Landau (Mike Manning), Ben Sheridan (Bald Bill King)

Synopsis. Bart and Dandy Jim Buckley join a mining camp in the Black Hills, where they await an opportunity to play poker with the other miners. While panning for gold, they meet prospector Genessee Jones, who has $8,000 in gold dust. But Jones is also a card shark who relieves Bart, Mike Manning and Joe Hayes (two other miners) of all their money. When Jones is found dead, Bart, Manning and Hayes become the likely suspects. Knowing they all will hang unless the real killer confesses, Bart proposes that the three of them cut cards — whoever draws the high card must confess to the crime. When Bart wins the draw, he apparently faces the gallows — but it's all part of a plan that he hopes will lead him to the real killer.

Bart seems to bring out the best in Dandy Jim Buckley, because his relationship with Buckley is not as acrimonious as brother Bret's. Bret's associations with Dandy Jim are always against his will; even when he does side with Buckley, he never lets his guard down (he usually addresses Buckley by his last name). Bart, on the other hand, knows that Buckley is slippery, yet he seems considerably less guarded with Jim, and they seem to enjoy a genuine friendship (Bart often calls Buckley "Dandy"). This plays out in later episodes — in "Shady Deal at Sunny Acres," it is Bart who enlists Buckley in the con game that helps Bret get his money back. (If the shoe were on the other foot, Bret probably wouldn't ask Buckley for any kind of help, simply because Bret doesn't trust Buckley — he *respects* him, but he certainly doesn't trust him.) Bart evens manages to convince Buckley to leave his job as camp clerk (along with all the camp's money). Buckley laughs, "Someone once said that money isn't everything, although I can't imagine who."

When the script for "High Card Hangs" called for someone to play an Indian woman who spoke French (a rather unusual combination), someone in casting suggested Lilyan Chauvin, "a French actress with the dark beauty of a Sioux maiden," according to a 1958 Warners press announcement. Chauvin later co-starred with Robert Colbert ("Brent Maverick") in the popular daytime serial *The Young and the Restless*.

Martin Landau, who plays Mike Manning, was several years away from his Emmy Award-winning role as Rollin Hand in *Mission: Impossible*. Today he is one of the most prominent character actors in motion pictures, including *Intersection*, *Crime and Punishment* and his Oscar-nominated performance in *Tucker*.

"High Card Hangs" was later redone on *The Alaskans* as the episode "Odd Card Hangs."

33. ESCAPE TO TAMPICO

(a.k.a. "Borderline")

ORIGINAL AIRDATE: OCTOBER 26, 1958

Written and Directed by: Douglas Heyes

Guest Cast: Gerald Mohr (Steve Corbett), Barbara Lang (Amy Lawrence), John Hubbard (Paul Brooke), Paul Picerni (Rene), Tony Romano (Chicualo), Ralph Faulkner (Herr Ziegler), Louis Mercier (Raoul Gireaux), William D. Gordon (Sam Garth), Nacho Gallindo (Carlos)

Synopsis. In New Orleans, aristocrat Raoul Gireaux offers Bret $6,000 to bring back Steve Corbett, who has fled to Tampico, Mexico after murdering Gireaux's youngest son. After finding work in the cantina that Corbett operates, Maverick befriends the fugitive and cancels the arrangement when he believes Corbett's claim of innocence. But Bret smells a trap when Amy Lawrence, the cantina's singer (and Corbett's girlfriend), convinces Corbett to join her on a trip to Corpus Christi, Texas. Suspecting that Amy was also hired by Gireaux, Maverick follows them in order to warn Corbett.

If you think La Cantina Americana, the club that Maverick visits in this episode, looks a lot like Rick's Cafe, the establishment owned by Humphrey Bogart in *Casablanca*, you're right — "Escape to Tampico" used many of the sets designed specifically for that Warner Bros. classic that won the Academy Award for Best Picture of 1942.

34. THE JUDAS MASK

ORIGINAL AIRDATE: NOVEMBER 2, 1958

Written by: Gene Levitt
Directed by: Richard L. Bare

Guest Cast: Anna-Lisa (Karen Gustavsen), Richard Garland (Elliot Larkin), John Vivyan (Walter Delourne), Mel Welles (Carlos), Nico Minardos (Enrico), James Hope (Poker Player), Robert Jordan (Willie), Bud Osbourne (Stagecoach Driver), Rosa Terrich (Happy Mexican Woman), Paul Fiero (Manuel), Mildred Von Holland (Adele), Cecil Elliott (Seamstress), Alegra Varron (Woman), Rocky Ibarra (Street Vendor), David Reynard (Telegrapher), Luis Gomez (Juan), Carlos Rivero (Spanish Man)

Synopsis. Bart wins over $20,000 playing poker in Silver City, New Mexico, and plans to buy half-ownership of the Bella Union with the current owner Walter Delourne. Karen Gustavsen, a showgirl at the hotel, steals Bart's money and flees to Mexico. Bart and Elliot Larkin (Karen's protective lover) follow her south of the border. Karen doesn't have the money (it's at a bank in Silver City), but she explains why she stole it: Delourne is a ruthless man who drove her sister, also a showgirl, to suicide. Karen convinces Bart not to purchase the hotel. But a jealous Elliot, afraid of losing Karen to Bart, summons Delourne to Mexico.

Just as Bret and Bart Maverick enjoyed a friendly rivalry onscreen, James Garner and Jack Kelly engaged in a playful ongoing competition off-camera. The game was called "Bang" and, as *TV Guide* wrote in 1959, the rules were simple: whenever and wherever they met on the set, the first man to see the other would draw his prop gun and yell "Bang!" — at which point, the other man who would have to drop what he was doing and raise his hands above his head. Kelly once claimed to have gotten the "Bang" on Garner while Garner was putting on his pants.

On a particularly hot and hectic day when four different production crews were filming on the back lot, Garner and Kelly teamed up for a stunt that eased a lot of tension. "We had four companies working at the same time, and I swear to you, the buttocks of the four camera operators weren't more than a yard apart," Kelly told Mick Martin in 1992. "The middle of summer in Burbank [where Warner Bros. is located] can get really miserable. It was terribly hot that day, and Jimmy came over to me and whispered something in my ear. I said, 'Let's go for it.'

"Jim and I went over to two fire hydrants, big stand pipes with large turn wheels, and we both took a hose and started hosing down all four companies, including our own. It broke a lot of tension that day, although the directors went crazy — every ten minutes they'd get a call from production, 'Hey, you got scene 41 in the can yet?' and they'd have to tell them, 'Well, no, you see, the Maverick boys are going crazy down here with fire hoses.' We must have gotten at least two-and-a-half hours behind that day."

"The Judas Mask" features what is probably the most famous **Pappyism** of all: "He who plays and runs away lives to run another day." However, this aphorism is usually remembered differently, as "He who *fights* and runs away lives to run another day."

35. THE JAIL AT JUNCTION FLATS

ORIGINAL AIRDATE: NOVEMBER 9, 1958

Television Story and Teleplay by: Marion Hargrove
Adapted From the Story "The Jail Break" by Elmer Kelton
Directed by: Walter Doniger

Guest Cast: Efrem Zimbalist Jr. (Dandy Jim Buckley), Patrick McVey (Morrison Pyne), Jean Allison (Madame Higgins), John Harmon (Saloon Keeper), Bert Remsen (First Deputy George), Claudia Bryar (Mrs. Pyne), Dan Blocker (Hognose Hughes), Jack Lomas (Bartender)

Synopsis. Much to his dismay, Bret bumps into the "new" Dandy Jim Buckley in Broken Wheel, Wyoming. Claiming that he's now making an honest living selling horses, Buckley promises Maverick double his money back if Bret joins him as his business partner. Reluctantly, Maverick loans Buckley $2,000 — and is quite shocked when he sees that Dandy Jim is actually buying horses. But Buckley's true colors show when he plants a rumor about a gold strike, then sells back the horses (at a profit) to anyone foolish enough to check out the "claim." After Buckley pays Bret his share (then immediately steals it back), Maverick finds Dandy Jim locked inside an apparently impregnable jail in nearby Junction Flats, where Buckley is accused of shooting the sheriff's nephew. In order to get his money back, Maverick must break Buckley out of jail.

"The Jail at Junction Flats" underwent a series of interesting, albeit somewhat complicated, changes before filming ever began. Marion Hargrove presented Roy Huggins with an outline for a story called "The Spanish Prisoner," wherein Maverick breaks a man out of a Spanish jail, then decides to put him back in upon realizing that the man is an unsavory character. Huggins didn't like the concept because he didn't think the prisoner was the kind of character that *Maverick* could have fun with. Hargrove revised the story, then presented Huggins with another version containing two significant changes: (1) the prisoner was now a grafter named Friendly Ferguson, who had a great sense of humor but a distorted sense of honor; and (2) the jail in the story was now a notorious prison with a reputation for being absolutely impregnable.

In the new story, now called "The Jail at Junction Flats," Maverick breaks Ferguson out of the jail for purposes profitable to him, but later finds himself locked in the jail and has to rely on Ferguson to free him. Huggins liked this version much better; however, as a precaution, he advised Warner Bros. to purchase the rights to "The Jail Break," a story by Elmer Kelton with a similar jailbreak plot. Hargrove insisted that his story, which he had designed as a comedy, was not an infringement on the Kelton story, which was more of a melodrama. Huggins lobbied successfully on Hargrove's behalf for the use of the Friendly Ferguson story, but the matter became further complicated when

Hargrove informed Warner Bros. that he had designed his story as a pilot for a possible series featuring the Ferguson character. Per its policy, Warners elected to purchase the Kelton story (as well as another story, "A Corner in Horses" by Stewart Edward White) rather than compensate Hargrove, although Hargrove retained "television story" credit for "The Jail at Junction Flats." The episode was reworked into a caper featuring Dandy Jim Buckley.

Several years later, Hargrove did write a pilot based on the Ferguson character (whom he now called Honest John Smith), but the project never got off the ground.

Ultimately, it doesn't matter whether the foil in "The Jail at Junction Flats" was named Ferguson, Smith or Buckley — what matters is that Efrem Zimbalist Jr. was available to play him. Zimbalist had just launched his own series for Warner Bros., *77 Sunset Strip*. "Efrem was perfect for Jim," said Hargrove. "He gave Garner someone who was good and who was smart to play against. They worked really well together." Later in the 1958-59 season, Garner had a cameo appearance–as himself—in "Downbeat," an episode of *77 Sunset Strip*.

Hargrove named the character "Hognose Hughes" after fellow *Maverick* writer Russell Hughes. Hognose was played by Dan Blocker, a few years away from becoming Hoss Cartwright on *Bonanza*.

36. THE THIRTY-NINTH STAR

ORIGINAL AIRDATE: NOVEMBER 16, 1958

Written by: Marion Hargrove

Directed by: Richard L. Bare

Guest Cast: Bethel Leslie (Janet Hilmer), John Litel (Judge Summers), Sam Buffington (Bigelow), Mark Tapscott (Farfan), William Phipps (Hazelton), Nestor Paiva (Louie), Roy Barcroft (Marshal), Robert Carson (Dixon), Guy Wilkerson (Desk Clerk), Alan Reynolds (Bartender), John Cliff (First Thug), Jack Williams (Second Thug), Mickey Simpson (Tiny), Peter Mamakos (Watchman), A. Guy Teague (Stagecoach Driver)

Synopsis. Bart celebrates the Fourth of July in a western territory that hopes to qualify for statehood. After the ceremony, Bart and several others take the stagecoach to Capitol City, where Bart inadvertently removes a suitcase identical to his own from the luggage rack. The suitcase belongs to Judge Summers, and it contains documents that link the territory's late Governor Steward to murder and corruption. Summers wants the documents kept secret because their disclosure could adversely affect the territory's chances for statehood — but the remaining members of Steward's political machine want the papers destroyed. When the suitcase is stolen from him, Bart finds his life in danger unless he can recover it.

This episode was one of the few *Maverick*s that was specifically written for Jack Kelly. "I think Roy came up to me one day and said, 'Marion, you really ought to write one for Kelly,'" recalled Marion Hargrove. "So I wrote the one that became 'The Thirty-Ninth Star.'"

As a rule, the "lighter" scripts (i.e., the scripts with more humor, or scripts where the humor is derived from Maverick's reactions) were reserved for Garner, while the "straight" scripts (stories that were more along the lines of a straightforward Western drama) were assigned to Kelly. Although both actors contended that either could play one or the other ("light" or "straight"), the consensus is that Garner had a natural flair for bringing out the kind of humor that made *Maverick* work.

"Garner was a constant source of delight and surprise to me," said Roy Huggins. "He never misread a line — he delivered them like an artist, giving it every touch it deserved. He was just incredible that way: he knew the Maverick character so well, and he knew how to say things the way that character would. I never did know why that character was so clear to him — I'm not sure *Jim* knows. But there's no question in my mind that he was the perfect vehicle for that character."

Jack Kelly was a more accomplished performer than Garner at the time, yet he just didn't have the same flair that Garner brought to *Maverick*. "Jack was a very bright, very intelligent, and *very funny* person in real life," said Hargrove. "But he just wasn't very funny on film."

Not that Kelly didn't try. "Jack was quite, quite good," added Huggins. "He made a significant contribution to the success of the show. He always gave his all. It was those lines that Jim Garner would have made funny and so right that Jack would sometimes deliver with too much care."

Keep an eye on the names listed in the hotel register when Bart asks to inspect it early in the episode. You'll see an entry for "Fred Bohanon," which is the name of one of the editors who worked on *Maverick*. Also early in the episode: the name of the gentleman who groused about losing money to Bart (and who was later found dead in his bedroom) is "Farfan," which was named after *Maverick* assistant director Robert Farfan.

Pappyism: "Work is fine for killing time, but it's a shaky way to make a living."

37. SHADY DEAL AT SUNNY ACRES

ORIGINAL AIRDATE: NOVEMBER 23, 1958

Teleplay by: Roy Huggins
Story by: Douglas Heyes
Directed by: Leslie H. Martinson

Guest Cast: Efrem Zimbalist Jr. (Dandy Jim Buckley), Diane Brewster (Samantha Crawford), Richard Long (Gentleman Jack Darby), John Dehner (John Bates), Leo Gordon (Big Mike McComb), Arlene Howell (Cindy Lou Brown), Regis Thomey (Ben Granville), Karl Swenson (Sheriff Griffin), J. Pat O'Malley (Ambrose Callahan), Joan Young (Susan Granville), Leon Tyler (Henry Hibbs), Jonathan Hole (Desk Clerk), Irving Bacon (Employee), Syd Saylor (1st Townsman), Jack O'Shea (1st Rube), Earle Hodgins (Plunkett), Val Benedict (Cowhand)

Synopsis. Bret wins $15,000 playing poker in Sunny Acres, Colorado. He deposits the money with the town's banker, John Bates, but when he tries to withdraw some of his money the following morning, Bates denies the entire transaction. Bates has been lifting funds from the bank in order to buy out his partner Ben Granville. Bret vows to recover his money within two weeks, but Bates is unfazed — he knows he has an impeccable reputation in town, and that the sheriff will be watching Maverick closely. Bret plays helpless, but actually orchestrates an elaborate investment scheme built around Bates' inherent greed. Playing key roles in the sting: Samantha Crawford, Dandy Jim Buckley, Gentleman Jack Darby, Cindy Lou Brown, Big Mike McComb, and brother Bart.

Roy Huggins wrote the majority of the stories on *Maverick*, then assigned a writer to do the teleplay. Yet, Huggins' name rarely appears among the writing credits for his shows — he almost always gave the credit to whomever wrote the teleplay. But Huggins' motives, by his own admission, were not exactly altruistic — they often served as a counter attack against another of Warner Bros.' staunch contract policies.

"When I joined Warners in 1955, I had a clause written into my contract that stated if I was ever required to function as a writer, I would have to be paid my established writer's salary of $1,000 per week — in addition to my producer's salary of $500 per week," he explained. "That was written into the contract, and initialed by Warners, and by me. I asked for credit on the stories because I was writing the stories.

"At some point, Bill Orr met with me and told me that Warners couldn't give me credit on the stories. Their rationale was, 'If we give you story credit, all of the other producers are going to demand story credit.' I said, 'Wait a minute, Bill. Are the other producers writing the stories?' He said, 'Well, they think they are.' And I said, 'Is there any evidence of that?' He said, 'Look, Roy, it's a matter of policy and principle. If I give you story credit, we're going to have to give them story credit. It's going to create a big problem.'

"I understood Bill's problem. But I had a problem, too. I had left feature films because I had believed that television was the wave of the future. I wanted to establish myself in television. I was off to a good start — I had done well on *Cheyenne* — but that wasn't enough. I wanted to have a big reputation, and I was willing to work hard for it.

"I couldn't afford to leave Warners at that point, so I accepted their decision. But I was also determined that Warners was not going to save a nickel — I was going to give the stories that I came up with to the writers so that Warners would have to pay for the story in any case."

Early in 1958, after the phenomenal success of *Maverick* solidly entrenched Huggins' reputation as a television hit-maker, Warners renegotiated his contract and more than doubled his salary.

"Shady Deal at Sunny Acres" marked the final appearances of Dandy Jim Buckley and Samantha Crawford — Efrem Zimbalist Jr. was busy starring in *77 Sunset Strip*, while Diane Brewster was about to launch her own series (*The Islanders*, produced by Richard Barc). In fact, with the exception of Gentleman Jack Darby, none of the supporting characters created by Roy Huggins and company returned to *Maverick* following Huggins' depature after the second season.

38. ISLAND IN THE SWAMP

(a.k.a. "Swamp Girl")

ORIGINAL AIRDATE: NOVEMBER 30, 1958

Written and Directed by: Montgomery Pittman

Guest Cast: Edgar Buchanan (Buddy Forge), Erin O'Brien (Victoria Forge), Arlene Howell (Ladybird), Lance Fuller (Oliver Gifford), Gage O'Dell (Herbert Forge), Richard Reeves (Anthony Gifford), Albert Carrier (Philip Thierot), Roy Engle (Sebastian), Joe Espitallier (Joe Espitallier), George Dee (Andre)

Synopsis. Set adrift in a lifeboat after he was robbed, Bret lands on an island outside New Orleans, where he meets Buddy Forge and his eccentric community of black market smugglers. Forge mistakes Bret for a government spy and holds him prisoner.

"Montgomery Pittman was an interesting, idiosyncratically talented man," said Roy Huggins. "He wrote the screenplay for *Come Next Spring*, for Republic Pictures, which I thought was a cinematic work of art. That's what brought him to my attention.

"Monte came from the South, and he had a take on life that was deeply regional. I'm sure he drew from that a great deal. Monte was quite good — he contributed something very special when he wrote a script."

Huggins made a director out of Pittman, and "Island in the Swamp" was one of the first shows Pittman directed. Pittman had a lot of imput in the casting of this episode. Needing someone to play a character who spoke French with a special accent, he remembered his friend Joe Espitallier, a former actor who was managing the Hollywood Masonic Temple at the time. Espitallier fit the role so perfectly that Pittman named the character after Espitallier. Pittman also cast his 2-year-old son Robert as Baby Forge.

39. PREY OF THE CAT

ORIGINAL AIRDATE: DECEMBER 7, 1958

Written and Directed by: Douglas Heyes

Guest Cast: Wayne Morris (Pete Stillman), Patricia Barry (Kitty), Barry Kelley (Sheriff), Yvette Dugay (Raquel Morales), William Gordon (Fred Spender), William Bryant (Chase), Syd Saylor (Clerk), James Anderson (First Deputy), William Yip (Chan), Morgan Sha'an (Second Deputy)

Synopsis. Bart suffers a broken leg when his horse throws him after it was startled by a mountain lion. Bart rehabilitates at the Star Trail Ranch, where he finds himself entangled in a triangle with Pete Stillman, whom Bart has befriended, and Pete's wife Kitty, who has fallen in love with Maverick. When his leg heals, Bart earns his keep by joining Pete and his ranch hands on a hunt for the mountain lion. When Pete is killed by a stray bullet, the ranch hands accuse Bart of murdering their boss in order to be with Kitty.

The first act of this episode takes place around Christmas time, as evidenced by the presence of a Christmas tree, as well as the playing of "Jingle Bells." Also, Pete Stillman finds a wheelchair which he "gives" to the bedridden Bart as a Christmas present so that Maverick can take part in the lodge's celebration.

40. THE SPANISH DANCER

(a.k.a. "The Dark Dancer" and "Accordin' to Law")

ORIGINAL AIRDATE: DECEMBER 14, 1958

Teleplay by: Robert Shaefer & Eric Freiwald and Robert Smith
Story by: Edward Seabrook & Homer McCoy and Oscar Millard
Directed by: James V. Kern

Guest Cast: Adele Mara (Elena Grande), Richard Long (Gentleman Jack Darby), Robert Bray (John Wilson), Tony Romano (Raoul Onate), Slim Pickens (Jed), Ben Morris (Harry), Mark Tapscott (Charlie), Fred Graham (First Miner), John Mitchum (Second Miner), John McKee (Third Miner)

Synopsis. While peddling goods in the New Mexico mining camp of Riverhead, Bart and Gentleman Jack Darby fall for exotic dancer Elena Grande, who hopes one day to buy back the ranch that her family once owned. When Bart wins a flooded mine from crooked camp owner John Wilson, he enlists Jack and Elena's help in an elaborate scheme to drain the mine at Wilson's expense.

Adele Mara was a perfect choice for the title role — earlier in her career, she performed as a classical Spanish dancer for renowned bandleader Xavier Cugat. Although she had previously danced many times on film (including her unforgettable performance in the "Seed of Deception" segment of *Maverick*), this episode marked the first time she performed an actual Spanish dance on film. In order to prepare for her role, Mara studied under famous flamenco dancer Martin Vargas; the dances she performs in this episode were authentic dances from the 1876 period.

John Mitchum is the brother of legendary screen actor Robert Mitchum.

"The Spanish Dancer" was later redone on *The Alaskans* as "Kangaroo Court."

41. HOLIDAY AT HOLLOW ROCK

ORIGINAL AIRDATE: DECEMBER 28, 1958

Written by: Howard Browne
Directed by: Richard L. Bare

Guest Cast: William Reynolds (Tod Blake), Saundra Edwards (Nora Taylor), Tod Griffin (Jesse Carson), Emile Meyer (Colonel Arnold Taylor), George O'Hanlon (Morton Connors), Hugh Sanders (Jed Snyder), Guy Wilkerson (Sam), Don Harvey (Clyde), Lane Bradford (Matt Hendricks), Don Kelly (Ira Swain), Chuck Cason (Pete), I. Stanford Jolley (Stableman), Roydon Clark (Chuck), Bob Steele (Billy)

Synopsis. Bret spends the Fourth of July in Hollow Rock, where he hopes to make some easy money by betting on Silver King, the prize quarter-horse owned by his friend Colonel Arnold Taylor, in the town's annual horse race. When crooked Sheriff Jesse Carson robs and beats Bret out of over $4,200, Maverick uses the race to even the score.

"George O'Hanlon, who had a part in "Holiday at Hollow Rock" and I go back a long way," said director Richard Bare. "George starred in the *Joe McDoakes* comedy shorts that I wrote and directed for Warner Bros., which are also what led to my getting a contract with Warners. I used George whenever I could."

If O'Hanlon's name doesn't sound familiar, his voice should: he's the voice of George Jetson on the long-running cartoon series *The Jetsons*.

Pappyisms: "Never play in a rigged game, unless you rig it yourself;" and "If you haven't got something nice to say about a man, it's time to change the subject."

42. GAME OF CHANCE

(a.k.a. "A Rope of Pearls")

ORIGINAL AIRDATE: JANUARY 4, 1959

Written by: Gene Levitt
Directed by: James V. Kern

Guest Cast: Marcel Dalio (Baron Dulet), Roxane Berard (La Contessa de Barot), Lou Krugman (Murdock), Jonathan Hole (San Francisco Jeweler), Fred Easler (German Jeweler)

Synopsis. In Denver, a French grifter and his charming niece use a phony string of pearls to fleece Bart out of $10,000. Bret helps Bart even the score by relieving the pair of the real pearls and a potential profit of $40,000. But the scheme backfires when a greedy jeweler robs the Mavericks of the necklace.

After Bart realizes that the countess has fleeced him of $10,000, he asks Bret to help him get his money back. At first, Bret declines ("That's your problem"), but Bart reminds him that "we all helped you" when the banker at Sunny Acres took Bret for $15,000. Bret admits that his brother has a point, so he agrees to help — for 17.5% of Bart's money.

Pappyism: "Never cry over spilled milk — it could've been whiskey." This is a funny line, although it seems odd insofar as the Mavericks rarely drank during the first two years of the show.

43. GUN-SHY

ORIGINAL AIRDATE: JANUARY II, 1959

Written by: Marion Hargrove
Directed by: Leslie H. Martinson

Guest Cast: Andra Martin (Virginia Adams), Ben Gage (Marshal Mort Dooley), Walker Edmisten (Clyde Diefendorfer), Reginald Owen (Freddie Hawkins), Gage Clarke (Kenneth P. Badger), Marshall Kent (Doc Stucke), Kathleen O'Malley (Amy Ward), Roscoe Ates (Barfly), Irene Tedrow (Mrs. Adams), Doodles Weaver (Lum), William Fawcett (Rube)

Synopsis. A 15-year-old letter from a Confederate Army captain leads Bret and a fellow grafter named Freddie Hawkins to Elwood, Kansas, where the captain buried

$500,000 in gold before he died. But Bret must contend with the town's marshal, the stalwart but dimwitted Mort Dooley, who is determined to run Maverick out of town for no apparent reason.

"*Maverick* is perhaps the only Western that could [poke fun at *Gunsmoke*] and get away with it," wrote Marion Hargove in 1959. "*Gunsmoke* can do nothing in retaliation. It cannot parody *Maverick* without endangering its own impressive dignity, and *Maverick* has no dignity to attack." *Gunsmoke did* threaten to retaliate (*Time* reported plans for an episode featuring a villainous character named "Huggins") but nothing ever came of it.

"Gun-Shy" is remembered for its lampoon of *Gunsmoke*, but Hargrove's script nudges another popular Western series, and also contains several other "in" jokes. Mort Dooley asks Doc if he remembers a gunman who handed out business cards — a sly reference to Paladin, the character played by Richard Boone in *Have Gun, Will Travel*. Meanwhile, Bret disposes of Mort with phony messages that either send him to nearby "Haglund's farm" (named after Oren W. Haglund, production manager for all Warner Bros. television series), or to Kansas City to capture Hognose Hughes, the character named after *Maverick* writer Russell Hughes. Also, Hargrove christened "Doc Stucke" after Carl Stucke, who was the assistant story editor on all Warners series.

Ben Gage was once married to champion swimmer and movie star Esther Williams. "Ben gave up a promising career in show business when he married Esther," said director Leslie Martinson. "He had been the singing announcer on Jack Benny's radio program. But I remembered him from when I was at MGM — I was the dialogue director on three of Esther's pictures — and I thought of him when I first read the script for 'Gun-Shy.' I visualized how to spoof [*Gunsmoke*'s] main title sequence, with the shootout, and I remembered that I had jokingly said to Roy, 'You know, I'd love to shoot that sequence through the legs, because Ben Gage has got just the can to make it work.' We didn't do it that way, of course — we shot it off the hip, and I used a wide-angle lens to film the shootout between Ben's legs."

At the time, Gage had been devoting most of his time to running his land development company in Yucca Valley, California, although he continued to act occasionally, including three more appearances on *Maverick*.

James Garner also co-starred with Andra Martin in *Up Periscope* for Warner Bros. in 1959.

44. TWO BEGGARS ON HORSEBACK

ORIGINAL AIRDATE: JANUARY 18, 1959

Written and Directed by: Douglas Heyes

Guest Cast: Patricia Barry (Jessamy Longacre), Ray Teal (Stryker), John Cliff (Sundown), Clem Bevins (Old Man), Will Wright (General Hoyt Boscourt), Roscoe Ates (Kibitzer), Duane Grey (Howie Horwitz)

Synopsis. Bret and Bart each carry a $10,000 draft from the Gannet Express Company, only to discover that the company is about to go bankrupt. But Jessamy Longacre has inside information: the Gannet office in Deadwood hasn't closed yet, and will remain open until a messenger brings the news by stagecoach. For $1,000 commission, Jessamy will lead the Mavericks to Deadwood — but since the Deadwood office only has $11,000 (enough to cover only one draft), it becomes a race between Bret and Bart to see who can beat the messenger to Deadwood and cash in before the office shuts down.

Douglas Heyes named the "Howie Horwitz" character after Warners writer/producer Howie Horwitz, whose credits included *77 Sunset Strip* (he later produced *Batman* for 20th Century-Fox). Horwitz also took over as producer of *Maverick* for one episode late in the fourth season.

According to this episode, **Pappy** told Bret, "When you're playing poker, don't trust anybody, not even your brother." (Bart chimes in, "What he meant was, *especially* your brother.")

45. THE RIVALS

ORIGINAL AIRDATE: JANUARY 25, 1959

Television Story and Teleplay by: Marion Hargrove
Based on the Play by Richard Brinsley Sheridan
Directed by: Leslie H. Martinson

Guest Cast: Roger Moore (John Vandergelt III), Patricia Crowley (Lydia Linley), Neil Hamilton (Brigadier General Archibald Vandergelt), Barbara Jo Allen (Mrs. Mallaver), Dan Tobin (Lucius Benson), William Allyn (Livingston), Sandra Gould (Lucy), Chet Stratton (Desk Clerk), Stanley Farrar (Doctor), Robert Carson (Hotel Manager), Ed Nelson (Classmate), Rand Brooks (Second)

Synopsis. Wealthy John Vandergelt III is a hopeless romantic in love with Lydia Linley, a charming young heiress who yearns for a man like Sydney Carton of *A Tale of Two Cities* — "a man of warmth, imagination, courage, and a sense of adventure." Van is the perfect mate for Lydia, but he knows she'll have nothing to do with him because he's filthy rich. Van hires Bret to switch identities with him: he hopes that Lydia will love and accept him for who he is before she realizes that he's also a Vandergelt. The plan goes along smoothly until Van's father arrives in town unexpectedly.

"Marion Hargrove had a bead on *Maverick* that no other writer had," said director Leslie Martinson. "It was a perfect marriage — Marion's scripts and Roy Huggins' concept."

Martinson found working on *Maverick* a unique television experience not only because Huggins allowed him ample time to prepare each script, but because Hargrove was also available for consultation. "It was a great marriage of mind between producer, writer, and director," he said. "Roy always gave you the time to talk things over with him — we'd meet regularly before the start of each show — so that when you went out to make the film, you already had a marriage of concept as to exactly where the episode was going, and which were the particularly important scenes, and so forth, so that there'd be no surprises when you watched the dailies in the projection room.

"Then, of course, Marion was more or less available for his episodes — which is not usually the case on television. Usually, the writer turns in the script, and moves on to something else, and is therefore not available by the time the director starts to film it. But Marion had an office at the studio, so he was accessible if I wanted to work something out with him."

Hargrove and Martinson shared a mutual respect and admiration for the other. "I loved Les' work, and so did Roy," said Hargrove. "Whenever possible, I'd try to get Les to direct my shows — and if he wasn't available, I'd want to know why."

Pappyism: "'Early to bed and early to rise' is the curse of the working classes."

46. DUEL AT SUNDOWN

ORIGINAL AIRDATE: FEBRUARY 1, 1959

Teleplay by: Richard Collins
Story by: Howard Browne
Directed by: Arthur Lubin

Guest Cast: Edgar Buchanan (Jed Christiansen), Abby Dalton (Carrie Christiansen), Clint Eastwood (Red Hardigan), Dan Sheridan (Doc Baxter), James Griffith (John Wesley Hardin), Clarke Alexander (Sheriff), Linda Lawson (Lily), Myrna Fahey (Susie)

Synopsis. Bret stops by Sundown to visit his old friend Jed Christiansen, a rancher who'd like to see Maverick break up the romance between his daughter Carrie and Red Hardigan, a smarmy bully more interested in Jed's wealth than his daughter. Bret refuses to become involved until he loses a $5,000 bet with Jed (not realizing that Jed had tricked him). Jed promises to erase the debt, and pay Bret $1,000, if he remains in town for one week. Maverick has to think fast when Red, the fastest gun in the county, challenges him to a duel.

Although Bret describes himself as an "average" gunshot in this episode, he doesn't appear worried until after he witnesses Jed's skill with a gun. In order to get out of the duel, Bret has Bart impersonate notorious gunslinger John Wesley Hardin, who supposedly rides into Sundown and challenges Bret to a duel. With Red and the entire town watching, Bret appears to gun down John Wesley Hardin. Red finds it hard to believe, but when the doctor (who's also in on the gag) pronounces "Hardin" dead, Red reverts to his natural cowardice and runs out of town.

"Of course, you knew that nobody in town knew what John Wesley Hardin looked like," Jed observes at the end of the story. "But I know what your brother Bart looks like, and from a distance, he looks like John Wesley Hardin." Jed adds that Maverick was taking quite a chance. Other than Jed's word, Bret had no way of knowing for certain that Red was a coward. What if he had guessed wrong? "Sometimes it frightens me what I'll do for money," Bret said soberly.

Bret tells Carrie (Abby Dalton) that when he was six years old, "my Pappy took my brother and me into a saloon, where the men who were playing Red Dog and Chuck-a-Luck and Wheel of Chance. 'Son,' he said, 'This is what's called gambling. Stay away from it. In games like this, you don't stand a chance. As long as you live, stick to poker.'"

This episode marks the second time in which Bret demonstrates how to play "Maverick Solitaire," where you can deal yourself 25 cards from a well-shuffled deck and come up with five pat poker hands. Bret had previously used "Maverick Solitaire" in "Rope of Cards," as a means of getting a stubborn juror to change his vote.

"Duel at Sundown" also features Clint Eastwood, whose character derisively refers to Bret as "Maver-ack" throughout the entire episode. A few years away from his breakthrough role as Rowdy Yates on *Rawhide*, Eastwood (like James Garner and Steve McQueen), was one of the few TV stars who became equally successful in motion pictures.

stars. Known for his roles as *Dirty Harry* and as the Man With No Name in the Sergio Leone spaghetti Westerns, Eastwood won the Academy Award for Best Director for 1992's *Unforgiven*.

47. YELLOW RIVER

ORIGINAL AIRDATE: FEBRUARY 8, 1959

Written by: Howard Browne
Directed by: David Lowell Rich

Guest Cast: Patricia Breslin (Abigail Allen), Peter Miles (Jean Baxter), Mike Lane (Horace Cusack), Sam Buffington (Professor von Schulenberg), Robert Richards (Fred Grimes), Robert Conrad (Davie Barrows), Harry Hines (Pete Mulligan), Kem Dibbs (Mills), Stuart Bradley (Asher), Tol Avery (Sawyer)

Synopsis. Charming but slippery Abigail Allen tricks Bart into detaining two men whom she cheated out of $2,000 (she claims they're outlaws). Bart catches up with Abigail outside Yellow River, where she and five men are trying to lead a herd of cattle to Kansas. When Bart discovers that the group needs a trail boss, he forces Abbie to hire him at an inflated price ($200 a month, plus one dollar for each head of cattle). Along the way the group encounter Jean Baxter, a mysterious woman whose father was murdered by two men. Abbie and Bart invite Jean to join them, but after she does, two of the trail members are found knifed to death. The group begins to suspect each other, until Bart discovers that the "woman" is really escaped killer Billy Young.

Patricia Breslin, who starred with Jackie Cooper on the popular mid-1950s comedy series *The People's Choice*, guest stars as Abigail Allen, the first of many wily female grafters (most of whom were played by Kathleen Crowley) who appeared on *Maverick* to fill the void created by the departure of Diane Brewster. Abbie's style is so familiar that on two occasions Bart asks her if she has any relatives named Crawford. Also, like Samantha, Abbie gets the last laugh: although Bart has earned $1,500 from her by the end of the cattle trail, Abbie breaks into his room and steals it. (Ironically, "Yellow River" was a remake of a *Cheyenne* episode, "The Dark Rider," that featured Brewster as a crafty con artist.)

Robert Conrad has been a television mainstay, starring in no less than eight series (including *The Wild, Wild West*, *Baa Baa Black Sheep*, and *High Mountain Rangers*) and numerous movies for television over the past three decades. Conrad's guest role in *Maverick* was one of his first TV performances, and soon led to a starring role in his first series, *Hawaiian Eye*.

48. THE SAGA OF WACO WILLIAMS

ORIGINAL AIRDATE: FEBRUARY 15, 1959

Teleplay by: Gene Coon
Story by: Montgomery Pittman
Directed by: Leslie H. Martinson

Guest Cast: Wayde Preston (Waco Williams), R.G. Armstrong (Colonel Karl Bent), Louise Fletcher (Kathy Bent), Brad Johnson (Karl Bent Jr.), Ken Mayer (Sheriff Boyd Tait), Harry Lauter (Bernie Adams), Lane Bradford (Jack Regan), Syd Saylor (Menzies), Stephen Coit (Charlie)

Synopsis. Bret delays meeting Bart in Denver in order to trail fearless gunslinger Waco Williams, who's scheduled to meet his partner, outlaw Blackie Dolan, in Bent City. Waco wants Blackie to go straight, while Bret wants to turn Dolan in and claim the $2,500 reward. But Waco's presence upsets some of the townspeople, particularly its founder, cattleman Colonel Karl Bent, who thinks Waco has been sent by cattle rustlers to take over the town.

Louise Fletcher won the Academy Award for Best Actress for her memorable portrayal of Nurse Ratched in the film adaptation of Ken Kesey's *One Flew Over the Cuckoo's Nest*, which also won the Oscar for Best Picture of 1975.

"The Saga of Waco Williams" was the highest-rated episode of the entire *Maverick* series, scoring a 35.3 rating and 51 share. Film editor Robert Watts received an Emmy nomination in 1958 for this episode (for Best Editing of a Film for Television), although the award went to Silvio D'Alisera, who won for "Meet Mr. Lincoln," a segment of *Project XX*.

49. BRASADA SPUR

ORIGINAL AIRDATE: FEBRUARY 22, 1959

Teleplay by: John Tucker Battle
Story by: Palmer Thompson
Directed by: Paul Henreid

Guest Cast: Julie Adams (Belle Morgan), Patrick McVey (Roy Stafford), Ken Lynch (Rufus Elgree), Ralph Neff (Horace Hogan), Hope Summers (Martha Abbot), James Lydon (Terry McKenna), Robert Griffin (Adam Sheppley), Gertrude Flynn (Dorritt MacGregor), Fred Kruger (Barnes)

Synopsis. In King City, Bart wines and dines Belle Morgan, the powerful town boss, in order to get a seat in an exclusive poker game with millionaire railroad men. But when Belle catches onto Bart's game, she retaliates viciously by impounding his winnings (over $13,000) and sticking him with the operation of the Brasada Spur, a floundering railroad company in which Belle controls most of the stock. After receiving a crash course in the railroad business from his new partner Roy Stafford, Bart tries to keep the company afloat and win back his money.

Roy Huggins created Bart as almost a kind of clone for Bret Maverick, in that both brothers would share the same characteristics — right down to their clothes. Originally, Bret and Bart were supposed to wear the exact costume, but this was eventually modified so that by the end of the first season, each brother had his own distinctive, albeit similar, wardrobe. Bret usually wore a ruffled shirt, string tie, light-colored vest, white slacks and a black dude coat in his shows, while Bart usually wore black coat and pants, light vest, and a short necktie in his shows. Sometimes their wardrobe varied: in several episodes during the first two seasons, each brother had an outfit consisting of tan dude coat, brown slacks and brown vest, although Bret would always wear a string tie, and Bart a short necktie. (This particular costume was similar to the one Roger Moore wore when he joined *Maverick* in the fourth season.) Bret also had a white three-piece suit which he wore occasionally ("Escape to Tampico," "Island in the Swamp," "Guatemala City").

Bart's costume in "Brasada Spur" is almost identical to the one most associated with Bret — dark coat, white slacks, and a vest. This is the only time in the series in which Bart wears this particular outfit. The brothers were also originally supposed to wear the same-colored hat, although this, too, was modified: Bret usually wore a black hat, while Bart's hat was tan. The Mavericks' headwear also varied: Bret sometimes wore a tan hat, while Bart also wore a black hat. Also, Bret had a Panama hat, which he wore with his white suit, while Bart owned a ten-gallon hat, which he wears in "Brasada Spur."

Huggins explained that there was a practical reason why the Mavericks' wardrobe occasionally altered. "Many times we would borrow footage — mostly long shots or establishing shots — from old Warner Bros. films to provide transition from one scene to another, and we would have to make sure that the costume we used on *Maverick* matched the costumes used in the older films," he said. "For example, the footage in 'Brasada Spur' [where the two trains collide] was taken from *Saratoga Trunk*, an old Gary Cooper film from 1945. We had to make sure that Jack Kelly was dressed to match what Gary Cooper wore in *Saratoga Trunk*." Other *Maverick* episodes borrowed from such Warners films as *Rocky Mountain*, *San Antonio*, *Stampede*, *The Command*, and *Calamity Jane*.

According to this episode, Bart promised Pappy he wouldn't marry until he was 38 years old. In "Duel at Sundown," Bret made a similar statement: he promised Pappy that on his 38th birthday, he'd look around for a wife, get married and raise twelve Mavericks. "Brasada Spur" also features the Pappyism "The two greatest evils are hard liquor and hard work."

50. PASSAGE TO FORT DOOM

ORIGINAL AIRDATE: MARCH 8, 1959

Written by: Roy Huggins
Directed by: Paul Henreid

Guest Cast: Nancy Gates (Mrs. Chapman), Arlene Howell (Cindy Lou Brown), Fred Beir (Lou Granger), John Alderson (Ben Chapman), Diane McBain (Charlotte), Sheila Bramley (Mrs. Stanton), Charles Cooper (Claude Rogan), Alan Caillou (Fergus McKenzie), Thomas B. Henry (Charles Stanton), Ron Hayes (Joe), Rafer Barnes (Frank)

Synopsis. Needing money, Bart finds work as a trail guide for a wagon train heading for Fort Brader, located in the Black Hills of the Dakotas. Among the members of the caravan is Cindy Lou Brown, who is hiding from outlaw Claude Rogan, who stuffed $30,000 in stolen money inside a doll that's now in Cindy's possession. Although Cindy Lou buries the money, Rogan and his gang catch up with the wagon train, but Bart and the men ward them off. While the caravan arrives at Fort Brader, they find the place completely deserted after a cholera epidemic wiped out most of the troops. When a tribe of Indians converge on the fort, Bart and the others must fight them alone.

"Passage to Fort Doom" features these pearls from **Pappy** Maverick: "Son, you're self-centered, shifty, and you know the value of a dollar — you're gonna die honored and wealthy;" "Make a lot of mistakes, son, but always make sure they're your own;" and "Love is the only thing in life you've got to earn — everything else you can steal."

This episode also marks Arlene Howell's third appearance as dance hall entertainer Cindy Lou Brown (she also played another character in "Island in the Swamp"). When we first met Cindy Lou, she was Gentleman Jack Darby's girlfriend, but that relationship apparently ended long ago. Arlene Howell was crowned Miss USA of 1958, and was named third runner-up in the Miss Universe Pageant later that year.

51. TWO TICKETS TO TEN STRIKE

ORIGINAL AIRDATE: MARCH 15, 1959

Written and Directed by: Douglas Heyes

Guest Cast: Connie Stevens (Frankie French), Adam West (Vic Nolan), Andrea King (Mrs. Miller), Lyle Talbot (Martin Stone), William D. Gordon (Eddie Burke), Roscoe Ates (Barker), John Harmon (Stranger), Duane Grey (Sheriff)

Synopsis. Frankie French, a somewhat ditzy young woman from Tucson, is summoned to Ten Strike by a mysterious benefactor — the town banker. Frankie doesn't realize that the banker is really her father, an escaped killer named Frankovich who surfaced in Ten Strike eight years earlier and assumed the identity of a deceased man named Stone. Only one person in town knows the banker's secret — saloon owner Mae Miller, who knew Frankovich from her days as a showgirl. When Frankovich learned he was dying, he set about taking care of his affairs, including establishing an inheritance for Frankie. Mae decides to kill the banker and pin the crime on Frankie.

James Garner always kept his eye out for the working people, particularly those members of the cast and crew who were on the low end of the totem pole. "Jim might be working on a movie, and he'd have a scene with an extra who had a 'silent bit' — Jim would ask him a question, and all the extra is supposed to do is nod his head," explained Luis Delgado. "Jim would say to the director, 'You know, to me, that's really ridiculous. I don't feel the scene. This man should say something to me, either 'Go to hell,' or 'Yes,' or something. He should say something.' And so, the director would say, 'Okay,' and the extra now had a line of dialogue — which would also make him some more money, because you get paid more for a one-line bit than you do for a 'silent bit.' Jim does things like that practically all the time."

According to **Pappy** Maverick, "There's just about three reasons why most men do anything — greed, curiosity, and anger." But Bret doesn't think that Pappy meant most men, because "he was lookin' right at me when he said it. And he was right."

This episode also features one of the most famous Pappyisms of all: "A coward dies a thousand deaths, a brave man only once. A thousand to one — that's a pretty good advantage."

Connie Stevens starred as lounge singer Cricket Blake in the Warner Brothers detective series *Hawaiian Eye.*

52. BETRAYAL

ORIGINAL AIRDATE: MARCH 22, 1959

Teleplay by: James O'Hanlon and Richard McCauley

Story by: Winston Miller

Directed by: Leslie H. Martinson

Guest Cast: Patricia Crowley (Anne Sanders), Ruta Lee (Laura Dillon), Morgan Jones (Buck Wilkerson), Don Barry (Sheriff), J. Pat O'Malley (Mr. Dillon), Michael Dante (Outlaw), John Dennis (Pete), Edward Marr (Drummer), Harry Jackson (Poker Player), Stanley Adams (Link)

Synopsis. Bart is among the passengers who are victimized by two men who hold up a stagecoach bound for Virginia City. Bart suspects a connection between the robbers and another passenger, Anne Sanders (she told them where Bart hid his money), so he trails Anne in the hopes that she will lead him to the holdup men (and the $1,500 they took from him). Bart's suspicions are well founded: after he captures the two men, Anne not only fails to identify them — she enables them to escape.

A filmed story is told three times: once by the writer; once by the actors and director, who interpret the writing; then finally by the post-production process, which includes editing. Because *Maverick* was based on a particular brand of humor, it was important that the film editors remain in sync with the show's concept, because a film cut the wrong way can tell an entirely different story than what was originally written or filmed.

During its first two seasons, *Maverick* went slightly over budget because producer Roy Huggins spent extra time in the editing and sound mixing of his shows. "One day when I was in the projection room at Warners, I noticed Jim Moore [the head of the studio's Editorial Department] sitting in the back row," Huggins recalled. "I wondered why he was there, but I didn't say anything, because we were friends. Then I noticed that Jim was beginning to show up frequently at my runnings, so I finally asked him. Jim told me, 'Bill Orr wanted to find out what the hell you were doing in post-production that was taking you so long.' I said, 'Oh. Have you found out yet?' Jim said, 'Yeah, I told him this morning. I told him that you were making the pictures better.'"

53. THE STRANGE JOURNEY OF JENNY HILL

ORIGINAL AIRDATE: MARCH 29, 1959

Written and Directed by: Douglas Heyes

Guest Cast: Peggy King (Jenny Hill), Sig Ruman (Professor Vegelius), William Schallert (Carl), Leo Gordon (Big Mike McComb), George Keymas (Sam), K.L. Smith (Starke), Mark Tapscott (Crowley), Michael Galloway (Jim Hedges)

Synopsis. Big Mike McComb is on trial for the murder of a stagecoach driver and two robbers. Mike claims that the real killer is a former friend named Jim Hedges, a man believed to have died six months earlier. Bret believes that Hedges' wife, saloon singer Jenny Hill, is also trying to locate him, so he follows Jenny as she plays out a series of one-night appearances in different towns. Maverick's role becomes more complicated when he realizes he's falling in love with her.

Maverick's cowardice is one character facet that has long been blown out of proportion. True, Bret has made many such proclamations in the past (including this episode, when he tells Jenny that his No. 1 rule is to "be cowardly at all costs"), but he usually resorts to such ploys in order to get out of undesirable situations (such as becoming sheriff in "The Sheriff of Duck 'n' Shoot"). But Maverick has displayed far more instances of courage than you'd think. Although it's easy to show this by looking back at past episodes (facing off Red Scanlon in "Day of Reckoning," standing in for Noah against Battling Krueger in "Stampede"), we really needn't look any further than Maverick's chosen occupation. Maverick has won numerous pots by sheer bluff. If he were really a coward, he would never take *any* chances.

Best known as the father on *The Patty Duke Show* and the English teacher on *The Many Loves of Dobie Gillis*, William Schallert is also an accomplished pianist and composer (he once studied music with Arnold Schoenberg), so he was an excellent choice to play Carl, the accompanyist to singer Jenny Hill.

JAMES GARNER AND JACK KELLY

JACK KELLY, ROGER MOORE, AND ROBERT COLBERT IN FOURTH YEAR EPISODE

THIRD SEASON: 1959-1960
PRODUCTION CREDITS

Starring James Garner as Bret Maverick
and Jack Kelly as Bart Maverick

Executive Producer: William T. Orr
Produced by: Coles Trapnell
Created by: Roy Huggins

Directors of Photography: Harold Stine, Jack McKenzie, Wesley Anderson, Ralph Woolsey, Roger Shearman, Lloyd Crosby, Bert Glennon, Ray Fernstrom
Supervising Art Director: Perry Ferguson
Art Directors: Howard Campbell, John Ewing

Supervising Film Editor: James Moore
Film Editors: Elbert K. Hollingsworth, Lloyd Nosler, David Wages, George C. Shrader, Carl Pingitore, Robert Watts, Walter S. Stern, Jim Faris, Clarence Kolster, Cliff Bell, Robert Watts, Byron Chudnow, George Eppich Noel L. Scott, George E. Luckenbacher, Robert Jahns, Henry L. Demon Milt Kleinberg

Music Supervision: Paul Sawtell, Bert Shefter
Music Editors: Erma E. Levin, Sam E. Levin, Joe Inge,

Charles Paley, Theodore W. Sebern, George E. Marsh,

Louis W. Gordon, Robert Crawford, John Allyn Jr., Donald K. Harris, Jack B. Wadsworth

"Maverick" Theme Music by David Buttolph,
Lyrics by Paul Francis Webster

Production Manager: Oren W. Haglund

Sound: Robert B. Lee, Howard Fogetti, Francis E. Stahl, Donald McKay, David Forrest, Sam F. Goode, John Jensen, Frank W. Webster, Harold Hanks, John Kean

Set Decorators: John F. Austin, Glenn P. Thompson, Steve A. Potter, Frank M. Miller, John Sturtevant, Jerry Welch, Edward M. Parker, Hal Overell

Assistant Directors: C. Carter Gibson, Victor Vallejo, Fred Scheld, Claude Binyon Jr., Ralph E. Black, Don Blair, Kenny Kessler, Dick L'Estrange, Richard Maybery, Henry Spitz, John F. Murphy, Bob Stone

Makeup Supervisor: Gordon Bau

Announcer: Ed Reimers

arion Hargrove recalled a prediction that James Garner had made about the future of *Maverick* about halfway through the show's second season. "It was around the time I was writing the story for *Life* on the 'Gun-Shy' episode," he said. "I was talking to Garner, and Garner said, 'I had a feeling when we did 'The Belcastle Brand,' this is the best we are going to do, and from here on, it's downhill. And I will predict to you that you will be the first to leave, Huggins will be the second to leave, and ol' Jimbo will not be far behind you.

"Well, as you know, Roy and I had been on each other's nerves ever since the 'Gun-Shy' episode. I finally left around the middle of the second season, after I had completed 'The Rivals.' That show got great reviews, so I was able to leave in a 'high dudgeon.' But it was just like Garner had said — I would be the first to leave."

Garner was right on the order of departure. Roy Huggins left *Maverick* at the end of the second season. Garner stayed on until the fourth season.

Huggins' exit from the series was partially prompted by a severe case of pneumonia. "I took a holiday shortly after I finished work on the second season, around late March of 1959," Huggins recalled. "I left town, and I discovered on a train going from New York to Detroit that I had double pneumonia. Adele took me off the train in Buffalo, New York. It was snowing, so we had a hard time getting to a hospital. I was in the hospital for ten days. I was in very serious trouble. I am still suffering from having had that bout with double pneumonia. I have fibrosis."

Upon his release from the hospital, Huggins returned to Los Angeles and rested at home for another week. While he was recovering, he did some "long, hard thinking. I thought about my career at Warner Bros. I took over *Cheyenne* — I improved the writing so that the show would now tell stories that adults would watch. By the end of that first season, *Cheyenne* was the only one left of those first three Warner Bros. shows — *Casablanca* and *King's Row* had been cancelled. I then moved on to *Conflict*, and among the shows that I wrote and produced for *Conflict* were the pilots for *Maverick*, *77 Sunset Strip* and *Colt .45*."

Going into the 1959-60 season, *77 Sunset Strip* and *Colt .45* were established hits, *Cheyenne* was still running strong, and *Maverick* was rated the No. 6 television program. Those series accounted for nearly half of the 7-1/2 hours of programming Warners was producing for ABC that year. Huggins had created three of those programs and saved the fourth, *Cheyenne*, from an early cancellation. Yet because of the drastic measures that the studio often took to avoid compensating writers for the creation of series (such as the previously mentioned instance wherein Warners purchased the treatment of *Antonia* in order to secure their claim that Huggins had based his pilot for *Maverick* on a specific work they owned), he was not able to reap any of the benefits of his work.

Considering that most of the remaining Warners shows were outright clones of either *Maverick* (*The Alaskans*, starring Roger Moore) or *77 Sunset Strip* (*Bourbon Street Beat* and *Hawaiian Eye*), Huggins could very well argue that he *was* Warner Bros. Television. "I remember that I was feeling very sorry for myself," he said. "I was feeling low, and a little put-upon. I looked at my life and I thought, 'Here I am, working 16-17 hours a day — because it takes time to write scripts. I worked at night. I worked at home. I developed the stories for most of the shows I did, and rewrote almost every script."

Huggins returned to the studio in late April 1959 and requested a meeting with William T. Orr. "I told Bill that I wanted out of my contract, which had a little over two years to go," Huggins continued. "I told Bill, 'It would be the classy thing for you to do to let me out of my contract. Every show you've got on the air is based on something I created.' Bill said, 'I can't do that, Roy.' I said, 'Well, I have to tell you — in that case, I will no longer write the stories, and I will no longer rewrite the scripts. That's why I got pneumonia. It was wearing me out.'"

Orr said, "Roy, what if I offered you a job in the Features Department? Would you take that?" Huggins said, "If you're asking me whether I want to take that, the answer is No. But if you're asking me if I will take that as a compromise, the answer is Yes, because you have twenty lawyers working for you, and I have none."

Huggins was put in charge of Warners' new "Exploitation Film Division," a unit devised by the studio to produce feature films that utilized the actors, writers and directors under contract at Warner Bros. Television. "I didn't want to make features," Huggins said. "But I figured that making features would be like going on a long, well-paid vacation. You make one or two features a year, whereas I was making 26 hour-long TV shows, which is like making 12 features a year, or worse — because no matter how you slice it, that's 26 stories you have to come up with. So I took the job as a way of getting my health back."

Huggins completed one picture, an adaptation of William Pearson's novel *A Fever in the Blood* starring Efrem Zimbalist Jr., Jack Kelly, Angie Dickenson, Don Ameche, and Robert Colbert. But he wasn't happy making movies and in 1960 he once again asked to be released from his contract. "I didn't have the autonomy in features that I had in television," he explained. "It wasn't easy, but we worked it out, and I was finally released from my contract in September of 1960." Over the course of the next 25 years, Huggins continued to shape the face of television as the creator of such groundbreaking shows as *The Fugitive, Run for Your Life, Alias Smith and Jones, The Rockford Files, Baretta,* and *Hunter*. In 1994, the Producers Guild of America honored Huggins with the Lifetime Achievement Award in Television.

Meanwhile, Huggins' departure from *Maverick* left the series not only without a producer, but with practically no scripts for the coming season. In May 1959, one month before shooting was scheduled to begin for the Fall, only one teleplay was ready to go ("Pappy"). Bill Orr worked furiously to find a replacement for Huggins. By this time, Orr had designed the entire Television Film Division at Warner Bros. into an intricately organized, high volume system that allowed no room for error. The cost-conscious studio simply could not afford to fall behind schedule. Such a delay not only risked the possibility of missing ABC's deadlines for airdates, it would also force the studio to incur additional expenses which would cut into the profit margin.

It was at this time that Coles Trapnell was called out to Warner Bros. Trapnell had spent many years at 20th Century-Fox, at both its New York and Los Angeles headquarters. "I started out in New York as a reader [of motion picture scripts], and then I became an assistant story editor, and after that was in charge of the Reading Department," he said. "Around the middle of World War II, I was asked to come out to the West Coast. Now, everybody in the New York office had one ambition, and that was to go to California, where the 'action' was, so I was very glad to go."

Trapnell moved his family to Hollywood, and continued working for Fox for the next ten years. But when the studio eliminated three-quarters of its West Coast Story Department, in a cost-cutting move, Trapnell found himself out of a job — but not for long. Dick Powell, the head of Four Star Productions, hired Trapnell as a writer and producer on the *Four Star Playhouse* anthology series. After four years at Four Star, Trapnell moved onto to the *Yancy Derringer* series, and wrote about a dozen scripts. He found himself unemployed again when *Yancy Derringer* was cancelled at the end of the 1958-59 season, but Trapnell found an opportunity waiting for him just around the corner.

"My agent set up an appointment at Warner Bros.," Trapnell remembered. "I didn't know what it was about, but I went, and when I arrived at the studio I discovered that two of my closest friends — Dick Bluel and Bill Koenig, both of whom I'd known at Four Star, then on *Yancy Derringer* — were now working at Warners as assistants to Bill Orr."

Trapnell was offered a job on the *Sugarfoot* series. "They wanted me to be an assistant producer under Harry Tatelman," he said. "It was a very pleasant meeting, but the job was not something I was interested in.

"However, before I left, I did say facetiously–*facetiously,* because I knew they'd been looking for 'big names' all over the place to succeed Roy Huggins — 'Gentlemen, the one thing at Warners that I would really be interested in is producing *Maverick*. I mean, anybody would have given his left you-know-what to do *Maverick*.. So everybody laughed politely, and I said goodbye and left.

"Less than a week later, Sylvia Hirsch from the William Morris office [Trapnell's agent] called me and said, 'Will you get over to Warners right away?' I said, 'Well, what for? I had a meeting just a few days ago.' Then she said, quite breathlessly, 'You will find out when you get there, but believe me, you want to go.' So I trotted over, and I was offered*Maverick* to produce."

The new producer had his work cut out for him. "I was hired in June 1959," Trapnell said. "We were scheduled to go on the air in September, and we had only one script ready to shoot ('Pappy'). We also had a 12-page outline, but not a script, for a story called 'The Sheriff of Duck 'n' Shoot,' by Bill Driskill. Bill did the screenplay for that one, so now I had two scripts to shoot. But the clock was running, and I was frantically trying to gather more stories."

At the same time, Trapnell needed writers. When Roy Huggins left, *Maverick*'s core group of writers — Marion Hargrove, Douglas Heyes, and Howard Browne — went with him. (Browne would return to *Maverick* and contribute two scripts for the fourth season.) Trapnell gradually built his own stable of writers, many of whom he'd known from his days at 20th Century-Fox: Catherine Turney, Leonard Praskins, Wells Root and Ron Bishop.

Trapnell had to contend with two other, less tangible matters. One was the inherent pressure linked with taking over the No. 6 show on television. With an Emmy Award under its belt, and an average of nearly 50% of the total TV-watching audience every Sunday night at 7:30, *Maverick* had just about reached prime time television's pinnacle of success — it could only go down. Whoever followed Roy Huggins as *Maverick*'s producer would be scrutinized as fiercely as a pro football coach taking over a team that had just won the Super Bowl. If he succeeds, it's assumed that he inherited a winning operation, and so he gets no credit. But if he fails, it's assumed that he fixed something that wasn't broken, and so he gets the blame. Either way, the successor is never quite judged on his own merits.

Marion Hargrove knew what Trapnell was up against. Hargrove himself had been asked to take over *Maverick*, but he declined for that very reason: "I received a phone call from Bill Orr while I was working on the screenplay for *Cash McCall*. Bill said, 'We've got a great job for you, Marion, and you're gonna love it.' And I said, 'What's that?' Bill said, 'Producing *Maverick*.' And I said, 'Bill, forget it! If it didn't work, you'd blame me for the rest of my life, and I would blame me for the rest of my life. And if it *did* work, Roy Huggins would never speak to either of us again."

But Trapnell had spent enough years in the film and TV industry to know what he was getting into. "Oh, you're concerned all the time," he said. "There's a line in an article on television, written by a television writer, that I heartily subscribe to: 'No one who does not enjoy the constant sense of impending disaster belongs in this business.'

"So, I enjoyed the pressure — and that sense of impending disaster — to the best of my ability."

The other intangible facing Trapnell was that he would not enjoy the kind of autonomy that Roy Huggins had as a producer. Warner Bros. Television had been placed entirely in the hands of Bill Orr, and Orr oversaw every aspect of production on every Warner Bros. series — with the exception of those shows produced by Huggins. By the sheer strength of his personality, Huggins convinced Orr to leave him to his own devices. While Orr may have objected to some of Huggins' methods (such as taking extra time in post-production), he couldn't argue with the results. But given the high volume of production scheduled for the 1959-60 season (Warners had to deliver 7-1/2 hours of programming to ABC each week), as well as Trapnell's relative inexperience as a producer, Orr took a more active role in the making of *Maverick* after Huggins' departure.

On the surface, 1959-60 was a successful year. Buoyed by the summer reruns of the second season, the first third-year episode ("Pappy") opened with a 49 audience share. Trapnell and his writers came up with some excellent stories ("The Ghost Soldiers," "The Goose-Drownder," "Maverick and Juliet," "Greenbacks, Unlimited"), and James Garner and Jack Kelly continued to sparkle as the brothers Maverick. *Maverick* again ranked among the Top 20 television programs, finishing its third season at No. 19.

But something was missing, and perhaps the difference can be explained in the approach to one character — Pappy, the patriarch of the Mavericks. Huggins had created Pappy as a safety device against some of the Mavericks' unconventional attitudes. Much of the boys' offbeat behavior was attributed to the aphorisms of "their dear old Pappy," such as "Work's fine for killing time, but it's a shaky way to make a living" (from "The Thirty-Ninth Star") and "'Early to bed and early to rise' is the curse of the working class" ("The Rivals").

Pappy and his zingers served as a sort of microcosm for the entire irreverent vision Huggins had on *Maverick*. Not surprisingly, many of Pappy's best lines came from Huggins himself. Marion Hargrove, Douglas Heyes and Howard Browne also understood the character, and each delivered "Pappyisms" with the requisite zip. When all four left *Maverick* after the second season, the Pappy character lost some of his teeth. The aphorisms of the last three seasons, as a whole, have nowhere near as much of the bite as those of the first two years.

But most importantly, Pappy was never intended to be seen. To give the character an extra dimension, Huggins insisted that the old reprobate always remain in the background. "That, for Roy, was like an Article of the Faith," explained Marion Hargrove.

But that all changed with the episode "Pappy," in which James Garner himself played the old man. While there really was no other actor who could have played Pappy (because, after all, Garner *was* Maverick), the episode comes off as gimmicky — particularly since Jack Kelly is also grayed up to play another older relative, Uncle Bentley Maverick, who appears briefly at the end of the show. At any rate, the perception of Pappy was forever changed, regardless of who played him, once the character appeared on-screen. There was no longer an air of mystery about him. (However, in fairness to Trapnell, the decision to bring Pappy to life had been made prior to when he took over as *Maverick*'s producer. "Pappy" had already been completed by the time Trapnell joined the series, so the script had been written sometime in the interim between Huggins' departure and Trapnell's hiring.)

"Pappy" was a gimmick that did not work, because the next week's episode ("Royal Four-Flush") registered a 39 share, ten points lower than the first episode's share. In just one week, *Maverick* had lost over 20% of its audience. Although *Maverick* had suffered a drastic loss of audience before (such as in the second season, when viewers reacted against "The Jail at Junction Flats"), the series usually managed to win back the audience within a few weeks. But this time, the viewers stayed away. *Maverick* continued to average around a 39-40 share during the first half of the season — a healthy figure, to be sure, but still far below the figures from the second season. Then *Maverick* suffered another significant drop in audience during the month of January. "The White Widow," broadcast on January 24, 1960, scored a 35 share (a decrease of nearly 13%), and the series hovered around that mark for the rest of the season.

Under normal circumstances, *Maverick*'s final seasonal average share of 34 (one-third of the total TV-watching audience for its time slot) would be considered respectable, at the very least. But the fact remains that the program continued to lose viewers at an alarming rate over the course of the year. By the end of the third season, *Maverick* had lost over one-third of its audience.

What happened?

Again, the answer is suggested in the "Pappy" episode. In addition to relying on gimmickry (graying up Garner and Kelly to play the older Mavericks), "Pappy" marked the beginning of a change in *Maverick*'s approach to humor. "Bill Orr had always liked the comedy aspect of *Maverick*, and he thought we ought to bring it out more," said Coles Trapnell. "And there's no doubt about it, we were broader, or looser, with the comedy than Roy had been. But Roy created the character, after all, and that's where the idea of comedy came from. That character."

True. But Huggins never intended to make *Maverick* a "comedy," per se. The humor of the first two seasons was derived from the Maverick character (and, more often than not, James Garner's impeccable instinct for delivering a funny line). But the humor of "Pappy," and the subsequent "comedy" episodes of the last three seasons, is on a more lowbrow, slapstick level — pratfalls and occasional muggings — that Huggins vigilantly avoided in his scripts.

It's a matter of conjecture whether the shift in humor is the main reason for the decline in audience. While the third-year approach has plenty of detractors among the fans and followers of *Maverick*, there are also those who clearly enjoy the looser brand of comedy. But it's also hard to ignore the ratings, and the fact remains that *Maverick* began to lose its audience. "That's always the problem with writing comedy — you have to know when not to 'go too far,' or not to be 'too funny,' so that you're straining for a laugh," said Trapnell. "I tried to keep an eye on the ratings, but I wasn't aware that they had slipped that badly during my first year. There may have been some shows where we went too far. If we did, and that turned away the audience, then obviously we made a mistake."

Another trend developed during the third season that actually reversed a pattern established during the first two seasons. When Roy Huggins produced *Maverick*, the audience figures remained remarkably constant regardless of whether the episode featured James Garner or Jack Kelly. In fact, the average audience share for Kelly's shows was slightly higher (less than one percentage point) than Garner's average. But the opposite held true during the third season. The average audience for Garner's episodes was 6% greater than the average audience for Kelly's shows. It's not a huge difference, but it does show that the viewers were beginning to make a choice — they would continue watching *Maverick*, even though the writing was not the same, so long as James Garner was on. This is significant, because when Garner left *Maverick* in 1960 after winning his legal confrontation with Warner Bros., what had remained of the show's audience, for all intents and purposes, left with him.

Garner also knew that something was missing from *Maverick* after Roy Huggins had left, but he never let it affect his approach to his work. "That was what was so beautiful about Jim," observed Huggins. "Jim would never say, 'I won't do that,' even if he thought the writing wasn't as good as it could have been. Even during that third season, when he easily could have said, 'I don't want to do it,' he never did. He never would do that."

Garner did try to coax Huggins back to the show, though. "Jim sent me a picture of himself, dressed in his Maverick costume," Huggins recalled. "He had his eyes crossed, and he wrote at the bottom of the picture, 'When you're worth a million bucks, it doesn't matter how you look.' And then, right below his signature, he added, 'P.S. — Please come back!'"

Familiar faces to look for in the third season include Troy Donahue, Peggy McCay, Buddy Ebsen, Richard Deacon, Patricia Crowley, Joel Grey, Nita Talbot, and Robert Redford.

54. PAPPY

ORIGINAL AIRDATE: SEPTEMBER 13, 1960

Written and Directed by: Montgomery Pittman

Guest Cast: Adam West (Rudolph St. Cloud), Troy Donahue (Dan Jamison), Henry Daniell (Reno St. Cloud), Virginia Gregg (Gida Jamison), Michael Forest (Jean Paul St. Cloud), Kaye Elhardt (Josephine St. Cloud), John Hubbard (Bronze), Chubby Johnson (Miller)

Synopsis. Dan Jamison, a friend of the Mavericks since he was a child, calls upon Bret and Bart when he discovers that their dear old "Pappy," Beauregard Maverick, plans to marry Josephine St. Cloud (pronounced "Sahn Clew"), the 18-year-old daughter of a prestigious Louisiana family. Initially more curious than concerned, the boys become suspicious once the St. Cloud brothers take an instant dislike to Bret during a chance meeting in a Texas saloon. Bart decides to infiltrate the St. Cloud family (by impersonating Dandy Jim Buckley) and soon discovers that Pappy's life is in danger.

"Pappy" features several pearls of wisdom from the old reprobate: "The only time you quit while you're winning is after you've won it all;" "The best time to get lucky is when the other man's dealing;" and "If you're ever served a rare steak that is intended for somebody else, don't bother with ethical details — eat as much as you can before the mistake is discovered." (The last aphorism is delivered by Pappy himself.)

James Garner played Pappy Maverick just once in the original series, but he reprised the role many years later. Garner again donned a gray wig and mustache to pose for the portrait of Pappy featured in *Bret Maverick*.

55. ROYAL FOUR-FLUSH

ORIGINAL AIRDATE: SEPTEMBER 20, 1960

Teleplay by: Bob Barbash
Story by: Gerald Drayson Adams
Directed by: Arthur Lubin

Guest Cast: Roxane Berard (Liz Bancroft), David Frankham (Captain Rory Fitzgerald), Arch Johnson (Placer Jack Mason), Roberta Shore (Judy Mason), Jimmy Baird (David Mason), Raymond Hatton (Harry), Tom Fadden (Silvan), Ray Walker (Hotel Clerk)

Synopsis. In Virginia City, Bart runs into a con artist acquaintance of his named Rory Fitzgerald, who owes him $4,000 but claims to be out of money. Bart becomes suspicious when he recognizes the glamorous "countess" whom Fitzgerald is escorting as Liz Bancroft, a card dealer from New Orleans. He later discovers that Fitzgerald and Bancroft are plotting to swindle wealthy Placer Jack Mason out of $200,000.

As it did with its other hit TV series, Warner Bros. parlayed *Maverick*'s success into a line of merchandise based on the show, including *Poker According to Maverick*, a textbook published by Dell Paperbacks that features numerous references from the TV series. Roy Huggins had a hand in the writing of *Poker According to Maverick*. "Warners, I think, had an old manuscript on poker lying around; it was a property they had somehow acquired over the years," Huggins recalled. "When *Maverick* was at its height of popularity, someone apparently found it and thought it'd sell if it was made into a *Maverick* book. I went over the manuscript and inserted all of the *Maverick* references, but I also found a few inaccuracies about poker which I corrected."

Other *Maverick*-related merchandise included the comic books distributed by Dell Publishing Company; the *Maverick* action figures issued by Hartland Plastics; the *Maverick Hide-a-Way Derringer* issued by Leslie-Henry Company; and the *Maverick Oil Painting-by-Numbers* set produced by Hasbro.

Pappyism: "Stay clear of weddings, because one of them is liable to be your own."

56. THE SHERIFF OF DUCK 'N' SHOOT

ORIGINAL AIRDATE: SEPTEMBER 27, 1959

Written by: William Driskill
Directed by: George Waggner

Guest Cast: Peggy McCay (Melissa "Missy" Maybrook), Chubby Johnson (Billy Waker), Jack Mather (Judge Hardy), Don Barry (Fred Leslie), James Gavin (Buck Danton), Hal Baylor (Bimbo), Irving Bacon (Andrews), Clarke Alexander (Jonah), Billy M. Greene (Herman), Richard Butler (Smitty)

Synopsis. The conniving judge of Duck 'n' Shoot (population 1,018) wants Bret as the town sheriff after apparently witnessing Maverick knock out a rowdy cowboy with only one punch. Bret explains it was all a mistake (the man was actually hit in the face by his horse) but the judge doesn't see it that way — he blackmails Maverick into taking the position by withholding his $5,000 poker winnings for six months. Although Bret proves to be an effective (if not orthodox) sheriff, he tries desperately to get out of the job. When he learns about a plan to rob the bank, Bret decides do it himself — by foiling the scheme and then returning the money, he hopes to bargain his way out of town. But when the plan backfires, Maverick lands in jail.

Bret Maverick may not enforce the law like Matt Dillon (or even Mort Dooley), but he certainly gets results. When Bimbo (the brother of the man knocked out by the horse) challenges Maverick, the new sheriff offers him a deal: "We'll play one hand of poker. If I win, you go to jail for a day. If I lose, you get to wreck the town." Maverick's three nines beat Bimbo's two pairs, so Bimbo had to go to jail. (Bret *did* have to cheat, but he also knew that Bimbo wouldn't catch on.) Then later in the episode, Maverick has to break up a bar fight between Bimbo and another rowdy. Again, he uses his smarts instead of his gun — whenever Bimbo or the other cowboy is knocked down, Maverick bets the other barflies whether he's going to get back up. (Again, he cheated a little — he once poured whiskey on Bimbo in order to revive him — but that beat having to use his gun.) The ploy works: Bimbo and the other man stop fighting once they realize Maverick is making money off them.

Pappyisms: "The worst crime a man can commit is to interrupt a poker game;" "Try everything once. If you don't succeed, then become a lawman;" and "The next best thing to money is a man's name on the dotted line."

57. YOU CAN'T BEAT THE PER-CENTAGE

ORIGINAL AIRDATE: OCTOBER 4, 1959

Written and Directed by: George Waggner

Guest Cast: Gerald Mohr (Dave Wendell), Karen Steele (Myra), Tim Graham (Pop), Dan Riss (Sheriff Bill Satchel), Joe Partridge (Dealer), Michael Harris (Charley), Ray Daley (Brazos)

Synopsis. Bart arrives in the town of Arroyo after receiving a letter from a saloon girl named Myra whom he met long ago in Missouri. Myra tells Bart that she plans to buy the saloon from Dave Wendell and that she needs Bart as a business partner. Maverick soon realizes that Myra plans to implicate him in the murder of her husband, a cowboy who has followed her from their home in Texas, so that she will become free to marry Wendell.

George Waggner enjoyed a diversified film career — he was an actor, screenwriter and songwriter prior to becoming a successful director and producer of horror and action films. His pictures include *The Fighting Kentuckian, Operation Pacific* (both of which he also wrote), *The Phantom of the Opera, The Ghost of Frankenstein* (both of which he also produced) and *The Wolf Man*.

58. THE CATS OF PARADISE

ORIGINAL AIRDATE: OCTOBER 11, 1959

Teleplay by: Wells Root and Ron Bishop
Story by: L.P. Holmes
Directed by: Arthur Lubin

Guest Cast: Mona Freeman (Modesty Blaine), Buddy Ebsen (Scratch Madden), Wendell Holmes (Mayor Uli Bemus), Lance Fuller (Faro Jack), Richard Deacon (Floyd Gimbel), Mervyn Vye (Captain Puget), Robert Griffin (Bartender), Earl Hansen (Mr. Wilkins), Reza Royce (Woman)

Synopsis. Bret goes into business selling cats to a town besieged by rats and mice. Bret doesn't realize that his charming partner, Modesty Blaine, is also a crafty and completely amoral con artist who robs him of $500 and nearly has him shanghaied. Maverick locates Modesty in Paradise, where he finds her conveniently protected by the town's two-faced mayor and its superstitious but equally corrupt sheriff.

When Efrem Zimbalist Jr. (*77 Sunset Strip*), Diane Brewster (*The Islanders*), and Richard Long (*Bourbon Street Beat*) each went on to star in their own series, they were no longer available to appear on *Maverick* as Dandy Jim Buckley, Samantha Crawford, and Gentleman Jack Darby, respectively (although Long did play Darby in the third season's "The Goose-Drowner"). Rather than recast these characters, Coles Trapnell and his writers decided to create new ones, such as Modesty Blaine (Mona Freeman), who appears for the first time in "The Cats of Paradise."

Although Modesty is supposed to be a Samantha-like character, in this episode she comes across more like Dandy Jim — an all-out grafter without any semblance of conscience. But even Buckley had his limits: the worst he'd ever done to Maverick was leaving him tied up at the end of "The Jail at Junction Flats" (and, in truth, he was merely retaliating for what Bret had done to him). The Modesty Blaine character, on the other hand, had absolutely no sense of restraint — at least, in the beginning. In "The Cats of Paradise," she thinks nothing of shanghaiing Maverick, or hiring gunman Faro Jack to kill him. What's worse is that Maverick doesn't seem to mind what she did to him, because at the end of the episode, we're left with the impression that Bret and Modesty will again go into business with each other.

Maverick's audience dropped nearly five percent the week after "The Cats of Paradise" aired, so apparently some of the viewers did mind. To his credit, producer

Coles Trapnell took heed. "Wells Root and Ron Bishop were good writers, but sometimes they got a little crazy," said Trapnell. "Sometimes they figured, with *Maverick*, the wilder the situation, the better. Occasionally, they had to be 'sat on.' They may have gone too far with the Mona Freeman character, because the next time we put her in a story [in 'The Cruise of the Cynthia B'], Bob Wright had cleaned her up — she became more subdued, and more of a lady."

Pappyisms: "A man who sticks his head in the sand makes an awfully good target;" "A fox isn't sly; he just can't think any slower;" and "You can be a gentleman and still not forget everything you know about self-defense."

59. A TALE OF THREE CITIES

ORIGINAL AIRDATE: OCTOBER 18, 1959

Teleplay by: Leo Townsend
Story by: Robert Wright
Directed by: Leslie H. Martinson

Guest Cast: Patricia Crowley (Stephanie Malone), Ben Gage (Sheriff Hardy), Edward Kemmer (Sherwood Hampton), Barbara Jo Allen (Mrs. Hannah Adams), Ray Teal (Sheriff Murray), Frank Richards (Sam), Leake Bevil (Pete), Louis Jean Heydt (Jim Malone)

Synopsis. A desperate young woman named Stephanie Malone robs Bart of the $800 he won playing poker. After tracking Stephanie down, Bart discovers why she stole his money. She needed it to repay the $1,500 her father owes to Sherwood Hampton, a card cheat who runs a gambling hall in a nearby town. After Stephanie promises to reimburse him, Bart tries to win back the money from Hampton.

Patricia Crowley and Barbara Jo Allen previously co-starred in the second season's "The Rivals." Crowley, no relation to frequent *Maverick* guest star (and then-Warners contract player) Kathleen Crowley, starred in the TV version of *Please Don't Eat the Daisies* in 1965, many years later, she co-starred with James Garner in the "Guilt" episode of *The Rockford Files.*

60. FULL HOUSE

ORIGINAL AIRDATE: OCTOBER 25, 1959

Teleplay by: Jerry Davis
Story by: Hugh Benson and Coles Trapnell
Directed by Robert Gordon

Guest Cast: Jean Willes (Belle Starr), Robert Lowery (Foxy Smith), Gordon Jones (Marshall), Gregory Walcott (Cole Younger), Joel Grey (Billy the Kid), Tim Graham (Willie Thimble), Kelly Thordsen (Sam Bass), Nancy Kulp (Waitress)

Synopsis. In Denver, Bret wins $2,000 playing cards with a man who is temporarily short of cash. Maverick wants the man's fancy tie pin as collateral, but the man is reluctant to give up what he calls his "good luck charm." After a struggle, Bret walks away with the tie pin, while the man is arrested. Later, in the nearby town of Bubbly Springs, Maverick discovers that the man with the tie pin is a renowned criminal operative named Foxy Smith, who has arranged to meet Cole Younger, Billy the Kid, Willie Thimble, Sam Bass, Black Bart, Ben Thompson, Jesse James, and Belle Starr to plan a big job. None of the outlaws have ever seen Smith — they only know him by his trademark tie pin. When Maverick arrives in town, they mistake him for Foxy Smith.

Look for Nancy Kulp in a small role as the waitress whose tears lead Maverick into a trap. Kulp was a few years away from her best-known TV role, that of Miss Jane Hathaway on *The Beverly Hillbillies*. Kulp died in 1991.

Executive producer William T. Orr first came up with the premise for this episode, which also features future Academy Award winner Joel Grey (*Cabaret*) as Billy the Kid.

61. THE LASS WITH THE POISONOUS AIR

ORIGINAL AIRDATE: NOVEMBER 1, 1959

Teleplay by: Catherine Turney
Story by: Roy Huggins
Directed by: Richard L. Bare

Guest Cast: Joanna Moore (Linda Burke), Howard Petrie (Mike Burke), John Reach (Phil Dana), Carole Wells (Cathy), Stacey Keach (Deevers), Francis J. McDonald (Pop Talmadge)

Synopsis. While riding a mare he won in a poker game in Denver, Bart meets — and immediately becomes attracted to — Linda Burke, a woman of great beauty, few words, and many secrets. Bart doesn't realize that Linda's husband is a mining tycoon with gubernatorial aspirations. Bart secretly meets Linda every day at a secluded spot in a nearby meadow, much to the suspicion of Phil Dana, the son of Burke's former partner — and Linda's secret lover. Bart and Phil soon become rivals in cards and in love. When Phil is found shot to death, Bart becomes the prime suspect. But the real killer is Linda.

This episode is a good example of how Warner Bros. recycled scripts from one series for use on another. "The Lass with the Poisonous Air" was originally filmed as a segment of *77 Sunset Strip* entitled "Lovely Lady, Pity Me." In both cases, the script was derived from a short story, also called "Lovely Lady, Pity Me," written by *Maverick*'s creator, Roy Huggins.

Although Huggins was given story credit for this episode (and, later, "Guatemala City") he did not, in fact, write any stories for *Maverick* after leaving the series at the end of the second season. The credits for the third-year episodes bearing his name were based upon stories he had previously written for other Warners series, and which then were adapted for *Maverick*. "I knew that Warners had been taking old scripts, including some of mine, and reshooting them for use on their other TV shows," said Huggins. "But I wasn't aware that they were giving me credit for any of the remakes."

62. THE GHOST SOLDIERS

ORIGINAL AIRDATE: NOVEMBER 8, 1959

Written by: Robert L. Jacks and Richard Carr
Directed by: Leslie H. Martinson

Guest Cast: James Westerfield (Sergeant Baines), Paul Clarke (Running Horse), Stuart Randall (Red Wing), Ted Otis (Corporal Daggett), Chuck Wassil (Lieutenant Jennings)

Synopsis. The discovery of gold in the Black Hills of the Dakotas brought on a stampede of prospectors — much to the resentment of the Sioux Indians, who retaliated by killing those who invaded their land. The U.S. Army responded by sending regiments into the Dakota Territories to protect the settlers. Bret finds himself in one such location awaiting an Army inquiry (he was caught fooling around with a colonel's wife) when the Sioux attack the fort. Only Bret, a veteran sergeant and a young corporal survive the massacre. In order to buy time while waiting for reinforcements, Maverick and the others, knowing that the superstitious Indians are scared of evil spirits, pretend to be ghosts. But when Running Horse, the Sioux leader, calls their bluff and murders the corporal, Maverick must impersonate the dead soldier in order to prove that the fort is "haunted."

63. EASY MARK

ORIGINAL AIRDATE: NOVEMBER 15, 1959

Teleplay by: Jerry Davis and Marion Parsonnet
Story by: Jack Emanuel
Directed by: Lew Landers

Guest Cast: Edgar Buchanan (Colonel Hamilton), Nita Talbot (Jeannie), Pippa Scott (Abigail), Wynn Pearce (Cornelius Van Rensselaer Jr.), Hanley Stafford (Van Rensselaer Sr.), Douglas Kennedy (McFearson), Frank Ferguson (Conductor), Carl Milletaire (Hakime), Jack Buetel (Phillips), John Zaccaro (Engineer), Ivan Browning (Porter)

Synopsis. Outside the desert of Santa Fe, Bart encounters Cornelius Van Rensselaer Jr., a Harvard graduate and the son of a railroad magnate. Corny takes Bart for over $1,000 in poker but offers him double his money back if Bart agrees to impersonate him for a few days. Corny is travelling to his father's company in St. Louis for an important shareholders meeting (his father faces the danger of being bought out by a rival named Hardiman), but he also needs to complete a paper on cacti he must deliver to a horticultural society. Maverick takes the job — and immediately finds himself the target of henchmen dispatched by Hardiman to derail Corny.

Hanley Stafford, who plays the senior Van Rensselaer in "Easy Mark," is best known as Daddy Snooks in the classic radio series *Baby Snooks* starring legendary singer-comedienne Fanny Brice.

Pappyism: "Love and love alone will send a man soaring into the depths."

64. A FELLOW'S BROTHER

(a.k.a. "The Code")

ORIGINAL AIRDATE: NOVEMBER 22, 1959

Written by: Herman Epstein
Directed by: Leslie Goodwins

Guest Cast: Diane McBain (Polly), Gary Vinson (Smoky Vaughn), Sam Buffington (Burgess), Bing Russell (Sheriff), Wally Brown (Enoch), Adam West (Arnett), Jonathan Hole (Marvin Dilbey), Emory Parnell (Bill Anders), Charles Maxwell (Russ Ankerman)

Synopsis. Needing a stake to get into a big poker game in Abilene, Bret decides to collect on some old gambling debts. One of the persons he visits is Ellsworth Haynes, a Wells Fargo agent in Red Rock Junction. Things become complicated when Haynes is murdered and the bank is robbed of $50,000. Because Haynes was last seen speaking to a man named "Maverick," Bret becomes wanted for murder and robbery.

Adam West, a few years away from becoming TV's *Batman*, has a small role in "A Fellow's Brother;" he had previously appeared in "Two Tickets to Ten Strike" and "Pappy." The episode also features this bit of advice from Pappy Maverick: "It's not how fast you draw that counts; it's what you draw and when you draw."

65. TROOPER MAVERICK

ORIGINAL AIRDATE: NOVEMBER 29, 1959

Written by: William Driskill
Directed by: Richard L. Bare

Guest Cast: Suzanne Lloyd (Catherine), Joel Sawyer (Sergeant Shumacher), Herbert Rudley (Colonel Percy), Charles Cooper (Captain Berger), Myron Healey (Benedict), Mark Tapscott (Sergeant Rogers), Sammy Jackson (Albert Heaven), I. Stanford Jolley (Dakota Cadman), Tom Middleton (O'Dell), Tony Young (Okando)

Synopsis. Whenever he's in the Dakota Territories, Bart drops in on the Army fort run by his friend, Colonel Sam Percy, so that he can check out the poker action between the soldiers and the local settlers. Maverick becomes suspicious when Sam, normally one of the card players, arrests him for gambling and sentences him to 180 days service. Behind closed doors, Sam explains why — a war with the Sioux Indians is imminent, and one of his soldiers has been funneling weapons to the other side. Sam needs Bart to uncover the spy and stop the smuggling.

"At the time of *Maverick*, Jack Kelly was a better actor than Jim Garner," said director Richard Bare. "Jack could do Shakespeare, and he could play mean, grisly heavies — you could run the gamut with Jack, because he was a trained actor.

"But Jim got all the fame, all the money, and all the career because he had one thing Kelly didn't have. Jim had the ingredients that all the great stars have — the Gary Coopers and the Clark Gables. They were personalities, *and you liked them* regardless of their acting ability.

"Jim also had a real ease about him — it was all built into that wry quality he conveys onscreen. And that's why *Maverick* really worked. It was a great, great wedding between two talents — Roy Huggins' writing, and Jim's interpretation."

66. MAVERICK SPRINGS

ORIGINAL AIRDATE: DECEMBER 6, 1959

Written by: Leo Townsend
Directed by: Arthur Lubin

Guest Cast: Kathleen Crowley (Melanie Blake), King Donovan (Mark Dawson), Tol Avery (John Flannery), Doris Packer (Kate Dawson), Sig Ruman (Professor Kronkhite), Leslie Barrett (Mr. Mason), Charles Arndt (Charley Peters), William Bakewell (Desk Clerk), Jim Hayward (Bartender)

Synopsis. After bailing Bret out of jail (he was arrested for playing poker with the mayor — and winning), Texas rancher Kate Dawson sends Maverick after her brother Mark, a lightweight gambler who is squandering away his fortune in Saratoga. Maverick finds Mark moments after he loses his share of the Queen's Ranch, the family spread, to a card cheat named Flannery. With the aid of Bart and an old card shark named Kronkhite, Bret reels Flannery into a bogus investment deal involving a luxurious resort built on worthless swamp land. The con works perfectly — until Kate shows up and inadvertently blows their cover.

In "Trail West to Fury," we discovered that the Mavericks cannot return to their native Texas until they were cleared of the murder of Jesse Hayden. Apparently, that matter was quietly resolved, because Bret's in Texas at the beginning of "Maverick Springs" (and in no apparent danger).

Pappyisms: "If you're gonna drop names, drop 'em hard;" and "If at first you don't succeed, try something else."

67. THE GOOSE-DROWNDER

ORIGINAL AIRDATE: DECEMBER 13, 1959

Written by: Leonard Praskins
Directed by: Arthur Lubin

Guest Cast: Richard Long (Gentleman Jack Darby), Fay Spain (Stella Legendre), Will Wright (Boone Gillis), H.M. Wynant (Rance), Robert Nichols (Red Herring), Clarke Alexander (Hurley), Billy M. Greene (Latimer)

Synopsis. Bart and Gentleman Jack Darby are stranded in the ghost town of Silverado, Nevada, where they spend the night with the town's lone resident, Boone Gillis. They are later joined by a hold-up gang that just robbed the stagecoach of its payroll. Among the passengers: a wounded gunslinger named Rance and his girlfriend Stella Legendre, a dance hall girl whom Maverick met six months ago in Abilene.

"The Goose-Drownder" is one of the best episodes of the third season. "There was little or no comedy in that show," said Coles Trapnell. "I remember that Maverick had to extract a bullet from the man who was shot, because somebody noticed that he had steady hands. That scene where he performs the 'operation' was pure melodrama, and it worked."

It certainly did. Jack Kelly's range as a dramatic performer is showcased in this episode. In addition to exhibiting cool under pressure during the "surgery" sequence, Kelly as Maverick displays a rare show of anger when Darby brazenly questions Bart's love for Stella.

In his teleplay, writer Leonard Praskins suggested that Trapnell use no music, but rather sound effects — such as that of rain, lighting and thunder — to establish the mood of the story and punctuate the dramatic scenes. "I admit fully this is a corny device I have merely borrowed from another hack writer who used this technique frequently — fellow by the name of Shakespeare," Praskins explained in 1959.

Pappyism: "He who lives by the gun, dies by the neck."

68. A CURE FOR JOHNNY RAIN

ORIGINAL AIRDATE: DECEMBER 20, 1959

Written by: Leonard Praskins
Directed by: Montgomery Pittman

Guest Cast: William Reynolds (Johnny Rain), Dolores Donlon (Millie Reid), John Vivyan (Tinhorn), Thomas B. Henry (Mayor Pembroke H. Hadley), Kenneth MacDonald (Sheriff), Bud Osbourne (Stagecoach Driver)

Synopsis. Johnny Rain is a hero to the townspeople of Apocalypse — the type of man who saves children from runaway horses, mends broken legs, and rides 30 miles through a blizzard to get a doctor for an ailing old woman. He's also responsible for a series of stagecoach robberies totalling $45,000 (including $5,000 from Bret). But Johnny's a heavy drinker who suffers blackouts — he only robs while he's drunk and has no recollection of what he's done once he sobers up. Hoping to recover the stolen money (and collect a 25% reward for himself), Maverick prescribes a "cure-all" tonic — 80% of which is alcohol! — so that Johnny can lead him to the money.

William Reynolds, who made his film debut as Laurence Olivier's son in *Sister Carrie*, had previously starred as a jazz concert player who doubled as an amateur detective in *Pete Kelly's Blues*, a 1959 series produced by Jack Webb (and based on Webb's 1955 film of the same name). Reynolds co-starred in series with two *Maverick* alumnae: he played opposite Diane Brewster in *The Islanders*, then later joined Efrem Zimbalist Jr. on *The F.B.I.*

Pappyism: "Gentlemen don't haggle over money."

69. THE MARQUESA

ORIGINAL AIRDATE: JANUARY 3, 1960

Teleplay by: Leonard Praskins
Story by: James Gunn
Directed by: Arthur Lubin

Guest Cast: Adele Mara (Luisa), Edward Ashley (Nobby Ned Wyngate), Jay Novello (Pepe), Maurice Ankrum (Judge Mason Painter), Carlos Romero (Manuel Ortiz), Belle Mitchell (Bufemia), Rodolfo Hoyos (Miguel Ruiz), Raymond Hatton (Charley Plank), Lane Chandler (Sheriff)

Synopsis. Bart wins the rights to the Lucky Lady cantina located in New Mexico territory, but he finds that his new property has been shut down — it was built on land owned by a wealthy family of Portuguese descent, and the apparent heir to the Marquesa has arrived to reclaim her land. Maverick suspects a charade — the Marquesa doubts her heritage (she claims she's merely a saloon girl named Lily Nightingale), while her associates display a murderous underside.

"The Marquesa" marks the last of Adele Mara's three appearances on *Maverick*, and the first of two shows featuring Edward Ashley as the Buckley-like character Nobby Ned Wyngate.

70. THE CRUISE OF THE CYNTHIA B

ORIGINAL AIRDATE: JANUARY 10, 1960

Written by: Robert Wright
Directed by: Andre deToth

Guest Cast: Mona Freeman (Modesty Blaine), Carl Webber (Quincy Smith), Maurice Manson (Rutherford Carr), Irene Tedrow (Mrs. Tutwiller), Gage Clarke (Montgomery Teague), Jack Livesey (Gillespie Mackenzie), Charles Fredericks (Jefferson Cantrell), Alexander Campbell (Abner Morton), Fred Kruger (Meacham)

Synopsis. Bret rescues Gillespie McKenzie, a charming Scottish salesman whom he finds hanging upside down from a tree. A grateful McKenzie sells Bret an old schooner called *The Cynthia B* at the bargain price of $1,000. Maverick soon discovers that McKenzie is a slippery forger who has pocketed over $8,000 by "selling" the boat to six other people (one of whom is his old adversary Modesty Blaine, who nearly had him shanghaied in "The Cats of Paradise"). When Bret and the other owners discover that *The Cynthia B* is worth $20,000 to its original designer, Abner Norton of Memphis, they decide to sail the boat to Memphis and split the money. *The Cynthia B* has long been known as "the death ship" because each of its first six owners died on board under mysterious circumstances. Although Maverick initially dismisses that as an old wives' tale, he becomes concerned when the new owners are murdered, one by one.

Like "Black Fire," "The Cruise of the Cynthia B" is a mystery in the genre of Agatha Christie's *And Then There Were None*. The story is fine, but what really makes this episode stand out is the difference in approach to Modesty Blaine, whose character was literally revolting when she first appeared in "The Cats of Paradise."

Maverick's attitude toward Modesty during the first half of "The Cruise of the Cynthia B" is cautious, and a little hostile (one of the first things he says to Modesty is "Oh, are you out on parole?"). Over the course of the story, however, it becomes clear that Modesty's character has been toned down considerably, and once Maverick realizes this, he backs off on his verbal attacks. This time, when Maverick becomes attracted to her (as he does by the end of the story), the thought isn't quite as repulsive as it would have been before. Credit goes to *Maverick* producer Coles Trapnell for recognizing an element that the audience clearly had found offensive, and doing something about it. (*Maverick* suffered a significant drop in audience the week after the character appeared in "The Cats of Paradise.")

"Bob Wright was one of my best *Maverick* writers," said Coles Trapnell. "He had a real feel for the show. The first thing he wrote for me was an outline for what became 'A Tale of Three Cities.' I then explained to Bob that he'd get paid a lot more if he could follow through on his outline with a screenplay. He did just that on the second one he wrote, 'The Cruise of the Cynthia B.' He sent me an outline, which I okayed, and then he wrote the screenplay, which was excellent."

At the time, Trapnell and Wright worked via long distance — Wright was still working as a technical writer for Boeing Airlines in Seattle, Washington. Wright also incorporated the Modesty Blaine character in "One of Our Trains is Missing," which he wrote for *Maverick*'s fifth season.

Pappyism' "A man does what he has to do — if he can't get out of it."

71. MAVERICK AND JULIET

ORIGINAL AIRDATE: JANUARY 17, 1960

Written by: Herman Epstein
Directed by: Arthur Lubin

Guest Cast: Carole Wells (Juliet Carteret), Steve Terrell (Sonny Montgomery), Rhys Williams (Mr. Montgomery), Marjorie Bennett (Mrs. Montgomery), Jack Mather (Mr. Carteret), Sarah Selby (Mrs. Carteret), Michael Garrett (Ty Carteret), Lew Brown (Jeb Carteret), John Zaccaro (Nat Carterat), Walter Coy (Preacher), Johnnie Collier (Jody Montgomery)

Synopsis. Juliet Carteret and Sonny Montgomery love each other, despite the bitter feud between their families. After helping the young couple when their wagon breaks down, Bret becomes involved in the dispute when the Carteret family mistakes him for a Montgomery. When Maverick discovers that the feud stems from a poker game (the Carterets claim they won land from the Montgomerys, while the Montgomerys claim they lost because of a bad deck of cards), he convinces the families to play another game to settle the matter once and for all. Bret assures the Carterets that he'll win. But the Montgomerys come up with a ringer of their own: Bart.

Coles Trapnell followed at least one tradition started by Roy Huggins — borrowing ideas for *Maverick* stories from classic works of literature. "The Marquesa" was based on *Anastasia*, Marcelle Maurette's play about an amnesiac who impersonates the daughter of a Russian czar. Trapnell then lifted "Maverick and Juliet" from an episode of Mark Twain's *Huckleberry Finn* in which Huck found himself embroiled in a feud between two families. "I figured if Twain could steal from Shakespeare, then I could steal from Twain," reasoned Trapnell.

Bret freely admits that there are only two people who can give him a run at playing cards; one is Pappy and the other is Bart. That's why he's legitimately concerned when he discovers that Bart is the other ringer. Bret's reaction to the news is priceless — James Garner says it all with just a look. "Garner had absolutely the greatest takes of anyone I've ever seen in this business," adds Trapnell.

Pappyisms: "If all the men who lived by the gun were laid end to end, I wouldn't be standing here;" and "There's only one thing more important than money, and that's more money."

72. THE WHITE WIDOW

ORIGINAL AIRDATE: JANUARY 24, 1960

Teleplay by: Leo Townsend
Story by: Coles Trapnell
Directed by: Leslie Goodwins

Guest Cast: Julie Adams (Wilma White), Richard Webb (George Manton), Russ Elliott (Mayor Cosgrove), Don Kennedy (Sheriff Jim Vaughan), Pilar Seurat (Pilar), C. Alvin Bell (Joel Barnes), Charles S. Buck (Depot Agent), Leo Turnbull (Bartender), Jack Bryan (John Brinks)

Synopsis. Bart wins $5,000 playing poker in Fairview and stores the money in a hotel safe. The next day, he discovers that the money has been stolen, and the hotel clerk killed. Needing money, he applies for a loan at the bank, where he discovers that the bank president, a widow named Wilma White, is being threatened. Wilma hires Maverick to protect her.

Pappyism: "So long as you stay away from women and temptation, you're no son of mine."

73. GUATEMALA CITY

ORIGINAL AIRDATE: JANUARY 31, 1960

Teleplay by: Leonard Praskins
Story by: Roy Huggins and Coles Trapnell
Directed by: Arthur Lubin

Guest Cast: Suzanne Storrs (Ellen Johnson), Patric Knowles (Sam Bishop), Linda Dangcil (Angelita), Tudor Owen (Sim), Charles Watts (Spelvin), John Holland (Tall Man), Robert Carson (Clerk), Nacho Galindo (Spanish Driver), Henry Hunter (American Consul), Mousie Garner (Newsboy)

Synopsis. In San Francisco, Bret's girlfriend Ellen, a mysterious woman who is always calling him "Bert," suddenly disappears. When Bret reads about a $250,000 jewel heist pulled off by a man named Adelbert Sawyer, he deduces that the thief is Ellen's "Bert" and that the two of them have run off together with the jewels. Maverick decides to go after Ellen and Bert, and collect the $25,000 reward for their capture.

Bret admits that he's not sure whether he's gone after Ellen because of the reward money or because he still loves her: "When it's a question of love or money, I sometimes get confused."

According to this episode, Maverick experienced four bouts of seasickness during his three-week trip to Guatemala; however, he'd made "The Cruise of The Cynthia B" without suffering any kind of setbacks.

Pappyism: "A penny earned isn't worth much anymore."

74. THE PEOPLE'S FRIEND

ORIGINAL AIRDATE: FEBRUARY 7, 1960

Written by: Robert Wright
Directed by: Leslie Goodwins

Guest Cast: Merry Anders (Penelope Greeley), R.G. Armstrong (Wellington Cosgrove), Walter Sande (Sheriff Burke), John Litel (Ellsworth Greeley), Francis deSales (Mayor Culpepper), John Zaremba (Gantry), Donald Kirke (Clayton), Allan Nixon (Cosgrove Crony #1), Dick Wilson (Crenshaw), Ruth Terry (Librarian), Dorothea Lord (Mrs. McCoy), Rex Lease (Poker Player #2)

Synopsis. Bart arrives in Silverdale as the town prepares to elect a new State senator. The candidates: reformist Ellsworth Greeley, and underhanded Wellington Cosgrove, who tries to have his opponent assassinated. Maverick deflects the gunman's bullet but when the shooting incapacitates Greeley, the Reform Party convinces Bart to run in his place. Cosgrove, disguised by a hooded mask, kidnaps Bart and threatens to kill him if he wins the election. On the day of decision, the votes are tied, and Maverick must cast the final ballot.

When it becomes apparent that Greeley's staff wants Bart to run for the Senate against Cosgrove, Maverick declines, saying "I do not choose to run." Penelope (Greeley's daughter), sniffs "That line will not go down in history," but it did, of course: President Calvin Coolidge said it in 1927 when he decided not to run for re-election in 1928.

"The People's Friend" features another well-remembered Maverickism. After Cosgrove and his goons threaten to kill him if he wins the election, Bart decides to drop out of the race. "Are you going to let a little thing like that stand in the way of your civic duty?" asks Penelope. "That little thing you're talking about is my life," responds Bart. "It may be little to you but it's mighty big to me."

Jack Kelly, of course, entered politics in real life. Running on the campaign slogan "Let Maverick Solve Your Problems," Kelly was elected to the Huntington Beach city council, where he served from 1980-88, and again from 1990 until his death in 1992.

75. A FLOCK OF TROUBLE

ORIGINAL AIRDATE: FEBRUARY 14, 1960

Teleplay by: Ron Bishop and Wells Root
Story by: Jim Barnett
Directed by: Arthur Lubin

Guest Cast: Myrna Fahey (Dee Cooper), George Wallace (Verne Scott), Tim Graham (Jensen), Armand Alzamora (Basco), Don Rhodes (Cain), Chet Stratton (Mr. Crabill), Irving Bacon (Honest Donald McFadden), Merritt Boan (Big Coley)

Synopsis. Bret catches a quick game with a rancher named Big Coley, a big man with a big reputation: nobody gets the best of him. Maverick learns this the hard way when Coley sells him three hundred head — of sheep. Bret soon discovers that he's inherited a land mine — there's a war between cattlemen and sheepherders. Compounding the matter: after the double-crossing Coley wires the cattlemen with details of the sale, Maverick finds himself the object of a $2,000 bounty.

Wells Root, whose career as a motion picture writer dated back to the twenties (he wrote the screenplay for *The Prisoner of Zenda*), loved Westerns but did not have many opportunities to write them until he turned to television in the 1950s. Root had toured the West many times, and had kept a notebook of stories that he began to use when he started writing Westerns for Warner Bros. and Four Star Productions.

Root enjoyed writing for *Maverick*, and for James Garner. "Garner was a joy to write for on *Maverick* because you knew what he would do with it; he took a joke and gave it extra life and vigor," Root told Tom Stempel in *Storytellers to the Nation: A History of American Television Writing* (Continuum Publishing Company, 1991). Root died in 1992.

At the time of this episode, Jim Barnett served as Executive Story Editor on all Warner Bros. TV programs.

According to Bret, when his brother Bart was born, **Pappy** Maverick looked down at his cradle and said, "Sometimes lightning strikes twice at the same place."

76. THE IRON HAND

ORIGINAL AIRDATE: FEBRUARY 21, 1960

Written by: Gerald Drayson Adams
Directed by: Leslie Goodwins

Guest Cast: Susan Morrow (Connie Coleman), Edward Ashley (Nobby Ned Wyngate), Anthony Caruso (Joe Vermillion), Antony Eustrel (Major Innescourt), Joan Elan (Ursula Innescourt), Robert Redford (Jimmy Coleman), Lane Bradford (Red), John Zaccaro (Slim), Lane Chandler (Marshal Richter), Terry Frost (Purdy)

Synopsis. In need of money after Nobby Ned Wingate cleans them out at poker, Bart and some cowboys convince Connie Coleman to hire them to help on a cattle drive to Abilene. Maverick recognizes Connie's foreman, a Cheyenne half-breed named Joe

Vermillion, but he can't quite place where. Bart negotiates with the Indians to pass through their land without charge, only to discover that Connie has sold the herd to a con artist named Innescourt, who pays her with counterfeit money, then resells it for a quick profit. Maverick suspects that Vermillion, whose heavy gloves conceal a murderous iron hand, is behind the operation.

Robert Redford became a major motion picture star whose films include *The Candidate, The Sting, The Way We Were, The Electric Horseman, Brubaker, All the President's Men, Three Days of the Condor, Out of Africa, Legal Eagles* and *Indecent Proposal.* His breakthrough film was 1969's *Butch Cassidy and the Sundance Kid* (written by William Goldman, who also wrote the screenplay for the 1994 *Maverick* movie). Redford won the Oscar for Best Director for *Ordinary People*, which was also named Best Picture of 1980.

77. THE RESURRECTION OF JOE NOVEMBER

ORIGINAL AIRDATE: FEBRUARY 28, 1960

Written by: Leonard Praskins
Directed by: Leslie Goodwins

Guest Cast: Nita Talbot (Bessie Bison), Joanna Barnes (Felice deLassignac), Charles Maxwell (Baron Thor von Und Zu Himmelstern), Donald Barry (Willie Saffron), Roxane Berard (Veronique deLassignac), Kelly Thordsen (Chief of Police), Harry Cheshire (Brother Ambrose), Bill Walker (Attendant), Forrest Lewis (Captain Nelson)

Synopsis. While sailing to New Orleans for the Mardi Gras, Bret runs into a woman claiming to be his childhood friend Felice deLassignac. Felice cons Maverick into playing blackjack and he immediately loses $5,000. Felice and her husband, an unscrupulous German baron, offer to pay Bret $10,000 to transport the remains of the Lassignacs' late majordomo, Joe November, from New Orleans to Europe. Maverick becomes suspicious when he meets the real Felice at the Lassignac estate and discovers that the casket contains millions in stolen jewelry.

Usually the right title is the very last thing to come to a writer. But not always. "Leonard Praskins went up to me one day and told me he wanted to write a *Maverick* called 'The Resurrection of Joe November,'" recalled Coles Trapnell. "I said, 'Fine. What's it about?' Leonard said, 'I have no idea — but isn't that a great title?' So we worked out a story for that show."

Maverick displays excellent fencing skills in this episode; he handles himself splendidly when the Baron challenges him to a sword fight. Apparently it runs in the family: according to *Young Maverick* (the episode "Big Deal in Deadwood"), Ben Maverick was the top man on Harvard University's fencing team.

78. THE MISFORTUNE TELLER

ORIGINAL AIRDATE: MARCH 6, 1960

Written by: Leo Townsend
Directed by: Arthur Lubin

Guest Cast: Kathleen Crowley (Melanie Blake), Alan Mowbray (Luke Abigor), Ben Gage (Sheriff Lem Watson), Emory Parnell (Fred Grady), Mickey Simpson (Charlie Turple), William Challee (Bartender), Chubby Johnson (Jailer)

Synopsis. Somebody using the name "Bret Maverick" swindled the citizens of Medicine Bow, Wyoming out of $15,000 in a phony land development scheme. The mayor of Medicine Bow travelled to the nearby town of Kyle to meet with "Maverick," but he was killed for his troubles. When the real Bret Maverick rides into Medicine Bow, he finds himself arrested in connection with the mayor's murder. Fortunately for Bret, Melanie Blake, his old acquaintance from New Orleans (the episode "Maverick Springs"), arrives in town and breaks him out of jail. Together they travel to Kyle to find out who has been impersonating Bret — and why.

Ben Gage, whose *glutenous maximus* was immortalized in "Gun-Shy," stars as another "Matt Dillon-type" in "The Misfortune Teller." Because Gage again plays a slow-taking, by-the-book lawman, this episode is occasionally mistaken as another deliberate parody of *Gunsmoke*. Adding further confusion is the fact that Gage basically repeated his "Gun-Shy" characterization in all four of his *Maverick* episodes (he was also in "A Tale of Three Cities" and "A Technical Error").

According to this episode, Bret's birthday is May 11 (although it'd been established as April 7 in "The Day They Hanged Bret Maverick"). Melanie Blake's birthday is January 8.

79. GREENBACKS, UNLIMITED

ORIGINAL AIRDATE: MARCH 13, 1960

Written by: Leo Townsend
Directed by: Arthur Lubin

Guest Cast: John Dehner (Big Ed Murphy), Gage Clarke (Foursquare Farley), Wendell Holmes (Colonel Dutton), Roy Engel (Marshal Ratcliffe), Jonathan Hole (Main Secretary), Robert Nichols (Driscoll), Patrick Westwood (London Latimer), Ray Walker (Bartender), John Holland (Tamblyn), Sammy Jackson (Junior Kallikak), Forrest Taylor (Propietor)

Synopsis. Colonel Dutton, president of the Denver State Bank, learns that a notorious safecracker is in town, but neither he nor the marshal knows what the man looks like. Because the bandit reportedly likes to play cards, Dutton hires Bret to locate him. Meanwhile, Maverick bumps into his old friend Foursquare Farley, a former bricklayer who has now become a very successful blackjack dealer. Foursquare tells Bret that he has a backer with unlimited funds — what he doesn't tell Maverick is that he lives behind the Denver Bank and has a door that leads him inside the bank vault. (Foursquare always repays whatever he "borrows.") When Maverick discovers that the safecracker — Big Ed Murphy — is about to hit the bank, he and Foursquare remove the money from the vault.

"Greenbacks, Unlimited" was the tenth *Maverick* directed by Arthur Lubin, who had established himself as a "comedy" director with the likes of the *Francis the Talking Mule* films. Lubin, who was under contract to Warner Bros. at the time, later developed the *Francis* movies for television as *Mister Ed*, which debuted as a syndicated series on Sunday nights in 1961. An immediate hit, *Mister Ed*, ironically enough, ran directly opposite *Maverick*, so Lubin had a hand in eventually pushing *Maverick* off the air.

The Hollywood Reporter lauded "Greenbacks, Unlimited" as "the funniest show of the year."

JAMES GARNER AND ED BRUCE IN (BRET MAVERICK)

ROGER MOORE, WHO PLAYED BEAU MAVERICK, AND WITH KATHLEENCROWLEY(BELOW LEFT)

FOURTH SEASON: 1960-1961
PRODUCTION CREDITS

Starring Jack Kelly as Bart Maverick
Roger Moore as Beau Maverick
and Robert Colbert as Brent Maverick

Executive Producer: William T. Orr
Produced by: Coles Trapnell, Arthur W. Silver, Howie Horwitz
Created by: Roy Huggins

Directors of Photography: Ralph Woolsey, Bert Glennon, Jack Marquette, Carl Berger, Walter Castle, Glen MacWilliams, Ray Fernstrom,) Willard van der Veer, Louis Jennings, Wesley Anderson, Perry Finnerman, Floyd Crosby, Edwin duPar, Ellis Carter, Harold Stine
Art Directors: William Campbell, John Ewing

Supervising Film Editor: James Moore
Film Editors: Cliff Bell, Fred M. Bohanon, John Hall, James W. Graham, Milt Kleinberg, Lloyd Nosler, Robert Crawford, Robert L. Wolfe, Victor C. Lewis Jr., Harry Reynolds, David Wages, James W. Graham, Clarence Kolster,John M. Haffen, Holbrook N. Todd, Norman Suffern, Stefan Arnsten, Leo Shreve, Robert Jahns, William W. Moore
Sound Mixers: Stanley Jones, Lincoln Lyons, Samuel F. Goode, Francis E. Stahl, Donald McKay, Tom R. Ashton, Ross Owen, Robert B. Lee, Charles Althouse, B.F. Ryan, M.A. Merrick, John K. Kean, Frank M. MacWhorter, Theodore B. Hoffman, Bill Crewe
Music Supervision: Paul Sawtell, Bert Shefter
Music Editors: Sam E. Levin, Erma E. Levin, Theodore W. Sebern, Joe Inge, John Allyn Jr., Jack B. Wadsworth, Donald K. Harris, George E. Marsh, Norman Bennett, Robert Phillips, Louis W. Gordon, Charles Paley, Norman Bennett
Song "Maverick": Music by David Buttolph, **Lyrics by** Paul Francis Webster

Production Manager: Oren W. Haglund
Set Decorators: Jerry Welch, Glenn P. Thompson, Ralph S. Hurst, Patrick C. Delaney, Gene Redd, Hal Overell, Fay Babcock
Assistant Directors: D. Jack Stubbes, Fred Scheld, B.F. McEveety, Victor Vallejo, Richard Maybery, Gene Anderson Sr., Sam Schneider, Claude Binyon Jr., Phil Rollins, Dick L'Estrange, James T. Vaughn, D. Jack Stubbs, John F. Murphy, Rex Bailey
Makeup Supervisor: Gordon Bau
Supervising Hair Stylist: Jean Burt Reilly
Announcer: Ed Reimers

The next pivotal chapter in the history of *Maverick* is closely linked to a major turning point in the history of Warner Bros. Television. Warner Bros. built its television division according to the studio system of its motion picture heyday. Rather than seek established talent who would demand competitive salaries, Warners sought unknown or untried actors, writers and directors whom they could develop relatively inexpensively. The studio utilized — and in some cases exploited — its employees to the fullest possible degree, particularly as the Television Division developed into a high-volume duplicative factory that churned out programs at a frenetic pace.

But the studio took a short-sighted approach to television: it saw its participation in TV merely as a means of generating more revenue for its motion picture division. By concentrating solely on the financial benefits of television, and refusing to relinquish control of the ownership of its programs, Warners planted the seeds of its own destruction. The studio's refusal to give writers "created by" rights to its TV series had already cost them its most innovative television mind, producer Roy Huggins. The hardline position it took with contract performers — particularly with regard to profit sharing — would not only cost them its most prominent television star, James Garner, but it effectively killed *Maverick*, the studio's most successful series.

TV historian Christopher Anderson, who spent an exhaustive number of hours researching the Warner Bros. Archives at both the University of Southern California and Princeton University, chronicles the rise and fall of Warners television in *Hollywood TV: The Studio System During the Fifties* (University of Texas Press, 1994). Citing correspondence between the studio's executives, Anderson reveals just how badly the studio took advantage of its television performers. "When not engaged in production, Warner Bros. TV stars still earned money for the studio," Anderson wrote. "When they made personal appearances, the studio received half of their earnings. In this way, the studio actually forced the actors to pay a percentage of their own salaries, since the money earned by the studio through an actor's personal appearances could be channeled back into paying the actor's salary. . . . The studio also earned money from its performers by licensing their likenesses for use on trademark merchandise such as comic books, games and toys — for which the performer received nothing more than the Screen Actors Guild minimum royalty. In addition, the TV stars were encouraged to exploit their popularity by launching recording careers, but they were obliged to record for Warner Bros. Records — which again channeled the largest portion of their earnings back to the studio. Warner Bros. justified these restrictive contractual conditions by arguing that the studio was almost completely responsible for the market value of its actors; its guidance and marketing skills had delivered them from anonymity to stardom."

Two of Warners' early TV stars tried to fight back. Clint Walker walked off the set of *Cheyenne* in 1958 in an attempt to renegotiate his contract to include, among other things, a greater share of profits from *Cheyenne*-related merchandise and the right to keep all monies earned from public appearances. Warners refused to capitulate and replaced Walker with Ty Hardin, who took over the lead of *Cheyenne* (as Bronco Layne) for the 1958-59 season. Walker's case weakened, however, when *Cheyenne* succeeded without him, and he returned to the series in 1959. Similarly, when Wayde Preston walked off the set of *Colt .45* in 1959, the studio simply replaced him with Donald May, and the series continued to succeed. Having established a precedent of sorts that no actor was bigger than the studio, Warners felt exceedingly confident when James Garner stood up to them in 1960.

In January 1960, the Writers Guild of America went on strike for the first time in its then 27-year history. At issue was the sharing of profits made by the major studios over the sale of movies made after 1948. The studios sold these films to television after they had completed their theatrical run for huge sums of money, but refused to share the profits with the actors, writers, directors and so forth who had worked on them.

In March 1960, James Garner and Jack Kelly had just finished filming an episode of *Maverick* called "The Maverick Line" when Warner Bros. suspended the two actors by invoking the *force majeure* clause in their contracts. This clause stipulated that the studio had the right to stop paying its actors if extraordinary circumstances forced a halt to series production. The studio claimed that it had to stop production of *Maverick* because there were no scripts available due to the Writers Guild strike, but that argument was a sham.

Maverick producer Coles Trapnell was among the many members of the Writers Guild who was not affected by the strike. "I was what they called a 'hyphenate,' because my contract listed me as a 'writer-producer,'" he explained. "If I had only been a writer, I would have had to honor the strike. But as a writer-producer, I was not affected. The Guild allowed producers to write and/or rewrite the scripts, particularly after the original writer had turned in the final draft, and was not available for last-minute revisions on the set. Warner Bros., of course, stretched this to the limit during the strike. But I was in pretty good shape — 'The Maverick Line' was 'in the can,' ready to go on the air, and I had two other scripts that were ready to shoot."

Apparently Warners had as many as 14 "hyphenates" who were able to write scripts during the time of the strike; these writers all used the pseudonym "W. Hermanos" (after the Spanish word for "brothers"). At the time the studio suspended Garner and Kelly, it had at least two *Maverick* scripts in development ("A State of Siege," "Arizona Black Maria"). Trapnell could produce a new script in 15 days, and rewrite an old one in as little as five; given the contingent of "W. Hermanos" writers at the studio's disposal, it was reasonable to conclude that Warner Bros. would have no trouble preparing scripts for the 1960-61 season. After all, Trapnell had only one teleplay ready when he took over *Maverick* in June 1959, yet he managed to get the episodes for the third year produced and delivered to ABC on time for the start of the new season in September. Despite its claims that the Writers Guild strike had "hampered" production of its TV series, Warners not only had the means to produce scripts, it in fact had sufficient time to prepare them. (Production of the 1960-61 episodes was not scheduled to begin for another two months, in May 1960.)

James Garner objected to his suspension on the basis that the studio was in no way hampered from continuing production, and he demanded payment of his salary. When Warners refused to capitulate, Garner countered by informing the studio that he now considered his employment contract terminated on the grounds that his suspension constituted a breach of contract. On March 31, 1960 Warner Bros. sued Garner (the studio argued that, by walking out on the contract, *Garner* had committed the breach); on April 26, 1960, Garner filed a cross-complaint against the studio, reiterating his claim that Warners had broken his contract.

Warner Bros., Inc. v. James Bumgarner did not mark the first instance of a major star taking a major motion picture studio to court. Marquee players had gone up against Warner Bros., and many, such as Bette Davis, had lost. If the court ruled for Garner, he would be declared a free agent; but if it ruled for the studio, Garner would be bound to his contract, or even faced with the possibility of never working in the film industry again.

The lawsuit also had an impact on other people who were close to Garner, such as Luis Delgado, the actor's longtime stand-in. "Warner Bros. had put out the word not to hire anybody who was connected to James Garner," Delgado recalled. "So I was kind of blacklisted. Fortunately, I'd become friends with a number of assistant directors who had worked on *Maverick*, and one of them was Bob Stone, who was now the A.D. on *Perry Mason*. Bob helped me find work on *Perry Mason* [where I stood in for Raymond Burr] during the time of Jim's lawsuit."

Although Jack Kelly was originally going to join Garner in his legal battle, Kelly later elected to settle with the studio. The risk of not working factored heavily in his decision. "Shortly after the start-up of the briefs and research to get the case ready, Jack Warner called me," Kelly told Mick Martin in 1992. "I guess he called Jim, too, but Jim didn't respond — he wanted out so badly that he could taste it. But I wanted *in*." Kelly knew that he did not have the same bargaining power that his co-star had — after all, Garner had established himself as a major box office attraction in addition to his status as the star of *Maverick*. Kelly wanted the security of regular employment and opted to return to work. Garner understood Kelly's position, and never held it against him. It was a good deal for Kelly — Jack Warner raised his salary and gave him top billing on *Maverick* for the remainder of the series.

In the meantime, the Writers Guild strike ended (Universal Pictures was the first studio to work out a settlement, and the other studios soon followed). Warner Bros. then announced that Roger Moore would replace Garner on *Maverick* by playing a new character, Cousin Beauregard. "Moore had signed a contract with the studio the year before, and they put him in a show [*The Alaskans*] that didn't last," said Coles Trapnell. "Jack Warner loved Roger Moore — he saw Moore as the next Errol Flynn — and he wanted us to put him in *Maverick*."

Doubtlessly confident because it had won its previous confrontations with TV performers, Warners went ahead with plans for the fourth season of *Maverick*. Yet there were flutters of doubt among the studio's top executives, who suspected that the circumstances in Garner's case were not quite the same. And they weren't. After all, Roy Huggins had designed *Maverick* specifically with James Garner in mind. Garner was the only performer Huggins could think of who had an unerring instinct for the kind of humor that *Maverick* delivered — humor that comes out of character, and humor that works only if you have an actor who intuitively understands that character. Garner had much to do with *Maverick*'s early success, but his true value was not revealed until after Huggins left the show. Garner carried *Maverick* through the third season — his presence countering the inadequacies of the scripts. *Maverick* had lost a sizeable chunk of its audience in that third season, but the Nielsen ratings clearly indicate that the episodes with James Garner were attracting a large enough audience to give the series a respectable overall rating for the 1959-60 season.

Kaiser Industries, *Maverick*'s primary sponsor, recognized the importance of retaining Garner. "Kaiser believed that Garner was so crucial to *Maverick*'s success that its representatives offered him half of the company's one-third share in the series, retroactive to the first episode," reports Christopher Anderson in *Hollywood TV*. Warners also entered the negotiations. "Retaining Garner became such a high priority that Jack Warner dispatched Steve Trilling, his right-hand man, to handle the delicate negotiations that soon involved not only Warner Bros., but also Kaiser and ABC. . . . Warner Bros. broke all precedent by offering to raise Garner's salary from its existing terms of $1750 per week and a $15,000 bonus for each feature film to $5000 per episode with his commitment reduced to thirteen episodes and a $100,000 bonus per feature. Under this contract, Garner would continue in *Maverick* for two seasons and then would work exclusively in features."

The prospective deal was the highest TV contract Warner Bros. had ever offered, but Garner turned it down for two reasons. He did not want to be tied to one studio, and he no longer wanted to do television. Garner wanted to pursue his film career, and he reasoned that his value as a performer would be ruined if he continued to subject himself to the grueling pace of series television.

Maverick producer Coles Trapnell recalled viewing the stalemate with mixed emotions: "I felt, as did a lot of other people, that Garner had been treated shamefully by the studio, so I can't honestly say that I was hoping he would lose his lawsuit. But, on the other hand, in the event that he lost, I would have been glad if he came back to *Maverick*, because he was carrying the show." (However, Garner had put out the word that, regardless of the lawsuit's outcome, he would not return to the series.)

Maverick opened its fourth season with "The Bundle from Britain," the episode introducing Roger Moore as Cousin Beau. Surprisingly, the series did not lose any of its audience throughout the first half of the season. From September through November, it averaged a 34.8 audience share, a slightly higher figure than the seasonal average of 1959-60. The engaging Moore put his own spin on the Maverick character, and the series also benefited from such episodes as "Hadley's Hunters" (featuring cameo appearances by many of the Warners TV stars) and "Bolt from the Blue" (written and directed by Robert Altman).

But the true reason for *Maverick*'s early success that year was probably linked to the national attention surrounding Garner's trial, which began in September 1960. The viewers hung on, perhaps hoping for a resolution that would enable Garner to return to the series. But that hope burst on December 14, 1960, when the Los Angeles Superior Court ruled in favor of James Garner. Although Warner Bros. would continue to appeal the decision for another year, the damage had already been done. Garner was now free to walk away from *Maverick*, and so now were the viewers. The series' total audience fell by nearly eleven percent after the ruling — younger viewers opted for the likes of *Dennis the Menace* and *The Shirley Temple Theater*, while the older ones returned to Ed Sullivan. *Maverick* finished the year with a respectable average audience share of 32.4, but that figure is, again, inflated because the show continued to lose viewers as the season progressed. *Maverick*'s audience hovered around the 30% mark for the remaining four months of 1960-61.

(Ironically, Garner *did* return to the series — for one episode. ABC aired "The Maverick Line," which had been completed nearly a year earlier, on November 20, 1960 — just a few weeks before the court handed down its decision.)

Roy Huggins had kept his eye on the entire matter. "Warners made a big mistake when they suspended Jim," he said. "They were always trying to take the fullest possible advantage of their personnel, but they did something with Jim that they really had no right to do. And Jim got a lawyer who was able to prove it."

Maverick underwent several other changes in personnel during the second half of the season. Roger Moore left the series prior to the end of the season (he appeared in 15 episodes). With several scripts yet to be filmed, the studio decided to introduce another Maverick brother, the heretofore never-mentioned Brent, who would be played by Robert Colbert. "I was under contract to Warner Bros. at the time," recalled Colbert, "and I was scheduled to do a film called *Black Gold*, which was really a nice film — I was really looking forward to it. I had a wonderful part, and it was going to be my breakthrough into features. I reported to the studio one day, and they sent me down to Wardrobe. I ended up walking out of there dressed up in one of the *Maverick* outfits. And I knew where I was headed, because Jim had just won his confrontation with the studio."

Although Colbert was fine in both his episodes ("The Forbidden City," "Benefit of Doubt"), he was never given a chance. Brent's appearance had "gimmick" written all over it, and not only because he dressed in his brother's clothes — Warners apparently hoped that Colbert's facial resemblance to Garner would appease the viewers who had sorely missed watching Bret. "As I first walked up that main studio boulevard [dressed in the Maverick outfit], a lot of heads were popping out of a lot of windows, and I heard a lot of people say 'Oh, he's back!'" Colbert continued. "I remember saying to the producers, when they called me in and looked me over, 'C'mon, guys, put me in a dress and call me 'Brenda' — give me a break!'"

William T. Orr, the head of Warner Bros. Television, ultimately selected Colbert. "I don't remember saying, 'We've got to get somebody who looks like Jim Garner,'" he said. "We weren't trying to fool the audience — you can't do that. As it happened, Bob did look like Jim, but I picked him because he was a good actor, he was under contract, and I thought he would fit in with the show."

Unfortunately for Colbert, he was thrown into a situation that was entirely beyond his control. Brent Maverick was never accepted by the viewers — his two episodes were the least-watched shows of the season. Colbert did not return to *Maverick* when the series was renewed for 1961-62.

Coles Trapnell also left *Maverick* before the season ended. "An opportunity came up for me to take over *Lawman*," he said. "Bill Orr asked Julie Schermer, the producer of *Lawman*, to become an executive producer and handle three shows. Since *Lawman* was very close to Julie's heart, he said he'd do it if he could hand-pick his successor. Julie asked me to be the new producer of *Lawman*. Now, this came at a very appropriate time for me, because *Maverick* was going down the drain, and so I gratefully accepted his offer."

Howie Horwitz replaced Trapnell for one episode ("Red Dog") before Arthur Silver took over as producer for the final episodes of the season. Arthur Silver was the man Warner Bros. had chosen to take over *Cheyenne* after Roy Huggins left that series at the end of its first season.

Familiar faces during Maverick's fourth season include George Kennedy, Lee Van Cleef, John Astin, Shirley Knight, Andrew Duggan, Dawn Wells, Alan Hale, Denver Pyle, Chad Everett, Peter Breck, and John Carradine.

80. THE BUNDLE FROM BRITAIN

ORIGINAL AIRDATE: SEPTEMBER 18, 1960

Teleplay by: Ron Bishop   Based on a Story by: Primo Saxon
Directed by: Leslie H. Martinson

Guest Cast: Robert Douglas (Herbert), Robert Casper (Freddie Bognor), Diana Crawford (Molly), Laurie Main (Marquis of Bognor), Clancy Cooper (McGee), Mickey Simpson (Pecos), Max Baer (Brazos), Rusty Wescoatt (Muldoon), Alberto Morin (Hotel Clerk), I. Stanford Jolley (Kratkovitch)

Synopsis. Introducing Roger Moore as Cousin Beauregard Maverick, the "white sheep" of the family, who had the embarrassing misfortune of earning a medal in the Civil War — accidentally. Bart greets Beau upon his return to America (Pappy had banished him to England for five years) and enlists his cousin to impersonate the weaselly son of the Marquis of Bognor, who has been indentured to work at a Wyoming ranch for six months. The Mavericks stand to earn an easy $4,000, but the plan goes awry when Beau is kidnapped by a man who wants to settle a grudge with the Marquis.

"The original concept of Beauregard Maverick was quite a funny idea," recalled Roger Moore. "Beauregard was supposed to have done something 'heroic' during the Civil War, but in fact hadn't done anything heroic at all–it was purely by accident. He'd been taken prisoner by the other side, and was playing poker with the colonels and the generals–his captors. They threw their cards down, and they said, 'Oh, you win! We give in'–and, at that moment, his side came through the tent flap, and they thought that the enemy had surrendered to him. And so, all of a sudden Beauregard Maverick was a hero–which made Pappy say, 'You leave the country,' because no Maverick has ever been a hero, and so he went off to England.

"That was a funny idea, except they never shot that episode–instead, they simply explained his background [as part of the exposition of the first show of the season]. It would have made quite a good show if the filmed his 'origin' as part of an episode."

Although under contract to Warners at the time, Moore was hesitant about joining *Maverick* for two reasons: he had just completed two other television series (the syndicated *Ivanhoe* in 1957-58; and *The Alaskans*, for Warners, in 1959-60); and he was afraid *Maverick*'s audience would resent him for replacing James Garner. "I had signed a picture deal with Warners [around 1958], and I made a fim called *The Miracle*, with Carroll Baker, and directed by Irving Rapper. I was then asked to do *The Alaskans*–that was supposed to be the only television series I was to do for the studio–but, of course, I found out that they wanted me to replace Jim Garner on *Maverick*.

"I really didn't want to do another television series. And I honestly did feel that Jim was so popular that anybody coming in would be resented. It's very difficult to follow somebody in an established role." (Moore knows a bit about this. In addition to following Garner on *Maverick*, he "took over" *The Saint* on television after George Sanders had played the role in many films. Later, of course, Moore succeeded Sean Connery as the lead in seven James Bond pictures from 1973-85.)

Not happy about the situation, Moore took "ill" and retreated to Las Vegas for some "therapy"–the kind where you manupulate your fingers on the crap table. "I couldn't afford to stay there long," he quipped. "When I returned to L.A., my agent told me that Jack Warner wanted to meet with me, and so I did. Warner started talking to me about money, and then he looked at me and said, 'Oh yeah, you're that mad sonuvabitch. You're not interested in money–you're just interested in scripts.' I said, 'Yes, quite honestly'–because while we were doing *The Alaskans*, there'd been a writer's strike, and we were being given *Maverick* scripts, where they just changed the names, some of the time, and my character, Silky Harris, was saying Bret Maverick lines (they even had 'My old Pappy used to say' in one script).

"I went on to play Beauregard with Jack Kelly. Jack and I had a lot of laughs doing it, I must say. I also remember Les Martinson directing the first episode. He thought we were both completely insane—at one point, he said,'I've got one sonuvabitch who's a clown, and another one who doesn't want to do it!'"

As part of its effort to appease Moore, the studio offered him a starring role in a Clint Walker film called *Gold of the Seven Saints* (1961). "It was a Western I'd wanted to do," he said. "Looking back, *Gold of the Seven Saints* was really sort of prophetic, because I went on the make a movie called *Gold* (1974), and then *The Man with the Golden Gun* (1974), and I was also 007 and *The Saint*."

81. HADLEY'S HUNTERS

ORIGINAL AIRDATE: SEPTEMBER 25, 1960

Teleplay by: Patrick Wallace   Story by: William Henderson and Jeanne Nolan
Directed by: Leslie H. Martinson

Guest Cast: Edgar Buchanan (Sheriff Hadley), Robert Wilke (McCabe), Andra Martin (Molly Brewster), Robert Colbert (Cherokee Dan Evans), Howard McNear (Copes), Herb Vigran (Pender), George Kennedy (Deputy Jones), James Gavin (Deputy Smith), Harry Harvey Sr. (Dad Brewster), Roscoe Ates (Albert), Gregg Barton (Boggs), Murray Alper (Gus), Craig Duncan (Wesley)

Appearing as Themselves: Clint Walker, John Russell, Will Hutchins, Edd Byrnes, Peter Brown, Ty Hardin

Synopsis. Bart rides into Hadley, a town named after its sheriff, a shrewd politician who has carefully crafted a reputation for apprehending notorious criminals. But the legend of Sheriff Hadley is a sham — Hadley's deputies pull the jobs themselves, then pin the crimes on innocent victims whom Hadley later arrests. When Bart stumbles onto a bogus stagecoach robbery (which springs a "criminal" named Cherokee Dan Evans), the crooked sheriff gives Maverick five days to capture Evans — or Bart will hang.

"Hadley's Hunters" is one of three fourth-year *Maverick*s featuring direct allusions to characters in other Warner Bros. TV series. In "Bolt from the Blue," Beau spends most of the episode trying to determine just where he's seen the young lawyer who's representing him (the lawyer is played by Will Hutchins, who played such a character on *Sugarfoot*). In "Red Dog," a character refers to a "Marshal Dan Troop" who gunned down a man in Laramie, Wyoming; Dan Troop is the name of John Russell's character in *Lawman*, which takes place in Laramie.

In "Hadley's Hunters," Hutchins, Russell, Clint Walker (*Cheyenne*), Peter Brown (Lawman) and Ty Hardin (*Bronco*) all make brief appearances playing their respective series characters. Edd Byrnes, the hair-combing parking lot attendant Kookie on *77 Sunset Strip*, also has a cameo, but his role has a twist — he's seen combing the mane of a horse while the theme from *77 Sunset Strip* chortles in the background. (The stable where Burns works is located at 77 Cherokee Strip.)

Pappyism: "If you can't fight 'em, and they won't let you join 'em, it's best to get out of the county."

The episode also features Robert Colbert, who became Brent Maverick later in the fourth season; and George Kennedy, who won the Academy Award for Best Supporting Actor for his role as Dragline in 1967's *Cool Hand Luke*.

82. THE TOWN THAT WASN'T THERE

ORIGINAL AIRDATE: OCTOBER 2, 1960

Teleplay by: Arthur Paynter   Story by: Dick Lederer
Directed by: Herbert L. Strock

Guest Cast: Merry Anders (Maggie Bradford), Richard Hale (Wilbur Shanks), John Astin (Joe Lambert), Forrest Lewis (Oldtimer), Craig Duncan (Jake Moody), Lane Chandler (Sheriff Crane), Jon Lormer (Sam Bradford), Alexander Campbell (Horatio Cromwell), Bruce Wendell (Henry Pitkin), Richard Cutting (Ralph Hobbs), Steve Pendleton (Marshal McCoy)

Synopsis. Beau wins ownership of the Silver Hill ore mine, only to discover that the mine is worthless. Meanwhile, a crooked railroad agent named Shanks tries to cheat the townspeople out of their land by offering them a price that is well below market value. Beau rallies the town together into relocating Silver Hill to a sheep ranch twenty miles away. But the plan backfires when a new vein of silver is discovered in the supposedly worthless Silver Hill mine, thus enabling Shanks to claim the land without cost. The town's only hope is to relocate back to Silver Hill before the railroad takes over the land.

In the tradition of his cousins Bret and Bart, Beau conjures up one of Pappy Maverick's old sayings, such as this episode's "There are things more important than money, but I've never found one." While Roger Moore proves that he can deliver these zingers as well as James Garner and Jack Kelly, the aphorisms that come from Beau sound just a little clumsy. This is no fault of Moore's, nor the writers — it's just that "As my old Uncle Beau said" (which how Beau puts it) doesn't quite have the same zip as "Well, as my dear old pappy once said" (which is how Bret and Bart would put it). Beau, of course, can't say "as my old Pappy said," because Pappy Maverick is indeed Beau's uncle. So the truisms that come from Beau are really more "Uncleisms" (or "Uncle Beauisms") than "Pappyisms."

At the end of the story, Shanks offers Beau $10,000 for his property, but Beau rejects the deal in order to force Shanks into negotiating with the citizens of Silver Hill. This is the first time since "The War of the Silver Kings," the very first episode of the series, that Maverick has turned down money in favor of people. Beau knows that he's done a decent thing, although he admits that if Pappy Maverick ever heard that he turned down $10,000, he'd send him back to England for sure.

John Astin was the original Gomez Addams. Astin starred as the patriarch of the ghoulishly eccentric *Addams Family* in the 1964-66 ABC series based on the cartoon figures created by Charles Addams for The New Yorker (Raul Julia took over the role in the 1990s for the popular Addams Family feature films). Astin later starred as Harry Anderson's father on the popular 1980s NBC comedy *Night Court*; his appearance on *Maverick* was one of his first TV acting roles. For many years, Astin was married to TV star Patty Duke; their sons Sean and Mackenzie are also actors.

83. ARIZONA BLACK MARIA

ORIGINAL AIRDATE: OCTOBER 9, 1960

Teleplay by: Arthur P. Paynter   Story by: R.G. Spang
Directed by: Lew Landers

Guest Cast: Joanna Barnes (Daphne Tolliver), Alan Hale (Captain Jim Paddishaw), Gary Murray (Redfeather), Donald Barry (Dishonest Abe), Terrence DeMarney (Fingers Louie), John Holland (Farnsworth McCoy), Harry Swoger (Rufus), Art Stewart (Lem), Charles Stevens (Indian Chief)

Synopsis. While camping in the Arizona desert, Bart finds himself the target of a determined Indian named Redfeather, who needs to collect one scalp in order to be named Chief. Two gunmen rescue Maverick in the nick of time, but they steal his water as payment and leave him to die of thirst. The next morning, Redfeather tries to scalp Bart again, only this time a federal marshal comes to the rescue. The marshal asks Bart to help him transport a wagonload of prisoners to the federal penitentiary. Redfeather's tribe overtakes the wagon, but agrees to let the marshal pass through if he turns over Maverick.

"Arizona Black Maria" features another of the most-remembered lines of the entire *Maverick* series. When Paddishaw decides to turn Bart over to the Indians, he tries to console *Maverick*: "You're a brave man, Maverick. At least you know that you won't have died in vain." Bart's response: "I'd rather live in vain, then die any way there is."

Alan Hale, who plays Paddishaw, was one of three future castaways from *Gilligan's Island* to guest star in *Maverick* (Dawn Wells appeared in the episode "The Deadly Image," while Jim Backus starred in "Three Queens Full"). Hale was also featured in the fifth season's "The Troubled Heir."

84. LAST WIRE FROM STOP GAP

ORIGINAL AIRDATE: OCTOBER 16, 1960

Teleplay by: Herman Epstein Story by: Primo Saxon
Directed by: Lee Sholem

Guest Cast: Olive Sturgess (Phyllis), Robert Cornthwaite (Wembly), Tol Avery (Hulett), Stephen Coit (Devers), Don Hardy (Sheriff), Lane Bradford (Beldon), John Cason (Clay), James Chandler (Ryan), Richard Reeves (Prospector), James Horan (Kibitzer)

Synopsis. On their way to Denver, Bart and Beau pick up $6,500 in a poker game at Stop Gap, then decide to wire the money to Denver through the Hulett Telegraph Company. They soon discover the company is a fake — the telegraph line leads to a cave two miles away, where the crooks stash the customers' money and send phony messages in return. The Mavericks devise a scheme to recover the money and put the company out of business.

One of the plot devices of "Last Wire to Stop Gap" — the phony telegraph company whose messages are relayed to a nearby cave — was later incorporated in the "Welcome to Sweetwater" episode of *Bret Maverick*.

According to this episode, another Maverick relative — Uncle Buck — lives in Arizona. "Last Wire to Stop Gap" also features these two well-remembered **Pappyisms**: "Hard work never hurt anybody — who didn't do it;" and "All men are equal before the law — but what kind of odds are those?"

John Cason was Jack Kelly's stand-in on *Maverick*. Like Luis Delgado (James Garner's stand-in), Cason appeared onscreen in a number of uncredited roles in many other *Maverick* episodes.

85. MANO NERA

ORIGINAL AIRDATE: OCTOBER 23, 1960

Teleplay by: Leo Gordon and Paul Leslie Peil Based on a Story by: Tom Kilpatrick
Directed by: Reginald LeBorg

Guest Cast: Myrna Fahey (Carla Marchese), Gerald Mohr (Giacomo Beretti), Anthony Caruso (Lieutenant Joe Petrino), John Beradino (Giovanni Marchese), Frank Wilcox (Chief Rawlins), Paul Bryar (Officer Noonan), Nesdon Booth (Hotel Detective), Arthur Marshall (Hotel Clerk), Edward Colmans (Alberto), Joe Garcio (Agostino), Jerome Loden (Calvini)

Synopsis. In New Orleans, an Italian shopowner dies at Bart's feet — the latest victim of a murderous band of extortionists known as *Mano Nera* ("black hand"), who have been terrorizing members of the Italian business community. Bart suspects that Giacomo Beretti, a prominent businessman, is linked to the organization after Beretti has Maverick beaten and robbed of $3,500. Bart helps his friend Joe Petrino, a police lieutenant, investigate the matter.

"Mano Nera" is the first of four scripts written by Leo Gordon and Paul Leslie Peil. Gordon, of course, starred as Big Mike McComb during *Maverick*'s first two seasons. "I'd known Leo since I'd been in television," said Coles Trapnell. "He did a number of shows at Four Star, as both an actor and a writer. If I remember correctly, Leo came to see me one day and said that he wanted to write a *Maverick*. I liked his idea, and so he went ahead with the script [for 'Mano Nera']. His first show was very well written, and then, of course, he went on to write more shows for me." Gordon and Peil also wrote the teleplays for "A Bullet for the Teacher," "Diamond Flush," and "The Deadly Image."

"Mano Nera" opens with stock footage of Mardi Gras celebrations, including some film once used in "The Judas Mask." Keep an eye out for the heavyset woman wearing cat-eyed glasses (she's seen, albeit briefly, revelling with a man and another woman). This must be a flub, because cat-eyed glasses didn't exist during the period in which *Maverick* took place (circa 1875). Only wire-rimmed spectacles were available during that era.

86. A BULLET FOR THE TEACHER

ORIGINAL AIRDATE: OCTOBER 30, 1960

Teleplay by: Leo Gordon and Paul Leslie Peil
Story by: Harry Franklin and Barry Cohon
Directed by: Lee Sholem

Guest Cast: Kathleen Crowley (Flo Baker), Arch Johnson (Ephrim Burch), Bing Russell (Luke Storm), Brad Johnson (Jim Reardon), Joan Tompkins (Mary Burch), Sammy Jackson (Walter Burch), Henry Brandon (Rand Storm), Lynn Cartwright (Ann Shepard), Carol Nicholson (Elvira), Max Baer (Cowboy), Fred Sherman (Clerk), John Harmon (Depot Agent), Tom London (Farmer)

Synopsis. Beau wins half-ownership of the Golden Wheel Casino in St. Joseph, Missouri. But the business venture is short-lived when his partner Rand Storm, a notorious ladies' man, is shot to death by Flo Baker, a female entertainer who was resisting his advances. Just before he dies, Rand tells his younger brother Luke that the shooting was an accident. But Luke, who has long wanted to own the casino, has Beau framed for Rand's murder so that he can take over the business.

Ronnie Dapo, Timothy Rooney, and Anna Marie Capri — who play three of the schoolchildren in this episode — all co-starred in *Room for One More*, the Warner Bros.-produced comedy series starring Andrew Duggan and Peggy McCay.

Max Baer, who also had small roles in "The Bundle from Britain" and "Kiz," later starred as Jethro Beaudine on the long-running CBS comedy *The Beverly Hillbillies*.

87. THE WITCH OF HOUND DOG

ORIGINAL AIRDATE: NOVEMBER 6, 1960

Written by: Mae Malotte
Directed by: Leslie Goodwins

Guest Cast: Anita Sands (Nancy Sutliff), Wayde Preston (Luke Baxter), Sheldon Allman (Ox Sutliff), William Corrie (Zack Sutliff), Phil Tully (Cyrus), Dorothea Lord (Miz Turner)

Synopsis. Bart lands in Hound Dog, Tennessee, where he tries to collect a $10,000 gambling debt from "Hound Dog" Harris. Maverick learns from the town doctor, Luke Baxter, that Harris died shortly after winning a hounddog named Peaches from Ox and Zack Sutliff, whose sister Nancy claims to be a witch. Harris kept his money in Luke's safe; one day, Ox and Zack broke into Luke's office and confiscated the entire safe. Maverick tries to recover his money from the safe without raising Ox and Zack's suspicions.

Bill Crewe, who was one of the sound technicians on *Maverick*, was also once a professional card dealer and magician.

Pappyism: "A man can stay out of trouble if he learns to do something with his hands."

88. THUNDER FROM THE NORTH

ORIGINAL AIRDATE: NOVEMBER 13, 1960

Teleplay by: Leo Townsend
Story by: Don Tait
Directed by: William Dario Faralla

Guest Cast: Andra Martin (Pale Moon), Richard Coogan (Hank Lawson), Janet Lake (Kitty O'Hearn), Robert Warwick (Standing Bull), George Keymas (War Shirt), Jack Mather (Colonel O'Hearn), John Zaccaro (Judd Marsh), Trent Dolan (Lieutenant), Gary Conway (Orderly), Miguel Landa (Swift River)

Synopsis. Two crooked Army shopkeepers named Marsh and Lawson have been cheating the local Indian tribes by supplying faulty or inferior goods, such as sick cows or contaminated flour. When a tribeswoman named Pale Moon threatens to report them to the Army Commission, the shopkeepers decide to start a war with the Indians, knowing that the Army will not investigate the claim at a time of war. Marsh and Lawson murder Pale Moon's brother, then decide to pin the crime on the stranger who won $1,500 from them the night before — Beau Maverick.

89. THE MAVERICK LINE

ORIGINAL AIRDATE: NOVEMBER 20, 1960

Written by: Wells Root and Ron Bishop
Directed by: Leslie Goodwins

Guest Cast: Peggy McCay (Polly Goodin), Buddy Ebsen (Rumsey Plum), Will Wright (Atherton Flayger), Charles Fredericks (Shotgun Shanks), Chubby Johnson (Dutch Wilcox), C. Alvin Bell (Bandy), Alan Reynolds (Phineas Cox)

Synopsis. Bret and Bart arrive in Snowflake to claim their inheritance from their late Uncle Micah — full ownership of the Maverick Stage Line. Although Micah had hoped that the boys would run the company, his will allows them to sell it if they can turn a huge profit. Polly Goodin, who had sold Micah exclusive right-of-way through her ranch property, offers the boys $1,000 each per month for life if they sell her 49% of the company. Bret and Bart are unaware that Polly has hired an operative named Shotgun Shanks to sabotage the stagecoach and thus negate the deal. Meanwhile, Atherton Flayger, Micah's scheming attorney, discovers a clause that *he* would inherit the company if the Maverick boys are killed. Flayger hires Shanks to do away with Bret and Bart.

James Garner filmed "The Maverick Line" in March 1960, immediately before the start of his confrontation with Warner Bros. The episode was originally scheduled for broadcast on September 25, 1960 (it would have been the season premiere), but it was held back in light of the legal battle between Garner and the studio.

This episode also marks the first and only mention of Uncle Micah Maverick.

90. BOLT FROM THE BLUE

ORIGINAL AIRDATE: NOVEMBER 27, 1960

Written and Directed by: Robert Altman

Guest Cast: Fay Spain (Angelica Garland), Will Hutchins (Lawyer), Richard Hale (Judge Hookstraten), Charles Fredericks (Starky), Tim Graham (Ebenezer Bolt), Percy Helton (Bradley), Owen Bush (Benson January), Arnold Merritt (Junior), Connie Van (Hotel Clerk)

Synopsis. Beau befriends a kindly old prospector named Ebenezer Bolt, unaware that he's the partner of notorious horse thief Benson January. An angry posse intercepts Maverick and mistakes him for January. Although the posse is determined to hang Beau, a young lawyer halts the proceedings until Maverick can have a trial. But Beau's conviction seems imminent when the lawyer locates a notorious "hanging judge" and a woman whose sister was engaged to January identifies Maverick as the horse thief.

Full of the wit and biting humor that characterized many of the early *Maverick* scripts, Robert Altman's "Bolt from the Blue" is by far the best episode of the fourth season. Altman was apparently such a huge fan of *Maverick* that he'd finished his script *before* he presented the idea to producer Coles Trapnell.

"Altman liked *Maverick* very much, and he came in one day with a complete script and told us that he'd like to direct it," recalled Trapnell. "He'd just completed a remarkable picture for Universal [*The Delinquents*] in which he'd used no additional lighting, except for street lights. We gave him *carte blanche*.

"Altman had nothing but good ideas for the show, and he was punctiliously polite, to boot! He always asked me what I'd thought, and of course, I would always agree with him. He really had a lot to do with the making of that *Maverick* — so much so, that the credit for that show should have read 'Written, Directed *and Produced* by Robert Altman.'"

Altman has since established himself as a major motion picture director, whose films include such critical box-office successes as *M*A*S*H, Nashville, The Player*, and *Short Cuts*. Altman also directed James Garner in 1979's *H.E.A.L.T.H.*

Roger Moore filmed "Bolt from the Blue" around the time of his 33rd birthday (October 14, 1960). In fact, the sequence in which Beau is about to be hanged was filmed on October 14, so Moore spent a good part of his birthday wearing a noose around his neck. "I hope this does not express the sentiment of my colleagues at the studios," he deadpanned at the time.

91. KIZ

(a.k.a. "Portrait in Terror")
ORIGINAL AIRDATE: DECEMBER 4, 1960

Written by: Leo Townsend and Laszlo Gorog
Directed by: Robert Douglas

Guest Cast: Kathleen Crowley (Kiz Bouchet), Peggy McCay (Melissa Bouchet), Whit Bissell (Clement Samuels), Tris Coffin (Dr. Pittman), Thomas B. Henry (Attorney Hanford), Claude Stroud (Henry), Max Baer (Ticket Taker), Don Beddoe (Fire Chief Thorpe), Emory Parnell (Hank), Gil Stuart (Poker Player)

Synopsis. In Virginia City, Beau crashes a party thrown by eccentric socialite Kiz Bouchet, who has a penchant for smoking cigars, playing poker, and fighting fires. Believing that her life is in danger, and recognizing Beau as a fellow free spirit, Kiz hires Maverick to protect her. Beau soon discovers that the real target is not Kiz, but her $2 million inheritance — her devious cousin Melissa, along with family doctor Pittman and attorney Hanford, are plotting to have Kiz judged incompetent so that they can split the money. Beau counters with a scheme to turn the tables on Melissa.

As a gag, director Robert Douglas asked Kathleen Crowley to wear the jet black wig needed for "Kiz" when she first reported to the set. The stunt worked. Crowley, who was certainly no stranger around Warners (she appeared in several episodes of many WB series, including *Maverick*), made such a convincing brunette that everyone on the set wondered who "the new actress" was.

Whit Bissell's character "Clement Samuels" is a take-off on renowned American humorist and satirist Mark Twain, whose real name was Samuel Clemens.

An accomplished sketch artist, Roger Moore often brought his pad to the *Maverick* set and drew likenesses of the various actors and members of the crew.

92. DODGE CITY OR BUST

ORIGINAL AIRDATE: DECEMBER 11, 1960

Written by: Herman Epstein
Directed by: Irving J. Moore

Guest Cast: Peter Whitney (Brock), Diana Millay (Diana Dangerfield), Med Florey (Deputy Nevers), Howard McNear (Dangerfield Sheriff), Harry Tyler (Shopkeeper), Kelly Thordsen (Customer), Mickey Morton (Rockford Sheriff)

Synopsis. In the mining town of Dangerfield, Bart wins $3,000, but he can't collect his winnings until the town banker returns with his money. A gunshot rings out just as Diana Dangerfield, whose father founded the town, arrives by stage. The startled horses go amuck, but Maverick rides to Diana's rescue. When they return to town, they find themselves implicated in the death of the banker, who was shot after someone robbed the bank. The spoiled and arrogant Diana, who didn't exactly appreciate Bart rescuing her, now must rely on Maverick to get her to Dodge City so that she can wire for help — while a bungling detective named Brock (the real killer) trails them.

Bart and Beau learn a few unusual card games from the Dangerfield locals, including "Jack and the Beanstalk," in which fives and one-eyed jacks are wild, and the low hand splits the pot with the winner; "Pass the Buck," where aces, black threes, the eight of hearts, and your lowest card are wild, and each player is allowed to pass his or her three worst cards on to the person to the left; and "Eight-Toed Slough," in which an "Apache nightmare" beats a "Texas tornado" (as long as the queen is black) — but only before midnight.

93. THE BOLD FENIAN MEN

ORIGINAL AIRDATE: DECEMBER 18, 1960

Written by: Robert V. Wright
Directed by: Irving J. Moore

Guest Cast: Sharon Hugueny (Diedre Fogarty), Arthur Shields (Terence Fogarty), Arch Johnson (Colonel Gaylord Summers), Lane Bradford (Major Sergeant Hogjaw Hanson), Jack Livesey (Patrick Hunter), Herb Vigran (Ed Cramer), James O'Hara (Sean Flaherty), Bert Russell (Orson Holt), Harvey Johnson (Charles Donovan), Mickey Finn (Mike O'Connell)

Synopsis. The Irish Revolutionary Brotherhood, also known as the Fenians, are trained soldiers sworn to free Ireland from British rule. The Fenians have gathered in Dakota City (under the banner of The First Annual Convention of the Sons of the Shamrock Chowder and Marching Society) to plan a march into Canada — they want to hold a small part of that British property hostage in exchange for Ireland's freedom. After England pressures the United States to intervene, a shrewd Army colonel "blackmails" Beau Maverick into infiltrating the Fenians' ranks.

The Fenians really existed. "They came to the United States at the time of the Civil War," said Coles Trapnell. "They fought on both sides — some for the Confederacy, some for the Union. After the war, they drifted up to the Northeast United States, and hatched their plot to take over Canada. The U.S. Secret Service nipped it in the bud, arrested all the Fenians, and deported them back to Ireland."

Trapnell kept this bit of history in the back of his mind for years because he thought it would make a great story. "One day, Bob Wright and I were noodling around with story ideas for *Maverick*, and I told him about the Fenians," he continued. "Bob thought it had wonderful possibilities for the show — all we had to do was get Maverick involved. So we decided that he'd somehow owe a favor to the Army, and that he would be induced to join the ranks of the Fenians."

Arthur Shields, the brother of Academy Award-winning actor Barry Fitzgerald (*Going My Way*), contributed a line to "The Bold Fenian Men" that became the slogan of the Fenian party. "Arthur played the leader of the Fenians, and in one scene he tries to get Maverick drunk," recalled Trapnell. "But Maverick knows what he's trying to do, and he keeps pouring his liquor into a flower pot. Shields keeps putting them away, and he becomes more and more drunk, until finally he passes out. But before he passes out, he's supposed to raise his glass in the air and give the Fenian slogan, 'Over the house stops Ireland forever,' which was an actual Irish slogan at the time.

"Shields said to Irving Moore (who directed the show), 'You know, that, of course, is authentic. But I wonder if we might get more of a laugh out of this: when I was a boy in Ireland, the slogan of the temperance movement was 'Ireland sober is Ireland free.' If I could say that just before I fall on my face . . . What do you think?' Irving thought that was great, so he called me up and ran it by me. I said, 'Wonderful, go ahead.' And that's how we shot it."

Jack Kelly was originally slated to star in "The Bold Fenian Men," but he was forced out of the production when he sustained a broken bone in his right hand after a fall in his home.

94. DESTINATION: DEVIL'S FLAT

ORIGINAL AIRDATE: DECEMBER 25, 1960

Teleplay by: Robert Wright
Story by: Neil Nelson
Directed by: James V. Kern

Guest Cast: Peter Breck (Sheriff Dan Trevor), Merry Anders (Marybelle McCall), Frank Ferguson (Deacon Curt Eaker), Richard Reeves (Bull Crumpitt), Patrick Westwood (Snake Randall), Chubby Johnson (Oscar), Harry Swoger (Conductor), Tipp McClure (Guard), Chuck Hayward (Guard), Helen Mayon (Mrs. Amber)

Synopsis. Wells Fargo authorities, long frustrated by the antics of train robber Incredible Clay Corey, dispatch undercover agents throughout the Kansas City railway to find the notorious bandit, whose description is unknown. The $2,000 reward for Corey's capture entices Bart, who finds himself flat broke (and extremely hungry) in the small town of Crenshaw, Kansas. Bart meets Marybelle McCall, an apparently reformed faro dealer who is travelling with her minister uncle — along with $50,000 in church donations — to Devil's Flat, Colorado, where they plan to build another mission. Maverick becomes suspicious when the sheriff of Crenshaw (who is really Clay Corey) takes a personal interest in the money's whereabouts.

Keep an eye on Jack Kelly when Bart takes on Trevor's henchmen toward the end of "Destination: Devil's Flat." Kelly sustained a nasty bump on the head when he was thrown into one of the prop "boulders" during the fight sequence for this segment.

Pappyisms: "When it comes to the game of life, by the time most of us are familiar with the rules, we're generally too old to play it;" and "It's fine to turn over a new leaf, but there's always someone trying to sneak through the old pages."

95. A STATE OF SIEGE

ORIGINAL AIRDATE: JANUARY 1, 1961

Teleplay by: Larry Welch
Adapted from the Story Pavilion on the Links by Robert Louis Stevenson
Directed by: Robert B. Sinclair

Guest Cast: Ray Danton (Don Felipe), Lisa Gaye (Soledad), Joe De Santis (Don Manuel), Raoul Leon (Don Roberto), Ref Sanchez (Yaquito), Slim Pickens (Stagecoach Driver), Bella Bruck (Mamacita)

Synopsis. Don Felipe Archelita owns the Santa Rita Grande hacienda in the southern part of the New Mexico territory. The land belonged to Felipe's family for over 200 years, but when the United States annexed New Mexico, it refused to recognize the original terms of the grant — a decision that was upheld in court. After Bart saves Felipe's life one night, the grateful nobleman offers him room and board at his hacienda any time. But Bart picks a bad night to take up the offer — he walks into a bitter family feud that is linked to Felipe's plan to revolt against the U.S. government and reclaim his land.

"A State of Siege" was directed by Robert Sinclair, an old friend of producer Coles Trapnell from their days at Four Star Productions. "What I remember about that show is how Bob and Jack Kelly kept staring at each other throughout the entire production, as if they'd known each other from someplace before," said Trapnell. "As it turned out, Bob had directed Jack as a child on the New York stage, in a play called *Saint Helena.*"

Robert Louis Stevenson's "Pavilion on the Links" was originally published in 1896, two years after the author's death in 1894.

96. FAMILY PRIDE

ORIGINAL AIRDATE: JANUARY 8, 1961

Written by: Catherine Kuttner
Directed by: John Ainsworth

Guest Cast: Anita Sands (Rosanne Warren), Karl Swenson (General Josiah Warren), Robert Cornthwaite (Honest John Crippen), Denver Pyle (Jerry O'Brien), Dorothea Lord (Mrs. Hale), Wallace Rooney (Mr. Wallace), Olan Soule (Hotel Clerk), Stacy Keach (Marshal)

Synopsis. In New Mexico, con artists Warren and Crippen, along with Warren's granddaughter Rosanne, take Beau for over $4,500 ($4,000 of which belonged to his friend Jerry O'Brien). Beau tries hard to recover the money, and finally takes the matter to court, but the threesome outsmart him every time. The constant defeats demoralize Beau to the point where he believes he's disgraced the Maverick name — until Rosanne tells him that her grandmother was a Maverick.

Character actor Denver Pyle has a familar face that you've seen in many Hollywood films, such as *To Hell and Back*, *The Man Who Shot Liberty Valance*, *Bonnie and Clyde*, *Five-Card Stud*, and *Cahill: U.S. Marshal*. Pyle has also been a fixture on television for over 30 years, including regular roles as Briscoe Darling on *The Andy Griffith Show* and Uncle Jesse on *The Dukes of Hazzard*. Pyle is also featured in the 1994 *Maverick* motion picture.

Director John Ainsworth was an "old chum" of Roger Moore; both were classmates at the Royal Academy of Dramatic Art in London.

Pappyism: "A Maverick outwitted is still worth two ordinary men."

97. THE CACTUS SWITCH

ORIGINAL AIRDATE: JANUARY 15, 1961

Written by: Fenton Earnshaw
Directed by: George Waggner

Guest Cast: Fay Spain (Lana Cane), Edgar Buchanan (Red Daniels), Peter Hansen (Lawrence Deville), Tom Gilson (Jimmy Daniels), Carolyn Komant (Flossie), Chubby Johnson (Andy Gish), Walter Reed (Ed Spencer), Lane Chandler (Sheriff Bill Wright), Gayla Graves (Dottie Rand), Brad Weston (Mutt Craven), Robert Logan (Ben Daniels)

Synopsis. In Green River, Bart prevents Lana Cane from committing suicide, then intervenes when he suspects a smooth talker named Lawrence Deville of swindling Lana out of her $6,500 diamond necklace. But it's Bart who's taken — he ends up in jail for fraud and has to pay Deville to drop the charges. When Maverick discovers that Lana and Deville are married, he stages Lana's kidnapping in order to force Deville to repay his money. The con works perfectly — until an escaped killer named Red Daniels intercepts Bart and threatens to kill him.

An ice cream truck caused some delay in the production of "The Cactus Switch." A sound technician continued to pick up the chiming of a Good Humor cart that was parked adjacent to the back lot of the Warner Bros. studios, forcing take after take of the same sequence. Director George Waggner finally solved the problem: the vendor promised to relocate afterWaggner purchased ice cream for everyone on the crew.

98. DUTCHMAN'S GOLD

ORIGINAL AIRDATE: JANUARY 22, 1961

Teleplay by: William Bruckner
Story by: Jerry Capehart
Based on the Song Dutchman's Gold by Jerry Capehart
Directed by: Robert Douglas

Guest Cast: Mala Powers (Charlotte), Jacques Aubuchon (The Dutchman), Sheldon Allman (Vern Tripp), Carlos Romero (Padilla), David Potter (Andy), Bob Grossman (Ramon), Frank Sully (Bartender)

Synopsis. Beau wins half-ownership of the Blue Bell Saloon in Arizona. In order to raise funds for the floundering business, Beau and his partner Charlotte become partners with a mysterious gold prospector known only as the Dutchman. Along the trail to Superstition Mountain, where the gold is located, Beau, Charlotte and the Dutchman encounter danger in the form of the bandit Padilla, who wants to know the location of the mine; Apache Indians, who would kill to protect the mine; and the gold itself, which according to legend brings death to whoever touches it.

This episode was based on the song *Dutchman's Gold*, which was released as a single in April 1960 by Dot Records. *Dutchman's Gold*, which became a Top 40 hit in 1960, was recorded by three-time Academy Award-winning character actor Walter Brennan, accompanied by Billy Vaughn and his Orchestra.

Robert Douglas often played villains in such adventure films as *The Adventures of Don Juan*, *The Flame and the Arrow*, *Kim*, *Ivanhoe*, *The Prisoner of Zenda*, *Fair Wind to Java*, and *The Virgin Queen*. Douglas became a prolific TV director in the 1960s, although he continued to act (he played the man who kidnaps Beau Maverick in "The Bundle from Britain").

99. THE ICE MAN

ORIGINAL AIRDATE: JANUARY 29, 1961

Teleplay by: Peter B. Germano
Based on a Story by: Palmer Thompson and Peter B. Germano
Directed by: Charles Hass

Guest Cast: Andrew Duggan (Calvin Powers), Shirley Knight (Nancy Powers), Bruce Gordon (Rath Lawson), Virginia Gregg (Abbey), John Kellogg (Ben Stricker), Nelson Olmsted (Eli Sayles), James Seay (Sheriff Gil McCrary), Sid Kane (Carl Stone), John Truax (Brazos), Clyde Howdy (Man at Glacier), Art Stewart (Tom Wales)

Synopsis. Bart arrives in Temple City, California just before the gubernatorial election between Reform Party candidate Calvin Powers and town boss Rath Lawson. Maverick has more than a passing interest in the race — he stands to collect $2,000 if Powers wins. But Powers' chances become cloudy after his workers unearth the body of Powers' former business partner, who was shot to death 20 years earlier. Powers killed the man in self defense, but he has never been able to prove it. When Lawson learns about the corpse, he tries to smear his opponent with the scandal.

According to Bart, Pappy told his boys to avoid trouble, but he was never much for running. This would seem a direct contradiction to one of the most-remembered Pappy-isms, "He who lives and runs away, lives to run another day."

The Mavericks frequently called upon the wisdom of their Pappy, and this episode is no exception ("Don't impose too long on a man's hospitality — he's liable to put you to work"). But they never mentioned anything about their mother — until "The Ice Man." "My Pappy said there would never be a day where you could beat an ace-high flush," Bart tells Nancy (Shirley Knight). "But my mother used to say that if you look into a well with someone you care for and make a wish, it will come true. She was always the romantic one in the family." (This is the only mention of the boys' mother in the entire series.)

"The Ice Man" also has an ironic exchange between Bart and Powers (Andrew Duggan) early in the episode. After explaining that his interest in Powers stems more from collecting $2,000 than in Powers' platform, Bart says "Can you imagine me backing a man on the Reform ticket?" Apparently Bart forgot that he once ran for senator on the Reform ticket (in "The People's Friend").

100. DIAMOND FLUSH

ORIGINAL AIRDATE: FEBRUARY 5, 1961

Teleplay by: Leo Gordon and Paul Leslie Peil
Story by: Coles Trapnell and Don Tait
Directed by: Andrew McCollough

Guest Cast: Roxane Berard (Danielle deLisle), Carl Esmond (Comte deLisle), Sig Ruman (Bockenheimer), Anna Lee (Helene Ferguson), Dan Tobin (Ralph Ferguson), Ted deCorsia (Amos Parker), K.L. Smith (Dave Dawson), Phil Tully (Tim O'Rourke), Charles Davis (Hotel Clerk)

Synopsis. A dapper con artist named Ferguson knocks Beau unconscious during an unsuccessful attempt to hoist a priceless diamond necklace from a French countess. Claiming that the countess' diamond is a fake, and that he was in the process of replacing it with the real thing when Beau startled him, Ferguson offers Maverick $5,000 to switch diamonds. Beau doesn't realize that Ferguson and his equally devious wife are setting him up for robbery.

"Diamond Flush" is the second episode in which we hear Beau whistle the theme from the *Maverick* series (he did the same in "Family Pride").

101. LAST STOP: OBLIVION

ORIGINAL AIRDATE: FEBRUARY 12, 1961

Written by: Howard Browne
Directed by: John Ainsworth

Guest Cast: Suzanne Lloyd (Laura Nelson), Buddy Ebsen (Nero Lyme), Virginia Christine (Verna Lyme), Donald Barry (Smith), Hampton Fancher (Tate McKenna), Maurice Manson (Bascombe Sunday), Rayford Barnes (Dirk Lyme), Robert Ross (Dave Lyme), Paul Birch (Sheriff Miller), Bud Osbourne (Sam Overman)

Synopsis. Aboard the Denver stage, Bart meets Laura Nelson, whose fiancé mysteriously disappeared on his way to San Francisco several months earlier. Bart, Laura and the other passengers spend the night at the stage station in Oblivion, an apparently friendly place operated by Nero and Verna Lyme. But the Lymes' warmth and hospitality mask a horrifying pasttime — they sniff out wealthy passengers and kill them for their money. When Bart and Laura discover that the Lymes murdered her fiancé, they fear for their lives.

Howard Browne's "Last Stop: Oblivion" is a taut melodrama that is further enhanced by the inspired casting of Buddy Ebsen (two years away from *The Beverly Hillbillies*) and Virginia Christine (Mrs. Olsen of the Folgers Coffee commercials) as the amiable, but ultmately deadly, Mr. and Mrs. Lyme. "It really was perfect casting, and I thought Ebsen in particular was great," said Browne. "But the credit for that goes to Coles — I just wrote the scripts, then let Roy or Coles decide which actors were best for whichever script. Some writers will make suggestions on casting, especially if they've written something with a particular actor in mind. But, in all the years I wrote for television and features, I never 'wrote for actors.' I always concentrated on plot and character development. That's the way I was taught to write."

Pappyisms: "There are only two times in a man's life when he should be noble: when he's caught dealing seconds, and when somebody slaps a lady;" and "What good's a yellow streak if you can't depend upon it?"

102. FLOOD'S FOLLY

ORIGINAL AIRDATE: FEBRUARY 19, 1961

Teleplay by: George F. Slavin
Story by: Coles Trapnell, Don Tait, and George F. Slavin
Directed by: Irving J. Moore

Guest Cast: Jeanne Cooper (Martha Flood), Michael Pate (Chet Whitehead), Alan Baxter (Judge John Scott), Marlene Willis (Sally Flood), Ric Roman (Emery), John Cliff (Elkins)

Synopsis. Amidst a blizzard outside Denver, Colorado, Beau and his friend Judge Scott find shelter in the home of widow Martha Flood and her niece Sally. Beau soon discovers that Martha and the judge are plotting to institutionalize Sally in order to take over her inheritance. But the judge is in for a surprise of his own — Martha's lover, a professional killer named Chet Whitehead, who wants to simplify matters by killing Sally, the judge, and Maverick.

Roy Huggins designed the Maverick character as a situational ethicist — someone whose ethics are not absolute, but rather flexible, depending on the circumstances. Coles Trapnell understood this key character facet, and tried to work it into his stories whenever possible, as he did with "Flood's Folly." Beau realizes he's in a tight spot (if Whitehead doesn't get him, the judge surely will), so he pretends to bargain with the judge: Make me your partner, give me half of what you stand to get from the inheritance, and we'll take care of the others. The judge asks Beau if his conscience will bother him, because becoming partners with the judge means betraying Sally Flood. "I'm very flexible with my conscience when my life is concerned," replies Beau.

George Slavin, who wrote the teleplay for "Flood's Folly," also understood the concept of situational ethics — it came into play in "Stage West," an early *Maverick* he wrote for Huggins.

Character actress Jeanne Cooper, who also guest starred in the episode "Naked Gallows," is the mother of *L.A. Law* star Corbin Bernsen. Cooper has another *Maverick* connection: for many years, she and Robert Colbert starred on the popular CBS daytime serial *The Young and the Restless*.

103. MAVERICK AT LAW

ORIGINAL AIRDATE: FEBRUARY 26, 1961

Written by: David Lang
Directed by: John Ainsworth

Guest Cast: Dolores Donlon (Clover McCoy), Gage Clarke (Myron Emerson), Tol Avery (Cyrus Murdock), James Anderson (Wooster), Kem Dibbs (McGaffy), Ken Mayer (Sheriff Starrett), Dan White (Poe)

Synopsis. Two outlaws enlist a mousy bank teller in their plans to rob the Bank of Ten Sleep, but the job is bungled when bank owner Cyrus Babcock catches the robbers in the act of looting his safe. The crooks get away, leaving the teller to stash the money in the first place he can find — inside Bart's saddle bags. Complicating the matter: although the crooks stole $5,000, the cheapskate Babcock reports a $10,000 loss (he pocketed the extra $5,000 before speaking to the sheriff). When the outlaws, who think they stole $10,000, find Maverick and the teller with only half the money, they demand to know what happened to the other $5,000.

As part of his scheme to trip up Murdock, Bart presents himself as an attorney from the law firm of Maverick, Benson and Bluel. This is an in-joke — Hugh Benson and Richard Bluel were executive assistants to William T. Orr, the Executive in Charge of Television at Warner Bros. Bluel also produced *The Gallant Men* for Warners in 1962.

Pappyism: "Don't play with strangers: the friends you have are dangerous enough."

104. RED DOG

(a.k.a. "The Cave")

ORIGINAL AIRDATE: MARCH 5, 1961

Written by: Montgomery Pittman
Directed by: Paton Price

Guest Cast: John Carradine (Judge), Sherry Jackson (Erma), Mike Road (Buckskin), Evan McCord (Kid), Lee Van Cleef (Wolf)

Synopsis. Beau stumbles onto the cave site meeting place of five outlaws who were summoned by another bandit named Jess in order to plan a big job. (Maverick passes himself as the notorious Texas outlaw "Red Dog.") When Beau declines to join the others in a $500,000 bank robbery scheme, they become suspicious and hold him hostage.

Prior to joining Maverick, Roger Moore had been assured that the scripts would be tailored specifically for him. In truth, the scripts were still being written for "Maverick" (and in all probability, James Garner, in the event that the studio won the lawsuit), and then doled out to whichever actor was available to play it. In addition, the studio continued to take scripts that were written for one series and turn them into *Maverick* episodes (the names of the characters would change, but little else). Moore found his experience very disappointing–he'd gone through it before on *The Alaskans*–and toward the end of the 1960-61 season, he asked out of *Maverick*. "Red Dog" marks his 15th and final appearance on the series.

"We finished *Maverick*, and they then said I was going to do something which was an exact duplicate of *Sugarfoot* where they wanted me to play an English 'stumblebum,'" he said. "At that point, I asked to be released from my contract–as a matter of fact, I think they offered me that show in order to get me to ask for my release. But, anyway, I went off to Italy and made some pictures."

Although Moore's personal experience as Maverick was not exactly pleasant, he turned in excellent performances in all his episodes. Moore never tried to "copy" James Garner; rather, he adapted the Maverick character to his own naturally engaging personality and made the role his own. A few years after *Maverick*, Moore became an international superstar as *The Saint* (and, much later, James Bond 007).

John Carradine was one of the greatest character actors ever known in the film industry. With his tall, reedy figure and gaunt features, he could play both sinister villains and, as in the case of this episode, an eccentric, offbeat ally. Carradine, who starred in over 170 films and nearly as many stage and TV productions, was the father of actors David, Keith and Robert Carradine.

Lee Van Cleef went on to become an internationally renowned box office star in the mid-1960s after his memorable performances in such "spaghetti Westerns" as *For a Few Dollars More* and *The Good, the Bad and the Ugly*.

Sherry Jackson, who played Danny Thomas's daughter on *Make Room for Daddy*, is the daughter of *Maverick* writer/director Montgomery Pittman. Mike Road, who plays Buckskin in this episode, starred in a series called *Buckskin* in 1958-59.

Pappyism: "Some men are afraid of the dark, and some are afraid to leave it."

105. THE DEADLY IMAGE

(a.k.a. "Killer Maverick")

ORIGINAL AIRDATE: MARCH 12, 1961

Teleplay by: Leo Gordon and Paul Leslie Peil
Story by: Coles Trapnell and Don Tait
Directed by: John Ainsworth

Guest Cast: Gerald Mohr (Gus Tellson), Abraham Sofaer (Papa Rambeau), Dawn Wells (Caprice Rambeau), Robert Ridgely (Lt. Reed), Bartlett Robinson (Captain Ranson), Kelly Thordsen (Hammett), Harvey Johnson (Sergeant Rafferty)

Synopsis. Rod Claxton, a onetime federal deputy marshal who found more profit in murder and robbery, is wanted both by the Army and a former gang member named Gus Tellson whom Claxton doublecrossed. (Tellson went to prison for Claxton for a robbery on the condition that Claxton provide Tellson's family with a share of the money; instead, Claxton kept the money and took advantage of the affections of a young girl named Caprice Rambeau — Tellson's daughter.) After the Army mistakenly arrests Bart — who bears an uncanny physical resemblance to Claxton — Tellson breaks Maverick out of prison. The two men head for Caprice's home to capture Claxton.

Jack Kelly had missed several weeks after breaking a bone in his right hand, and as a result scripts that would have gone to him were sent on to Roger Moore. "We needed a story for Kelly for when he came back to work," recalled Coles Trapnell. "Don Tait and I bounced around the idea of doing a show where Jack would play two parts — Maverick and a bad guy who was his lookalike. Don came up with the story (although he gave me co-credit), then I passed it onto Leo Gordon, who wrote the script."

Kelly's hand was still in a cast when he reported to the set for "The Deadly Image," but Trapnell simply wrote the injury into the script. "We added a scene in which Maverick is shot in the hand at the beginning of the show," said Trapnell. "He would have to get patched up, and that would explain the cast on Kelly's hand."

106. TRIPLE INDEMNITY

ORIGINAL AIRDATE: MARCH 19, 1961

Written by: Irene Winston
Directed by: Leslie H. Martinson

Guest Cast: Peter Breck (Doc Holliday), Alan Hewitt (George Parker), Charity Grace (Mrs. Parker), Ed Nelson (Bill Parker), J. Edward McKinley (Sam Landry), Don Beddoe (Dr. Whalen), Laurie Mitchell (Ellen), Nick Pawl (Slim), Bob Wiensko (Jones), Mickey Simpson (Cabella), Alberto Morin (Chef)

Synopsis. Bart wins $800 from George Parker, the mayor and owner of the town Parkerville — and a notorious bad loser. After George has Maverick robbed and beaten,

George's younger brother Bill, who has long held a grudge against his sibling, convinces Bart to help him even the score. After Bill and his mother set up Maverick as a cattle buyer, Bart takes out a $100,000 life insurance policy, then arranges to have himself "killed." George, who owns the company, discovers Bart's plan and refuses to pay the claim. But that move, as Maverick points out, could cost the company millions in cancelled policies — so George is forced to keep Bart alive. But the charade backfires when a greedy undertaker tempts Doc Holliday into killing Maverick for $50,000.

"Triple Indemnity" marks Peter Breck's first of five appearances as Doc Holliday, who was played by Gerald Mohr in two first season episodes ("The Quick and the Dead" and "Seed of Deception"). Breck and fellow *Maverick* confederate Richard Long later co-starred with Barbara Stanwyck in *The Big Valley*.

Pappyism: "No matter what a man does in life, he always has a guilty conscience. But the smart man suffers his guilt pangs in luxury."

107. THE FORBIDDEN CITY

(a.k.a. "The Guilt-Edged Bond")

ORIGINAL AIRDATE: MARCH 26, 1961

Teleplay by: Wells Root
Story by: Coles Trapnell and Don Tait
Directed by: Richard C. Sarafian

Guest Cast: Nina Shipman (Joanne Moss), Lisa Montell (Andalucia Rubio), Jack Mather (Mayor Moss), Jeff deBenning (Dave Taylor), Thomas B. Henry (McGuire), Robert Foulk (Sheriff Shadley), Gertrude Flynn (Nettie Moss), Vladmir Sokoloff (Robbins), Bill Erwin (Hotel Clerk), Craig Duncan (Val Joyce)

Synopsis. The first of Robert Colbert's two appearances as Brent Maverick, Bret and Bart's younger brother. Brent finds himself arrested for gambling in Sunburst, a town that prohibits all vices. His cellmate Rubio has just served a 20-year sentence for a murder he didn't commit. Rubio has proof of his innocence that he plans to present to the town judge, but three men break into the jail and kill him. Brent and Joanne Moss, the town historian, also investigate, but neither are aware that Joanne's uncle — the mayor of Sunburst — is linked to Rubio's death.

Not much is known about young Brent Maverick, the "other brother" who came and went after only two appearances. A publicity release issued by Warner Bros. in early 1961 describes him only as "a strapping new relative of the irrepressible Mavericks." Wells Root's teleplay for "The Forbidden City" doesn't provide much more — the script merely depicts Brent as "a gambler trapped in a sinless city" who is "dressed as his brother Bret used to be."

Robert Colbert is to be commended for his fine work on *Maverick*, considering that he joined the series at a particularly difficult time. In the wake of James Garner's victory against Warner Bros., *Maverick*'s total audience dropped another ten percent. "Roy was gone, Jim was gone, and much of the humor of the show was gone," said Colbert. "I don't remember many of the particulars of those two episodes, but it doesn't matter — I'm a part of the page of the past. I was a part of that series, and a part of the 'Legend of the West.'"

Pappyisms: "In the midst of life, we are in jail;" and "Never debate the innocence of a drinking woman or a man in jail."

108. SUBSTITUTE GUN

ORIGINAL AIRDATE: APRIL 2, 1961

Teleplay by: Howard Browne
Story by: Berne Giler
Directed by: Paul Landres

Guest Cast: Coleen Gray (Greta Blauvelt), Joan Marshall, (Connie Malone), Robert Rockwell (Tom Blauvelt), Carlos Romero (Clete Spain), Walter Sande (Sheriff Coleman), Jack Searl (Smiley), Norman Leavitt (Ezra Gouch), Harry Seymour (Piano Player), Joseph Hamilton (Stableman)

Synopsis. While passing through Spearhead, Kansas, Bart bumps into Robert "Smiley" Drake, a professional gunman whom he met in a St. Louis gameroom long ago. Afraid that Maverick will discover his business in town, Smiley tries to kill Bart, but the sheriff, who had become suspicious of Smiley's behavior, trails the gunman and shoots him dead. The sheriff asks Maverick to impersonate Smiley in order to find out who hired him. Bart's only clues: the professional and personal animosities between rival gambling house owners Tom Blauvelt and Clete Spain; and Smiley's dying words, "Get Blauvelt."

Bart, who was hired by Blauvelt, suspects a ruse when he notices Spain meeting with Tom's bookkeeper, who had been studying the roulette wheel at Blauvelt's casino and making notes on probable winning combinations. "When a roulette wheel gets a lot of use, the spindle begins to wear one way or the other," he explains. "If you can guess which way, and bet those numbers, your odds go way up." Spain tries to cash in (at Tom's expense), but Bart trips him up by switching the wheel — "a little trick an old riverboat gambler taught me," he later tells Blauvelt. As a result of Bart's chicanery, Spain lost over $11,000.

"Substitute Gun," which was originally made on *Cheyenne* as the episode "Hired Gun," features this word of advice from Pappy Maverick: "Never make friends with a man who has no enemies."

109. BENEFIT OF DOUBT

ORIGINAL AIRDATE: APRIL 9, 1961

Written by: David Lang
Directed by: Paul Landres

Guest Cast: Randy Stuart (Mavis Todd), Elizabeth McRae (Emily Todd), Mort Mills (McGaven), Trevor Bardette (Bert Coleman), John Alderson (Zindler), George Wallace (Sheriff Joe Holly), Slim Pickens (Roscoe), Steve Raines (Sims), Fred Krone (Walt)

Synopsis. Three men rob the American Mail Company in Amber Flats of over $7,000. The robbers are gunned down, but the money disappears. Sheriff Joe Holly claims there was a fourth man who got away, but Holly himself lifted the money after shooting one of the bandits, and mailed it to the nearby Midway station. Holly never gets a chance to pick up the money — he was shot on his way to the station. Brent Maverick, who was stranded at Midway after losing all his money the night before, recovers the money and decides to return it to Amber Flats. But when a posse intercepts him and finds the money in his saddle bags, Brent finds himself arrested for the robbery.

While he was starring in *Maverick*, Robert Colbert was a restaurateur — he owned and operated The Corner, in Beverly Hills. Colbert went on to star in *The Time Tunnel* and *The Young and the Restless*.

Pappyism: "Patience is the best remedy for every trouble — but money is better."

110./111. THE DEVIL'S NECKLACE
(TWO PARTER)

(a.k.a. "To Kill a Brigadier")
ORIGINAL AIRDATES: APRIL 16 AND 23, 1961

Teleplay by: William Bruckner
Story by: Coles Trapnell and Don Tait
Directed by: Paul Landres

Guest Cast: John Dehner (Luther Cannonbaugh), Sharon Hugueny (Tawny), John Hoyt (General Bassington), Steve Brodie (Captain Score), John Archer (Major Reidinger), Kasey Rogers (Angel Score), Rita Lynn (Mrs. Reidinger), Michael Forest (Bob Tallhorse), Mark Tapscott (Enlisted Man), Chad Everett (Lieutenant Gregg), Rayford Barnes (Corporal Sean), Jerry O'Sullivan (Lieutenant Torrance)

Synopsis. After his horse breaks down in the Arizona heat, Bart seeks shelter at Fort Distress, operated by his friend Major Reidinger. A greedy peddler named Luther Cannonbaugh suckers Bart into buying a wagon containing illegal whiskey — and the Indian squaw Tawny, whom Cannonbaugh kidnapped to sell into slavery. An angry Bob Tallhorse, the Apache warrior to whom Tawny is betrothed, threatens to attack the fort unless she is released. Maverick tries to return Tawny to her tribe, but Tallhorse captures him. Meanwhile, Cannonbaugh (whom the Apaches had also imprisoned) bargains his way of trouble by offering Tallhorse "strong medicine" — a beartooth necklace that makes its wearer impervious to bullets. The conniving Cannonbaugh demonstrates the neckpiece's "power" by testing it himself (using blank cartridges). Bart warns Tallhorse of the fraud, but Cannonbaugh shoots him with a real bullet that grazes him in the temple. As Maverick lies unconscious, Tallhorse and the Apaches launch a massive attack on Fort Distress.

Best known to *Maverick* fans as the greedy banker in "Shady Deal at Sunny Acres," John Dehner was a marvelous character actor who had no limitations. "John was a consummate performer who could do just about anything," said director Leslie Martinson. "He was under contract to Warner Bros. at the time, and they would use him in all their shows.

"John was what we called a 'money in the bank' actor. You never had to worry whenever he was in one of your shows, and I did so many things with him over the course of my years at Warners. Sometimes, as I was watching John in the dailies, the producer of whatever show I was directing would say 'That was a great, great scene,' and I'd say, 'Yeah, I thought it was rather good — and, of course, I got it for nothing.' That was John Dehner — you'd only have to turn the camera on and turn him loose." Dehner, who later starred as Marshall Troy on *Young Maverick*, passed away in 1992.

The only two-part episode of the original *Maverick* series, "The Devil's Necklace" also features Chad Everett, who later became a major TV star on the long-running CBS hosptial drama *Medical Center*.

Pappyism: "You can tell a fortune or make a fortune with a deck of cards.

JACK KELLY AND RUDOLPH ACOSTA

FIFTH SEASON: 1961-1962
PRODUCTION CREDITS

Starring Jack Kelly as Bart Maverick
and James Garner as Bret Maverick

Executive Producer: William T. Orr
Produced by: William L. Stuart
Created by: Roy Huggins

Supervising Producer: Arthur W. Silver
Directors of Photography: Louis Jennings, Harold Stine, Robert Tobey, Jack Marquette
Art Directors: William Campbell, John Ewing, LeRoy Deane, Carl Macauley, Stanley Fleischer
Film Editors: Robert Jahns, Clarence Kolster, Fred M. Bohanan, John Joyce, Harry Reynolds, Robert Crawford, Cliff Bell, Byron Chudnow

Music Supervision: Paul Sawtell, Bert Shefter
Music Editors: Erma E. Levin, Sam E. Levin, Joe Inge, Theodore W. Sebern, George E. Marsh, Donald K. Harris, Louis W. Gordon, John Allyn Jr.

Song "Maverick" — Music by David Buttolph, **Lyrics by** Paul Francis Webster

Production Manager: Oren W. Haglund
Sound: Francis E. Stahl, Howard Fogetti, Everett A. Hughes, Stanley Jones, Sam F. Goode, B.F. Ryan, Gary Harris, Robert B. Lee, Frank McWhorter
Set Decorators: Alfred E. Kegerris, Jerry Welch, John P. Austin, Hoyle Barrett, Bertram C. Granger
Assistant Directors: William Kissel, John F. Murphy, Rex Bailey
Makeup Supervisor: Gordon Bau
Supervising Hair Stylist: Jean Burt Reilly
Announcer: Ed Reimers

Filmed at Warner Bros. Studios in Burbank, California

William L. Stuart took over as *Maverick*'s producer (the show's fourth in less than one year) for the fifth and final season. Arthur Silver, who had replaced Coles Trapnell late in the fourth season, had been promoted to the role of "supervising producer," which in effect made him

Maverick's executive producer. William T. Orr was still executive producer, as he was on all Warners shows — that was part of his capacity as the studio's Executive in Charge of Television. But in 1960, at the peak of Warners' early TV success, Orr found that the volume of production had become so great that he needed assistance in the overseeing of all of the studio's programs. To relieve some of that burden, Orr created a new line of management, the "supervising producer," who was assigned to manage the work of individual producers on two or three series.

In a sense, *Maverick* went back to its roots for its fifth season. For the first time since the early first-year episodes (before the introduction of brother Bart), the series became a solo vehicle. Jack Kelly was now the unquestioned star, the only Maverick in town — there's no mention of any brothers or cousins on the horizon in any of the 13 fifth-season episodes. But the show had a haggard look to it. "[*Maverick*] seems to have a difficult time in starting new trails," noted *Weekly Variety* (September 27, 1961). "The names and places are different, but it has an aura of having been thataway before. The plot seems familiar and the treatment has worn thin throughout the years." Compounding the familiarity was ABC's decision to rotate the new Kelly episodes with reruns from the first two seasons. The repeats featured James Garner, perhaps in an attempt to lure the Garner fans back to the series. (Garner's name, in fact, continued to appear in the opening sequence of the fifth-year shows — only now it followed Jack Kelly's.)

Maverick did introduce two new characters to the series: Kathleen Crowley and Mike Road appeared in two episodes as grafters Marla and Pearly Gates ("Dade City Dodge," "The Troubled Heir"). Although Crowley and Road were fine in their roles, the characters didn't work, and again the problem had to do with familiarity — Marla and Pearly were simply two more clones in the long line of duplicate characters patterned after the long-departed Samantha Crawford (Diane Brewster) and Dandy Jim Buckley (Efrem Zimbalist Jr.).

Peter Breck also joined Kelly in four episodes as Doc Holliday (Breck had taken over the role from Gerald Mohr in *Maverick*'s fourth season). The approach to Doc Holliday reflects the difference in approach to *Maverick* before and after Roy Huggins. Mohr's Holliday, who appeared in the first season ("The Quick and the Dead"), was a somber, calculating, and philosophical character, much like the real Doc Holliday. Breck also played the gunman as an intellectual, but more humor was written into his character. (Purists, however, will likely cringe if they should catch Breck in "The Maverick Report." Holliday's legend takes a beating in this episode, in which Doc enters a rowing competition — without knowing anything about handling a rowboat. Holliday proceeds to sink the boat, in the truest tradition of slapstick comedy.)

The fifth-season episodes also feature a goosed-up version of the *Maverick* theme song. The new rendition has a more upbeat tempo, and features such accoutrements as bells (after the lyric "Riverboat, ring your bell") and horns ("Fare thee well, Annabelle").

In the meantime, *Maverick*'s decline coincided with that of the entire Warner Bros. Television Department. Just two years after its peak period — 1959-60, when it placed four series (*77 Sunset Strip, Lawman, Cheyenne*, and *Maverick*) in the Top 20 — the studio was facing major problems. Although all four series were still on the air, their audiences were dwindling, and nothing seemed capable of bringing them back. The high-volume production system demonstrated that Warner Bros. knew how to manufacture stories quickly, but the material was often recycled from one series to another. No one seemed capable of creating something new (or something new that worked) — the studio's strident policies against profit sharing and ownership of series continued to keep the truly "creative" talent away.

ABC, which had entered an exclusive agreement with Warner Bros. in 1955, was growing concerned. "ABC went to Jack Warner and said, 'We want to change this situation,'" said Jack Kelly to Mick Martin in 1992. "J.L. told them to stuff it. But ABC had one power that nobody else could control, and that was scheduling the time the show went on. We went from 7:30 p.m. Sunday, where we had been a hit, to an hour earlier at 6:30 p.m. And we got killed by, of all things, *Dennis the Menace*! They threw us smack into a family hour. Not that *Maverick* wasn't a family show, but *Dennis the Menace* was an unpaid babysitter on Sunday nights. That put us down the drain."

Dennis the Menace was actually a 7:30 show, but Kelly was correct on all other accounts. The two shows ran head-to-head in the 1959-60 and 1960-61 seasons. *Maverick*, as previously noted, suffered a considerable decrease in audience during both years. (For the record, two of the series against which *Maverick* competed in its 6:30 time slot were *Mister Ed* and *The Bullwinkle Show*, both of which had the hip, biting humor that *Maverick* had in its first two years. *Maverick* faced another "unpaid babysitter" in *Lassie*, which ran on CBS from 7:00 to 7:30.)

Maverick suffered another blow when Kaiser Industries withdrew its sponsorship. "Henry Kaiser pulled out because he was paying for a 7:30 time slot, not 6:30," Kelly continued. "We had no crutches whatsoever. We just went to hell in a handbasket, and the show was soon over." *Maverick* once again lost nearly one-third of its viewers — the series' total audience had dropped to just 22 percent (down from its fourth-season average of 32.4). Not even reruns of such venerable *Maverick*s as "Shady Deal at Sunny Acres," "Gun-Shy," and "The Saga of Waco Williams" — all of which had pulled monstrous audience figures during their original broadcasts — could not lure back the viewers. ABC quietly cancelled the series at the end of the season. *Maverick* had its final prime time telecast on July 8, 1962.

"For that show to die as inelegantly as it did . . . that was hard to take," said Jack Kelly to Mick Martin in 1992. "But we had some good stuff, and we had some good times. And I will never look back on those days with anything less than a charming retrospective delight that I was involved in it."

Kelly's sentiment has been shared by many, many fans and followers of the series. It is also at the heart of why *Maverick* has continued to endure for over 30 years. "*Maverick* was such a huge success, especially in its second year, that the show took on mythic proportions," said Roy Huggins. "Myths have always have strange perceptions attached to them, and as a result the facts often become idealized."

Maverick, in other words, was more than "the Legend of the West." *Maverick became* a legend unto itself. The series made such an impact on television during its phenomenally successful first two seasons — it put a different spin on television by injecting a sense of humor into the Western; it launched Huggins on the way to becoming one of the most successful producers in the history of television; and it gave us James Garner — that its struggles during its final three years are often overlooked.

Maverick also had an enormous influence on such people as Stephen J. Cannell, who became a protegé of Roy Huggins. Cannell and Huggins created and produced *The Rockford Files*, James Garner's second hit TV series. Cannell joked that he often came up with ideas for *The Rockford Files* by "stealing" ideas from *Maverick*; in fact, Cannell has said that he based the *Rockford* character Lance White (the picture-perfect private detective played by Tom Selleck) on none other than Waco Williams. Also, blues artist George Thorogood recorded a version of the *Maverick* theme for his 1985 album *Maverick*. "I had to do it," Thorogood once said. "Growing up, [Bret Maverick] was the coolest guy in my life."

"*Maverick* was so important that it became an idealized cult image in the lives of many people," said Huggins. "Something has to be pretty special to have that done to it."

Familiar faces in *Maverick*'s fifth season include Jack Cassidy, John Hoyt, Ed Nelson, John Dehner, Kasey Rogers, and Jim Backus.

112. DADE CITY DODGE

ORIGINAL AIRDATE: SEPTEMBER 17, 1961

Written by: George F. Slavin
Directed by: Irving J. Moore

Guest Cast: Kathleen Crowley (Marla), Mike Road (Pearly Gates), Ken Lynch (Sheriff Clark), Gage Clarke (Harper), Charles Arnt (Mason), Guy Wilkerson (Kerns), Robert Burton (Judge Kincaid), Edward J. Moore (Sykes), Mickey Morton (Sheriff Hiram Tiray).

Synopsis. At a horse race in New Orleans, smoothtalking hustler Pearly Gates and his accomplice Marla talk Bart into betting $5,000 on a longshot. But Pearly never placed the bet — he fled with the money. Following a tip from Marla, Bart heads for Dade City, Texas, where he hopes to catch up with Pearly. After a crooked sheriff and three card sharks take him for $4,000, Maverick decides to kill two birds with one stone: he convinces the foursome that Pearly is a notorious bank robber named Diamond Mike, whose capture is worth $10,000. But the plan goes awry when the greedy card sharks, eyeing the $50,000 that Diamond Mike recently heisted, plot to break Pearly out of jail, lead them to the money — and then kill him.

Pearly Gates (Mike Road) and Marla (Kathleen Crowley) were two more attempts to fill the void left by Efrem Zimbalist Jr. and Diane Brewster when both left *Maverick* and took their characters with them. Like Dandy Jim Buckley and Marla, both Pearly and Marla are all-out grafters who operate without any kind of ethical code. Maverick, on the other hand, has a conscience, as we see in "The Troubled Heir." Bart wants to get back at Pearly for cheating him of $5,000, but once he realizes that he's put Pearly's life in danger, Bart tries to save him (Pearly's death might cost him a few night's sleep). If the shoe were on the other foot, Pearly — like Buckley — would likely ditch Maverick as soon as he could.

Mike Road, who starred in *The Roaring Twenties* for Warner Bros., was also the voice of Race Bannon on *Jonny Quest*.

113. THE ART LOVERS

ORIGINAL AIRDATE: OCTOBER 1, 1961

Written by: Peter B. Germano
Directed by: Michael O'Herlihy

Guest Cast: James Westerfield (Paul Sutton), Jack Cassidy (Roger Cushman), Maurine Dawson (Ann Sutton), John Hoyt (George Cushman), Leo Belasco (Cosmo Nardi), Stephen Chase (Taber Scott), Stanley Farrar (Leighton Borg), John Alderson (Captain Bly), Laurie Main (Crimmins), Gertrude Flynn (Rheba Sutton), Lou Krugman (Larouche).

Synopsis. In San Francisco, Bart becomes a servant to railroad tycoon Paul Sutton in order to pay off a $25,000 gambling debt. Sutton faces bankruptcy — a new railroad project has encountered delays, and the board of directors has denied his request for another loan of $500,000. Sutton's one asset, an apparently original daVinci *Mona Lisa*, can't help him because he bought it from a dealer who claims it was stolen. When Maverick recognizes the dealer as a con artist friend (whose specialty is forging daVinci's), he devises a scheme to sway the board members into changing their vote.

Jack Cassidy often played suave, dashing (and often cold-blooded) villains in numerous TV series, such as *Mission: Impossible* and *Columbo*, but he was equally adept at comedy — he starred as the egotiscal star of "Jetman" on *He and She*, and was Ted Baxter's equally vain brother on *The Mary Tyler Moore Show*. Cassidy, who died in 1976, was once married to singer/actress Shirley Jones; one of his sons (David) co-starred with Jones on *The Partridge Family*, while the other (Shawn) co-starred with Jack Kelly on *The Hardy Boys Mysteries*.

Pappyisms: "There are a lot worse things in life than being broke, although I must admit I don't know of any;" and "Travel broadens the mind."

114. THE GOLDEN FLEECING

ORIGINAL AIRDATE: OCTOBER 8, 1961

Written by: Charles B. Smith
Directed by: Irving J. Moore

Guest Cast: Paula Raymond (Adele Jaggers), Olive Sturgess (Phoebe Albright), John Qualen (Henry Albright), J. Edward McKinley (Loftus Jaggers), Myron Healey (Frank Mercer), Richard Loo (Lee Hong Chang), Charles Meredith (Seth Carter), Herb Vigran (Mr. Butler), Harry Harvey Sr. (Captain Owens)

Synopsis. Bart enters the stock market when he oversees the investment of a mining company owned by the Albrights, a family of Quakers who rescued Maverick from drowning in the Sacramento River. Maverick must then protect the Albrights' interests when a greedy industrialist and his equally covetous daughter plot to take over the company.

Jack Kelly always had a keen eye for business. He invested most of his *Maverick* earnings in real estate, and by the time the series ended he had created a nice financial empire. Kelly at one point owned so much property in Southern California, James Garner once cracked that his former co-star "owned all of Orange County."

Pappyisms: "There's nothing like a boat trip if you're going somewhere by water;" and "The most important thing to know about any gambling game is when to quit."

115. THREE QUEENS FULL

(a.k.a. "Three Brides for Three Brothers")

ORIGINAL AIRDATE: NOVEMBER 12, 1961

Teleplay by: William Bruckner
Story by: William Bruckner and Robert Hamner
Directed by: Michael O'Herlihy

Guest Cast: Jim Backus (Joe Wheelwright), Merry Anders (Cissie), Kasey Rogers (Emma), Allyson Ames (Lou Ann), Evan McCord (Small Paul), Jake Sheffield (Moose), Larry Chance (Henry), Frank Ferguson (Sheriff Mattson), Harry Lauter (Brazo), Willard Waterman (Whittleseed), Don Kennedy (Humboldt)

Synopsis. In this loose parody of the popular Western series *Bonanza*, wealthy rancher Joe Wheelwright hires Bart to chaperone the three brides he purchased for his sons Henry, Moose and Small Paul. Maverick soon discovers that the women are linked to a man named Brazo, a rival of Wheelwright's who hopes to buy his way into the family fortune.

Because it also attempts to satirize a top-rated network Western series, "Three Queens Full" ranks among *Maverick*'s most-remembered episodes, although the episode received nowhere near the tremendous advance publicity that benefited "Gun-Shy." But as a parody, "Three Queens Full" fails in the same way that "Gun-Shy" failed—it reduces the Cartwright family of *Bonanza* (or "Wheelwrights," as they're known in this episode) to dunderheaded caricatures without really poking fun at the conventions that made *Bonanza* so popular (it was the No. 2 show on television in 1961, en route to becoming No. 1 for five consecutive seasons in the mid-1960s).

"Three Queens Full" does, however, kid the Cartwright family's closeness and sanctimonious reputation. The Wheelwrights stick together because Joe Wheelwright's father swindled the Indians of their land — that's how he built the Subrosa Ranch, and the Wheelwrights stick together in order to protect the family secret. But the episode missed an obvious target. Ben Cartwright and his sons owned a fabulous 600,000-acre spread (the Ponderosa), but they were always so busy becoming involved in other people's problems that they never seemed to work on their own ranch. The Ponderosa apparently ran by itself.

Jim Backus, a few years away from becoming millionaire blowhard Thurston Howell III on *Gilligan's Island*, plays Joe Wheelwright in a similar blustery, gruff way. He's the best reason for watching "Three Queens Full." Backus was also the voice of the near-sighted octogenarian *Mister Magoo* in numerous cartoons during the 1960s.

116. A TECHNICAL ERROR

ORIGINAL AIRDATE: NOVEMBER 26, 1961

Teleplay by: Irene Winston and David Lang
Story by: David Lang
Directed by: Marc Lawrence

Guest Cast: Peter Breck (Doc Holliday), Reginald Owen (Major Holbrook Sims), Jolene Brand (Penelope), Alma Platt (Mrs. Hennessey), Ben Gage (Sheriff), Galay Graves (Holly), Frank DeKova (Blackjack), Stephen Coit (Mr. Craft), Frank London (Sonny), Jake Sheffield (Deputy), Paul Barselow (Ferguson)

Synopsis. In Junction Corners, Bart wins ownership of the Bank on the Square from Major Holbrook Sims, who seems suspiciously eager to unload the bank. Maverick soon discovers why: the bank is short $20,000 due to a bookkeeping error. When the word leaks out, the angry townspeople threaten to make a run on the bank. Bart's problems increase when Doc Holliday "borrows" the money from Blackjack Carney and his gang of thieves, who demand $25,000 in return.

Reginald Owen, who previously guest-starred in "The Belcastle Brand" and "Gun-Shy," appeared in dozens of major films in a career that spanned nearly five decades, including such classics as *A Christmas Carol*, *The Call of the Wild*, *A Tale of Two Cities*, *Mrs. Miniver*, *Kidnapped*, *Woman of the Year*, *National Velvet*, *Five Weeks in a Balloon* and *Mary Poppins*. Owen, who also co-starred with James Garner in *Darby's Rangers* and *The Thrill of It All*, died in 1972.

Jolene Brand was one of comedian Ernie Kovacs' repertory of players — she appeared on many of Kovacs' television series as "the girl in the bathtub" in numerous comedy blackout sketches. Brand also played opposite Guy Williams (*Lost in Space*) on *Zorro*.

Pappyism: "Money's always the same — it's the pockets that change."

117. POKER FACE

(a.k.a. "The Short Career of Sebastian Bolanos")

ORIGINAL AIRDATE: JANUARY 7, 1962

Teleplay by: Fred Eggers
From a Magazine Story by: Jennings Perry
Directed by: Michael O'Herlihy

Guest Cast: Rudolph Acosta (Sebastian Bolanos), Carlos Rivas (Luis), Tol Avery (George Rockingham), William Fawcett (Stallion), Doris Lloyd (Lady Florentine Bleakly), Nancy Hsueh (Rose Kwan), Richard Hale (Dr. Robespierre Jones), I. Stanford Jolley (Chauncey), Anna Novarro (Maria), Jorge Moreno (Captain Renaldo)

Synopsis. Outside Yuma, Bart boards a stagecoach whose passengers include George Rockingham, an American businessman; Dr. Robespierre Jones, a missionary; Lady Florentine Bleakly, a woman of British nobility; and Rose Kwan, an Asian woman en route to Mexico City to fulfill an arranged marriage. Rockingham, Bleakly, and Jones look down upon Bart (because of his profession) and Rose (because of her race). But they all change their opinion quickly after Mexican bandit Sebastian Bolanos kidnaps them and holds them for $70,000 ransom. Their lives are in Bart's hands when Bolanos challenges Maverick to a high stakes game of poker for their freedom.

According to this episode, Maverick has a second supply of emergency money — a $50 gold piece that he keeps inside his boots. Maverick's usual source of emergency funds is his "pin money" — the $1,000 bill he keeps pinned inside his coat. "Poker Face" is the only episode of the series that mentions this gold piece.

At the time she filmed "Poker Face," Nancy Hsueh (who played Rose Kwan) was studying to become an English teacher — she took acting jobs during the summer to pay her tuition at UCLA. Although Hsueh spoke fluent French, Italian, German, Spanish and English, she couldn't speak a word of Chinese. Hsueh also starred in the CBS daytime serial *Love is a Many Splendored Thing*.

Pappyism: "There's imperfection in all of us; it just shows more in some, is all."

118. EPITAPH FOR A GAMBLER

ORIGINAL AIRDATE: FEBRUARY 11, 1962

Written by: George F. Slavin
Directed by: Irving J. Moore

Guest Cast: Marie Windsor (Kit Williams), Fred Beir (Sheriff Ed Martin), Robert Wilke (Diamond Dan Malone), Joyce Meadows (Linda Storey), Adam Williams (Sam Elkins), Frank Albertson (Harvey Storey), Don Haggerty (Lucky Matt Elkins), Wes Hellman (Whitey), Harry Harvey Jr. (Wes Taylor)

Synopsis. In Sunrise, Nevada, Bart wins $12,600 playing roulette at Diamond Dan Malone's gambling parlor. Dan is $10,000 short, so he writes Maverick an I.O.U. and offers to pay him once a week out of the casino's profits. Bart becomes suspicious when he discovers that Dan has been holding back funds due him in order to pay blackmail money to a gambler named Elkins. Maverick leans on Dan to settle his account first (the I.O.U. could shut down Dan's business), but Elkins refuses to negotiate. When Elkins is found murdered, Dan becomes the prime suspect.

As far as the TV series was concerned, Bret Maverick literally took a ride on the trail to who-knows-where. After "The Maverick Line" episode, he was neither seen nor heard from again (although Bart did name him as the beneficiary in the life insurance policy he took out in "Triple Indemnity"). But Bret Maverick continued to live on — at least in the world of comic books. Bret's character appeared in "The Diamond Mine," a story featured in *Maverick* No. 18, published by Dell Comics in January 1962. *Maverick* No. 18 was the final issue of the comic book series.

Pappyism: "You can tell more about a town by looking at its gambling emporium than any other area."

119. THE MAVERICK REPORT

ORIGINAL AIRDATE: MARCH 4, 1962

Written by: Irene Winston
Directed by: Irving J. Moore

Guest Cast: Peter Breck (Doc Holliday), Lloyd Corrigan (Senator Porter), Jo Morrow (Jeanie Porter), Patricia Crest (Molly Malone), Ed Nelson (Gary Harrison), George Neise (Jonesy), Kem Dibbs (Ames), Don Harvey (Sheriff Bentley)

Synopsis. In Colorado, Bart wins ownership of the *Porterville Clarion* newspaper from his friend Jonesy, who owes him $15,000. Bart enables Jonesy to buy back the paper; as collateral, Jonesy offers information implicating Senator Porter in a scheme to purchase Indian lands for profit (after the Senator had previously condemned them). Jonesy assures Maverick that he can prove his allegations, but when Porter retaliates with a $100,000 libel lawsuit, Bart decides to sell the newspaper as soon as possible. Maverick heads for Jonesy's place — but discovers Jonesy is dead.

Jack Kelly owned a newspaper in real life —*The Huntington Beach News*.

120. MARSHAL MAVERICK

ORIGINAL AIRDATE: MARCH II, 1962

Teleplay by: James O'Hanlon and Arnold Bellgard
Story by: Arnold Bellgard
Directed by: Sidney Salkow

Guest Cast: John Dehner (Archie Walker), Peter Breck (Doc Holliday), Gail Kobe (Theodora Rush), Earl Hammond (Billy Coe), Willard Waterman (Mayor Oliver), Med Florey (Wyatt Earp), Herb Vigran (Elkins), Jerry Hausner (George), Kay Kuter (First Creditor), Greg Bendict (Keno), Zack Foster (Cowhand)

Synopsis. Archibald Walker, a cowardly bartender who believes his life is meaningless (he likens himself to the hole in a doughnut), arrives in Abilene under the guise of Wyatt Earp, whose trademark revolver he stole when Earp wasn't looking. Deputy Bart becomes Archie's protector when gunslinger Billy Coe challenges "Earp" to a showdown. (Bart was heavily in debt to the previous marshal, who was shot to death by one of Coe's men in the middle of a poker game. When Maverick shot down the gunman, the mayor named Bart temporary marshal to pay off the debt; when "Wyatt Earp" took over, he insisted on keeping Maverick as a deputy.) Archie's problems multiply when the real Wyatt Earp shows up.

Maverick's cancellation at the end of the 1961-62 season did not spell the end of Jack Kelly's career — he continued to star in movies and television for the next 20 years before following another path in 1980. "I was campaign chairman for a buddy of mine who was running for county supervisor in Huntington Beach," Kelly told Mick Martin in 1992. "Then people I'd had working on behalf of my candidate tried to interest me in running for city council. So I did and got elected."

Kelly served two four-year terms on the Huntington Beach City Council; after sitting out two years (the city's laws prohibited him from serving three successive terms), he was re-elected to the council in 1990, where he continued to serve until his death in 1992.

Pappyism: "If you don't go when the going's good, you're gonna get got."

121. THE TROUBLED HEIR

(a.k.a. "A Will is Better Than a Way")

ORIGINAL AIRDATE: APRIL 1, 1962

Written by: George F. Slavin
Directed by: Sidney Salkow

Guest Cast: Kathleen Crowley (Marla), Mike Road (Pearly Gates), Alan Hale (Big Jim Watson), Chick Chandler (Oliver "Slippery" Perkins), Will Wright (Sheriff Chester Bentley), Frank Ferguson (Sheriff Luther Hawkins), Gordon Jones (Ward Quillan), Will J. White (Hub)

Synopsis. Bart renews acquaintance with the crafty duo Pearly Gates and Marla, whom he last encountered in "Dade City Dodge." Pearly and Marla lure Maverick into a poker game with some other players — one of whom is wanted outlaw Big Jim Watson. After Pearly and Marla create a smoke screen, they sneak off with the $5,000 pot, but Bart and Watson soon catch up with them. When Watson discovers that Pearly's already spent the money (he and Marla invested in a mine that turned out to be worthless), the outlaw orders Pearly to turn him in for the $10,000 reward money — in exchange, Pearly would receive $2,500 after Watson's men break him out of jail. But Maverick discovers that Watson intends to kill Pearly.

Once again (as in "Dade City Dodge"), Pearly Gates takes advantage of Bart's good nature. Once again, Bart faces a dilemma between conscience and self-preservation when he inadvertently puts Pearly in danger. Once again, Maverick rescues Pearly, but this time his motives are more pragmatic. "I'm not a sentimental slob where Pearly's concerned, but common decency dictated his being apprised of his imminent demise," Bart observes. "Besides, if he was killed, I'd never get my money back."

122. THE MONEY MACHINE

ORIGINAL AIRDATE: APRIL 8, 1962

Written by: Robert Vincent Wright
Directed by: Lee Sholem

Guest Cast: Andrew Duggan (Big Ed Murphy), Kathy Bennett (Jacqueline Sutton), Patrick Westwood (London Louis Lattimer), Ted de Corsia (Cannonball Clyde Bassett), Henry Corden (Professor Raynard), Sig Ruman (Jonckbloet), Frank London (Bellboy), Charles Fredericks (Marshal Hedgkins), Guy Wilkerson (Mark Conway), Nesdon Booth (Hal Smythe)

Synopsis. Bart meets his cousin Jacqueline Sutton in Kansas City to collect the $10,000 that Pappy owes to a bruiser named Cannonball Clyde Bassett. But Jackie quickly loses the money when she purchases a phony money-making machine from con artist Big Ed Murphy. Bart and Jackie trail Murphy to Denver, where they decide to beat him at his own game.

Director Lee Sholem was known throughout the television industry as "Roll 'em Sholem" as a result of his unfailing capacity to deliver his shows ahead of schedule. "Lee was absolutely reliable in that regard," recalled Roy Huggins. "And he did not do bad work. In fact, I have often discovered, in my years in television, that speed does not necessarily mean lack of quality — it's really a necessity in some respects, and Lee Sholem understood that. He was also a very nice guy."

"Big Ed Murphy" was also the name of the safecracker played by John Dehner in "Greenbacks, Unlimited."

Pappyism: "The easiest man to con is a con man."

123. MR. MULDOON'S PARTNER

ORIGINAL AIRDATE: APRIL 15, 1962

Teleplay by: William Bruckner
From a Magazine Story by: Lee E. Wells
Directed by: Marc Lawrence

Guest Cast: Mickey Shaughnessy (Mr. Muldoon), Janet Lake (Bonnie Shea), Terrence deMarney (Terrance E. Rafferty), Timothy Rooney (Timmy), John Alderson (Simon Girty), Marshall Reed (Hatfield), Ray Teal (Sheriff Bundy), Mikki Jamison (Irish Girl), Charles Lane (Proprietor)

Synopsis. Down on his luck in Desert Gap, Bart meets a leprechaun named Muldoon, who grants him five wishes after Maverick freed him from a bottle. But Bart's troubles only increase after Muldoon grants his first wish (for $22,409) — the money that Muldoon bestowed on Maverick turns out to be stolen. Bart soon finds himself running not only from the sheriff, but from the crooks who robbed the money.

Timothy Rooney, who also appeared in "A Bullet for the Teacher," is the son of screen legend Mickey Rooney.

Pappyism: "Beware of regular employment — it just leads to clean living."

124. ONE OF OUR TRAINS IS MISSING

ORIGINAL AIRDATE: APRIL 22, 1962

Written by: Robert Vincent Wright
Directed by: Lee Sholem

Guest Cast: Kathleen Crowley (Modesty Blaine), Peter Breck (Doc Holliday), Alan Hewitt (Skinner), Barry Kelley (Diamond Jim Brady), Gage Clarke (Montague Sprague), Kevin Hagen (Justin Radcliff), Mickey Simpson (Leroy Haod), Emory Parnell (Clarence), Greg Benedict (Tim Hardesty), Glenn Stensel (Rufe)

Synopsis. In Whipsaw, Kansas, Bart walks into trouble when he encounters Modesty Blaine, who doesn't tell him that she's now the fiancé of wealthy Amos Skinner, who owns the St. Joseph/Denver Railroad Company. Skinner gives Maverick a choice — leave town by midnight, or spend a year in jail. Bart catches a ride on the next train out, along with Diamond Jim Brady and Montague Sprague, who have wagered $100,000 on whether the train crosses the state line by midnight; and Doc Holliday, who stands to make $2,000 if the train is delayed. Further complicating the trip for Bart: a neurotic safecracker named Justin Radcliffe, and the larcenous Modesty herself, who are both trying to lift the $100,000 from the train's safe.

Kathleen Crowley returns to *Maverick*, this time in the role of Modesty Blaine, who had been played by Mona Freeman in "The Cats of Paradise" and "The Cruise of the Cynthia B.," two third-season episodes. Something of a *Maverick* chameleon, Crowley appeared in several "Samantha Crawford-like" roles during the last three seasons: she also played Marla, the female counterpart to Pearly Gates; Melanie Blake, in two third-season shows; the showgirl who poses as a teacher in "Bullet for the Teacher;" and the eccentric Kiz Bouchet in the memorable fourth-season episode "Kiz."

This final episode of the series leads us to believe that there is a history between Modesty and Bart — Modesty tells Bart "There's never been anyone else but you," while Bart winces "Every time I get involved with you, I get in trouble." The truth of the matter (at least, on screen) is that this episode marks Bart's first encounter with Modesty Blaine — she plagued brother Bret in her two previous appearances.

"One of Our Trains is Missing" also features the final **Pappyism** of the original *Maverick*: "Any man who needs to make out a will isn't spending his money properly."

JAMES GARNER, SUSAN BLANCHARD, AND CHARLES FRANK

PART III:
THE NEW MAVERICKS

The lure of the legend that became *Maverick* explains why all three major television networks attempted to bring back *Maverick* in the late 1970s and early 1980s (it also accounts for the production of the 1994 *Maverick* feature). But in order for a revival to succeed, you have to understand what made the original work. The secret to *Maverick*'s success would seem obvious — Roy Huggins' concept, (as well as his supervision over story and script), and an actor in James Garner who completely understood the concept—yet no one seemed to realize this until the time of the third *Maverick* revival (NBC's *Bret Maverick*, 1981-82).

The following is a look at all three reincarnations of *Maverick*: ABC's *The New Maverick*, a 1978 made-for-TV movie; CBS's *Young Maverick*, which ran from November 1979 to January 1980; and NBC's *Bret Maverick*.

THE NEW MAVERICK
(ABC, 1978)

After winning his lawsuit against Warner Bros. in 1960, James Garner concentrated on his motion picture career. He completed several major films over the next ten years, including *The Children's Hour*, *The Great Escape*, *36 Hours*, *Move Over Darling*, *The Thrill Of It All*, *Grand Prix*, *Support Your Local Sheriff*, *Skin Game*, and (his personal favorite) *The Americanization of Emily*. Garner's freedom further manifested itself in 1964 when he formed his own company, Cherokee Productions, which Garner named after his maternal grandfather, a full-blooded Cherokee Indian. Cherokee Productions has produced nearly all of Garner's films ever since.

Garner returned to television — and to Warner Bros. — in 1971. Jack Warner had long left the film business, and the studio was now taking a less rigid approach to television. Cherokee Productions was among the many independent companies now working with Warner Bros. to produce movies and TV series. Garner produced and starred in *Nichols*, which lasted one season on NBC (1971-72).

After making a few more pictures (*They Only Kill Their Masters*, *One Little Indian*, *The Castaway Cowboy*), Garner decided to do another television series. He approached Roy Huggins and asked if he would develop something for him. Huggins decided to update *Maverick* as a private detective series, so he and Stephen J. Cannell designed *The Rockford Files* around the kind of character-driven humor that made *Maverick* so successful during its first two seasons. *The Rockford Files* was an immediate hit — it was the 12th most-watched series on television its first year — and remained a mainstay on NBC for six years (1974-80).

The tremendous popularity of *The Rockford Files* also had an impact on *Maverick* in the mid-1970s. Independent television stations throughout the country began showing *Maverick* reruns once again, so the series was now introduced to a new generation of viewers. Doubtlessly hoping to capitalize on the new wave of interest, Warner Bros. Television decided to produce an updated version of *Maverick* as a pilot for a possible series. *The New Maverick* would depict the adventures of young Ben Maverick, who had quit his Harvard education in order to roam the West in the tradition of his father Beau and his cousins Bret and Bart. Juanita Bartlett, one of the regular writers on *The Rockford Files*, scripted the pilot, which aired September 3, 1978 on *The ABC Sunday Night Movie*. James Garner and Jack Kelly reprised their roles as Bret and Bart, while Charles Frank played Ben.

The reviews were mixed at best. "The great charm of *Maverick* was that it spoofed the hard-bitten mystique of the cowboy at a time when the breed was treated with reverent awe on the tube," wrote *Weekly Variety* (September 6, 1978). "There has been a generation of satire and varied treatment of Westerns since then, however, and the concept has lost its freshness.

"James Garner's considerable appeal in the original series has been on display since, and he reprised the role in *The New Maverick* with acceptable results. But [the movie] relied on charm too much — too many wonderful smiles and too few interesting or believable scenes."

Although *The New Maverick* was intended to introduce Charles Frank, the movie clearly focuses on Garner. So when the pilot drew a respectable audience share, ABC found itself with a problem: it couldn't design a new series around Garner because he was still busy filming *The Rockford Files*. In addition, Frank hadn't exactly established himself in the pivotal role of Ben Maverick — there didn't seem to be much to the character (at least in the pilot) beyond Frank's toothy grin.

ABC eventually passed on the prospective new series, but Warner Bros. apparently kept the project in development. The studio ordered at least two scripts for *The New Maverick*, including one — "Silver Threads Among the Gold" — featuring Bart Maverick, whose relationship to young Ben had suddenly changed from cousin to uncle. (The pilot had ended with the hint that Ben would get together with Bret and/or Bart for future adventures.) Finally, in the summer of 1979, CBS ordered another two-hour pilot, again starring Charles Frank and Susan Blanchard (Frank's wife, who had played Ben's foil in the first pilot). The new series, now called *Young Maverick*, debuted as a mid-season replacement on November 28, 1979.

YOUNG MAVERICK
(CBS, 1979-80)

One of the most popular programs of the 1979-80 season was NBC's *Real People*, a lighthearted salute to "typical ordinary Americans" who happened to have ususual talents, professions and/or lifestyles. Sort of a forerunner to the likes of today's enormously popular *America's Funniest Home Videos* and *America's Funniest People*, *Real People* knocked off several competing programs on its way to becoming the 15th most-watched show of the year.

CBS scheduled *Young Maverick* for Wednesdays, 8:00 p.m. — directly opposite *Real People* — so therein lies a partial explanation as to why the series failed. (CBS cancelled *Young Maverick* after six episodes.) But there's more to it than that.

"That show faced a rather uphill fight all the way," said *Maverick* veteran Leslie Martinson, who directed one episode of *Young Maverick*. "It was a difficult thing to attempt a follow-up to *Maverick* — even with a young Maverick — because the original show had a certain magic of its own that just captivated everybody's fancy. The original *Maverick* worked because of what Roy Huggins had conceived, and because Jimmy Garner was Maverick. Jim had a built-in personality for that character.

"As I recall, the writers on *Young Maverick* tried very hard to capture the flavor of the original show, and Charley played it for what it was worth — whatever was inherent in the scripts. The rest was in his personality, and what he brought to the role. But Charley had a hard task in front of him. I don't know anybody who could possibly capture audiences the way Jimmy did in that part."

Perhaps the hardest task facing Charles Frank was that he was miscast. There's more to playing Maverick than having a winning smile. "Frank brought good looks to the role," noted *Weekly Variety* (December 5, 1979), "but the charisma the Maverick character is supposed to have came from script references to such qualities, not from portrayal." *Young Maverick* could have worked if it had someone like Tom Selleck in the lead — the kind of performer whose subtle, natural charm (like Garner's) exudes in every character he plays.

In Frank's defense, however, the early scripts of *Young Maverick* left much to be desired. Probably the best episode of the series — in terms of both telling a good story and capturing the feel of the Maverick character — was "Half Past Noon," in which a conniving mayor hoodwinks Ben Maverick into facing a recently paroled gunslinger who has threatened vengeance against his hometown for sending him to prison. Maverick uses elemental means to get out of the situation non-violently — he dispatches Nell McGarrahan (Susan Blanchard's character) to get the gunman drunk. When he discovers that his opponent is a better shot drunk that he is when sober, Ben calmly moves on to Plan B (Maverick always has an ace in the hole) — he arranges for the town to throw a "welcome home" party for the gunslinger. Ben then rides out of town, figuring that if the town is nice to the gunman, he'll forget why he was angry. "What if he doesn't?" asks Nell. "That's not my problem," replies Ben.

Unfortunately, "Half Past Noon" never aired. *Young Maverick* was cancelled two weeks before it was scheduled for broadcast.

Young Maverick also might have worked had the producers consulted Roy Huggins. But nobody did. "Well, they didn't have to, because from a legal point of view, I don't own *Maverick*," Huggins said. "Warners owns the show. Still, the original *Maverick* was a success only in its first two seasons. The other three years it was a failure. You'd think they'd want to know why the show worked spectacularly for two seasons, and then failed, spectacularly. I don't remember exactly what I was doing when *Maverick* was first resurrected, but you'd think they might've talked to me."

BRET MAVERICK
(NBC, 1981-82)

Apparently NBC determined that the difference between the *Maverick* that worked and the *Maverick* that didn't was in James Garner himself, even though *Maverick*'s third season had proven otherwise. Garner's absolute understanding of Roy Huggins' concept was still there that year, but without the core group of writers who also grasped what Huggins was doing, the series lost nearly one-third of its original audience. Nevertheless, in October 1980, NBC announced plans for yet another attempt to introduce *Maverick* to the next generation. James Garner would star as *Bret Maverick*, which would premiere in the Fall of 1981.

The wave of nostalgia first hit prime time television in the late 1970s, when several old favorites of the 1950s and '60s — *Gilligan's Island, Father Knows Best, The Addams Family, The Wild, Wild West, The Many Loves of Dobie Gillis, The Avengers, The Millionaire*, to name a few — were brought back as either TV-movies, full-fledged series, or (as in the case of *Star Trek*) major motion pictures. In the Fall of 1981, the networks carried the trend a step further by casting many of the stars of these old favorites — such as Lorne Greene (*Bonanza*), Mike Connors (*Mannix*), Tony Randall (*The Odd Couple*), James Arness (*Gunsmoke*), and Robert Stack (*The Untouchables*) — in new series. In James Garner's case, there was an added twist: *Bret Maverick* was a new series featuring an old favorite in his original role.

Bret Maverick was beset with problems from the start. Another writers' strike in 1981 crippled the television industry, delaying the season premieres of all network programs from the traditional September until December or January. (*Bret Maverick* debuted December 1, 1981.) Darleen Carr replaced Marilyn Hassett as newspaper-woman M.L. Springer, one of Maverick's foils on the new show. And an injury to James Garner shut down production of the pilot episode, "The Lazy Ace," for three days. (Keep an eye out for the sequence, very early in the pilot, where Bret's horse goes ballistic after hearing gunshots. Garner was on a mechanical horse to film part of that sequence; he was thrown from the horse, and suffered nine broken ribs as a result.)

Whereas Maverick roamed from town to town in the original series, in *Bret Maverick* he decided to settle down after a wistful exchange with his longtime friend Doc Holliday. (In "The Lazy Ace," Holliday was also Maverick's *old* friend — he was at least twenty years Bret's senior, even though they were the same age in the original show. Also, the real Doc Holliday didn't live past 35, while John McLiam, who played Doc in "The Lazy Ace," was 63 at the time.)

The desire to settle down was actually rooted in the original series. "Maverick always had a latent desire to settle down, but it was always a matter of 'not yet,'" said Roy Huggins. "I think, in a couple of the early shows ['Point Blank,' 'Hostage!,' 'A Rage for Vengeance'], we had him mention the idea in passing, but we never developed it beyond that. But that desire was always there in the back of his mind — and it was certainly in the back of *my* mind as we continued to shape the character."

By placing Maverick in one town and having him interact with the various residents, *Bret Maverick* became an ensemble show. Having a regular group of characters in every episode meant that James Garner would not have to carry the entire load, which was the case when he starred in *Maverick* and *The Rockford Files*. Garner was ably supported by old friend Stuart Margolin (Angel Martin in *The Rockford Files*), Darleen Carr, Ed Bruce, Priscilla Morrill, Richard Hamilton, Ramon Bieri, and longtime "Garner company" members Luis Delgado and Jack Garner (Jim's older brother).

But the format had its disadvantages. "There were *a lot* of characters on that show," said Marion Hargrove, who wrote two episodes of *Bret Maverick*. "Somehow you'd have to work in all the characters — or the producer or story editor would do it for you — sometimes to the detriment of the script.

"I also remember that in practically every episode of *Bret Maverick*, Garner ended up in jail, charged with murder or what-have-you. That got old in a hurry."

One of the motifs of *Bret Maverick* addressed the perception of *Maverick* itself. "People think they know me, and then they get their backs up when [they find] I'm not what they expect," observes Maverick in "The Lazy Ace." "It's a rare man who'll admit that it's his own expectations that have caused the problem. Of course, you can't exactly blame them, with the press conjuring all that nonsense."

Maverick is speaking about himself, of course, but his thoughts can be applied to *Maverick* as well. The legends surrounding the original series (that it was designed as a comedy; that Maverick was a coward; that Samantha Crawford was *Maverick*'s mother in spirit) do not bear out when you look at the series as a whole. Even when *Maverick*'s approach to humor changed after its second season, the majority of episodes remained straightforward Western dramas. Similarly, in *Bret Maverick*, Maverick finds that people are more inclined to perceive him as they think he is (i.e., according to his legend) rather than accept him for who he really is. In "The Ballad of Bret Maverick," Bret tries to sell a legitimate silver mine, but he can't find any buyers because everyone's afraid he's running a scam (regardless of the fact that he never ran a con unless he, or someone he knew, had been cheated). "I know all about being a prisoner of the past," Maverick observes in that episode. "The truth doesn't seem to get you anywhere, anymore."

Bret Maverick premiered with a healty 23.2 Nielsen rating, but the audience diminished as the initial curiosity factor waned. Scheduled for Tuesday nights (first at 9:00 p.m., then at 8:00 p.m.), the show held its own against its primary competition — ABC's comedy juggernaut of *Happy Days*, *Laverne & Shirley*, and *Three's Company* — but it wasn't exactly inflicting damage on them, either. By the end of the season, it ranked somewhere in the middle of the year-end list of all network programs.

Knowing that the show was a borderline case for renewal, producer Gordon Dawson used the final episode of the season, "The Hidalgo Thing," to introduce changes to *Bret Maverick* that would go into effect if NBC picked up the series for a second year. Maverick would return to his roots by travelling more — and Jack Kelly would join the series as Bart Maverick.

"Gordon Dawson and [executive producer] Meta Rosenberg called me and said they wanted me to do the last show of the season," Kelly told Mick Martin in 1992. "It was for a 30-second spot that would appear at the end of the show. At first I didn't want to do it, because it would have meant an entire day of shooting, and I would've had to go up to L.A. [from Huntington Beach, where Kelly had been serving as a city councilman].

"But then Slick [James Garner's longtime nickname] got on the phone and said, 'Hey, you — get your fat ass up here! We've written ourselves into a tunnel, and you're the only one who can trip the trigger on the joke.'"

In "The Hidalgo Thing," Bret decides to foil a crooked accountant who tries to cheat a Spanish noblewoman out of her land by having Kate Hanrahan (Marj Dusay) impersonate the woman, who would "sell" her land to the accountant for $2 million. The accountant arrives — only, to Bret's surprise, it's none other than brother Bart, who was apparently attempting the same swindle, only from the other end.

"I didn't really like the play because it wasn't the essence of *Maverick*," Kelly admitted. "He was providing scams to make a living out of scams, whereas the real Maverick *never* did that.

"But, at any rate, I reported to the set at 7:00 a.m. that day. Meta, Jim, and a bunch of people were there to greet me, and then, out of nowhere, they threw six scripts at me. They wanted me to become the brother again and run the saloon while Jim was on the road doing his con-game routine. They already had six scripts that I would co-star in. I thought I'd died and gone to antique actors' heaven."

The new *Bret Maverick* would have drawn even further back on its past, because James Garner wanted Roy Huggins to produce the second season. "Both NBC and Jim asked me to become involved," Huggins recalled. "I had to think about it. I didn't think there was anything I could do to help, because I knew they weren't doing *Maverick*. And I also knew that Jim did not want to do *Maverick*. Jim did not want to work that hard — when he was doing *Maverick*, he was in every scene.

"But I had a problem — I didn't want to say No to Jim. I hadn't said No when he asked me — I said I'd think about it. But, as things turned out, I never had to give an answer. Three days later, I learned that NBC had cancelled the series."

Although every attempt to revive the *Maverick* series has failed, the Maverick character has enjoyed "more lives than an alley cat."s NBC aired reruns of *Bret Maverick* in prime time during the summer of 1990, while Jack Kelly made a cameo appearance as Bart in the the 1992 TV-movie *The Gambler Part 4: Luck of the Draw*. Other than James Arness as Matt Dillon, Garner and Kelly are the only actors who have played the same character on prime time over the course of five decades (1950s, '60s, '70s, '80s and '90s). Garner is also one of the few actors who has appeared as the same character on three different networks — he made a brief appearance as Bret in the first episode of CBS' *Young Maverick*.

"The Hidalgo Thing" provided a sense of closure to the *Maverick* saga when Bret and Bart heartily embraced each other in the closing moments of the show. Marion Hargrove, however, wrote a "second" ending to the *Bret Maverick* series in a script that was never produced. NBC cancelled *Bret Maverick* shortly before Hargrove finished the teleplay for "Our Man in Sweetwater," which had Maverick signing with the phone company in order to bring the telephone to Sweetwater. The entire town thinks Bret's been taken in, but Maverick knows better: he figures he can build himself a nice financial nest egg with the money he'll make off commissions.

Hargrove picks up the story. "Gordie Dawson called me and said, 'Marion, I've got good news and bad news. The bad news is that we're cancelled, but the good news is that all you have to do is finish writing, and you'll get paid full money.

"Now, I had this happen to me at least twice before — I had been writing for both *My World and Welcome to It* and *I Spy* right at the time they were cancelled, and I got the same pitch: 'Just finish 48 pages of anything and you'll get paid.' I never had the heart to finish them. But this time, I felt different — I went back to the typewriter, and it just sang!

"It's the final scene of the story. Maverick's in his office at the saloon, counting the money he's made off sales to new telephone customers. The door bursts open. Luis Delgado, who played the card dealer on *Bret Maverick*, rushes in and says, 'Jimbo! Jimbo! Jim!' Maverick looks up and says, 'Shifty, it's Maverick. *Bret Maverick*, remember?' And Delgado says, 'Not anymore, Jimbo. We were just cancelled!' And Garner says, 'What the hell you mean cancelled?' And Delgado says, 'I was up at Meta's office when the call came from the network. We're through, finito, nada.'

"Maverick thinks for a second, then he goes back to counting money, and he says, 'Fuck 'em, Louie, we can buy and sell the bastards.'

"And that was the last line I ever wrote in television."

Warner Bros. Pictures
A Warner Communciations Company

Presents

JAMES GARNER

in

THE NEW MAVERICK

AN ABC SUNDAY NIGHT MOVIE

ORIGINAL AIRDATE: SEPTEMBER 3, 1978

Starring Charles Frank as Ben Maverick
Jack Kelly as Bart Maverick
Susan Blanchard as Nell McGarrahan

Guest Starring Eugene Roche as Judge Crupper
Susan Sullivan as Poker Alice
George Loros as Vinnie
Woodrow Parfrey as Leveque

Co-Starring Gary Allen as Dobie
Helen Page Camp as Flora Crupper
Jack Garner as Homer
Graham Jarvis as Lambert
Malcolm McCalman
B.J. Ward
Luis Delgado

Executive Producer: Meta Rosenberg
Produced by: Bob Foster
Written by: Juanita Bartlett
Directed by: Hy Averback

Music Composed and Conducted by: John Rubinstein
Director of Photography: Andrew Jackson

Art Director: John Jefferies
Film Editor: George Rohrs, Diane Adler
Unit Production Manager: Robert Beche
Assistant Directors: Cliff Coleman, Russ Llewellyn
Script Supervisor: Marshall J. Wollins
Set Decorator: Herman Schoenbrum
Men's Wardrobe: Charley James
Women's Wardrobe: June Lynn Smith
Special Effects: Joe Unsinn
Property Master: Bill Fannon
Make-Up: Dick Blair
Hairdresser: Gloria Montemayor
Sound Mixer: John Carter
Sound Effects: Ron Tinsley
Music Editor: Don Harris
Casting: Karen Ray Grossman
Filmed at: The Burbank Studios, Burbank, California
Distributed by: Warner Bros. Television

Synopsis. Bret Maverick rides into New Las Vegas to collect a $1,000 debt from brother Bart, who has owed him the money for nine years. Although Bret gets a message from the hotel clerk that Bart has been shot and killed, he quickly determines that his brother is still alive — the coffin is only five feet long ("If that was Bart in there, they'd have to fold him"). Bret soon learns from his cousin Ben, whom he hasn't seen in nine years, that Bart's running from three men who lost money from him in a poker game the night before. Meanwhile, banker Austin Crupper hires the three men — one of whom is a transplanted New Yorker named Vinnie — to rob a train shipment of Gatling guns. Crupper hopes to parlay his "recovery" of the stolen arms into a seat on the Senate, but his plans are thwarted when Vinnie keeps the guns for himself. When Bret and Ben learn about the robbery, they each make plans to recover the stolen arms in the hopes of collecting the $25,000 reward money.

YOUNG MAVERICK

Starring Charles Frank as Ben Maverick
Susan Blanchard as Neil McGarrahan
and John Dehner as U.S. Marshal Edge Troy

Executive Producer: Robert Van Scoyk
Supervising Producer: Andy White
Produced by: Chuck Bowman
Developed for Television by: Juanita Bartlett
Executive Story Consultant: Norman Liebman
Director of Photography: Edward R. Plante
Associate Producer: Ric deAzevedo
Art Director: Steven Sardanis
Film Editor: Dick Wormell
Sound Effects: Echo Film Services, Inc. and John Kline
Music Editor: Anthony Milch
Music Supervision: Lee Holdridge, Samuel Lober, John Berkman
Theme Composition by: Jay Livingston, Ray Evans
"Maverick" Song by: David Buttolph, Paul Francis Webster
Unit Production Manager: F.A. Miller
Assistant Directors: Don White, Bradley Gross
Set Decorator: Ed Bare
Makeup: Melanie Levitt
Hair Stylist: Janice Cook
Men's Wardrobe: Dick Butz
Women's Wardrobe: Barbara Sebern
Script Supervisor: Stephen Dorsch
Property: Kenny Orme
Sound Mixer: Don Rush
Special Effects: Walter C. Dion
Casting: Vivian McRae, Melissa Skoff

Filmed at the Burbank Studios
Burbank, California

Warner Bros. Television
A Warner Communication Company

1. CLANCY

ORIGINAL AIRDATE: NOVEMBER 28, 1979

Written by: David E. Peckinpah and Chuck Bowman
Directed by: Bernard McEveety

Guest Cast: Denny Miller (Clancy Flannery), Dick O'Neill (Hobbs), Warren Berlinger (Doyle), Morgan Woodward (Dalton), Burton Gilliam (The Barbary Kid), Joanne Nail (Rose), and Dave Cass, Joseph Michael Cala, Terrance Hines, Gordon Hurst, Tom Middleton

Synopsis. Ben thinks he's found the perfect opponent for a barnstorming prizefighter — Nell's mammoth cousin Clancy. James Garner appears briefly as Bret Maverick.

2. A FISTFUL OF OATS

ORIGINAL AIRDATE: DECEMBER 5, 1979

Written by: Norman Liebman
Directed by: Don McDougall

Guest Cast: J. Pat O'Malley (Uncle Malachy), Clifton James (Judge Stubbins), Tom McFadden (Jubal Moffit), Vito Scotti (Cardenas)

Synopsis. Nell's uncle faces the gallows after he accidentally spooks the horse of a hanging judge.

3. HEARTS O' GOLD

ORIGINAL AIRDATE: DECEMBER 12, 1979

Written by: Robert Van Scoyk
Directed by: Leslie H. Martinson

Guest Cast: Bill McKinney (Smoky Trumbull), Audrey Landers (Saralou Mullins), Robert Hogan (Billy Peachtree)

Synopsis. Young Maverick follows Billy Peachtree, a lousy poker player who ran out on a gambling debt, into the town of Saddlehorn, where he learns that Peachtree is planning a bank robbery.

4./5. DEAD MAN'S HAND
(TWO-PARTER)

ORIGINAL AIRDATES: DECEMBER 26, 1979 AND JANUARY 2, 1980

Written by: Robert Van Scoyk
Directed by: Hy Averback

Guest Cast: Howard Duff (Herman Rusk), James Woods (Lem Franker), John McIntire (Vernon Maywood), Donna Mills (Lisa), George Dzundza (Cal Spahn), Alan Fudge (Amos Layton)

Synopsis. Ben inherits a pat hand from a gambler who died during a high-stakes poker game. The matter becomes more complicated when the gambler's widow falls in love with Ben — and a hired gun tries to kill him.

6. MAKIN' TRACKS

ORIGINAL AIRDATE: JANUARY 16, 1980

Written by: Norman Liebman
Directed by: Ralph Senensky

Guest Cast: Victor Jory (Pony That Waits), John Hillerman (McBurney), Morgan Fairchild (Selene), Ray Tracey (Russell Two Eagles), Andrew Robinson (Sangree)

Synopsis. An 80-year-old Indian cardsharp will grant railroad officials right-of-way through his land — if they can beat him in poker.

Unaired Episodes

7. HAVE I GOT A GIRL FOR YOU

SCHEDULED AIRDATE: JANUARY 23, 1980

Written by: Jerry Ross
Directed by: Bob Claver

Guest Cast: Richard B. Shull (Montague), Melinda Naud (Monica), Patch McKenzie (Alice), Misty Rowe (Betsy), Gary Grubbs (Kincaid)

Synopsis. Ben and Nell try to put a crooked marriage broker out of business.

8. HALF-PAST NOON

SCHEDULED AIRDATE: JANUARY 30, 1980

Written by: Lois Hire
Directed by: Hollingsworth Morse

Guest Cast: Howard Platt (Mayor Waldo Leggett), Dennis Buckley (Julius Higgins), Guy Raymond (Leander Berry), Jerry Hardin (Purnell Sims), Vincent Schiavelli (Snake Speevey), Cliff Norton (Ambrose)

Synopsis. A small community that thinks Ben is a master gunman bends over backwards to keep him around so that he can take on a vicious ex-convict who has sworn vengeance on the town for sending him to prison.

Unproduced Scripts

SILVER THREADS AMONG THE GOLD

Written by: Elliott Lewis

Synopsis. Uncle Bart sticks Ben with a barren spread in the Arizona Territory, but both Mavericks soon discover that the land may contain a fortune in gold.

THE GREAT BEEF BONANZA

Author Unknown

Synopsis. In order to trip up an unprincipled cattleman named Wilks, Ben enables a rival buyer to steal one of Wilks' herds and force Wilks into a bidding war over his own cattle.

DOUBLE-TROUBLE IN TEXAS

Written by: Andy White

Synopsis. A scientist's attempt to cross-breed Mexican cattle with Brahma bulls faces stiff opposition in the person of a murderous cattleman who stands to lose his fortune if the experiment succeeds.

THE BELLES OF VINEGAR WELLES

Written by: Norman Liebman

Synopsis. Holdup artist Packy Guffin becomes smitten with Ben — she plans her robberies around his activities in order to see him. Although Packy never robs Ben, she causes him nothing but trouble: her father wants to kill him, while Marshal Troy suspects that Maverick is part of her gang.

BIG DEAL IN DEADWOOD

(a.k.a. "The Wheel of Miss Fortune")

Written by: Andy White

Synopsis. Young Maverick tries to stop a fraudulent lottery run by a crooked French countess and her equally devious brother.

James Garner
in

BRET MAVERICK

Starring Ed Bruce as Tom Guthrie
Ramon Bieri as Elijah Crow
Richard Hamilton as Cy Whittaker
John Shearin as Sheriff Mitchell Dowd
David Knell as Rodney Catlow
and Darleen Carr as M.L. Springer

Co-Starring Jack Garner as Jack the Bartender
Luis Delgado as Shifty Delgrado
Tommy Bush as Deputy Sturgess

Executive Producer: Meta Rosenberg
Supervising Producer: Gordon Dawson
Produced by: Charles Floyd Johnson, Geoffrey Fischer
Developed by: Gordon Dawson
Executive Story Consultant: Lee David Zlotoff
Associate Producer: Mark Horowitz

Music by: J.A.C. Redford and Murray MacLeod
Art Director: Scott T. Ritenour
Directors of Photography: Andrew Jackson, Frank Thackery
Unit Production Manager: Sam Freedle, Larry Aubucher
Assistant Directors: David L. Beanes, Don Wilkerson, Glenn Surgine Jr., Robert Jones, Leonard Garner

Film Editors: George Rohrs, Clay Bartels, Paul Dixon, Diane Adler
Sound Mixers: Charles L. King III, Dean Gilmore
Music Editor: Jay Alfred Smith
Sound Effects Editors: Joe von Stroheim, Larry Kaufman, Al Kajita, Jerry Jacobson, Gene Elliot
Set Decorator: Robert L. Zilliox
Property Master: William Fannon

Costume Supervisor: Le Dawson
Special Effects: Larry Fuentes

Assistant to Mr. Garner: Maryann Rea
Makeup: Charlene Roberson
Hair Stylist: Charlotte Harvey

Main Title Photography: Ron Grover
Poker Game Photography: Gene Trindl (for pilot film)

Song "Maverick Didn't Come Here to Lose"
Music and Lyrics by: Ed Bruce, Patsy Bruce and Glenn Ray
Sung by: Ed Bruce (series), Ed Bruce and James Garner (pilot only)
Casting by: Dodie McLean
Location Facilities Provided by: The Burbank Studios

A Cherokee Production **
in association with

Warner Bros. Television
A Warner Communications Company

**Erroneously listed on the credits as "Comanche Productions"

1. THE LAZY ACE
(TWO-HOUR PILOT EPISODE)

ORIGINAL AIRDATE: DECEMBER 1, 1981

Written by: Gordon Dawson
Directed by: Stuart Margolin

Guest Cast: Janis Paige (Mandy Packard), Bill McKinney (Ramsey Bass), John McLiam (Doc Holliday), Stuart Margolin (Philo Sandeen), Billy Kerr (Blue-Eyed Kid), Sid Bakey (Lyman Nickerson), Bill Gross (Dembro), Richard Moll (Sloate), Chuck Mitchell (Joe Dakota), Duane R. Campbell (Lucas), Ivan J. Rado (Wolfgang Mietr), David H. Banks (Delta Fox), Ruth Essler (Townswoman), Norman Merrill Jr. (Teller), Al Berry (Townsman), Kirk Cameron (Boy #1), Max Martin (Boy #2)

Synopsis. Bret Maverick rides into Sweetwater, a town located in the Arizona territory, to participate in a high-stakes poker game with legendary players Doc Holliday, Ramsey Bass, Joe Dakota, Lyman Nickerson, the Delta Fox, and Mandy Packard. After winning the $100,000 jackpot and ownership of Mandy's saloon, the Red Ox, Maverick purchases a 100-acre ranch which he christens *The Lazy Ace*. However, Bret doesn't realize that he also inherited liability toward a $50,000 loan which Mandy took out from the bank against the saloon's mortgage. To make matters worse, no sooner does Bret deposit his money with the bank, the bank is robbed.

2. WELCOME TO SWEETWATER

ORIGINAL AIRDATE: DECEMBER 8, 1981

Written by: Gordon Dawson
Directed by: Rod Holcomb

Guest Cast: John Randolph (Frenchy Montana), Russ Marin (Garrick), Roger Torrey (Schroeder), Priscilla Morrill (Mrs. Springer), Lesley Woods (Miss Rose), Virgil Frye (Luke), Chester Grimes (Charles Decker), Mickey White (Alex Decker), Dan York (York), Stephen Morrell (Stubbs), Danny Butch (Telegram Boy), Dean Smith (Jack Denner), Wayne Van Horn (Zeke), Roy E. Andrews (Laborer), Ken Strong (Stranger)

Synopsis. No sooner does Maverick settle into his new home than he faces a fight: a railroad company plans to build right in the middle of his land.

3. ANYTHING FOR A FRIEND

ORIGINAL AIRDATE: DECEMBER 15, 1981

Written by: Lee David Zlotoff
Directed by: Ivan Dixon

Guest Cast: Lawrence Dobkin (Mondragon), Glenn Withrow (Billy the Kid), Charles Hallahan (McShane), Stuart Margolin (Philo Sandeen)

Synopsis. Bret and Tom protect a wounded Billy the Kid from bounty hunters by hiding the outlaw at *The Lazy Ace*.

4. THE YELLOW ROSE

ORIGINAL AIRDATE: DECEMBER 22, 1981

Written by: Lee David Zlotoff
Directed by: William Wiard

Guest Cast: Marj Dusay (Kate Hanrahan), Keye Luke (Lu Sung), Anthony Eisley (Banniker), Linda Lei (Rose), Priscilla Morrill (Mrs. Springer), Marcia Rodd (Captain Saffer), Stuart Margolin (Philo Sandeen)

Synopsis. Maverick wins a Chinese girl in a poker game, but decides to free her — only the girl doesn't want to leave him.

5. HORSE OF YET ANOTHER COLOR

ORIGINAL AIRDATE: JANUARY 5, 1982

Teleplay by: Lee David Zlotoff
Story by: Lee David Zlotoff and Geoffrey Fischer
Directed by: Ivan Dixon

Guest Cast: Simon Oakland (Delwood Crestmore), William Hootkins (Theodore Roosevelt), Holly Palance (Dolly O'Hare), Allan Arbus (Phineas Swackmeyer), Ray Tracey (Geronimo), Jim Cosa (Joe Ferns)

Synopsis. Maverick wins a horse in a poker game, but the animal is stolen property — it was supposed to be presented to the Indians by Congressman Theodore Roosevelt as part of a peace treaty. If the horse isn't returned within two days, the safety of the territory is at stake.

6. DATELINE: SWEETWATER

ORIGINAL AIRDATE: JANUARY 12, 1982

Written by: Ira Steven Behr
Directed by: William Wiard

Guest Cast: Ed Nelson (Andrew Tyndall), Richard O'Brien (Stephen A. Hennessey), Joshua Bryant (Busted Bill Farley), William Bryant (John Davis), Priscilla Morrill (Mrs. Springer), Bryon Morrow (Shaw), Roy Jenson (Monte), Brady Rubin (Mrs. Davis), Barry Cahill (Moran), Charles Hutchins (Osheroff), Norman Merrill Jr. (Desk Clerk), Howie Allen (Peter)

Synopsis. A con artist with a trick neck plays a pivotal role in Maverick's scheme to thwart a ruthless financial corporation from taking over Sweetwater.

7. THE MAYFLOWER WOMEN'S HISTORICAL SOCIETY

ORIGINAL AIRDATE: FEBRUARY 2, 1982

Written by: Lee David Zlotoff
Directed by: Ivan Dixon

Guest Cast: Jenny O'Hara (Samantha Dunne), David Young (Aaron Sylvane), Neva Patterson (Emma Crittenson), Priscilla Morrill (Mrs. Springer)

Synopsis. After a research librarian for a historical society breaks Maverick out of a St. Louis jail, she forces him to sign a contract granting her organization exclusive rights to produce goods (guns, hats, playing cards, etc.) bearing Maverick's likeness. Maverick tries to dissuade the woman by concocting a phony con game, but the plan backfires when the historical society demands a piece of the action.

8. HALLIE

ORIGINAL AIRDATE: FEBRUARY 9, 1982

Written by: Marion Hargrove
Directed by: John Patterson

Guest Cast: Dixie Carter (Hallie McCulloch), Geoffrey Lewis (Barney Broomick), William Sanderson (Kenneth Broomick), Eldon Quick (Clerk), F. William Parker (Captain Rufus Pinkerton), David Bond (Sloatman), Frank Loverde (Waiter)

Synopsis. Bret and Tom travel to a wine auction in Tucson to bid on a shipment of a rare French vintage, only to discover that the auction was a fraud and their $2,000 was stolen by Hallie McCulloch, an old con artist acquaintance of Bret's. Hallie needs the money to pay off two men who want to kill her.

9. THE BALLAD OF BRET MAVERICK

ORIGINAL AIRDATE: FEBRUARY 16, 1982

Written by: Gordon Dawson
Directed by: Jeff Bleckner

Songs "The Ballad of Bret Maverick" and "Dolores"
Music and Lyrics by: Alex Harvey
Vocals by: John Bennett Terry

Guest Cast: James Whitmore Jr. (Justice Smith), Sandy McPeak (Voorsanger), Cliff Emmich (Titus Openshaw), Howard Caine (Turtious Openshaw), Priscilla Morrill (Mrs. Springer), Dan Barrows (Jacob Voorsanger), Donegan Smith (C.P. Whitfield), Keith Walker (Holsten), Lawrence Laktin (Grainger)

Synopsis. Bret's reputation hurts him in his efforts to sell a silver mine — everyone thinks he's running a con. Meanwhile, a vagabond balladeer who thinks that Maverick led his father to suicide arrives in town determined to kill Bret.

10. A NIGHT AT THE RED OX

ORIGINAL AIRDATE: FEBRUARY 23, 1982

Written by: Lee David Zlotoff
Directed by: William Wiard

Guest Cast: Savannah Smith (Addie), Paul Koslo (Fletcher), Murray Hamilton (Cobb)

Synopsis. Bret, Tom and M.L. are held hostage by a woman who believes Tom murdered her husband 20 years ago.

11. THE NOT SO MAGNIFICENT SIX

ORIGINAL AIRDATE: MARCH 2, 1982

Teleplay by: Geoffrey Fischer
Story by: Shel Willens
Directed by: Leo Penn

Guest Cast: Stuart Margolin (Philo Sandeen), Joseph Sirola (Nimrod Bligh), Kelly Ward (White), Jesse Vint (Willie Trueblood), Kario Salem (Virgil Le Fleur), Ross Hagen (Farnsworth), Ed Bakey (Tulsa Jack), Art LeFleur (Deacon Tippett), Joseph Chapman (Jasper Weems), Shawn Stevens (Sidney Bent), David Banks (Sam Durham)

Synopsis. Novelist Nimrod Bligh engages six gunslingers in a deadly contest, with Maverick as the prize — whoever can kill the legendary gambler will have his life immortalized in Bligh's next book.

12. THE VULTURE ALSO RISES

ORIGINAL AIRDATE: MARCH 16, 1982

Written by: Gordon Dawson and Rogers Turrentine
Directed by: Michael O'Herlihy

Guest Cast: Stuart Margolin (Philo Sandeen), Monte Markham (Captain Dawkins), Peggy Walton-Walker (Eloise), John Anderson (General Frye)

Synopsis. Sweetwater calls in the cavalry after the stagecoach is apparently attacked by Apaches — but the massacre was really staged by a cavalry payroll master.

13. THE EIGHT SWORDS OF DYRUS AND OTHER ILLUSIONS OF GRANDEUR

ORIGINAL AIRDATE: MARCH 23, 1982

Teleplay by: Gordon Dawson
Story by: Gordon Dawson and Larry Mollin
Directed by: John Patterson

Magic Advisor for This Episode: David Avadon

Guest Cast: Cliff Potts (The Great Malooley), Sarah Rush (Princess Athena), Sid Haig (Sampson), W.T. Zacha (Cutler), Pete Munro (Cowboy)

Synopsis. Professional illusionist The Great Malooley is also a professional killer whose performance at the Red Ox masks a plan to exume the legendary Kirschfeld Diamonds, which he believes are buried underneath the saloon. To keep Maverick out of the way, Malooley frames him for the murder of a drunk who had threatened Bret the night before.

14./15. FAITH, HOPE AND CLARITY (TWO-PARTER)

ORIGINAL AIRDATES: APRIL 13 AND 20, 1982

Teleplay by: Lee David Zlotoff
Story by: Paul Ehrman and Lee David Zlotoff
Directed by: Leo Penn

Guest Cast: Robert Webber (Everest Sinclair), Stuart Margolin (Philo Sandeen), Marj Dusay (Kate Hanrahan), Jameson Parker (Whitney Delaworth III), James Staley (Workman), Simone Griffeth (Jasmine DuBois), Tony Burton (Arthur), Priscilla Morrill (Mrs. Springer), Richard Libertini (Fingers Wachefsky), Kathleen Doyle (Angela)

Synopsis. Everest Sinclair, a utopianist with an eye on making Sweetwater the center of his "new society," purchases all of the town's mortgages and immediately forecloses on them. In order to win back their land, the townspeople rally behind Maverick, who hatches an elaborate "sting" aimed at Sinclair.

16. THE RATTLESNAKE BRIGADE

ORIGINAL AIRDATE: APRIL 27, 1982

Teleplay by: Geoffrey Fischer
Story by: Gordon Dawson and Barton Dean
Directed by: Fernando Lamas

Guest Cast: Stanley Wells (John Henry), Arlen Dean Snyder (Colonel Bang), J. Edward McKinley (Snow)

Synopsis. A band of desperados trick Bret and Tom into protecting a gold shipment.

17. THE HIDALGO THING

ORIGINAL AIRDATE: MAY 4, 1982

Written by: Gordon Dawson
Directed by: Thomas Carter

Guest Cast: Jack Kelly (Bart Maverick), Hector Elizondo (Senor Gomez), Marj Dusay (Kate Hanrahan), John Dennis Johnston (Burt Full Moon), James Gallery (Fortune Hunter), Dub Taylor (Toothless Tom Teal), Sandra DeBruin (Screaming Woman)

Synopsis. An unscrupulous accountant withholds a grant naming a Spanish noblewoman as owner of the Arizona territory so that he can purchase the land himself. Maverick decides to trip up the crook by passing Kate off as the noblewoman and "selling" the land for $2 million.

Unproduced Scripts

SHERIFF WHO?

Written by: Geoffrey Fischer

Synopsis. With Mitch Dowd away from town, and a $100,000 gold shipment expected to arrive, Elijah Crow appoints Tom temporary sheriff. But Tom soon becomes the target of a hit man hired to gun down the sheriff of Sweetwater.

DEAD RINGER

Written by: Larry Mollin

Synopsis. An ambitious actress and her geologist husband believe that a gold mine is nesting underneath the Lazy Ace. When Maverick refuses to sell the ranch, they have him framed for attempted murder and sentenced to 20 years' hard labor — so that they can dig up his property. This script was later revised and produced as "The Eight Swords of Dyrus and Other Illusions of Grandeur."

THE SENSIBAUGH GANG

Written by: Del Reisman

Synopsis. Harry Sensibaugh and his murderous band of bank robbers use *The Lazy Ace* as a hideout while Maverick is out of town.

FAIR GAME

Written by: Paul Ehrman

Synopsis. Maverick sets up an elaborate con to trip up the crooked land agent who swindled Cy Whittaker out of his property. This script was later revised and produced as "Faith, Hope and Clarity."

OUR MAN IN SWEETWATER

Written by: Marion Hargrove

Synopsis. Maverick signs with the phone company as part of an effort to bring the telephone to Sweetwater — and set up a comfortable nest egg for himself. Meanwhile, Hallie McCulloch, in trouble once again, calls on Bret to help her out of a $10,000 scrape.

JAMES GARNER AND JACK KELLY

THE TRAIL TO WHO-KNOWS-WHERE

T he successful adaptation of *Star Trek* as a series of major motion pictures begat a trend in movie-making. Producers began looking at other popular TV series of the 1950s and '60s to see if they, too, could be brought to the big screen. The past ten years have seen the making of such "movies made from television" as *The Untouchables, The Twilight Zone, The Addams Family, Dragnet, Get Smart, The Naked Gun: From the Files of Police Squad!, The Beverly Hillbillies*, even *The Flintstones*. Roy Huggins got in on the act in 1993 — he was executive producer of *The Fugitive*, which he had created in 1960 (Quinn Martin produced the TV series from 1963-67). The *Fugitive* movie received an Academy Award nomination for Best Picture of 1994.

Maverick became the latest "movie made from television" when Warner Bros. released a feature-length adaptation in 1994. Mel Gibson and Richard Donner, who had brought a fortune to Warners courtesy of their *Lethal Weapon* series (a trio of action comedies that were all a smash at the box office), teamed up once again for *Maverick*. Gibson starred as Bret Maverick, and also produced the film, while Donner directed it. William Goldman (*Butch Cassidy and the Sundance Kid*) wrote the screenplay based on the series created by Huggins. Gibson and Donner had asked Huggins to join them on the picture, but Huggins was unable to participate. "Gibson and Donner are a couple of charmers, and I really appreciated their offer," Huggins said, "but I was involved in something I couldn't walk away from."

However, the feature film has the other important link to the original series — James Garner, who plays U.S. Marshal Zane Cooper, Maverick's primary foil in the picture. Garner's role has a twist that's sure to please the fans of the TV show.

The story puts a slightly different spin on the Maverick character, in that Maverick travels to take part in a championship poker tournament not for the money, but "for the knowing" — i.e., just to know how good he is. Although there have been instances in the original show ("The War of the Silver Kings," "The Town That Wasn't There") where Maverick has done things for reasons other than money, his primary motive has always been *profit*. But there's another element of the script that's "true *Maverick*." Early in the story, Maverick informs Annabelle Bransford, one of his rivals in the poker tournament, that she has two habits that betray her whenever she's bluffing; Maverick points out both habits, but he still manages to knock Annabelle out of the game. "Actually, you have three," he tells her. "You never want to give everything away."

Two-time Academy Award winner Jodie Foster (*The Accused, The Silence of the Lambs*) stars as Annabelle. *Maverick*'s cast also features a passel of Western movie and TV veterans, including James Coburn, Doug McClure, Dan Hedaya, Robert Fuller, Michael Chane, Bill Williams, Will Hutchins, Denver Pyle, Charles Dierkop, Bert Remsen, Bill Henderson, Reed Morgan, Alfred Molina, Gary Frank, William Marshall, Henry Darrow, William Smith, Dennis Fimple, Steve Liska, Richard Blum, Carl Bartlett, Donald Gibson, and country-western singer Clint Black. Remsen ("The Jail at Junction Flats") and Pyle ("Family Pride") also have links to the original show.

The movie also features the original TV theme, some authentic Pappyisms ("If you dare to come back with a medal, I'll kill you with my bare hands"), and a spectacular sequence in which Maverick singlehandedly tries to stop a runaway stagecoach.

The legend of *Maverick* has now spanned two generations. The original series has remained in circulation for over 30 years, and both the *Maverick* movie and the 30 episodes available through Columbia House (see below) will likely bring new fans to the fold. While the *Young Maverick* and *Bret Maverick* series are not as widely distributed as the original *Maverick*, the pilots for these shows (*The New Maverick* and *Bret Maverick: The Lazy Ace*) often appear on independent stations in two-hour movie slots.

JAMES GARNER AND LOUISE FLETCHER

APPENDIX

MAVERICK ON HOME VIDEO

To date, Columbia House has released 30 episodes, mostly from the first three seasons of the original *Maverick*, as part of its *Maverick: The Collector's Edition* series:

Volume 1	The War of the Silver Kings Point Blank
Volume 2	According to Hoyle The Wrecker
Volume 3	The Day They Hanged Bret Maverick Shady Deal at Sunny Acres
Volume 4	Duel at Sundown The Saga of Waco Williams
Volume 5	Pappy Greenbacks, Unlimited
Volume 6	Ghost Rider The Jeweled Gun
Volume 7	Stampede The Quick and the Dead
Volume 8	A Rage for Vengeance Day of Reckoning
Volume 9	Rope of Cards Seed of Deception
Volume 10	The Sheriff of Duck 'n' Shoot Full House
Volume 11	A Fellow's Brother Two Tickets to Ten Strike
Volume 12	The Cruise of the Cynthia B The Resurrection of Joe November
Volume 13	Stage West Comstock Conspiracy
Volume 14	Relic of Fort Tejon Hostage!
Volume 15	The Jail at Junction Flats The Rivals

Additional volumes of episodes may become available in the future.

BIBLIOGRAPHY

Books

Anderson, Christopher, *Hollywood TV: The Studio System in the Fifties*. Austin: University of Texas Press, 1994.

Brooks, Tim, The Complete Directory to Prime Time TV Stars, 1946-Present. New York: Ballantine Books, 1987.

Brooks, Tim and Earle Marsh, *The Complete Directory to Prime Time Network TV Shows, 1946-Present*. New York: Ballantine Books, 1988. Fourth edition. First published in 1979.

Broughton, Irv, *Producers on Producing: The Making of Film and Television*. Jefferson, N.C.: McFarland & Company, Inc., 1986.

Buscombe, Edward (editor), *The BFI Companion to the Western*. New York: Da Capo Press, Inc., 1988.

Castleman, Harry, and Walter J. Podriziak, *Harry and Wally's Favorite TV Shows*. New York: Prentice Hall Press, 1989.

Watching TV: Four Decades of American Television. New York: McGraw-Hill Book Company, 1982.

Gianakos, Larry James, *Television Drama Series Programming: A Comprehensive Chronicle*, Vols. I-III, VI. Meutchen, NJ: The Scarecrow Press, Inc.

Goldberg, Lee, *Television Series Revivals: Sequels or Remakes of Cancelled Shows*. Jefferson, N.C.: McFarland & Company, Inc., 1993.

Goldenson, Leonard H., with Martin J. Wolf. *Beating the Odds*. New York: Charles Scribner's Sons, 1991.

Huggins, Roy, *Tears from a Glass Eye*. A work in progress.

Inman, David, *The TV Encyclopedia*. New York: Perigee Books, 1991.

Johnson, Catherine E. (editor), *TV Guide 25-Year Index: April 3, 1953-Dec. 31, 1977, by Author and Subject*. Radnor, PA: Triangle Publications, Inc. 1979.

Katz, Ephraim, *The Film Encyclopedia*. New York: Thomas Y. Crowell, Publishers, 1979.

McNeil, Alex, *Total Television*. New York: Penguin Books, 1991. Third edition. First published in 1980.

O'Neil, Thomas, *The Emmys: Star Wars, Showdowns, and the Supreme Test of TV's Best*. New York: Penguin Books, 1992.

Parish, James Robert and Vincent Terrace, *The Complete Actors' Television Credits, 1948-1988, Volume I: Actors*. Meutchen: The Scarecrow Press, Inc. 1989. Second edition.

Rose, Brian, *TV Genres: A Handbook and Reference Guide*. Westport, CT: Greenwood Press, 1985.

Slide, Anthony, *A Collector's Guide to TV Memorabilia*. Lombard, IL: Wallace-Homestead Book Company, 1985.

Stallings, Penny, *Forbidden Channels: The Truth They Hide From TV Guide*. New York: Harper Perennial, 1991.

Steinberg, Cobbett S., *TV Facts*. New York: Facts on File, Inc. 1980.

Stempel, Tom, *Storytellers to the Nation: A History of American Television Writing*. New York: Continuum Publishing Company, 1992.

Strait, Raymond, *James Garner: A Biography*. New York: St. Martin's Press, 1985.

Terrace, Vincent, *Encyclopedia of Television: Series, Pilots and Specials. Volumes I and III*. New York: New York Zoetrope, 1986.

The Ultimate TV Trivia Book. Boston: Faber and Faber, 1991.

Marc, David, and Robert Thompson. *Prime Time, Prime Movers*. Boston: Little, Brown. 1992.

Variety Television Reviews, 1923-1988, in 15 volumes. New York: Garland Publishing Company, 1988.

West, Richard, *Television Westerns: Major and Minor Series, 1946-1978*. Jefferson, NC: McFarland & Company, Inc. 1987.

Woolley, Lynn, Robert W. Malsbary and Robert G. Strange, Jr., *Warner Bros. Television: Major Shows of the Fifties and Sixties, Episode by Episode*. Jefferson, N.C.: McFarland & Company, Inc., 1985.

ARTICLES

From TV Guide:

"Can He Outdraw the Champs? *Maverick*'s Jim Garner Hopes to Give Ed Sullivan and Steve Allen a Fast Shuffle," November 9, 1957.

Johnson, Bob, "Funniest Brother Act Since the Marxes: Like Those Comedians, Garner and Kelly Kid Each Other — and *Maverick*, Too," January 17, 1959.

"Code of the Westerns? Bah! *Maverick*'s Producer Sneered at the Rules and Created a Couple of Cowardly Heroes," August 1, 1959.

"Kelly Get Your Gun: The Story of the Duplicate Hero Who Was Rushed into *Maverick* to Keep the Series Going," May 17, 1958.

"The Last of the Mavericks: Jack Kelly Finally Becomes Top Hand as the Western Series Heads for the Last Roundup," June 2, 1962.

Nolan, Tom, "Though a Stalwart Hand at Playing *Maverick*, James Garner Was Told 'Get Out of Prime Time by Fall,'" August 7, 1982.

"Shooting for Laughs: Jack Kelly Would Like More Comedy Time on *Maverick*," September 9, 1959.

"Still a Maverick: James Garner, Who Kicked Over the Traces at Warner Brothers, is Now Happily Romping All Over the Place," March 25, 1961.

"The Understanding Type: Diane Brewster Spends Her Time Playing a Girl a Man Can Depend On," December 14, 1957.

"White Sheep of the Mavericks: With Roger Moore, TV's Best Known Brother Act Becomes a Cousin Act," October 8, 1960.

Whitney, Dwight, "The Cowboys' Lament, as Voiced by a Couple of Disgruntled Hired Hands — Namely, Clint Walker and Jim Garner," November 21, 1959.

"For the Record: James Garner and Warner Bros. Feud Over Contract," November 26, 1960.

"For the Record: James Garner Wins Suit Against Warner Bros.," December 10, 1960.

From other periodicals:

Brown, Gary, "A Look at *Maverick*," *Remember When*, Issue 14, 1974.

"Freewheeling Slick," *Time*, December 30, 1957.

Gould, Jack, "Heavy-Handed Satire," *New York Times*, January 12, 1959.

"Happy Larceny," *Newsweek*, January 19, 1959.

Hargrove, Marion, "This is a Television Cowboy? Stumblebum Hero Stars in *Maverick*," *Life,* January 19, 1959.

Huggins, Roy, "Television: What's the Difference," *Television Quarterly*, 1967.

Linderman, Lawrence, "James Garner: A Candid Conversation with the Easygoing Star about *Maverick, Rockford,* Funny Commercials, His Bizarre Childhood, and Corruption in Hollywood," *Playboy*, March 1981.

Martin, Mick, "Jack Kelly: Memoirs of a Maverick," *Filmfax*, August/September 1993.

Martin, Pete, "I Call on Bret Maverick: The Star of TV's *Maverick* Sets the Record Straight on His Real Life as Jim Garner, and Tells Why He Didn't Want to Become an Actor," *Saturday Evening Post*, October 11, 1958.

O'Flaherty, Terence, "Never Play Poker with the Mavericks," *San Francisco Chronicle*, November 28, 1979.

"Parodies Regained," *Time*, January 19, 1959.

Pond, Steve, "So You Think It's Easy Being James Garner?," *New York Times*, March 14, 1993.

"The Soft Touch Out West: TV Cowboys Take on Domestic Chores," *Life*, April 14, 1958.

Shanley, John P., "*Maverick*'s Creator: A Cynical Approach," *New York Times Magazine*, April 5, 1959.

"TV Goes Wild Over Westerns: Cowpokes' Clashes Fill the Programs as Horses, Camels and Clashes are Taken for a Ride," *Life*, October 28, 1957.

Other Sources

Warner Bros. Pictures, Inc. v. James Bumgarner, decided November 27, 1961, California State Court of Appeal, 2nd Appellate District, Division One, Docket No. 25519. Published in *California Appellate Reports, 2nd Series*, Volume 197 (November 14, 1961 to December 13, 1961). San Francisco: Bancroft-Whitney, 1962.

Huggins, Roy, "Breaking Traditions for Fun and Profit." Publicity item written in 1957.

"The Maverick Persuasion." Publicity item written in 1958.

"A Ten-Point Guide to Happiness While Writing or Directing a *Maverick*", 1957.

INDEX OF NAMES AND EPISODES

Carr, Michael 86
Carradine, John 137, 152
Carrier, Albert 93
Carroll, Laurie 54
Carroll, Bickford 41
Carson, Robert 50, 84, 91, 98, 124
Carter, Dixie 188
Cartwright, Lynn 140
Caruso, Anthony 126, 140
Cason, Chuck 71, 95
Cason, John 139
Casper, Robert 136
Cassidy, Jack 161-162
"Cats of Paradise, The" 115-116, 122-123, 170
Challee, William 128
Chance, Larry 164
Chandler, James 139
Chandler, Chick 168
Chandler, Lane 47, 122, 126, 138, 147
Chane, Michael 194
Chapman, Joseph 190
Chase, Stephen 162
Chauvin, Lilyan 88
Chefe, Jack 63
Chekenian, Iris 11, 31, 40
Cheshire, Harry 62, 127
Christy, Ken 62
Chudnow, Byron 159
"Clancy" 180
Clark, Roydon 95
Clarke, Gage 61, 96, 122, 128, 151, 162, 169
Clarke, Paul 118
Cliff, John 51, 84, 91, 97, 150
Coburn, James 194
Coffin, Tris 143
Coit, Stephen 101, 139, 164
Colbert, Robert 11, 88, 131, 135, 137, 151, 154-156
Collier, Johnnie 123
Collier, Richard 51
Colmans, Edward 140
Comiskey, Pat 56
"Comstock Conspiracy" 45, 59-60
Connors, Mike 49, 58, 174
Conrad, Robert 84, 100
Conried, Hans 69
Contreras, Roberto 60, 69
Conway, Gary 141
Conway, Russ 61
Coogan, Richard 141
Cooper, Jeanne 58, 150
Cooper, Maxine 54
Cooper, Clancy 136
Cooper, Charles 70, 102, 119
Corden, Henry 168
Cornthwaite, Robert 139, 147
Corrie, William 141
Corrigan, Lloyd 166
Cosa, Jim 187
Coy, Walter 123
Crane, Richard 52
Crawford, Diana 136
Crewe, Bill 131
Crosland, Alan Jr. 67
Crowley, Kathleen 45, 56, 96, 100, 116, 120, 128, 140, 143, 160, 162, 168-170, 191
Crowley, Patricia 79, 84, 94, 97-98, 100, 104, 112, 116, 166
"Cruise of the Cynthia B, The" 116, 122-123, 125, 170
Cugat, Xavier 94

"Cure for Johnny Rain, A" 121
Curry, Mason 63
Cutting, Richard 58, 138

D'Alisera, Silvio 101
"Dade City Dodge" 160, 162, 168
Dalio, Marcel 96
Dalton, Abby 99
Dangcil, Linda 124
Daniell, Henry 112
Dante, Michael 53, 60, 104
Danton, Ray 146
"Dark Rider, The" 66
Darrow, Henry 194
Darwell, Jane 69
"Dateline: Sweetwater" 188
Davis, Betty 131
Davis, Jerry 116
Davis, Charles 149
Dawson, Maurine 162
"Day of Reckoning" 26, 65, 105
"Day They Hanged Bret Maverick, The" 45, 74, 84, 128
de Marney, Terrence 56, 63, 139, 169
de Corsia, Ted 50, 168
De Santis, Joe 146
Deacon, Richard 115
"Dead Man's Hand" 181
"Dead Ringer" 192
"Deadly Image, The" 139, 153
deBenning, Jeff 154
DeBruin, Sandra 192
Dehner, John 92, 128, 156-157, 167, 179
DeKova, Frank 164
Delgado, Luis 11, 34-36, 59, 61-62, 103, 133, 139, 174, 176-177, 184
Dell, Myrna 68
Demon, Henry L. 107
deSales, Francis 68, 125
"Destination: Devil's Flat" 145-146
"Devil's Necklace, The" 60, 156
"Diamond Flush" 149
"Diamond in the Rough" 63
deToth, Andre 122
Dibbs, Kem 54, 100, 151, 166
Dickinson, Angie 109
Dierkop, Charles 194
Dillaway, Don 58
Dobkin, Lawrence 187
"Dodge City or Bust" 144
Dolan, Trent 141
Doniger, Walter 75, 90
Donner, Richard 44, 194
Donovan, King 120
Donovan, Margaret 42, 61
Dortort, David 30
"Double-Trouble in Texas" 182
Douglas, Robert 136, 143, 148
Douglas, Gordon 67
Driskill, William 114
"Duel at Sundown" 27, 99-100, 102
Dugay, Yvette 94
Duggan, Andrew 149, 168
Duncan, Pamela 56
Duncan, Craig 137-138, 154
Durant, Don 54
Dusay, Marj 187, 191, 192
"Dutchman's Gold" 148

Earnshaw, Fenton 147
Eastwood, Clint 99
"Easy Mark" 118
Ebsen, Buddy 115, 142, 150

Edmisten, Walker 96
Edwards, Ralph 85
Edwards, Saundra 70, 95
Ehrman, Paul 193
"Eight Swords of Dyrus and Other Illusions of Grandeur, The" 190-191
Eisley, Anthony 187
Elan, Joan 87, 126
Elhardt, Kaye 112
Elizondo, Hector 192
Elliott, Russ 124
Elliott, Cecil 89
Ellsworth, Stephen 63
Emanuel, Jack 20, 118
Emmich, Cliff 189
Engel, Roy 128
"Epitaph for a Gambler" 166
Epstein, Herman 139, 144
Erwin, Roy 84
Erwin, Bill 154
Esmond, Carl 149
"Escape to Tampico" 88, 102
Espitallier, Joe 93
Essler, Ruth 186
Eustrel, Antony 126
Evans, Ray 179
Everett, Chad 136, 156-157
Ewing, John 107, 131

Fadden, Tom 113
Fahey, Myrna 99, 126, 140
"Fair Game" 193
Fairchild, Morgan 181
Fairfax, Robert 63
"Faith, Hope and Clarity" 191, 193
"Family Pride" 147, 149, 194
Fancher, Hampton 150
Fannon, William 178, 184
Faralla, William Dario 141
Farfan, Robert 42, 74, 91-92
Faris, Jim 107
Farmer, Robert 41, 140
Farrar, Stanley 98, 162
Farrell, Tommy 52
Faubion, Elmer 41
Faylen, Frank 60
"Fellow's Brother, A" 18, 119
Ferguson, Frank 71, 88, 118, 145, 164, 168
Fernstrom, Ray 107
Fiero, Paul 35, 67, 89
Fimple, Dennis 194
Finn, Mickey 144
Fischer, Geoffrey 184
Fisher, Herbert 73
"Fistful of Oats, A" 180
Fitzgerald, Barry 145
Fletcher, Louise 101
"Flock of Trouble, A" 126
"Flood's Folly" 150-151
Florey, Med 144, 167
Flynn, Errol 134
Flynn, Gertrude 101, 154, 162
Fonda, Henry 17
Fogetti, Howard 107, 159
Foran, Dick 60
"Forbidden City, The" 135, 154
Forest, Michael 112, 156
Foster, Zack 167
Foster, Jodie 194
Foulger, Byron 68, 84
Foulk, Robert 49, 154
Frank, Charles 172, 173, 177, 179
Frank, Gary 194

JAMES GARNER AS BRET MAVERICK AND DARLENE CARR AS A NEWS PHOTOGRAPHER IN "WELCOME TO SWEETWATER"

JACK KELLY AND JAMES GARNER

ABOUT THE AUTHOR

Ed Robertson was born and raised in San Francisco, and earned his B.A. in English and Drama at Saint Mary's College of California.

Ed is the author of *The Fugitive Recaptured*, the best-selling companion guide to *The Fugitive*, which *TV Guide* proclaimed "the definitive guide to the series." He has been featured on such television programs as *Entertainment Tonight, CNN, Showbiz Today*, and *Inside Edition*.

Ed lives and writes in San Francisco.

PHOTOGRAPH © THOMAS ANDERSON

The photographs in this book, unless otherwise credited, are from The Personal Collection of the author, Ed Robertson; The Personal Collection of Leslie H. Martinson; The Personal Collection of Ann Mathis, and The Milton T. Moore, Jr. Collection.